THE PLEASURE CHAMBER

The whipping halted. Beatrice lifted her wrists.

'Turn around.'

Mary turned to face her mistress. She felt nervous as her wrists were hung up again. Now her tender breasts and naked belly were exposed; was the softest, smoothest skin she knew so much better than the unseen flesh of her back now going to be lashed dry? She looked warily at the bundle of wands. The leaves had almost all been shredded away, and now the instrument looked likely to produce a far more painful result.

The chatelaine ran a finger across Mary's stomach. Droplets of water still stood out. Then she flipped her hair back out of the way again.

'You are still wet, child.'

She drew her arm back. Mary closed her eyes and heard the whoosh of the birch.

By the same author:

CHAINS OF SHAME

THE PLEASURE CHAMBER

Brigitte Markham

Nexus

This book is a work of fiction.
In real life, make sure you practise safe sex.

First published in 1999 by
Nexus
Thames Wharf Studios
Rainville Road
London W6 9HT

Typeset by TW Typesetting, Plymouth, Devon

Printed and bound by
Cox & Wyman Ltd, Reading, Berks

ISBN 0 352 33371 5

One

Mary Coppen pressed the bell outside Laura Jenkins's flat for the third time in less than a couple of minutes. It was just before ten-thirty on a Thursday morning in late June.

'Come on, come on!' she called under her breath. At last she heard some movement within. She ceased the nervous tapping of her right foot and drew breath to tell Laura the news. Locks rattled, and finally the door opened.

'Laura, we've passed!' She threw her arms round the slim, tousle-haired girl standing bleary-eyed before her.

'Oh, great. Wonderful. What time is it?' Laura sounded sleepy and unimpressed about being woken so early.

'Half-ten, sleepy head. I rang earlier but couldn't get a reply.'

'Sorry, I was out late.' Laura turned away, into the cool dimness of her flat. 'I'll put the kettle on.'

'Isn't it great? No resits, and back in the autumn. I didn't think I'd do so well. You got really good grades – all As and Bs.' Mary chattered on in a nervous rush, her Yorkshire accent unusually noticeable in the excitement.

Laura's soft Welsh accent came from the tiny galley kitchen. 'What about you?'

'All As,' Mary almost whispered, embarrassed by her success.

'Told you so. I never knew what you were worried about.' Laura filled the kettle and clicked the switch. 'Toast?'

'No, thanks.' Mary tried sitting down, but her feet couldn't stay still. She walked round the living-room. She

1

knew why she'd been so worried. Mary had been raised and educated in an isolated religious community. As the only child of her age group, she had always sat exams on her own, so the act of sitting the end of first-year papers in a hall full of students had been absolutely terrifying, and made worse because she lacked any confidence in her own ability. That was too much to explain to a sleepy Laura, so all she said was: 'I've never been good at exams.'

Laura came back in with a mug of tea. Mary thought she looked lovely: quite short and slim, her short fair hair only slightly messed up after brief finger-combing, a neat little figure in a pale yellow silk slip worn as a nightie. 'So, we're free from care all summer. What will we do with all that time?'

Mary was about to explain that she had to go back home to the Community when the doorbell rang again. Laura went to the door. 'Hello. What's this?'

A delivery man, red-faced from climbing six flights of stairs with a big cardboard box, thrust a delivery note and pen into Laura's hands. As she signed, he leered. 'Thanks, sweetheart.'

Laura shut the door quickly, and Mary caught a glimpse of his leer turning to frustration. 'M, give me a hand.'

Mary helped her drag the box inside. It was surprisingly heavy. 'What is it?'

Laura finished positioning it by the table. 'I don't know.' She began investigating. FRAGILE, THIS WAY UP and address stickers adorned every face of the package. Laura scanned the delivery note for a clue. 'Pass me those scissors.'

Mary looked round. Laura directed her more accurately. 'Over there, on my desk.'

She spotted them in the pot beside Laura's computer, brought them over and watched the box reveal its secret. First came a layer of bubblewrap, then a tight packed mass of straw. Mary, always practical, brought a bin-bag from the kitchen, and they began baling the straw from box to bag. Gradually, something began to emerge out of the mass of straw: a pair of bronze arms, tied at the wrist.

Laura muttered, 'Ah, so that's what she did.' Mary didn't understand.

Laura baled the straw faster, moving round and obscuring Mary's view. Finally, Laura stood up and back. 'Give me a hand.'

Laura gripped the statue. Mary held on to the box. Laura heaved but failed. 'It's too heavy.'

Mary was taller, bigger and stronger than Laura, even though the smaller girl worked out regularly. 'Let me try.'

They swapped places. Mary was used to manual labour; the Community farmed their land without the aid of modern, powered machinery. She took hold of the statue's torso. It came away easily.

'Can you put it on the table?'

Mary turned and set it down, suddenly aware that she was gripping the statue's bare breasts. Embarrassed, she snatched her hands away and blushed as she realised who the model was. 'Laura! It's you!'

The half-scale statue was completely naked, standing, legs apart and bound to rings set in a stone plinth. The arms were upstretched, breasts high, vulva hairless and explicit. Mary's jaw dropped, and her knees went wobbly. Oh my, she thought, she's beautiful. She turned to look at the real Laura standing beside her. Under that silk nightie, was she really as gorgeous? Mary was struck by an inexplicable urge to ask Laura to take her slip off. She had to have a breath of fresh air, but there was nowhere to go without making a scene. What was she thinking of? Why did she want to see Laura naked? She closed her eyes and took deep breaths, reached for her mug and drank some tea.

'Mary, what's the matter? You look flushed.' Laura sounded concerned.

'Oh nothing. Running about in all this heat, I expect.' She felt the need to justify her statement, to cover her confusion with embellishments. 'It's terribly hot again, and I ran most of the way back.'

'You'd better sit down. I'll open some windows. It is a bit stuffy in here.'

3

Mary sank gratefully into the armchair and stared at the statuette while Laura let full daylight in before going off to the bathroom. A lazy breeze moved the air and ruffled a few bits of straw still clinging to the bronze. Without thinking, she leant forward to remove them. One was caught in something at the tip of the right breast. She grabbed the straw carelessly, taking both ends, and tugged. The bronze rocked. The straw did not come away. She leant even closer to find the cause. Her eyes widened. The straw was threaded through a tiny ring in the nipple. Carefully, Mary teased it free, and then she looked closely at the rest of the statue. There was another ring in the left nipple, and three more down below, clearly depicted. Mary gasped. The intricately detailed ridge splitting the smooth, hairless pubic mound was pierced at the peak and on each side.

Laura spoke from over her shoulder, startling her. 'Incredibly detailed and amazingly accurate. Leila's really done a good job. It looks far more sexy than I actually was.'

'You mean this was taken from life?' Mary was astounded. It was so explicit, so erotic, how could it be real?

'Of course. Leila's really good.'

'Who's Leila?'

'Just a friend. She had me pose when I stayed with her last summer. I didn't think she'd send me a cast, though.' Laura sounded very matter of fact.

'So this isn't some figment of her imagination?'

'No.'

Mary shook her head; they didn't do things like this in the Community. No one was ever seen naked in the Community, except babies, of course, and, she supposed, married couples in the privacy of their own bedrooms. At least, she guessed, the more passionate and younger married couples might undress in each other's company. The older ones were so straight-laced they had probably never shown anyone their legs let alone their loins. Nudity, like sex, was sinful, and to make a work of art out of it, well, she didn't know what to think.

4

'Laura, do you really have rings in your –' Mary couldn't bring herself to say the dirty words. 'You know, in your –'

'In my nipples and pussy? Yes, I do.'

Mary thought she sounded inordinately proud of such a disgusting thing, but at the same time she wondered what it was like. 'And you haven't any hair . . .' Mary pointed at the junction of thighs and body on the bronze.

Laura sat down opposite, a wry smile playing across her lips. 'Yep, smooth as a baby's bum.'

'But why, how? It's all wrong, it's, it's . . .' She trailed off, defeated by the depths of Laura's depravity.

'I've never pretended that I'm some kind of saint.'

'I know, but, but –' But what? she thought. But you should have said you were a slut? Then I'd never have made friends with you; never found the best friend I've ever had. I'd never have learnt so much about living in London, about real people or all the things they didn't teach me in the Community. I'd have continued to be afraid of the palaver of going into clothes shops and never learnt how to fend off unwanted advances or how to socialise with strangers. It was disappointing to discover that your best friend had held things back when you had bared your soul. Well, almost.

She heard a noise in the kitchen, looked up and realised that Laura had left her to think alone. There was a loud pop, and Laura returned with two long-stemmed, narrow glasses filled with clear, slightly golden bubbling liquid. She gave a glass to Mary.

'Champagne, to celebrate our results.' Laura smiled and then drank.

Mary, obeying in shock, felt the bubbles bursting cold against her nose and then felt them slide over her tongue and down her throat. Almost at once, her mood lifted. 'That's lovely.'

Laura giggled. 'It's good for shocks and all sorts of things. They always use champagne in Victorian novels, especially to revive young ladies affected by the vapours.'

As Laura drank again, Mary watched her body under

5

the silk. Yes, she could see it now, the imprint of rings in the material. Laura sat down, lying back on the sofa, legs slightly apart. The slip rode up, exposing more thigh. Mary knew she ought to avert her eyes. Laura wasn't wearing knickers under the silk. If the silk rode up just a little more, and if the light fell right, Mary would be able to see the real pouting, shaven, ringed naughtiness. Mary blushed. Laura lay back a little more, and she could see.

For a moment or two Mary looked at the thick, bright pink glistening lips with their fine gold rings. She felt a surge of emotion, something like love, and her own naughtiness, an area of her body she never took notice of, nudged her by feeling hot and swollen. Laura giggled again and tugged down her slip.

'Sorry, Mary. All uncovered. What must you think of me?'

'I think you're gorgeous.' Did I say that? thought Mary. She rushed to cover up. 'I mean, any man would be mad not to . . .' Had the drink loosened her tongue that quickly? 'Oh, I don't know what I mean – it must be the champagne.'

Laura leant forward, her voice suddenly soft, a little thick, almost husky. 'Mary, what's wrong?'

Mary tried to gather her thoughts. 'I don't really understand. I feel rather . . . odd, you know, mixed up. Part of me wants to call you a bad girl, but another wants to, wants to . . .' Tears of frustration about her inability to express herself welled up in her eyes.

Laura was by her side in a moment, arms around her, soothing her with whispered words of comfort. 'It's all right, my love. Let it all out.'

Mary's head fell sideways, on to Laura's bosom. She felt the firm little mounds and the hard point of a ringed nipple. She had to explain. She looked up, straight into Laura's gentle, loving, blue eyes.

'Laura, I –' she whispered, but Laura never let her complete the sentence. She covered Mary's mouth with her own and kissed her.

Mary had never been kissed on the mouth before. She

6

had read about it in novels, and since arriving in London had seen it on films and television, but nothing could prepare her for that first kiss. She felt as if her life was being sucked from her, while simultaneously a new, completely different life flooded in. The sensations gathering in her body for the last few minutes were explained. The swelling of her nipples and the wet heat between her thighs were sexual arousal. The revelation came as a shock, as did Laura's tongue, forcing her lips apart. She let it progress, and she tasted champagne in Laura's saliva. Her breath came in gusts through her nostrils. The invader began moving in her mouth, rolling over her tongue, along her teeth, and she sucked at it.

Her hands began to reach out to Laura, pulling her closer, down on to her. She felt the silk slipping over skin. Laura's hands began to move too, stroking her shoulder and neck, and down, down on to her breast. Mary froze as the hand cupped her there. No one had ever touched her so intimately before, and she didn't know what to expect or how she should react. Her breasts seemed so big, almost hard against her bra. Her nipples ached, craving that hand's touch. Laura's palm closed, gently hefting the heavy mound. Mary groaned into Laura's mouth, and wanted even more as she began to panic; short of breath, assailed by novel sensations, her mind rebelling against the terrifying fact that she was having sex.

Laura let the kiss break, and they recovered their breath. She held Mary's head to her bosom again. Mary's hand stroked down Laura's body and, just as she met the rise of her hip, felt naked skin. Laura kissed her forehead and eyes, her ear and neck, pushing her collar away to taste her shoulder. Mary stroked Laura's haunch. Laura spread her thighs, inviting her hand round to that briefly glimpsed, exotic, mysterious place. Mary's fingers accepted the invitation and ran over smooth skin until they touched hot, soft, sticky flesh. Clumsily, Mary felt along the parted lips until she touched metal. So strange, so alien.

'Hey,' Laura whispered, 'this isn't the most comfortable. Come on, sweetheart, we can be more comfortable in bed.'

7

Mary should have stopped it there. It was her last chance to assert reason over curiosity, lifelong belief over lust. Instead, like a sleepwalker, she let Laura take her hand and lead her away. The sheets were still disturbed from the night, the light muted by pale curtains, and the bed was something else: a gleaming, brass-framed, ornate construction canopied with white drapes that might have been designed to enchant her romantic soul.

For a few moments Mary stood still and unresisting, not knowing what to do or expect but impatient for it to happen. Then Laura drew her to the edge of the bed and began, slowly, to unbutton her denim shirt. The shirt gaped, from the waistband of her long denim skirt to her shoulders. She made only one move of assistance, to kick off her sandals. Laura unbuttoned her skirt, drew down the zip, and the skirt fell away. An almost sacrificial urge left Mary strangely distanced from events. She felt her shirt slide down her arms to join her skirt at her feet. Laura reached up a little to kiss her again. Her fingers pushed the bra straps off Mary's shoulders. Laura's hands were at her back, feeling for the catch. Mary sucked in her breath and closed her eyes, afraid of being completely naked, frightened to expose her big, clumsy, pale body to view. She felt the bra go, her breasts fall loose and unrestrained. They blossomed, relaxed, and Laura's mouth and hands were at them.

Laura took Mary's nipples, one after the other, into her wet mouth and cooled their fire but made them harder, sucking and almost, but not quite, biting them. Mary sucked in her diaphragm as Laura's tongue tickled down to her navel. The cool, wet trail reached the elastic at the top of her boring white knickers. Mary opened her eyes. Laura was kneeling at her feet, and Mary had to fight the impulse to flee as fingers began to pull down her knickers. For a moment she held her knees together, then relaxed and parted them.

'Oh, God, Mary.' She felt Laura's words on her thighs. 'You don't know how long I've wanted this.'

'Me too.' Her own words shocked Mary, but it was true.

At first her attraction to Laura had been pure friendship, but it had grown, though she had tried to deny it. She had followed Laura like a puppy, waiting open-mouthed for her approbation, for any sign of love.

She felt her knickers descend, unwilling to look, frightened by her own sinful lusts, as though watching would make the dream real. The elastic brushed her pubic hair. She trembled. Warm breath stirred her ginger bush. She closed her eyes tight as Laura exposed her most secret, intimate place. The realisation struck that, at least since puberty, she had not looked as closely at her naughtiness as Laura did now. Mary had never even explored herself, having been taught that exploration was masturbation and therefore a sin. The knickers coiled round her feet, soft but humid. Without conscious thought, her feet stepped out of her knickers.

Laura stood up. 'Why have you hidden yourself from me for so long, Mary?'

Laura was talking to herself. She knew the answers, understood Mary's deep-rooted beliefs. Mary herself wondered why. Laura was right: she did have a good figure. It wasn't fashionably waif-like, but her weight was correct for her size, she was fit, and went in and out in all the right places.

Laura coaxed her down the path to ruin. 'Lie down, my love, lie down.'

Mary obeyed, ceding control to Laura, knowing she was in experienced hands. She lay on her back, unable to move, transfixed by the enormity of what she was about to do. She moved only her eyes and watched Laura shimmy out of her slip. At last she could see Laura's breasts, gold rings hanging from the rosy tips of pointy mounds, her slightly rounded abdomen and shaved pubis. Mary's eyes held to the delta as Laura mounted the bed and climbed over her until her knees bridged Mary's hips. The ridge of flesh parted, the tiny weight of the rings pulling the inner lips out and down, and Mary gasped as she saw that the ring at the top actually pierced the bead of Laura's clitoris.

Mary's hands moved to stroke the outside of her lover's

9

thighs. Laura replied by putting her hands again to Mary's breasts. Mary closed her eyes as Laura gently stroked and rubbed, and her own hands slid up Laura's body to reach her bosom. Her breasts were so firm and elegant, and the cooler gold hoops against her palms so exciting. She pinched their rubbery mountings, which grew harder. Her own nipples stiffened as Laura first manipulated and then took them in her mouth once more.

Laura kissed her mouth again. As she did so, she took hold of Mary's wrists and pushed them away until they lay fully outstretched. Laura let go of her right arm, but Mary left it lying outstretched, wondering what Laura was doing to her left. Something looped close, but not tight, about her wrist. When Laura turned her attention to Mary's other hand, still kissing her mouth, Mary tried to move her left, but could not. Though disturbed, Mary understood that her arms were tied. Laura moved away then, and Mary knew her legs must also be restrained. She looked at what held her wrists: cuffs of suede, attached to the bed frame by short chains. There was enough slack in both chains and loops to let her release herself, but she knew she had no wish to do so. It was a surprising revelation. Mary did not want to be free to do this thing. She wanted to be passive, to let Laura lead, not only because she had no idea what to do but also because she did not trust herself to go through with it all the way. Complicity was a sin, but submission provided the excuse when she came to explain herself.

While her mind found peace, her body, so long suppressed, exploded into action. A great longing flowed from her swollen, eager naughtiness; her breasts yearned for Laura's touch. Hands began stroking the insides of her calves, her hips writhed, her knees flexed to the maximum degree allowed by her bonds. Mary closed her eyes and surrendered.

Laura licked her lips and looked down on the pale-skinned and natural meal laid out before her. Perfumes, depilatories, tweezers: none of the paraphernalia of cosmetic beautification had ever been used in the preparation of Mary's body. All her hair – the great cascade of wavy ginger spreading over the pillows around her heart-shaped face, the darker, finer stuff at her armpits, the loose bush at her groin, and the soft, almost invisible hairs on her legs and forearms – was a complete contrast to Laura's own highly controlled, depilated, shaved and trimmed growths. Mary's full, heavy breasts and pale, edible pink nipples, rounded hips and buttocks were all so much more substantial than Laura's slim frame. Laura wanted to consume her, possess her, and afterwards keep her kneeling at her feet for ever.

Laura moved between Mary's outstretched thighs and stroked the soft skin before the gateway to her innocent body. Mary quivered. Laura remembered when she, too, had been untouched, had never known the thrill, the pregnant threat, of imminent, intimate contact. Laura leant forward and inhaled deeply the dense fragrance of arousal. It was salty, sweet and undefiled. She bent closer and kissed the softest creases beside the humid ginger forest. Mary gasped. Laura slid her hands under Mary's taut buttocks, raised them to steady her untutored pupil and then kissed those creases again.

The scent of arousal grew stronger. Laura's own juices flowed more strongly, and she fought the impulse to bury her face in Mary's quim. Instead, she moved up, seeking the peripheral delights of Mary's body. She sucked again at her nipples, enjoying the thickening resilience. She drew them out with her teeth gently, causing Mary to murmur. She looked on her work and cherished the wide pink haloes now developing shape and density. She touched each little bump with the very tip of her tongue and then bit, below the left disc, sucking hard. Mary groaned and shook as Laura left a small red mark of ownership. She licked from breast up to shoulder, watching a ripple of goosebumps on Mary's soft skin. Then she switched and started again at Mary's fingertips, sucking each one and kissing her palm. Her tongue ran all the way up the delicate inner skin from wrist to armpit. Mary's arm writhed. Laura licked the salty hair, tasting, laving the little bush flat. She repeated the

11

gesture on the other side and nipped her way across Mary's neck, testing the elasticity of the translucent skin.

Laura could restrain herself no longer. She dived back to Mary's belly and, gently at first but with increasing hunger, began licking, kissing and sucking the gaping slit. Mary's inner lips grew thicker. Laura pulled them out and they hung wide and long. She eased the hood back from the erect clitty and wondered at its size for an organ so new to stimulation. She dipped her tongue into the cup of the virgin entrance and drank the pure essence. Her tongue wandered down into the crease below, the musty, fine hair-fringed crease hiding Mary's rose. When she licked that rose, Mary bucked her hips. She licked again and held her tight, accustoming her protégée to the most intimate touch.

Laura's eyes lingered over Mary's vulva and loved the brightness of every glistening fold, churning limb and clenching orifice. Then she returned to orchestrate Mary's first orgasm. Her fingers now played at front and back; spreading and pressing, stroking and gripping. Her tongue and lips isolated, nibbled, licked and sucked every segment, each sensitive morsel. She drank away the pouring honey but left the proud clitty alone. Lubricated by saliva and honey, her finger wormed its way into Mary's bottom. Her mouth exhorted Mary's vulva to thrust and grind. Her ears heard the cries and gasps, groans and incoherent imprecations of a girl at risk of losing her mind. Then, and only then, did her fingers spread the folds away from Mary's retreating, super-sensitive clitoris. She sucked it up and tickled the tip with her tongue. Her thumb pressed the entrance below, and Mary exploded against her, heaving and crying.

Laura's thighs still arched above Mary, who could smell and see Laura's glistening arousal at the apex. Laura looked down, an expectant, hungry look in her eyes. Neither spoke, but Mary knew what was expected of her. She licked her nervous lips repeatedly. She had received the gift of pleasure from Laura. Now she must repay the

12

compliment, but she had no good idea how to do so. She tried hard to remember what Laura had done to her, but the extremes of emotion and sensation fogged her memory.

Laura bent forward until her breasts hovered above Mary's face and her thighs squashed down on her chest. Mary reached up, straining, seeking a gold ring and a hard nipple. Her lips just reached the ring as it hung. They gripped as best they could and pulled. The nipple came lower, and now she could feel the odd contrast of cool metal and hot flesh. It was intriguing, sensuous. She sucked harder, and Laura moaned. Her tongue played with the ring, and Laura moaned again. She sucked harder and trapped the nub between her teeth; it grew bigger. She felt Laura undulating above her, and she let the nipple go, reaching for the other.

Laura crawled forward. Mary felt a flutter in her tummy as butterflies took wing. She peered upward at the approaching shadowy delta, the rings, the folds and the juiciness. Laura lowered herself.

'Stick out your tongue.' Mary summoned up her courage. She wanted this, though she had never imagined she could desire anything so lewd. She opened her mouth and stuck out her tongue. The tip entered the cup-like entrance of Laura's vagina. Honey dripped on to her lips, and she swallowed, savouring. Laura moved over her tongue, introducing her contours, wriggling as Mary's tongue touched rings or clitty. Mary strained, wanting to put her lips to the swollen folds. She murmured her frustration. Laura relented, and her hips descended.

That moment altered Mary's entire life, even more than her first orgasm. The intimate communion between her mouth and Laura's sex opened a locked door in her head. Almost instantly she lost her scruples, her sense of what was proper. Released by the act of giving, physical sexual pleasure entered her life. She tasted the fruit forbidden by her aunts and found she wanted more.

Laura made Mary work a long time, grinding Mary's face in juices and flesh, before she had changed the focus of action. It happened suddenly, shocking Mary into immobility. One moment Mary was happily thrusting her tongue inside Laura's sheath, the next her tongue licked into the tight bowl of her bottom. Mary shrank back into the bed, trying to escape the appalling demand. Her nose pressed against Laura's slit, the rings hard against her face.

Laura spoke with absolute authority. 'Your tongue, Mary. Give me what I want.'

Mary gathered up all her fortitude. There was no escape. Mary felt obliged to obey, for Laura had done the same for her. Mary opened her mouth again and touched tentatively. She shivered as the knot of muscle pulsed. It tasted strange; not nasty but strong and dark. She pointed her tongue and probed around the firm, smooth rosebud, pressing back the softer skin. She tapped the centre of the muscle. The knot relaxed and she entered a little way. Laura moaned loudly and ground her hips. Mary grew adventurous and opened her lips around the muscle. The knot opened wider. Mary kissed it, sucking slightly. The knot spread and dilated. She thrust her tongue. It went inside, and Laura groaned deeply. Mary shivered again and wanted Laura to touch her in the same place. Then she felt a fingernail against her face, and Laura bucked. She glimpsed Laura's fingers playing with her clitty. Fingers and tongue struck up a rhythm. Laura began grunting. Sparks of pleasure shot around Mary's body, seeking release in friction. Still tied down, there was no relief available; Laura had no thought for Mary's pleasure as her own reached climax.

Much later, Mary discovered that her arms and legs were free. She could smell Laura's sex as she inhaled, the scent applied as she had buried her head between Laura's thighs. Laura offered her a glass of champagne and toasted her.

'To you, my love.'

Mary drank thirstily. Her limbs were tired yet full of life, her breasts and sex heavy with passing arousal. Perhaps there was soreness too, but too little to cause discomfort and undermine the glow.

'Let's have a shower. I think we need it.'

Mary nodded her assent; she felt sticky and matted from her exertions. Hand in hand they walked naked to Laura's small, white-tiled bathroom. Two large white towels already hung on a rack behind the door. Laura turned on the shower and tested the temperature. Mary expected to have to take her turn, but Laura did not let go of her hand as she stepped into the cubicle.

Water flowed in a heavy rain, plastering hair to scalps, washing away salty sweat and sweet honey. Laura produced shampoo and poured some over Mary's head. Mary closed her eyes as fingers conjured a lather, teasing out tangles as they went. Water sluiced away the foam. Laura applied conditioner, and then shower gel to Mary's shoulders, burrowing under her arms. Her breasts bloomed again as Laura worked a generous dollop of gel into the fragile mounds, lifting them to soap the under-creases. Soapy hands plunged between her legs, worming round, reigniting the fires. Mary reached for the shampoo, and as her hips writhed she tried to concentrate on washing and conditioning Laura's shorter hair. Soon they were soaping each other, slippy fingers entering and moulding, smoothing and rubbing in slow circles.

Mary grunted as a finger pushed into her bottom. She gasped as it moved round, and her knees buckled. Laura moved behind her, and still impaling, scrubbed her back and buttocks. Mary had never imagined that her bottom could be a source of sensual pleasure; now she did not want it to stop. An itching, perhaps caused by soap on her delicate membranes, added to her wriggles, and when Laura came round in front again she wrapped her in her arms and repaid the debt. For some time they rocked together, pubis to pubis, fingers pinning them together, spare hands stroking buttocks and thighs. Mary sought Laura's mouth, and under the streaming water they kissed deeply. Mary was sad when it ended.

Kneeling, Laura washed Mary's thighs. As she did so she rested her forehead against Mary's belly. A full feeling grew inside. Mary regretted having a second glass of champagne; she needed to pee. When Laura stopped

15

soaping, she remained kneeling and pressed the heel of her hand just above Mary's bush and slipped a finger back inside her bottom. The need grew, became desperate.

Her plea came out in gasps. 'Laura, I need to use the loo.'

Laura looked encouragingly upward. 'Go ahead.'

Mary was horrified. 'But –'

Laura's eyes narrowed and her tone became commanding. 'Mary, pee. I know you need to.'

Mary could see no means of escape. Laura began massaging her slit, between the lips, below her clitoris, at the very opening of her bladder. Soap began to irritate the tiny hole. Mary wriggled as the finger moved within her bottom. The need came on stronger. Laura held her eyes and mouthed encouragement. Her control started to crack. She heard herself gasp, 'Oh, God.' The flow started. Laura spluttered and gasped as the water hitting her face altered colour. She closed her eyes in happiness. Mary shook her head as her flow increased, unable to comprehend Laura's reaction but suspecting that one day she would. Laura spread Mary's labia wide and urged her belly forward with that finger behind. Mary murmured, suddenly feeling rude and sexy. Laura touched Mary's clitoris. She cried, shuddered and keened as sharp, exquisite pleasure shot through her body. Her flow spluttered and splattered, receded, ceased.

Laura stood up and kissed her full on the mouth as she took Mary's hand and pressed it to her own mound. Warmer water flowed through Mary's fingers, and she knew Laura's moan as Laura's flow hit her thighs and disappeared down the drain.

Two

Mary's knees were still weak with a mixture of shock and the aftermath of that small orgasm when Laura turned off the water and began to towel her dry. They kissed frequently but uttered no coherent words. Astonished by everything that had happened since she rang the doorbell that morning, Mary could not hold a thought long enough to grasp it. Back in the bedroom, they drank more champagne as they dressed. Mary had to go back downstairs to the flat she shared with Philip; he would be back from work soon and, at least for the moment, her liaison with Laura could not become public.

All too soon it was time to part. They kissed for the last time, lingering, stretching the moment.

'Until tomorrow night, then.' Laura stroked her cheek. Mary felt desperately sad. Tomorrow night was so far away. 'Wear something special – I will.'

And then the door closed behind her. Those two words 'Until tomorrow' echoed mournfully in her ears. They planned to have an end-of-term meal together tomorrow night; Laura, Mary and Philip, who would be the only one of them staying in London for the summer. Laura was off to France to stay with her friends Penny and Jack. Mary had to go back to the isolated peace of the Yorkshire Dales, back to long hours of hard work and prayer. A grey gloom began to gather, clouding her happy, satisfied mood. She heard Laura's door open again.

'Mary!'

She turned and ran back, like a puppy to her mistress.

Laura stood with a finger in her mouth, smiling wickedly. 'I was thinking. Why don't you come to France with me?'

The sun came out again. 'That'd be great!' And then the full import of the concept sank in. 'But how can I? I gave my word I'd go back home. If I break it, they'll most likely cut me off without a penny.' Her mind began working overtime, trying to find a way round the obstacles. 'On the other hand, I might be able to convince them a trip to France would be educational.'

Laura seemed happy to wait on her final reply. 'You don't have to say yes now. Sleep on it, and we'll decide tomorrow.'

They kissed, as sisters, and Mary skipped away, new hope in her heart.

Philip came home before seven. Usually he was tired from a long day in the office, but this evening Mary noticed a spring in his step.

'Hi, Mary, get your results?'

She smiled, no longer so modest. 'Mm, I'll be back in the autumn.'

'Great!' He even kissed her on the back of the head. 'I've got some news too.' He delved into his briefcase and gave her a large buff envelope. 'Have a look at that.'

Mary read the top letter. It was from a solicitor.

Dear Philip,
Please find enclosed a letter from your father and other documents pertaining to your true identity.

This will be a surprise to you, because as far as I am aware until this moment you have been under the impression that you were an orphan. This was at the insistence of your father, Comte Henri du Bantonne, who has financed your upbringing and education.

Your employer has, as you will see, granted you indefinite leave of absence. Also enclosed are tickets and directions to your true home, your family's estate in France.

If you have any questions, please feel free to call or
visit me.

Your obedient servant,
Harold Cartwright-Hobley

For a few moments Mary did not know what to say; her
credulity was already exhausted by the day. No wonder he
was excited. Mary had often dreamt of waking up to find
her own parents' death had all been a bad dream. Unlike
Philip, Mary had always known what had happened to her
parents: killed in a car crash when she was four. Afterward,
she had been brought up in the Community. Philip had
been raised nearby, by his mother's family, though they
had met only last summer. She looked again at the letter,
and this time noticed the way the letter was addressed:
Philippe du Bantonne. He was no longer plain Philip
Banton.

Philippe, as she now thought him, sat down. 'You can
read the rest if you want, but it only confirms what old
Hobley says.'

'And you are going?'

'Of course. Soon as possible. Do you want to come with
me?'

Mary's jaw dropped. Another invitation to France, and
one the Community might find easier to accept. When she
met Philippe, she was trying to sort out some accommodation in London and not doing very well. The Community's
isolation was so extreme that she had no idea where to
start, nor did the Elders who were supposed to guide her.
Walking and worrying one hot afternoon, she had stopped
to bathe her feet in a stream forming one boundary of the
Community's land. A handsome young man appeared on
the other side and introduced himself. Shyly, Mary
answered, and they fell into conversation. It turned out
that Philippe, who already worked in London, was looking
for a flatmate. It was the answer to her prayers. He
managed to persuade the Elders that he had no designs on
Mary, nor would he lead her from the path of
righteousness, and they let Mary take up his offer. They

19

respected his word and good character, and neither he nor Mary had given them cause to reconsider, so they might allow her to go to France with him. If that were the case, she reasoned, later she could join Laura without them ever knowing.

'I'd like that very much. I'll write to my aunts right away. Mind, I might not get a reply until Tuesday at the earliest.'

'No problem. The tickets are open-ended.'

What a day! Mary could not believe it. She retired to her room to compose her plea.

Mary could not sleep, the result of neither the oppressive heat and humidity nor the remnants of intense arousal still affecting her vulva and breasts: it was guilt.

She had said her prayers as usual, reviewing the day through the filter of her creed, and found herself terribly wanting. She had broken vows of chastity outside marriage, plotted to deceive her aunts and done some very rude and disgusting things. She had fallen asleep, for a while, but sleep had been a riot of disturbing erotic dreams based on the events of the day. Disembodied, she had seen herself writhing under Laura's assault. Her nipples had grown enormous, the setting for great hoops of iron. Her vagina had been the receptacle for a huge sausage of flesh that she imagined a penis to be – she had never seen one. She woke then to find her fingers playing around her sex and bottom. She was wet and hot, and her nipples were almost painfully erect again.

Cold water did not cool the furnace; nor did more prayer. She struggled with her conscience and found the cause of her problem: her love of Laura. Comprehension produced the answer: the affair must be brought to an immediate end before she burst with self-loathing. At four in the morning Mary made up her mind, even though it hurt. The following morning she would tell Laura they could remain friends but not lovers. She would still try to go with Philippe, but she would not try to deceive her aunts by going on to join Laura. With her mind settled, she fell into a dreamless sleep.

* * *

The time to go out to the restaurant was fast approaching, and Mary had still not managed to contact Laura. She had knocked on her door first thing and used her key to enter, just in case she was still in bed, but there was no sign of her. Mary wondered where she might be. Perhaps she had gone to an end-of-term party, or out clubbing. Mary avoided both; she did not like drink and drugs. She left a note in a prominent place, and for the whole day she kept her ears open in case Laura came in.

Mary decided, after all, to put on her party frock, a frilly long white dress with a daring, for her, nipped-in waist that showed her figure. She had debated the matter long and hard. Although she was no longer trying to look her best for Laura, she decided to wear it anyway; it was the only opportunity before she left it behind for the summer.

She heard footsteps going up the stairs. Mary dashed out after Laura.

'Laura!'

Laura stopped halfway through the door and turned, beaming with delight. 'Mary, you look lovely!'

As she approached, Laura spread her arms in expectation of a cuddle. Mary stopped short. 'I must talk to you.'

Laura's smile faded, and Mary knew she had got the tone right. 'You'd better come inside.'

She waited until the door shut behind her. 'Laura, I've been doing some thinking and praying.'

Laura flopped into an armchair. 'And you're having second thoughts, right?' She looked disappointed, almost defeated.

'I'm sorry, L, but it's wrong. Yesterday, I broke almost every vow I've ever made, and my conscience won't let me do it any more.'

'So you want to cool it? Stay friends but cut the love?' Laura shook her head. 'I thought you felt the same for me as I feel for you.' She rubbed her face. 'You do, don't you?'

Mary felt a tear. She was in love with Laura, deeply in love. Her throat choked with tears, she could only nod.

21

Laura became vehement. 'It isn't wrong. I know it isn't wrong for two people to love each other even though they're the same sex.'

Determined to hold her position, Mary denied her heart's desire. 'It's women and men who make love, for procreation and nothing more. That's what God made sex for.' It sounded pompous, it was deliberately cruel, and it helped her come to terms with her decision. But as she said it she knew she was lying to herself. She ran away from Laura and her unhappiness.

As she ran out of the door, Laura called after her. 'M, we can still have dinner together tonight, can't we?'

She sounded so forlorn. Mary had to reply through her tears. 'Yes, yes.'

Laura stood under the shower. Running it cold, she numbed the pain and her tears stopped. What a lousy, rotten twenty-four hours this had turned out to be. After Mary left, she had been totally unable to settle, so she had gone to a party. People had talked and danced until daybreak, when they all went out for breakfast before crashing out for a few hours, since when they had watched tennis on television. It had been a good day, until Mary dropped her bombshell.

Running on autopilot, she dried off and began to dress. She poured a stiff Scotch and got down to some positive thinking.

It was obvious that Mary still loved her; certain that Mary did not, deep down, really believe all that crap about procreation and chastity. Therefore, there was still hope. After all, she was wearing that very un-Mary-like dress. She was not dolled up for Philip; more like brother and sister, those two. He clearly likes her, but he gave his word of honour, an unusual trait in modern man, and he won't break it unless Mary makes a move. However, Mary will not encourage him because she loves me. She won't tempt him into breaking a vow, and she has made a vow too.

Right then! On with the war-paint and off with the underwear – I'm going to change her mind.

Laura hung sapphires from all five rings under her dress and her earrings, decided not to wear stockings, and fetched out her tightest, shortest evening dress, a black silk number with shoelace shoulder straps. Strappy sandals, light eye-shadow and lipstick, and subtle, musky perfume completed her ensemble. So armed, but running a good quarter of an hour late, Laura went out to win back her lover.

The restaurant was just round the corner, an intimate Italian spot well known to them. The others were there already, and she noticed that Mary's eyes, like her own, had lost the puffiness of tears. She looked desirable, in a modest way. Laura thought that natural simplicity and lack of obvious allure were what had originally attracted her. Underneath, they were quite similar: fish out of water. Laura had not been entirely happy with her choice of university. She had only come to London because Penny's flat was available, and it was a long way from her family in Wales. The coincidence of Mary living downstairs and doing the same courses had been a godsend. Laura had needed a friend, and Philip was a bonus; he too had become a good friend, as well as being rather attractive.

'Philippe's got some terrific news,' Mary said as they perused the menu.

Laura wondered about the change of pronunciation. She looked up expectantly and realised that she had ignored the excitement bottled up behind his handsome, lively face.

'It appears I have a rich father and estates in France,' he announced with a wry smile and heavy irony.

Laura was stunned. The lucky bugger! She listened intently as he told the story, until he concluded: 'And Mary's going to see if she can come with me.'

Her heart dropped through the floor. For a moment she felt despair and betrayal, then anger and tears. She tried to cover up as tears gathered again. 'I am very, very happy for you, Phil. Can you excuse me a moment. I must powder my nose.' It was very hard not to run home and hide.

The bitch! She got a better bloody offer, and now she's

off to shag him instead of me! She stared hard in the mirror. Do I stay or do I go? How much more humiliation can she heap on me?

The door opened behind her. 'Laura, are you all right?' Mary's concern was completely genuine. Could she be more cruel?

Mary continued, checking Laura's vicious response. 'I know how it looks, but it wasn't like that. I don't even know if I can go with him yet.' She reached out her hand towards Laura's shoulder. Laura twisted away.

'Laura, please.' Mary's distress pierced Laura's anger. 'I love you.'

They embraced, both in tears. Laura had no idea what to say.

Mary cried into her ear. 'Why do things have to be so complicated?'

'I don't know, sweetheart. Hormones, probably.' Laura reluctantly broke away. 'Come on, dry your eyes. Phil will be wondering where we've got to. He might even think we're having a grope.' It was a feeble joke, but they both smiled. 'Maybe I should go – leave you two alone.'

Mary sniffed and found a tissue to blow her nose on. 'No, you stay. I'm very tired, and I need to be alone.' She smiled. 'It's funny, but Philippe's news has made me think about Mum and Dad and what I've missed.'

Embarrassed by this typical generosity, Laura offered her help. 'You sure? I'll walk home with you if you want.'

'No, better this way. I'll be all right. Come on, I'd better make my excuses to Philippe.'

They returned to the table. He looked concerned. Laura kept quiet while Mary explained. 'Phil, I'm not feeling very well. I think I'll get off home.'

'Oh, Mary, I'm sorry.' He stood up. 'Let me see you safely back.'

'Thanks, but you keep Laura company. You might not get the chance to see each other again until the autumn.' Mary kissed him on the cheek and left.

The starters arrived, and Philippe started a cheerful conversation. Laura slowly relaxed and began to enjoy herself. So, Philippe du Bantonne was going to be rich? He was certainly attractive, with his curly black hair, neat little bum and cheerful, gentlemanly disposition. Maybe he might be the one to see the other five sapphire settings tonight?

Mary took a glass of milk, the remains of a packet of chocolate biscuits, and tucked herself into bed. Had she made a mistake about Laura? She felt miserable and guilty again. She had spoilt Laura's summer, and her own would not be a bundle of laughs. The deceit implicit in the letter to her aunts had so far prevented her from putting it in the post. She wanted to go with Philippe; she would miss him otherwise. But now she didn't think she could bear his happiness when every moment she was being reminded of her loss. She wanted to go with Laura too, even now.

Seeking escape from her problems, she switched on the television and flicked through the channels. A drama caught her attention; a young girl's struggle to find love in her Newcastle home in the 1920s. Slowly, Mary sank inside the story, drank her milk and munched the biscuits. When the heroine lost her lover in error, she began to cry in sympathy. Next she watched a film, cried when a jealous suitor parted the lovers, and again cried, but with joy this time, when they were reunited in the last reel. She switched off, cuddled her pillow and cried some more. Mary realised now that she was in love with Laura. She would make it up with her when she got home, and until she heard Laura's feet on the stairs she would keep herself awake by reading a good book.

Time passed, and her eyes grew heavy and began slithering across the page. An image came to her: a scent, a mood, a memory from the previous afternoon. She closed her eyes, trying to recapture the essence of that lewd and glorious moment she first brought Laura to orgasm.

As her memory of every sensation returned, Mary's right hand reached for her ticklish mound, spreading thickened lips and pressing down beside the nub of her excitement. Her left hand went to her right breast and squeezed. She

25

plucked at her nipples and plunged into her vagina. In her mind's eye she saw Laura's reddened, dripping gash, and her mouth remembered the flavour of metal in honey. Her hand cupped her sex, rubbing deep between her lips, her thighs spread wider. Juices flowed hot and thick, her fingers became slick, her inner lips thick.

Gasping, she gripped and twisted a thick, hard, hot nipple, and then the other. She arched her hips, pressing against her plunging fingers. Wanting more, she rolled over and ground down. The empty ache came to her bottom again, and she tugged her other hand from her breasts. Laura's orgasmic cries echoed in her head. She wet a finger in her own juices and plunged it inside her bottom. All the time, other fingers plunged inside her sheath. Her thumb rubbed down hard on her clitty. Mary opened her mouth, uttering silent cries as stars burst inside her and she came under her own control for the first time.

Laura and Philippe crept up the stairs to her flat, intuitively agreeing that Mary must not know. She let him in.

'If you'd like a glass of wine, there's a bottle of white open in the fridge. I'm just going to my room.'

'Yeah, sure.'

She smiled as she turned away. He was trying to be cool, but he just couldn't keep the excitement from his face. Quickly, she tossed away her dress and found some underwear. She wanted to hit the right note; she felt sure he was a virgin, and to find her naked under her dress might be a little intimidating. Philippe was a difficult man to get inside; always aloof, always holding something back, but never in a secretive, unfriendly way. Laura decided to take it easy. There would be no bondage, no surprises for him. She chose one of her very few bras, a soft peach silk, and a pair of matching French knickers. Then she opened the door and posed, one arm reaching up the jamb, her hips curving out.

His face was a picture, eyes wide, the wine glass immobile at his lips. He swallowed nervously. 'Are you ready for your late birthday present?' He had celebrated his twenty-first just a few weeks ago.

It was all he could do not to choke. 'Er, yes, um, er –'

Laura smiled and held out her hand. 'Then come on, then.'

He stood up. She wished he was wearing tight jeans – he had such a tight, firm bum and a prominent bulge. Unfortunately, tonight he wore chinos. As he reached the door she began undoing the buttons on his shirt, revealing his firm, lightly tanned chest and V of dark hairs, the clearly delineated muscles of his stomach and shaded navel. He put up no resistance as she unbuckled his belt and unbuttoned his waistband. Laura pulled him close and forced him to kiss her. His lips were firm; at least he had kissed before. His hands found her back; they were strong, but already she knew he could never dominate her the way she needed. He held her, but did not crush her to him. Her forefinger traced the line of hair from his navel to the top of his boxers. She hooked that finger in the waistband and drew him to her bed.

Laura rested her head on his chest and nibbled a nipple as she drew down his zip and dropped his trousers. She licked down his centre line as she dropped to her knees and lifted his feet, one at a time, out of his trousers and removed his shoes and socks. She could feel his erection now, hard against her head. She pulled down his boxers and freed him. His cock pulsed as she held it. It was good and thick, the same colour as his tanned chest. She held his balls, heavy, almost hidden by almost black, thick hair. She peeled back his foreskin and kissed the purple plum. He groaned.

Calm down, she told herself. He'll come in seconds. She pulled away as she stood up again and ushered him on to the bed. She climbed over him, much as she had crawled over Mary. She wished Mary could be here to share him. His cock stood up against his stomach. She held it as she kissed his mouth, his neck, nipples and navel. She took his cock in her mouth. He took her head and moved it away. Laura did not let go with her hand.

27

'I can't last if you do that.' He looked so worried.

'You're a healthy boy, Philippe. Don't worry. I want you to – that way you'll last longer when we really get down to business.' She grinned.

He closed his eyes and she took him again into her mouth. He tasted strong, salty, healthy. He jerked and grew harder still. She cupped his balls and gently rolled them. They tightened. She sucked him further in. He was bigger than she had realised, and she had to breathe through her nose to stop from gagging. Her tongue ran around and she sucked a little. He jerked again, but though his fingers were still in her hair he did not pull her off again.

Laura tickled his crack and ridge, and slowly eased up and down his length. He gasped and moaned. She ringed the base of his stem with forefinger and thumb and pushed down as she moved away. His balls tightened further. His hips began bucking to her rhythm. His breathing grew harsh. She held tight and moved her lips up to the rim. She jerked her hand up and down, and he filled her mouth with jets of thick, salty, luscious sperm. She swallowed, and still it came. She swallowed some more, but some escaped. He subsided, and she licked up as much as she could, kissed the tip of his magnificent cock, and then lay beside him as he recovered.

Noises from upstairs disturbed Mary's sleep. She woke, annoyed at missing Laura's return and the chance to make up. She jumped from her bed, straightened her nightdress, put on slippers, located the spare key to Laura's flat and crept upstairs. Only at the top of the stairs did she wonder why there was no sign of Philippe in their flat, but dismissed it as unimportant. She let herself in. She wanted to surprise Laura in bed, sneak in and wake her with pleasure.

The bedroom door was open. From inside came faint sounds. She peered in. The candlelight was sufficient for Mary to see every detail. Two bodies entangled on the sheets; Laura with her back to the door, squatting over a

28

pair of muscular, male legs. Mary could see only his legs and hands. Laura's hips moved in a slow, circular motion. Mary tried to work out what she was doing, but whatever it was it made the couple grunt and moan with pleasure.

Laura bent forward to kiss her lover's chest. Jealousy stabbed. That was where she wanted to be: under Laura; with Laura; making love to Laura. A wave of intense emotion flooded through her and, though she wanted to leave, she had no confidence in her limbs to carry her away silently. She could not tear her eyes away in any case. This was another important part of the mysterious world she had entered yesterday in the same room, on the same bed. This was what men and women did together, what she had been trying to find out for years, ever since puberty started. The smell and sounds of sex mingled with the scented candles. Weak at the knees, she stayed where she was.

Laura raised her hips and began to work up and down. Mary suppressed a gasp. A thick, slick column of flesh came into view. At first it seemed to be a tube linking both bodies, but as Laura rose higher she saw Laura's inner tissues distend around the pillar. It was an erect penis. The real thing, not the sausage of her imagination. At its base between his thighs, a bush of black curly hair flattened by wetness, and his testicles, two tight balls of potency. Laura did not stop raising her hips until the penis began to narrow somewhat. A crown, almost purple, began to emerge. Mary thought it must pop out. It was so thick and long. How could Laura fit it all in?

Laura sat back down, swallowing the column. She grunted, sat upright, and began to plunge up and down, cooing soft words to her companion.

'Easy now, let me do the work. Oh, that's great. Oh.'

Included in the aura of sensuality, Mary stood transfixed. She felt a dampness between her thighs, and the now-familiar fullness returned. In concert with the rising arousal below, her nipples pricked into life. Unthinking, she put her hands to her breasts, cupping and massaging them. Her own feelings grew as perspiration appeared between Laura's shoulders. The penis came into view

29

repeatedly. She remembered other words she had heard but never voiced, even silently in her head, to describe it: cock, dick, willy, prick. No, it looked nothing like a prick. A prick sounded too small and insignificant. Willy sounded soft and useless, something that merely passes urine like a small boy's. Dick? That wasn't the image either. A dickhead seemed to be an idiot, and this thing was not idiotic. The column of hard, shining flesh had power, strength and virility. It was a cock, strutting and confident, a brash symbol of fertility, a phallus, a phallic symbol. The phrases flowed in her head as she came to realise what they really meant.

Mary's right hand left her breast and stroked her belly through her nightdress, scrunching the cotton into her sex. Hot wetness penetrated the material. She pulled it up, out of the way, and her fingers dug into her excitement. She began to imagine this act afresh, a living, pulsing, thick long cock inside her. She inserted a finger into her own tight sheath, the thickest thing that had ever been there. Could she stretch to take such a thing? She tried a second finger, and her vagina took it easily.

What about Laura's part in all this? The words Mary had been using to think of her own sex also seemed inadequate to the act to which she was witness. Vulva, vagina, clitoris, intercourse; none suited the deed. Vulgar expressions, the words of street-talk and abuse had appropriate vitality: fuck, cunt, screw. Old, Anglo-Saxon words that made sense now. They were the words of *Lady Chatterley's Lover*, a book proscribed by the Community but which Mary had read just as soon as she could.

She bit her lip, suppressing a moan. Laura and her partner mumbled to each other. Laura lay herself full-length without releasing his cock. They rolled over. Laura's legs spread wide, her knees bent and her feet gripped her lover's back as he knelt and began to thrust. His balls now hung between his thighs and swung back and forth as he drove into her. His back arched. Laura's hands came up, gripping his shoulders and scratching deep as her fingers clutched into talons. His head came up then, curly black hair swinging. She saw the left side of his face set in a grimace, and knew who it was.

Mary's heart went cold. Every drop of excited, heated blood fled from her face. Her hands froze. It was Philippe. The mild jealousy of a few minutes ago was nothing as compared with this. The blade plunged to her heart. Philippe? No, no, no. Not my Laura, and my Philippe!

Mary ran from the flat, tears pouring down her cheeks, not caring whether they noticed or not.

At six-thirty the next morning Mary wrote a note to Philippe. It was not an angry, emotional note. Instead, she simply told him that she could not go with him to France but had to go home. She left the reasons to his sense of honour and to Laura's conscience. Maybe, she thought, maybe I'll be back, but they'll have to beg my forgiveness. She put the note on the table, anchored it with a bottle of brown sauce, and left with her bags. She walked in the cool, clean early-morning air to the station. By teatime she would be back in the bosom of the Community.

Three

The rain had not let up since ten in the morning, but that didn't worry Mary. It gave her the excuse she needed to stay away from the rest of the Community. They would be indoors sheltering or getting on with their chores while the rain kept them from the fields. Mary, on the other hand, was doing what she wanted, reading and making notes for next term. It was the first opportunity to put in some solid hours since she came home almost a week ago.

Mary gazed through the window. Across the dale she could just about make out the village they all lived in. She was in her little study cottage, an old two-room stone building on the edge of the dale which had once been a keeper's cottage. This was Mary's private retreat, renovated three years ago to give her somewhere quiet to study away from the bustle. It had been a haven of peace, but after London the village itself was so quiet that that problem had disappeared. Now, Mary valued her cottage even more. The Community had become a prison. She felt cut off, blinded and deaf. At least here she could sneak a look beyond the high stone wall that surrounded the Community's land. Mary had smuggled a radio inside her baggage, though to conserve the batteries she listened only to the news.

Despite the rain, it was hot and sultry in the stone cottage. Mary undid the top three buttons of her blouse. The uniform, once a symbol of security, annoyed her. Women and girls all wore the same homespun garments: dark, dull long skirt, long-sleeved thick cotton blouse buttoned all the way to the neck, apron, headscarf and boots or sandals, depending on the weather. In winter, skirts were woollen, in summer, linen. Underneath, long shifts and bloomers were the norm, with the option of a laced bodice as support for the breasts; bras were too modern, and elastic was unknown. The headscarves were the only colourful item, though black had to be worn to chapel. Her head itched hot, so she removed her scarf and tied up her hair.

She turned back to her book. The Elders would not like this one little bit, she thought; too much sex and blasphemy. It was a set book, and she had to read it before next term. The rain poured down, she lost herself in the complex prose, occasionally sipping from a jar of ginger beer and chewing on some bread and cheese. Once in a while her pencil made notes. The rain poured on, and the tone of the prose became more and more erotic. Mary responded, nipples stiffening, rubbing on her linen shift. Unconsciously, she opened her blouse and reached in to adjust her breasts. They felt full. Little spasms of pleasure shook her body as she tried to make her nipples lie more comfortably. She rubbed her sore nubs, and the spasms reached her clitoris.

The prose built towards a climax. Her left hand reached down between her spreading legs. She was wet to the touch. Her fingers unbuttoned the front of her skirt and wormed inside, seeking the slit in her old-fashioned bloomers. Her fingers found her naughtiness. Mary closed her eyes as her fingers spread her lips. She knew what she liked now. At least once a day since coming home she had played with herself, revelling in her novel capacity for pleasuring herself. Each time, that pleasure had been accompanied by images of Philippe or Laura, though never at the same time. If she saw Philippe, she was the woman with him, his cock inside her, his mouth at her breasts. If she saw Laura, then their mouths and hands invaded each other.

Now the images came from the book. She felt the man's tongue running down her spine, his hands moulding her buttocks and stroking her thighs from behind. Her middle finger bent and ran up the length of her gaping slit. She let go of the book and closed her eyes. Her free hand lifted her right breast from her bodice and gripped her nipple, twisting. Her other hand rubbed over her mound, a finger dipping, bird-like, into the cup of her entrance.

The door slammed open. 'Naughty Mary.' Aunt Beverley's voice froze Mary into immobility.

'Yes, naughty little Mary,' Aunt Grace echoed.

Mary dragged her hands free and sat up, blushing, as the two women continued their intimidating double-act.

'Playing with herself.'

'All on her own.'

'In her private place, where none of us are supposed to come.'

'But she comes here, doesn't she, Beverley dear?' Grace emphasised the word 'comes', crudely, cruelly punning, laying on the sarcasm with a trowel.

'Yes, Grace, she comes here all on her own. Keeps it all to herself. Now that's not very generous, is it?'

'No, sister, not generous at all.'

'And she's breaking the rules, isn't she, Grace?'

'Yes, sister dear. So what shall we do about it?'

Mary was surrounded now, the two women behind and to each side. She could not escape.

'Perhaps Mary knows the answer. Does she want us to take her to the Elders, to have her sin announced in chapel?'

'Or does she want us to punish her privately?'

They both leant over her, sticking their faces in front of her face, and spoke in chorus. 'Privately or publicly? Speak up, girl. Cat got your tongue?'

Mary could not speak. Publicly? Shamed in front of the Community as she confessed? No. Privately, then. But what did that mean?

'She can't make up her clever little mind, Grace. All that education, and she's nothing to say.'

Mary finally managed to whisper her answer. 'Privately.'

'Sorry, niece, we didn't hear that.'

'Privately. Punish me privately.' Mary hung her head, defeated.

'Well, you'd better come with us, then.' They pulled her from the chair and thrust her out of the door. Grace did not let go of her right arm.

'Hey! I'll get soaked. Let me get my cape.'

Aunt Beverley locked the door behind her and pulled her own hood over her head. 'A little rain won't harm a fit young thing like you.'

'And naughty girls deserve what they get,' added Aunt Grace, nipping her arm spitefully.

Mary considered breaking away, sure she could overpower Grace, who was twice her age and lighter, but Grace tightened her steely grip and Beverley took a firm hold of her left arm. Already, Mary's clothes were getting wet, and they were still partially sheltered by trees. Once out in the open she would get soaked through. Her blouse gaped, and cold rain spattered on her chest. As they marched across the fields, the spatters became a steady drumming, and a rivulet ran down her cleavage. Her hair plastered to her skull, water dripped down her neck. Her skirt grew heavy, entangling her legs as she struggled to keep up the pace they were setting. Her sandals, which she had been wearing for comfort inside the cottage, grew slippery and gritty in the mud, the leather harsh and cutting. Thoroughly miserable and wretched, Mary was shoved through the door of their home some twenty minutes later.

'Stand still, girl!' roared Beverley as the two aunts removed their capes and Mary made for her room to change out of her soaking clothes. 'You'll stay where you are or it'll go even worse for you.'

'What a pathetic sight! Get those sandals off. I don't want muddy footprints all over the place.' Mary kicked them off. Grace grabbed her wrist. 'Come on, girl, into the parlour.'

The parlour was at the back of the house, overlooked by no one. 'Now you can strip.'

Mary fought back tears of humiliation and dutifully

undid the last blouse buttons. She tugged it off. Underneath she wore only the bodice, now wet and harsh against her skin. Beverley took the blouse.

'Now the skirt.' Mary dragged the buttons loose and handed it over.

'Bloomers.' Mary untied the soaking drawstring.

Aunt Beverley waited for them. 'Grace, I can't remember the last time we saw our little girl naked.'

Mary blushed again as she stepped out of her bloomers.

'Nor can I. Must have been years ago. I don't remember those rounded hips and all that hair.'

'Isn't she hairy? A real hairy Mary.'

'Almost as hairy as you, Beverley dear.'

'Unlike you. I think it's time to see those tits she was playing with. Come on, girl!'

Mary found their remarks puzzling. So unlike her staid, prim and proper aunts to be so crude or so intimate. Beverley's performance was particularly strange; she was usually so nice. It was Grace who had dished out any punishment for misdemeanours. Not that there had been many; an occasional smack on the bottom when she was very small, and through her clothes. Nothing like this.

Mary finished unlacing her bodice and it fell open, revealing her cold, rain-stiffened nipples. 'My, my, Gracie, aren't they nice and meaty.'

'Mm, and firm, like yours used to be, though not quite as big. Right girl, over the chair.' Grace pointed at her favourite high-backed wooden armchair. As she did so, Grace removed her thick leather belt from her narrow waist.

Mary stared at her, suddenly comprehending what was happening. They were going to belt her bottom. 'You ... no, you can't.'

'But you said you wanted to be punished in private. What did you think we were going to do, send you to bed so you can diddle yourself some more?'

'But –'

'But nothing, my girl. It's this, or we go to the Elders and tell them you want to confess your sins in chapel.'

Anything was better than standing up in front of the whole Community and confessing her precise sin. Mary turned and took hold of the arms of the chair.

'That's it. Head down on to the seat.' Mary lowered her head. 'No, dip your spine.'

Mary blushed as she pushed her bottom higher. She felt a foot tapping at her ankles. 'Part your legs. Your toes should be level with the feet of the chair.'

Mary groaned silently. Her thighs parted, and her bush peeked out. 'Keep your legs straight, no knee-bending.'

'How many strokes is she going to get, Gracie?'

'How many do you think she deserves, Beverley?'

'Well, it's got to be at least six for playing with her fanny, and another two for groping her tits. Then, of course, she tried to argue the toss, so I should think another couple, plus two more for not wearing her headscarf and looking like a tart.'

'A round dozen then? Right on the bottom.'

'And thighs. She ought to remember this.'

Mary felt foolish, bent over with her bum waving in the air.

'You keep count then, sister. Ready, Mary?'

'Ow!' The first stroke, admittedly not hard, snapped across her cheeks.

Beverley admonished her. 'What a crybaby. One. My granny hit me harder than that.'

'Just warming up, sister.' The second stroke was harder. Mary bit her lip as a broad strip of fire burst across her bottom. Her hands automatically flew to her bottom.

Aunt Grace stood back. 'Oh dear, Beverley, our little girl's a sissy. Mary, can you keep your hands down?' Mary had to rub her bottom. 'I don't think she can. Beverley, get something to tie her down, will you?'

A few moments later, Aunt Beverley's blonde head appeared beside her. She took hold of Mary's hand, looped a strip of cloth around her wrist and tied it to the arm of the chair. Mary swallowed nervously, remembering the highly erotic effect of Laura tying her to the bed. In a trice, Mary's other wrist was tied. Now her bum was humiliatingly elevated and exposed. Grace resumed the punishment. Mary's buttocks burnt, the heat suffusing her body. Oh no! It was happening again.

The third stroke was harder still, jolting Mary across the chair, breasts crushing into the polished wood. A surge of sensation radiated from her tender nipples. The fourth stroke was much lower, blazing across the top of her thighs and brushing her bush. Her clitty tingled. The fifth stroke was further down her thighs, urging her on to tiptoe. The next stroke came before her heels hit the floor again, stinging her inner thigh. Her legs opened wider in reflex, and her sticky, hot labia parted. How can I feel like this? she asked herself.

A cool hand on her bottom, stroking her untouched inner thigh, right up close to her bulging mound. A finger touched her lips. Mary realised she was wet.

Grace murmured. 'How about that? Our little girl's hot for it, randy little bitch.'

'But she's a virgin, isn't she? Never touched, innocent?'

'We caught her diddling, and now she's all hot after a little beating. That's not normal. Someone has been playing games with our little girl.' Grace stroked Mary's hot, sore bottom, fingers pressing closer and closer to her exposed, peeking sex.

Beverley joined in, her hand joining her sister's. 'Do you think it was that nice Philip she's living with?'

'No, no, not Philippe,' Mary protested.

Grace ignored her. Her fingers pressed closer, into the tight, wet sheath. 'Beverley, you can be dense, sometimes. Of course it wasn't him, or any other man. She's still a virgin. No man has been here, has he, Mary?'

'No, no.' Mary was defeated, embarrassed and nervous.

'But she's wet. Was it your friend Laura? The nice girl upstairs you wrote love letters to?'

Mary said nothing, too ashamed and frightened to be angry that they had read her letters. Grace's hand cupped her sex now, squeezing gently, one finger pressing between her lips, fingertip just touching the bump at her apex.

'Yes, it was Laura, wasn't it? No innocent she – and nor is our little Mary now, is she?'

39

Beverley stroked Mary's buttocks, gently, insistently. 'No longer innocent.' Her hands parted Mary's cheeks. 'Did she touch her there, do you think? Did her finger gently push inside this little pink ring?'

Mary gasped as a finger began pressing her there, just as Laura's had done. 'Did she wet her finger first, using Mary's juice, or her own spit?'

The finger left her for a moment, returning wet and cool. 'Or perhaps she used her tongue, curling it hard, and stabbing in, and tasting Mary's muskiness?'

Grace took up the conversation as Beverley's finger entered, making Mary grunt. 'And did Mary use her tongue on Laura, licking her hairy cunt?'

The vulgar language shocked Mary, insulted Laura and herself. 'It isn't hairy.' Mary spoke out loud, and then regretted it.

'Isn't hairy?' Grace's voice was full of scornful curiosity. 'Shaves her cunt, does she? A tart, is she? Fucks all the girls, I suppose. Does she fuck the boys too? Has she fucked your lovely Philippe?'

Mary began to cry. To admit that Laura and Philippe had, as her aunt put it with such vulgarity, fucked would betray all three of them.

'Do you think little Mary –'

'Not so little any more, Grace.'

'– would like to fuck us? To make up for her lies and deceptions? To show us what she's learnt in the big city?'

'I'm sure she would, Beverley, I'm sure she would. Wouldn't you, Mary?'

Mary shook her head. This was all wrong.

Grace whispered in her ear. 'Six more strokes, Mary? Or will you come upstairs with us?'

Mary shook her head again, bemused. The belt scorched her bottom ferociously.

'Another five like that, or are you coming upstairs?'

One of Beverley's soft hands stroked her buttock. It was a tender lover's touch. Mary felt lips on her burning flesh. Mary was tempted to take the soft way out, but with her aunts, the women she had treated as parents? No, anything

40

was better than that. She licked her lips and tasted salty tears, shook her head and gritted her teeth. The blows started immediately, thick and fast. Her body bumped and rubbed across the chair, her belly filled with a deep, dark red pulsing excitement. She moaned. The final stroke snapped vertically between her wriggling, sore cheeks, the tip sinking into her wet, pulsing vulva. The excitement blossomed and broke, and she cried with shame as she came.

It was as if the afternoon had never happened. The aunts bade her good night, and Mary escaped to her room. She undressed and lay face down on her bed to ease her sore bottom. Though her breasts and sex still felt congested, she did not touch herself because her mind was now deeply troubled.

So, her maiden aunts did have a sex life. All that preaching about chastity, virginity, purity and self-control was mere hypocritical claptrap disguising their lewd habits. Were the rest of them hypocrites? If she went outside now and peeked through the windows, would she find everyone rutting? Did the Elders and adults all indulge in unusual forms of fornication? What did anything mean any more? The Community made every effort to keep Mary all to themselves, imprisoning her in their little den of iniquity, and Mary did not want to be a part of it any longer. The Community had made solemn promises, and now they had broken them. The Community claimed to be the better way, claimed moral authority and ownership of its members' lives, but for Mary at least those claims lay in tatters.

Mary climbed to her feet, opened the window and looked out on the night. The breeze brought the clean, pure scent of the countryside after rain. The sky was clear, and moonlight illuminated the village and the road out of the valley. It went south, towards London and France, towards Laura, Philippe and the future. She had no idea where Laura might be, but she remembered Philippe's address.

41

Moving quietly, Mary closed the curtains, lit the lamp and dug out her outside clothes. She had almost a hundred pounds in her wallet, another hundred or two in her account, and an untouched credit card the bank had persuaded her to accept. Enough, she hoped, to get to France. She dressed quickly, picked up the keys to the flat, and crept out of the house. It would take at least a couple of hours to walk to the nearest town, more than three to reach the nearest railway station. It was one in the morning, and no one saw her leave the Community for the last time. Mary marched down the road, stopping only to retrieve her books from her study.

Four

Laura looked out over the Loire from her bedroom windows. The sun twinkled on the languid water, a slight breeze ruffled the plane trees that lined the road, and the vines gleamed in their low ranks along the contours of the slopes below. Closer at hand, the gardens burst with vibrant colour, and butterflies fluttered round the rose bushes adorning her balcony. Ice tinkled in her orange juice, and the croissant tasted buttery and fresh. She breathed in the scent of the roses, brushed a crumb from her silk slip and sighed sadly.

It was all so perfect and peaceful. Everything she could possibly want was available: two pretty maids at her beck and call, excellent food, a hunky gardener, video and sound systems in her room, an on-line computer, a full library, a swimming-pool, Jacuzzi, sauna, massage parlour, gym and a well-stocked wine cellar. You name it, Jack and Penny's home had it. Perhaps that was why Laura sighed. The chateau was their home, just like the flat she used in London and the car she arrived in a couple of days ago. Laura had some money of her own, but the fact that all the good things in life were gifts from Penny and Jack rankled.

Not that Laura resented Jack and Penny; she loved them, and they loved her. That last point now seemed to need some clarification. Laura and Penny loved each other in both a sisterly and physical way. Penny was a natural submissive, bringing out the dominatrix in Laura as no one other than Mary could. At the same time, Penny was the

43

sort of assertive, career-minded woman Laura aspired to be. Although distant cousins, they had first met two years before on the island run by the unpleasant Mr Tostides. At first, Penny acted like an older sister, helping Laura cope with her training in sensuality, but gradually they had become lovers. There, too, Laura met Jack, Penny's then master and now husband. He had taken the gift of Laura's virginity and was the first, and up to now the only, man Laura had ever felt any love for. Something in that relationship had changed, however. Perhaps it was Penny's impending motherhood; she was some five months pregnant. Maybe he found the task of educating new maids to his particular needs more interesting, or possibly it was Laura's failure to bring Mary for her initiation. Laura could not be sure. What was certain was that he seemed quite uninterested in her now.

A knock on the door interrupted her line of thought. Laura crossed the length of the room, bare feet stepping on polished marble and deep soft carpet, to let in her visitor. It was Penny, glowing, full and smiling with morning sunshine.

Her cheery disposition failed to rub off on Laura. 'Hi.'

'What's up, darling, still missing your lovely Mary?'

Laura had spilt her heart about Mary the evening she arrived. 'No, not really.' She returned to her breakfast.

Penny followed, sat opposite and poured herself a glass of juice. 'The doctor says I shouldn't drink too much coffee. Makes me want it all the more.' She wore a long, white, billowing dress that showed off her natural dark colouring but disguised her bump. 'So what's up, then?'

'Oh, nothing really.' Laura looked up. Penny waited patiently for more. Laura sighed. 'It's Jack. He doesn't seem interested in me any more.'

Penny let her eyes drop for a moment in silent acknowledgement of the validity of Laura's remark.

Laura continued. 'Is it because Mary didn't come with me?'

'Maybe. He was looking forward to helping you train her. I'm not sure that's all, though. I think it's the baby.'

44

Penny stroked her swollen tummy. 'He's spent all his life getting himself in and out of adventures, and suddenly he's got someone else to worry about, someone who needs him to be around for a long time.' She smiled. 'My little boy's having to do some quick growing up.'

'But marrying you didn't stop him wanting me.' Laura remembered how they made love only minutes before the ceremony, and again that night with Penny lying chained beneath them.

'I used to enjoy it too.'

The implication that Penny no longer wanted to share Jack with Laura was plain. 'Have you changed, then?'

'No. Absolutely not.' Penny's eyes dared Laura to contradict her as she stood up and took Laura's hand. 'He's a bit mixed up. I think this business with Natasha has made him think.'

Natasha was the newest maid, a Russian girl conned into coming West, rescued from a short, horrid life of prostitution and drugs by Jack's intervention during a follow-up to the Tostides affair. Laura let Penny lead her to the bed. 'What was so different about Natasha?'

'The cruelty of the traffickers, I think. They had no thought for the women. They were just a commodity, animals to be broken and traded. When he found Natasha, she was drugged up to the eyeballs, her mouth and eyes taped over, in a tiny cage in the back of that truck. Something changed inside him. He got angry, lost control, and killed three of the men. He'd never lost it before, and it frightened him. And when I told him I was expecting, he started to think about his child and its future – what if it's a girl and she gets mixed up in something nasty?'

Laura thought about their own brush with a man who treated women as mere objects and shuddered. Tostides had threatened to sell them to a Russian warlord. They had been saved only at the last minute by his trusted assistant, the beautiful, black and dangerous Donna. She had spent one night with the Russian, and his treatment of her so horrified Donna that she helped Jack rescue Laura and Penny. Penny suddenly hugged Laura tight. Laura rested her head against Penny's fuller, heavier breasts. Penny hugged her close.

'Laura, I didn't come here to talk about Jack and Natasha, I came to see you. You've been back two whole days but we haven't even kissed properly yet.'

Guilt swept through Laura. 'I'm sorry, Pens, lovesick and feeling low.'

She turned her face up and sought Penny's lips with her own. The tender kiss and the feel of her first love's soft, full body raised her spirits. Passion rose, and she opened her mouth for tongues to move. Laura's strength returned, and she began to take charge. She exposed Penny's right shoulder and kissed her brown skin. She pushed the other shoulder strap down, and her mouth sought the rise of Penny's breasts. She licked into Penny's full cleavage and along the top of the cotton where it cut into the swollen, milk-heavy gourds. Penny moaned. Laura pulled the dress down further, until it cut across the swollen nipples.

Laura stepped back. 'Kneel, slave, and use your tongue.'

Penny sank to her knees, her arms held tight to her sides, and bowed her head until she was below the hem of Laura's slip. Then she rose again, lifting the silk, until her mouth was level with Laura's pussy.

'Thank you, mistress,' Penny whispered softly, before beginning to lick Laura's slit from base to tip, tickling each ring as she went. Laura parted her thighs to let Penny's tongue part her lips and begin a heavenly, gentle arousal.

Laura caressed her own breasts and closed her eyes. There was a knock on the door. Laura did not stop, or let Penny halt. 'Come.'

The other maid, Corinne, entered. She stopped, embarrassed and confused by seeing them. 'What do you want?'

Corinne's English was very good. 'I came to take your breakfast away, mistress, if you have finished.'

'Well, go on then.'

Laura watched the maid go over to the window and bend to tidy everything on to the tray. She wore a tiny uniform which showed the lower curves of her buttocks

46

below the hem. A narrow line of white betrayed knickers, which struck Laura as unusual in a house run by Jack.

'Do you always wear knickers, Corinne?'

The maid straightened abruptly, and her hands tugged down her skirt as she turned, blushing. 'No, mistress.'

'Then why are you wearing them now?' Penny's tongue slowed as she listened to the exchange. Laura waited for an explanation.

'I thought you might be offended, mistress.'

'Me, offended by your bare bum? I am offended by your failure to follow house rules, Corinne. Remove the knickers at once, take away the tray, and return immediately with a bottle of champagne and two glasses.'

Corinne quickly pulled down her knickers, put them on the tray and fled.

'Stand up.'

Penny rose to her feet. Laura turned her round and unbuttoned her dress. It fell away to reveal Penny's flawless back. From here, there was not a sign of her bump, except she now had a dimple at the base of her spine. 'You've put on a bit of weight.' Laura smacked the offending spot. 'Your bum's getting big.'

'It must be lack of exercise since I gave up work.'

Laura stroked Penny's buttocks. 'But it's still very smackable.'

She kissed Penny's shoulder and turned her round. Penny looked absolutely lovely. Her breasts had really grown, now bulging and drooping under their extra weight. Her nipples were thicker, their haloes glowing and darker, almost purple. Her belly rose, proud and firm, before swooping back to her shaved, prominent mound. Only one of her rings, the wedding ring in her clitty, remained.

'You've removed your rings.'

'My nips were getting sore, and the ones in my lips would have had to come out sooner or later anyway.'

Laura decided to tell her what was going to happen next. 'When Corinne gets back, I'll put cuffs around your breasts, tie you to the bed and have her use a feather on

47

your nipples. If she makes you come, I'll smack her bottom. Then she can tongue me while I make you come again.'

Penny stroked her own breasts. 'Don't tie them too tight – they can get very painful.'

Laura kissed them. 'Of course not.'

Laura kissed Penny softly on the lips and snuggled down beside her. Beyond the rise and fall of Penny's bosom, she could see Corinne's naked form chained to the wall. Clamps gripped her nipples and outer labia, and a faint buzzing came from the vibrator in her bottom. She wriggled and gurgled behind a gag. Laura had no desire to be distracted by moans of pleasure while she and Penny recovered.

'L, why don't you go back and make it up with Mary?'

'I did something very silly, and I'm sure she doesn't want to see me.'

'What did you do?' Penny rolled over to look at her.

'When she broke it off, I got jealous and seduced her flatmate, Philippe. I think she must have found out, 'cos otherwise she would have gone with him to his father's place.'

'Why did making love to Philippe upset her so much?'

'She's been in love with him for ages, though she never realised.' Laura sighed. 'It was spiteful of me. And stupid – I didn't even want him that much.'

'Then you must make it up with her, for your own self-respect.'

Laura closed her eyes for a moment and imagined the scene: Mary in her Community clothes running down the path to Laura's car as she pulled up, tears and smiles in both their eyes.

'All right, I will.' She leant over and kissed Penny. 'Thank you.'

Three days later Laura drew up at the heavy farm gate that divided the Community from the outside world. The gate was set in an imposing dry-stone wall that flowed over the hillsides. Beyond the gate, a rough track wound away between parallel stone walls towards a belt of woodland beyond which she could see the roofs of the village, perhaps two or three miles away. Wheel ruts in the track had made such a high ridge down the centre that there was no way she could take the car further, and in any case she knew the Community abhorred motors. She parked to one side and locked up. It was a fine afternoon, and she had come prepared for a walk. She took her shoulder bag, put on a straw hat as protection against the sun, tied the arms of her rainproof jacket round her waist, clambered over a stile beside the gate and set off down the track. Laura had no illusions that she would be welcomed by Mary's people, but she had made an effort not to be too provocative, wearing a long loose skirt, a baggy lumberjack shirt picked up in a camping shop in Skipton, and no make-up. She had even put on a bra.

There were no people in sight, just sheep. All the fields appeared to be set aside for grazing sheep or cattle. As the track dipped and turned, she was able to look down on the village. No church spire, but otherwise it looked like all the other villages she had driven through during the day: a huddle of cottages in a terrace on either side of the street, and a couple of shops. Above the houses, a neoclassical chapel imposed itself on the inhabitants. Smoke drifted from chimneys, reminding her there was no electricity or gas, so all their hot water and cooking must be fuelled by wood or coal.

The track emerged from between the walls as it neared the trees, and for the first time she saw another human being. A tall man in black trousers, straw hat and collarless shirt leant on his scythe and watched her. He looked casual and relaxed, as if he knew all about her. Laura suddenly felt apprehensive. Up to now she had only been worried about confronting Mary, but something in the brooding atmosphere suggested she was unwelcome. She tried to fight the urge to smoke, but lost. Smoking was not a habit, but she always carried a packet just in case. It was another trait she had picked up from Penny, though of course Penny had given up.

49

Her lighter scraped the flint with unnatural loudness as she entered the shaded final stretch to the village. As she reached the end, two male figures appeared, black shapes blocking her passage. Both wore wide-brimmed hats, long coats and held shepherds' crooks in their hands.

'Good afternoon, miss. May we help you?'

She was close enough to see their faces. The tall speaker had a long grey beard and his long hair trailed below the rim of his black hat. She put on a smile and lightness of voice she did not feel to tell her little white lie.

'Good afternoon, sir. I'm Laura Jenkins. I was just passing, and I thought I'd pop in and see my friend, Mary Coppen.'

The other man looked sharply at his companion. Laura sensed a defensive reaction.

Greybeard replied. 'Ah, yes, Mary. Come with me, Miss Jenkins. I'll take you to her aunts. I'm sure they'd be pleased to meet you.'

They walked together, with the second man a few steps behind. People turned to watch her, and she wondered when the last visitor from outside had passed through. One young man came down to the street, his eyes out on stalks, until Greybeard chased him away.

'Be about your business, Thomas Thwaites.' Thomas ran away like a scolded child, but not before Laura had seen a look of naked lust in his curious eyes.

'Here we are, Miss Jenkins. I'll just tell them you're here.'

He strode up to a detached cottage and rapped on the door with his crook. The door opened and a tall, thin woman greeted him. Laura was too far away to hear their conversation; all she could do was to smile pleasantly every time the woman shot her a look. After some while, Greybeard beckoned her to join him.

'Miss Jenkins, this is Miss Grace Haverthwaite. I'll leave you in her hands.'

'Thank you. Oh! I didn't catch your name.'

He glowered at her, all amiability banished. 'The Reverend Nathaniel Goodman.'

Laura almost jumped backward in her attempt to avoid the hatred pouring from his eyes. The woman took her elbow.

'Come in, Miss Jenkins.' She was led into a pleasant parlour.

The woman called up the stairs. 'Beverley, we have a visitor, come to see our Mary.' She turned to Laura. 'Please take a seat. Would you like a cup of tea or lemonade?'

'Tea, please.'

Aunt Grace went off to make the tea as Aunt Beverley appeared at the foot of the stairs. She was rounded and, Laura thought, must have been quite pretty as a girl.

'So, you're Laura Jenkins. Not quite what I imagined. Welsh, if I'm not mistaken.'

Laura smiled pleasantly. 'Yes, from outside Cardiff.'

Grace returned with a tray she put on the sideboard. 'Rather short and skinny.'

'And no make-up. I think she's trying to impress us,' Beverley sneered. 'She can't impress us, can she Gracie?'

'We're not impressed by tarts.' Mary's aunts stood side by side.

'Or whores.'

Why are they talking like this? Not very Christian, thought Laura.

'This slut's come to steal our niece.'

Laura pressed herself back into the chair as the two women advanced.

'Maybe she doesn't know.'

'I'm sure she doesn't.'

'So what does she know?' they chorused, their faces close to hers, and waited for her answer.

Laura tried to play cool. 'What don't I know?'

'That her little lover's run away.'

'Taken all her money and run.'

Laura felt cold all over. Mary gone already? Then where was she? Not at the flat. Laura had spent last night there.

'Where's she gone, you little tart? Where's our pretty niece, the one you turned against us, the one you fucked?'

51

Laura looked down at her hands. 'I don't know. I thought she was here.'

'Is she in London?'

'No, or at least she wasn't there this morning.' She looked up, suspicion forming in her mind. She could not remember if Mary knew where Penny and Jack lived, but she knew where Philippe was. 'When did she go?'

The aunts retreated, giving her space now she was co-operating. Grace stared at her. 'Early Saturday morning. Why, do you know where she's gone?'

Laura might have an idea, but she wasn't going to tell these two harridans. If Mary had run away, she obviously had good reason, and it was not Laura's place to betray her. 'I have absolutely no idea.'

'No idea. Do you hear that, Gracie? The little tart's got no idea. But it's all her fault, isn't it? Little slut turns our Mary's head, corrupts her, and she has absolutely no idea.' Beverley gave a passable impersonation of Laura's light Welsh accent.

Laura felt menace in her words, a menace confirmed as Grace grabbed her wrists and pulled her from the chair with surprising strength.

'I think she needs to be taught a lesson, reminded of her responsibility for leading our little innocent astray.' Laura opened her mouth to protest, but Beverley interrupted.

'She might be willing to help, sister. Perhaps she will help bring Mary back, if we can persuade her.'

Laura stared bleakly at the backs of her hands. No amount of persuasion could make her bring Mary back to this, but she could play along in the hope of picking up clues.

'Can I see her room? She might have left some kind of clue for me.'

A pause. Laura looked up. Some sign had passed between them, because they both smiled strangely.

Grace took her hand. 'Come on. Show us how clever you are.'

Laura followed Grace up the stairs. Beverley followed close behind. Grace opened a door on the landing and

Laura was bustled inside. Laura looked around the simple bedroom. A double bed, a big built-in wardrobe, a chest of drawers and a bedside cabinet, all old-fashioned, solid, heavy and functional oak. There was not one familiar object. Mary's clothes, Bible and books, all missing. The door closed behind her as she realised it was not Mary's room. She had been tricked.

Grace held Laura's arm. 'The blindfold, I think.' Beverley went across to the wardrobe, opened the door and went inside.

Laura swallowed. 'What do you think you're doing?'

Grace tugged her further inside the room. 'We are going to teach you a lesson.'

'What kind of lesson?'

'You'll soon find out.'

Beverley reappeared with a suitcase, opened it, and produced a strip of black velvet. Laura's muscles turned to water, her heart thudded in her chest. Beverley came forward, tied the blindfold around her head and the room was blacked out. Hands grabbed at her clothes. Laura pulled away, and a hand slapped her bottom.

'Ow!'

'Stand still, or you'll really feel something!'

Quickly, but without tearing buttons or zips, the sisters removed Laura's clothes. Once nude, she felt soft hands on her breasts and buttocks. Beverley whispered with excitement, and Laura began to understand what they wanted.

'Oh my, Gracie, she's got little rings in her teats.' A hand slid between her legs, and Laura felt a familiar tingle of anticipation.

'And she's as smooth as a baby's bum. No wonder Mary fucked her, she's a little gem. Hey, she's got rings in her cunt!'

'Leave her, Bev. Help me get things ready.'

For a few minutes Laura heard them undressing and sorting out the room. Then she was pulled towards the bed.

'Now, my dear, it's time to see what you know. Lie down.'

The aunts made her lie on her back, stretched out her arms and fastened them with cords. They joined her on the bed, one on each side. They were naked. Grace, all bones and angles to her left, the soft bulk of Beverley to her right. Their hands roved across her body, kneading her breasts, and parting her thighs to probe between her legs. At first she lay still and stiff, numbed by the speed of events. Then a mouth closed on her left breast. Softly and gently, lips, teeth and tongue began to work away. The other mouth closed on her right breast. This mouth worked more aggressively, teeth sharper, sucking harder. The tingling grew and spread, and her breathing became rapid. Her shoulders and hips moved.

The mouth quit her left breast, fingers rolling the nipple instead, and she was kissed on the mouth. She gasped. Teeth trapped her bottom lip and bit insistently, sucking hard. The other mouth moved to her thighs; fingers rolled her right nipple. Both nubs were pulled, stretching her breasts up. Then the fingers let go, and her breasts bounced back. Hands slapped her breasts from each side. Her cry of dismay was swallowed by the kissing mouth. A glow filled her. Lips and tongue sucked in her ringed labia, chewed and flickered. Laura's hips jumped, and then her mouth was against a breast. It was small, but the nipple was very long.

Grace whispered. 'Suck, little girl, bite. Get it hot.'

Laura obeyed. The nipple tasted dry. She sucked, and it grew to the diameter of a little finger. She grabbed it with her teeth and licked the tip. Satisfied, Grace inserted her other breast. This nipple was not so round and a little knobbly, but Grace's reaction to Laura's nibbling suck was much stronger. She groaned and thrust her bosom hard against Laura's face.

Down below, Beverley was no longer working on Laura's sex. Her hands were under her bottom, raising it. Laura felt a cushion shoved under her. Her ankles were pulled apart and tied to the foot of the bed. Excitement, brought on by her vulnerability, enhanced by the blindfold and the aunts' silent routine, grew. Grace pulled away, and

54

Laura lost track of who was where. Hands adjusted her position, and then she felt something being tied round her waist. A strap was pushed down between her legs and fastened tight to the belt at the back. She felt a snug weight on her sex, something that moved when she wiggled her hips. She heard Grace laugh.

Beverley spoke. 'Shall we let her see?'

Her head was lifted, the blindfold removed, and light flooded in. She looked down, blinking. Rising from her groin was a polished wooden phallus that must have been almost a foot long and about two inches across. Grace knelt over her and held the tip to her slit. Laura looked up at her small breasts and long, purple nipples. Her body was very pale, with stark black pubic hair streaked with a few grey hairs. Grace murmured, spread her lips, and sank down on the phallus. Laura took her weight. The leather base of the phallus ground against her delta. Grace worked herself slowly up and down, and Laura felt each movement, each impact. Her clitty and lips began to throb. Grace rubbed her own sex, roughly.

Beverley, who had been kneeling beside her, suddenly blocked her view. Her breasts, heavy, soft and rose-tipped, swayed above her rounded tummy. She moved up, above Laura's head, and then knelt across her face, watching Grace screwing herself up and down the length of wood.

Laura's hips were moving now, responding to the rhythm, enjoying the stimulation. Then her sight was blocked out as Beverley lowered herself over her face.

'Give me your tongue, Laura.'

Laura hesitated. Beverley's sex was almost completely obscured by a thick, unruly thatch of pale-brown hair stretching between her legs and down her heavy thighs. The heady odour of arousal pervaded the small space between them.

'We know you like it. We know you've done it before.'

Laura swallowed. Beverley took hold of her nipples and twisted gently. Laura murmured. She twisted harder. Laura groaned and wriggled. Beverley pulled her left breast up, stretching the tissue into a cone. Laura grunted as shocks of excitement sparked out from her tortured nub. Beverley smacked the taut cone. Laura cried and opened her mouth. She stuck out her tongue and met Beverley's bush as it descended.

It was all so wrong, having sex with Mary's aunts, but also rude and arousing. Her clitty felt like a golf-ball-sized knot of energy, super-sensitive and greedy. Her breasts, despite the smacks, were swollen with lust, her bitten bottom lip thick and throbbing, now rubbed against Beverley's thick, long inner lips. Beverley tasted earthy, robust and unrefined. Laura stuck her tongue into the dripping heat and felt the tight walls pulsing around her. Beverley moved, pushing her clitoris down to Laura's tongue. It was long and thick, even before Laura's mouth began to work. It grew as big as the end of a little finger. Laura sucked and tickled the tip. Beverley juddered and cried.

Grace, meanwhile, had not let up her screwing motion, and Laura began to suck or lick in time to the thrusts as she heard Grace's grunts, feeling the bump of the dildo against her own clitty. Beverley would gasp or grunt as her clitoris was sucked hard. Beverley shifted again, this time offering her vagina for a few moments before sitting further forward. Laura understood what was wanted, but the looming bulk of those generous buttocks, and the brush of curly hairs against her nose and lips, reminded her of darker, more dangerous times. She hesitated again.

Beverley gripped her nipples hard in warning. Laura took a deep breath but still rebelled. Beverley tugged her left breast into a cone again. Grace stopped moving.

'Come on, girlie, get your tongue moving.'

Laura yelped as Beverley's hand smacked her breast, and yelped again as Grace pinched the insides of her thighs high up near her groin. She pushed her tongue into the dark cup and tickled the tight, twitching rose. The tension broke, Grace resumed her screwing up and down the phallus and Beverley released Laura's breast, settling down to enjoy her questing tongue.

It was not, after all, unpleasant. Quite the reverse. She

could feel Beverley's pleasure and excitement through the way her anus twitched and softened, and hear her sighs. At the same time Beverley began to give her pleasure, caressing her breasts and gently squeezing her ringed nipples. Laura began to ride on the wave of sensuality; her clitty bumped and ground as Grace's cries reached a crescendo. Her own climax began to build, and when Beverley shifted her focus back to her sex, Laura's whole being was devoted to the giving and receiving of sexual excitement. Her mind gave itself over to the multiple stimulation, and she was about to burst when, quite suddenly, they climbed off.

'All change.' Grace declared happily. Laura sighed her disappointment. Grace noticed. 'Bev, make sure she doesn't come too soon.'

'OK, sister dear.'

Laura looked down to see the phallus being removed. Beverley mounted Laura's hips with her back to her sister. Grace held another phallus. Beverley bent forward, presenting her bottom. She reached back with her hands and spread her buttocks. Grace pressed the tip of the fat, eight-inch black phallus to her sister's lubricated rose and pushed. Laura stared as the smooth rod slid inside, stretching the shining muscle, until just an inch was left outside. This last inch was a bulb of greater diameter.

Beverley settled her weight on to Laura's hips and began, gently, to rub her wet sex over Laura's thighs. Grace knelt behind Laura's head. Laura looked up. Grace was slim and hard, her breasts almost flat, with only the purple tips visible above the rising dome of her tummy. Amid silky pubic hair, red-purple lips showed as a streak of vibrant, wet colour. Grace bent forward and gave her nipples to Laura's mouth before lowering her sex.

For the next few minutes, Laura licked and sucked as the two older women undulated over her. When Grace presented her bottom, Laura lapped at it without hesitation. Slowly, much more slowly than before, Laura's excitement began to climb again, but Beverley, while taking as much as she could from Laura, was careful not to stimulate Laura's sex more than a little. The older women came to their pleasure, Grace grunting, Beverley sighing, before leaving Laura, wet-faced, perspiring and frustrated.

For a while they lay on either side, stroking and kissing each other and Laura, titillating her nipples and sex but never letting her climax. When Laura began to whimper with frustration, they left her and dressed. Once more the picture of conformity, they pulled Laura to her feet, released her wrists and smacked her bottom all the way to another bedroom.

Grace held a door key. 'This is Mary's room, so I'm sure you'll feel at home. You can stay here until we decide what to do with you.'

Laura stared as the door was locked. Naked, she was imprisoned, and she cursed.

Five

The taxi turned and sped away down the hill. Mary looked at the great wrought-iron gates, opened to her by unseen hands. She felt sure they had been closed when she had first glimpsed them from the last bend only a couple of hundred yards back. Not a soul around, not a sound, not even a bird singing in the dense wood bursting over the high stone wall that enclosed the top of the ridge. She looked back over the broad, almost limitless plain towards the heat-haze-hidden horizon. Below, a plume of dust blossomed from the heart of the small hamlet as the taxi returned home.

That's odd; the telegraph poles stop at the edge of the village. Perhaps the château is fed electricity and telephones from the other side. A movement caught her eye. High above, a buzzard circled on a thermal, a hunter seeking prey. Mary seemed to be the only moving, living thing, and she wondered if she was its supper. She shivered despite the late-afternoon heat, turned, and set foot inside the estate. Before she had taken five paces, she was in a world of shadows, the sun unable to penetrate the overhanging branches. She heard a clang behind her. Through no discernible human or mechanical agency, the gate was shut again. She took a deep breath, summoned her courage and walked on.

The drive wound through dark, thick, tangled wood, paved with rough stones interrupted by sand, weeds and rank grasses growing where wheels never ran. As she walked, the fading afternoon closed in. Soon she could see neither the gate behind nor the destination ahead. Nothing changed on either side: fir trees, thick bushes and bramble tangles seemingly uninhabited by small animals or birds. She recalled Bilbo Baggins and the Dwarfs marching through Mirkwood. She peered into the gloom, half expecting to see elves or giant spiders. Sweat gathered on her face and began to trickle, her eyes smarting. She felt awfully dusty and tired on the endless path. Time and again she swapped hands to carry her case, ever more quickly as her shoulders tired, and she ruminated on how unfit university had made her.

Head down and almost blind with fatigue, suddenly she burst out of the trees. In front was a wide grassy space bisected by the drive. At the end of the drive was the château. She stopped, dropping the suitcase, and gazed on her journey's spectacular end. It was like a fairy-tale castle. Rising from a terrace, four round towers soared up from the many-windowed main building. Steps led up to an entrance thrust out of one tower. There was no one in sight. The manicured grounds looked as if the gardener had just packed up for the day.

Crossing the open space, she searched the windows. As far as she could tell, with the dying sun reflecting golden shards of light from the windows, not a curtain twitched nor a face looked out. At the end of her strength, she climbed up the steps to the imposing doors and dropped her suitcase. She looked for a bell pull but found only a great knocker. It weighed a ton, and the ground seemed to shake under her hot, travel-swollen feet as the reverberations shook the still evening. The echoes died, and silence descended. The evening was drawing on, the light fading so much more quickly than the dawdling summer evenings of home. For all her earlier determination, Mary began to question her sanity in travelling hundreds of miles to a foreign land, with only a few pounds in her pocket, to a place she did not know. But this must be Philippe's château. It must!

The door opened, startling her from her reflections. A tall, somewhat oriental, statuesque woman stood waiting for an explanation for this interruption. Mary spoke in French, uncomfortably aware of her schoolgirl accent and hoping the woman would speak slowly so she could understand.

'Good evening, madame. My name is Mary Coppen. I have come to find my friend, Philippe du Bantonne.' As she waited for a response from the woman, Mary felt a need to embellish her simple statement. 'He invited me.'

The woman nodded, looking her up and down and wrinkling her nose at Mary's dusty, creased clothes and travel-streaked face. 'Come in, Mademoiselle Coppen. I will inform Le Comte you have arrived.' Mary made to pick up her case. 'Leave it. A maid will take it to the room prepared for you.'

Mary blinked. Expected? She followed the woman into an intimidating, grand, cool entrance hall. The woman opened a door to the left.

'If you would wait in here?'

Mary entered a soft, pleasant, relaxing sitting-room. In the window stood a plain wooden chair, a sanctuary for her grubbiness among an array of silk-covered sofas and armchairs. Gratefully, she lowered her bottom and took the weight off her tired feet. The room was decorated in pale colours. The dying light allowed her to make out Old Master-style landscapes. It was all just as French as she could have imagined, the piano and furniture painted in blues, yellows, roses and gilt. A crystal chandelier dominated the ceiling. She looked for the light-switches, but there were none, only candles. There was no television – not surprising given that this seemed to be the music room – but there was no sign of any kind of record player either. She heard footsteps pass the door, the outer door open and close, and the footsteps fade again.

It was like being in a doctor's waiting-room. Mary swallowed nervously. Her throat was dry. She spotted a decanter and glasses on a side table and went over to see what there was to drink. She lifted the decanter's stopper and confirmed the contents as water. There was also a crystal jug of a thick, pale lemony syrup. She was parched and persuaded herself that the severe woman would not begrudge her a drink. She poured a slurp of syrup into a glass and topped it up with water. Heaven. Soft, slightly sweet, sharp lemon cleaned her palate, immediately lifting her spirits. She wandered around the room, looking at the pictures and small ornaments. Everything was beautiful, old and expensive, but it was no museum. Everything was happily used, in its chosen place, harmonious.

Above the fireplace hung one particularly large and impressive painting. The landscape was classical – plunging green hills and ancient ruins. Figures – men, women and mythical fauns – capered. The women were young and almost naked in diaphanous robes, flowing in dancing lines. The men were equally young, and naked, but blindfold. The fauns orchestrated the movements and played pipes and drums. All fauns and men sported erect members. Mary blushed and retreated to the window, looking out on the dark trees while her blush faded.

'Mademoiselle Coppen? I am Count Henri du Bantonne.'

The old man's silent entrance made her jump. 'Oh, I'm sorry.'

She put down the glass and moved toward him. He was stooped and incredibly old, but his eyes, far from being dulled and filmed over, were as bright as the clearest blue sky over the sea.

She reverted to French, said, 'Yes, Mary Coppen. How do you do?' and held out her hand, aware that it was grubby, but she had to be polite.

He took it. His fingers felt like chilly, dry sticks. Instead of shaking her hand, he bent his silver-haired head and kissed her fingers.

'Enchanté.'

The touch of his lips and the single word were like bolts of pure energy. Mary's eyes popped wide open. She was rooted to the spot, electrified. He straightened up slowly but without strain, his stoop less marked as he drew himself up to something like his full six feet. He did not let her hand go. His face was illuminated by the last light of the day, its flesh like flexible porcelain, his lips aglow. He smiled, briefly showing perfect white teeth, and then she looked into his eyes. Before he began speaking again, she was aware of him probing. He searched her, seeing inside.

'Philippe told me he had asked you to accompany him. I know he wanted you to come, and so we have been waiting. It is a pity you did not send word ahead, for I could have had someone meet you. But that is the way of the young of today – all impulse and rush.' He shook his head sadly. 'But now you are here, welcome.'

'Thank you, sir. It was a sudden decision.'

Still holding her hand and her eyes, he continued. 'You have changed since you went to the big city. Your aunts should have realised you would be different from the schoolgirl they waved away last autumn.'

Mary felt the blood drain from her face. How could he know what had happened in the last few days?

'Do not be frightened, Mary. I am gifted, some say cursed, with the gift of insight. Sometimes I can read a whole life story from the merest kiss. Philippe has told me much about you, and the rest I could see in your eyes.' For a few moments longer he held her hand. His nostrils twitched as if seeking her scent, like a cat encountering something new. 'Yes, my child, you can find happiness here.' His eyes suddenly sparked fire. 'I am very pleased that you have come – it is not often that such a beautiful innocent visits these days.' The fire died, replaced by a hungry look. 'You will make an old man very happy.'

Mary did not know what to say or how to react to those last few words. He seemed so old and gentle, but so knowing and disconcertingly sharp.

'Now, I expect that you would like to see Philippe. You caught us unprepared, and he is otherwise engaged. He asked me to pass on this message.' Le Comte reached into his long black coat.

Mary finally noticed how oddly he was dressed. His coat was antique, tailed, with lace lapels and flap pockets, and his trousers were tight, buttoned at the knees above white silk stockings and buckled shoes. His shirt was high-necked and flounced. He was dressed as if it were two hundred years ago, but without a powdered wig.

He handed over an envelope. The paper was thick, embossed and creamy. A single word graced the front. '*Mary*.' Inside, in Philippe's hand, she read:

Dear Mary,
I cannot be with you until later. Please forgive the delay. My father and Beatrice, our chatelaine, will make you welcome. The château, you will find, is a bit odd at first, and so are its rules and habits, but don't worry. Please do anything they ask.
   Yours, Philippe

She reread the note, seeking a clue to the odd rules and habits and what he was doing that was so important he could not welcome her himself. She looked up to see Le Comte waiting for her response.

He clearly knew what was asked of her and saw the questions racing through her mind. 'Since our reunion, Philippe has had to confront many difficult problems about his identity and purpose in life. His mind is in something of a turmoil, although I am sure that your presence will lift his mood – you are the closest friend he has from his life before. I am sure you understand.'

Mary and Philippe had briefly discussed the effect of meeting his father. Now the old man's words made her feel guilty she had not been here to help him. 'Yes, of course I understand. I'll do my best to fit in.'

His face showed his genuine concern and worry. 'Are you sure, my dear? You will do anything we request?'

Mary felt as if her integrity was being impugned. 'Of course I will.'

He smiled with pleasure and rang a little bell on the side table. Immediately, the tall woman appeared. 'This is Beatrice. She is in charge of all my domestic arrangements, and her word is my wish in all things. Please go with her to your room. I will see you again for dinner.'

Beatrice beckoned, and Mary found herself following

the forbidding woman from the room. They crossed the entrance hall to a great staircase. Beatrice walked ahead, clearly unwilling to talk to her new guest. Mary watched her going up the stairs. She wore flat black shoes, black stockings that disappeared under the calf-length grey dress, and a thick black belt that emphasised her hourglass figure. She looked well over forty, with grey-streaked long black hair drawn into a tight bun. The only sign of any adornment was the heavy gold rings in her earlobes. Her broad shoulders, set jaw and hands hinted at unusual strength.

They turned left at the top of the staircase into a long, dark, panelled passage. Beatrice picked up a candelabrum with three fat candles already alight. Mary wondered if there had been a power cut, but as they walked on she realised that, like the reception room, there was no sign of electric light. It was like being back in the Community, but whereas she understood why the Community rejected modern technology she did not understand it with all this wealth. The walls were hung with indistinct portraits and armorial displays. Here and there, battle flags and pennons, faded and torn by battle, hung against the ornate panelling. A shuttered window formed the end of the passage. They stopped outside the last door on the left. Mary worked out that she would be at the front, in one of the towers. Beatrice opened the door and ushered her inside.

The bedroom was dominated by a four-poster bed draped in muslin and heavily brocaded covers. The windows, reaching from floor to ceiling, looked out towards the encircling woods and the rapidly advancing darkness beyond. Beatrice fussed about for a few moments, and then light flared from a candelabrum on a table near the door. A few moments later and three more spots of light illuminated the room, and Mary could see how richly the room was decorated. She looked round, taking in the painted ceiling, tapestry wall-hangings, deep, soft carpet, a huge wardrobe, a door off to the side, the blanket box at the foot of the bed, a bookcase full of leather-bound volumes, vases of flowers and a washstand.

'It's a lovely room. Thank you.' Beatrice made no reply.
Mary pointed to the side door. 'Is that the bathroom?'

The chatelaine nodded. Mary remembered dinner and
knew that she needed a shower and a change of clothes.
She wanted rid of the lurking, silent woman so she could
wash and change in private.

Beatrice finally spoke. 'I will return in a few minutes to
prepare you for dinner. If you would like to use the
bathroom, please use it now.'

Surprisingly, there was a shower, next to a more
traditional Continental toilet, a low pedestal over which
she had to squat. Mary ran the shower hot and washed
herself down, hurrying to avoid the woman's wrath. She
had just begun drying off when knuckles rapped on the
door.

'Aren't you ready yet?'

She emerged, shoulders and arms glowing pink above
the towel wrapping her torso. Beatrice led her to the
dressing-table and began to brush her hair dry.

Beatrice was suddenly complimentary and friendly. 'You
have lovely hair, Mary. It is very unusual. Red, thick, curly
and so long.' The brush worked through the tangles,
tugging them loose, then burnishing the locks to a shine,
the colour becoming lighter as the hair dried.

'Now, my dear, we will get you dressed.'

Mary stood up, expecting Beatrice to leave her. Instead,
she waited.

'Won't you leave, please?'

'It is the custom that I attend to female guests, and I
understand that you assured my master you would do
anything I request. Please do so now. I have to get you
dressed properly. Take that towel off or I'll get angry.'

Mary realised suddenly that her carelessly given promise
possessed deep consequences, and she was always faithful
to her word. Reluctantly, she stood up and unwrapped the
towel. Beatrice took it and frankly appraised her naked
body. Mary blushed under the examination.

'You are a very attractive young woman. A little rough
round the edges, perhaps, and I do not think you take

66

much care of your appearance.' Beatrice looked particularly at Mary's pubic hair and bushy armpits. 'Your breasts are firm, as they should be, and no flabbiness, though your waist is rather thick. Now, your costume.'

Laid out on the blanket box at the foot of the bed was a very long white silk dress with lace and flounces. To its side was a strange-looking panelled sheet of satin with tapes and buttons, to the other almost transparent white silk stockings. On the carpet were a pair of white slippers like ballet shoes. None of these things were Mary's.

'Where are my clothes?'

'You won't be needing them while you are here. Le Comte desires that you be as beautiful as possible, and for that you must wear the right clothes. Please raise your arms.'

In a daze, Mary obeyed, and Beatrice wrapped the odd-looking panelled thing around her waist and began buttoning it up the front. It was tight, almost rigid from the top of her buttocks to her shoulder blades, and she had to breathe in, sucking in her tummy. Before the buttoning was completed, Beatrice gently lifted her breasts into the small satin-lined cups on which they lay, blooming, bulging, nipples exposed. The final buttons were done up.

'Turn round and look at yourself in the mirror.'

Mary looked at a very different figure, a woman whose hips flowered and breasts billowed, and whose waist was sharply nipped. The tapes, hanging at the back, were in Beatrice's hands.

'A little tighter, I think.'

'Ahh, ahh.' The tapes tugged, nipping her waist even more. For a moment she struggled to breathe. The tapes tugged again and then were tied off.

'Not bad, for the first time.' Beatrice ran a tape measure round her newly narrowed waist. 'Fifty-five centimetres – about twenty-two of your inches. It's about time you English gave up your silly measurements.'

Mary was too short of breath to explain that the metric system came naturally to her.

Beatrice continued. 'I wish I could have started on you

when you were eleven or twelve, then we could have got you down to a much more acceptable forty-six. But you certainly look much better now, don't you think?'

Eighteen inches? That could not be possible. Mary shook her head in disbelief. Her body had bloomed and did look really good. Mary was getting used to the constriction and her breathing returned to something like normal.

The chatelaine smiled and nodded her head with satisfaction. 'Yes, my dear, most alluring. Now we must get your stockings and dress on.'

'Don't you have any knickers for me?'

'No. They are not appropriate for this costume. Le Comte maintains that they are a nasty modern invention. If the weather were cold, you could wear a chemise, but as it is warm you won't need them. Sit down.'

Mary lowered herself on to the dressing-table stool. It was difficult not being able to bend. Beatrice smoothed the stockings up her legs and held them in place with elasticated garters. Mary slipped her feet into the soft, elegant slippers. They fitted perfectly. She was puzzled. How could they know her size?

'Now for the dress. I think you'll like it.'

It was gorgeous. Below the waist it flowed away, hanging in a circle almost to the floor in many layers of built-in petticoats. Above, the bodice fitted tight, barely covered her nipples, leaving the upper swells of her breasts burgeoning in the frame created by side panels leading up to puffed shoulders and short arms. Around her neck, Beatrice placed a choker of pearls, and then she flicked back Mary's hair.

'Oh, you have not piercings in your ears. I will have to use clips for these earrings. Later, we will have to correct that deficiency.'

Mary grimaced as heavy strings of pearls were clipped to her earlobes. Bracelets of yet more pearls encircled her wrists. Although she had never made use of it before, Mary expected perfume to finish. She looked over the table. Beatrice must have divined her thoughts.

'Le Comte does not like us to use perfumes. They upset his delicate senses. He prefers the natural scent of his female acquaintances. Please look in the mirror.'

Mary could not believe that it was her reflected in the tall gilded mirror. She seemed to have grown several inches and become someone completely different. The gorgeous dress was so unlike anything she had ever worn before, so opulent and, for all the yards of silk, revealing. She wondered if her nipples would stay hidden. A dull, far-off sound reverberated through the château.

'It is time for dinner.'

Feeling like a princess, Mary descended the grand staircase behind her companion and floated into the dining-room opposite the music room. It was lit by three grand candelabra spread the length of a long mahogany table. Crystal and silver glittered from the three places set, one at the head of the table, the others to either side. Left alone for a few moments, Mary gazed round the room. Against the opposite wall stood a sideboard loaded with steaming dishes and tureens. In the shadows above it, and continuing round all four walls, paintings and tapestries decorated the walls right up to the high, ornate ceiling. The picture over the fireplace to her right caught her eye because it was illuminated by extra candles to each side. She went to get a better view.

It appeared to be another version of the picture in the music room, perhaps later in the same pagan rite. The young women and girls now danced round a golden pole while the young men circled them. Beyond, hooded men drank, and all were under the eye of a god and his satyrs. All the dancers were naked, all the spectators displayed huge erections. To the left, a girl with auburn hair straddled a golden phallus, vigorously sacrificing her virginity as she was whipped, her face ecstatic, her thighs bloody. The trickle of blood ran down the phallus into a chalice. Further left, a red-haired girl lay on her front over a stone. Her back and buttocks were streaked with cuts, and a satyr thrust his huge phallus between her thighs. Her face was turned to the viewer. Mary did a double take. The girl was obviously enjoying a huge orgasm.

Mary licked her lips, nervous with a strange, naughty excitement. She looked back to the dancing group in the centre. A girl was being drawn from the circle towards the golden phallus, tears in her eyes, while one of the young men was taken to the right. She followed his path. Old, witchlike women belaboured a boy with bundles of twigs. His erect penis was held between a witch's hands, its spouting end directed towards a second goblet. The goblets were being taken to the god, who drank from them. At the extreme right, a satyr sodomised another young man.

The story of the scene was clear; the deflowering of virgins amid an orgy of pain and ecstasy. In the background, women gave birth to children who joined the dance as they matured, becoming the witches and servants to a god who grew fat on the contents of the goblets. The pagan imagery disturbed her, but at the same time, as her eyes returned again and again to the girls over to the left, she felt a strange empathy with girls who seemed so happy to be treated with such ritual sadism.

'It is called *The Cycle of Life*, Mademoiselle Coppen.' Mary jumped. Le Comte stood right behind her. Mary had no idea how he had managed to cross the squeaky polished floor in absolute silence. 'I believe the allegory has much to say to us.'

She turned her head. His eyes glowed with fire, and his nostrils twitched. He took her scent as he looked down at her almost exposed bosom. Mary became aware that her erect nipples were only just hidden from his sight.

He spoke again, in an intimate whisper. 'I think the scene has touched you, has it not?' Mary blushed. 'Please, mademoiselle, take your seat at my left hand.'

As he helped Mary take her seat, the door opened. Philippe entered. Mary beamed, but he only smiled distantly, as if preoccupied with weighty and troubling matters.

'Philippe!'

Philippe, like Le Comte and Beatrice, replied in French. 'Hello, Mary. I am pleased you changed your mind.'

He came to her and shook her hand in a delicate, formal manner. Bewildered at his lack of animation, Mary watched him round the table, help his father into his chair and take his own seat. Like his father, he wore clothes in the style of the early nineteenth century: long dark coat, grey, pearl-embroidered waistcoat, tight buckskin breeches and stockings. She found herself looking at the prominent bulge in his breeches and remembering her brief sight of what lay beneath. His hair seemed to have grown very long in such a short time. Now it was tied back. He even moved differently; languid, affected and lacking in enthusiasm – unlike his eyes, which burned with new passion.

'Does not Mademoiselle Coppen look fetching in her new costume, Philippe?'

'Indeed, Father. The style suits her very well.'

'Are you refreshed after your journey, my dear?'

Bewildered by Philippe's oddly detached manner, Mary was slow to answer, struggling to find the right words in French. 'Er, yes, thank you. I'm just hungry now, though I don't know if I can fit much in with this corset on.'

Le Comte smiled. 'You will soon become accustomed.'

He rang a bell, and a dark-haired girl in a low-cut white blouse and long skirts materialised from an alcove by the sideboard. 'Yvette, the wine, please.'

Mary guessed this must be the maid. She smiled at her, but the girl kept her eyes lowered. As she bent forward to pour her master's wine, Mary was given a glimpse of her dark-tipped breasts.

Once the glasses were filled, Le Comte proposed an odd toast: 'To beauty and virginity!' He exchanged a smile with Philippe.

Mary was suddenly struck by her self-imposed vulnerability. OK, she knew Philippe, but her trust in him had been dented by his welcome. Otherwise she was on her own and in the hands of a strange old man, whose main preoccupation seemed to be her virginity, and a woman who was unbelievably frank about naughty things.

Yvette served each with a plate of opened oysters set on a bed of salt crystals. Mary looked blankly at the pale, raw,

71

sloppy morsels, not knowing what to do. She looked up at Philippe. He winked, lifted a shell to his lips and tossed it back. Mary copied him, and shuddered as a salt-sea, squidginess slid down her throat. She sipped her wine and courageously tried another. This one was bigger, fat and soft, and she felt she had to chew it. The salty creaminess was much more intense, but no more appetising.

Her host must have spotted her distaste. 'Oysters are one of the greatest treasures of the sea, my dear. It is said they have aphrodisiac qualities. Though I know of no proof for that claim, the experience of swallowing a creamy, soft, fresh oyster is certainly sensuous. Please persevere, Mademoiselle Coppen. I am sure you will find the effort efficacious.'

Mary tried another, this time following Philippe in squeezing a little lemon juice first. Slightly better, but she had no time for more. Le Comte had finished, and at once her plate was removed. The next course was served, and the old man began to talk between small forkfuls.

'As I explained earlier, Philippe is engaged on learning how an aristocrat of the old blood carries himself in society. Mine is an ancient line, established before the Duke of Normandy –' his tone implied that William the Conqueror was some mere upstart '– made your country his own, although the present title was granted only in 1763.' He spoke wistfully, as if recalling that lost era of family power: balls, revels, audiences with kings and queens. 'Before, though our influence was great, our lands were small. Of course, the Revolution was an evil time for us. Many of our estates were confiscated, but we managed to hold on to this one, and a few valuable properties elsewhere, to provide a comfortable income.'

He paused to taste the succulent duck on his plate. Mary sipped at the burgundy and nibbled on the duck. She was feeling full already, and a little light-headed.

'As my only son and heir, Philippe has much to do before he can earn the rewards of his heritage.' He smiled at Philippe. 'He will take a suitable wife and in due course, when my time comes, as one day it must, Philippe will be the master of our future.'

She looked at Philippe when his father mentioned his taking a wife. He smiled smugly. Mary looked away hurriedly, confused by the sudden impact of the double realisation that she might be his idea of a suitable wife and that she wanted him as her husband.

Le Comte continued. 'Suitable young women are so hard to come by these days. Chaste, of good breeding and manners, willing to give their body, heart and soul to a master thoroughly schooled in the arts of love. Mademoiselle Coppen, could you be such a wife?'

Mary answered honestly. 'I think so, sir. I have been brought up to believe that a wife should honour, cherish and obey.'

He sat back and wiped his lips with his napkin. 'A good wife needs to be able to anticipate her husband's needs and desires. She must be his hostess, mistress of his house and educator of his children. I have heard that many of these skills have been lost in the headlong rush of the modern world towards instant self-gratification. And then there is the misguided proposition that women are in all ways equal to men.'

He sat forward, looking directly into Mary's eyes. 'Would you be prepared to train for this task?'

His eyes burned into her soul, stripping away any pretence, seeking her sincerity. She found herself considering his question deeply. It seemed to be an offer of marriage to Philippe, but somehow with strings attached. Could she become a countess, ordering maids and cooks about their business, entertaining important people with the finest wines and foods? Could she do whatever Philippe asked, without question, satisfying his desires? An image of herself, crouching naked over Philippe's erect cock, yielding her virginity, flashed into her mind. She felt as if Le Comte had put it there as a test.

Abruptly, his eyes abandoned their probing. Released, she looked at Philippe. He smiled encouragingly. She took a deep breath. 'I would be honoured to be so prepared for marriage.'

'Good. Beatrice will commence in the morning.'

73

Satisfied, he suddenly dropped the subject. 'Is not the duck absolutely excellent?'

From that moment, the talk turned to inconsequential chat about the weather, the state of the vines and the quality of the food and drink. Although Mary ate sparingly, unable to ingest as much as she would normally, she did not feel hungry or short-changed, nor did she feel any more intoxicated by all the wine she drank. However, as the meal drew to a close she began to feel sleepy, and she was quite happy to accept Beatrice's offer of an escort to her room when father and son withdrew for cognac and coffee.

Once back in her room, Beatrice helped her undress and gave her a long, embroidered white nightdress. Mary managed only a brief prayer before falling into a deep sleep, leaving one candle alight.

The candle had not burned down far when she awoke, but she felt surprisingly refreshed. The noise that had broken her sleep came again, a resonant female moan. It seemed to float in the air above her head. She looked round, seeking the source. Another moan echoed. Now it seemed to float from the corridor outside, as if a woman leant against the door with a lover between her thighs. Mary was troubled by her ready imagining of sex, but she was also curious to discover who had disturbed her night's rest. She slipped out of bed and slid her feet into the slippers left by Beatrice.

Taking the candlestick in case the corridor lights had been extinguished, she poked her head out of the door. The empty corridor was lit by a torch at the end. A male grunt floated from the dimness. She followed her ears to a door across the way. No light escaped. She turned the handle and entered an empty passage leading to a descending spiral stair. Her candle cast a moving glow around her as she crept down stone steps towards the source of the noises. The stairs went down and down, and she soon lost count of her steps and the changes of direction. At last she reached the bottom. The way forward sloped away, lit by three dim candles, each a diffused pool of light too feeble to meet the next. At the end, the passage went sharp right.

Mary stopped as she turned the corner. Ahead, the left-hand wall was blank stone. To her right, light seeped through a carved stone lattice from a room below. She put down her candle. Aware she was snooping, Mary had no wish to risk discovery as she crept forward to look. She had to bite her lip to prevent an exclamation from escaping.

On a bed in the room below, Philippe rolled naked with Yvette. Jealousy jagged through her heart once more, tempered with just a modicum of understanding. This was, as Le Comte had explained, part of Philippe's education.

Once again, Mary knew she should go back to her room, but once again the sight of Philippe making love acted like a magnet. She watched as Yvette took Philippe's erect cock in her small hand and slowly slid it up and down, unable to encircle it completely. Mary touched her breast, squeezing her nipple through her nightdress. He seemed so much bigger than he had been with Laura, and she struggled to believe it could ever fit into Yvette, let alone her own narrow slit.

Yvette let Philippe roll her over. Her narrow waist, flaring hips and splayed thighs framed a hairless, glistening cherry-red sex. He took her dark nipple into his mouth and bit hard. Yvette groaned. Mary's right hand rubbed her sex through the cotton. It was wet and tender, pining for her newly discovered talent for self-gratification. Philippe pushed Yvette's thighs up until her knees crushed her breasts. He held his cock to Yvette's sex and drove into her. Mary's hands rucked up her nightdress and plunged into her soaking, yearning vagina. Her thumb reached for her nub, her other hand twisting her nipple as Philippe thrust deep until his balls met Yvette's uptilted buttocks. Yvette's hands clawed his back, and Mary's hand clawed her breast, copying unconsciously.

A hand closed over Mary's mouth, and another dragged her back into the passage.

Beatrice whispered viciously in her ear: 'Just what do

75

you think you are doing?' Mary was dragged away. 'Spying? Playing with yourself? Back to your room, young lady. I'll deal with you there!'

Mary hurried along in front of the chatelaine.

'Did I not tell you to stay in your room?' Mary had been so tired, she could not remember a word said by Beatrice. 'Did anyone give you permission to wander around?'

Mary had no answer. All she felt was shock and shame.

They almost ran up the steps and back into her room. Beatrice threw her on her bed.

She curled up and looked back at her accuser. 'I'm sorry. I didn't mean anything.'

'And I suppose you did not enjoy your game?'

Again, Mary had no answer. She watched Beatrice remove a leather strap with a wooden handle from her belt.

'Your training was supposed to start in the morning but a lesson learnt is never wasted. You have broken one of the strictest rules. You must never go where you have not been invited. Put your feet on the floor and your face on the bed.'

Mary guessed she was about to be punished, but it didn't seem fair. 'Why?'

Beatrice ignored her. 'I am going to give you four strokes of the tawse, as you would call it.'

Mary meekly took the desired position, scrunching the bedspread in her fists in anticipation of the pain to come.

'This is your first lesson. Your legs must be parted and straight, back dipped. You must always present yourself thus for discipline.' Beatrice stroked her rounded globes, fingers just inches from the unsatisfied slit. 'Later, I will introduce you to the delights of the cane, the birch and the whip.'

Mary shuddered, but her honey poured, her lips opened and, humiliatingly, she felt her sheath clench.

'Have you ever been beaten before?'

Mary whimpered. 'Yes, once.'

'It seems to have made a deep impression.' The fingers caressed closer to her hungry, dripping cleft.

Suddenly, the tawse seared across her right cheek. Mary

yelped and tensed her buttocks, the fire stoking the furnace between her legs.

'Be silent, child.'

The second stroke seared her left cheek, balancing the fire. The third stroke made a cross on her right cheek, and the fourth completed the cross on her left. Beatrice helped her up and wiped the tears from her cheeks.

'Now we can't have you wandering or playing with yourself again tonight. Lie down on your back.'

Wincing as her buttocks touched the sheets, Mary obeyed. Beatrice took her wrists, drew them above her head, and Mary heard the rattle of chain as they were manacled to the bed-head. Silent but wriggling, Mary let Beatrice spread her legs apart and chain to the foot of the bed, then the chatelaine left her in darkness to ponder her guilt and the events of the day.

The fire in her bottom diminished but spread, uniting with the residual heat in her sex and breasts. She could feel a trickle of honey running very slowly from her slit and an itch that would not be ignored. Her nipples, hard and pointed, rubbed against the embroidered bodice of her nightdress. She wriggled, and the itching grew. She wanted to reach down and assuage the itch, but the chains were taut. She tried to close her thighs to squeeze the irritation, but her ankles were held firmly apart. She sighed and muttered. Sweat broke out on her brow. The material of her nightdress touched her sex with a maddening lightness, insufficient to give relief, sufficient to maintain the super-sensitivity of her inflamed membranes. Mary drifted in and out of sleep and in and out of disturbing, erotic dreams in which those satyrs and fawns laid their whips on her skin, fed their immense cocks into her body, but never gave her the satisfaction she craved.

Six

Laura could smell a good breakfast; eggs and bacon, toast, fried tomatoes and, she was sure, sausages were cooking downstairs. Her empty stomach rumbled, and her mouth tasted like an old sock. She heard the front door open and close, and, for the umpteenth time, footsteps passed the door to Mary's room. This was, she concluded, the most awful torture.

A key turned in the lock, and the footsteps scuttled away. The front door opened and closed again, and she looked out to see the two women hurry off towards the chapel. Laura opened the door. Outside, on a chair, she found her clothes neatly piled. On top lay a note. *'Please dress, eat and go. If you find Mary, tell her we love her.'*

Laura dressed quickly and descended the stairs to find a marvellous breakfast waiting. Almost an hour later, with thirst and hunger satiated, Laura walked back to her car without seeing a soul. At the first town, she stopped and, after a search of the telephone directory, rang Philippe's foster-parents. It was news to them that Philippe had left the country, so they had no idea where he had gone, and good riddance to the ungrateful little swine. From there she drove directly to London, stopping only for petrol and a cup of tea. Perhaps she could find a clue in Mary's flat. Laura had a key for Mary's flat.

It was nearly dark when she got back to town. She stopped at the first floor to let Mrs Theodopolous know she was back and would be in both her own and Mary's flat, just to stop her worrying. Dropping off her bag, she found Mary's spare key and went to start her search. For almost an hour, Laura scoured Philippe's room for clues; all she found was a note he must have left in a final hope that Mary would still join him. It said simply, '*Please come to my father's house as soon as you can. Philippe.*'

Laura sighed with frustration, found a can of beer in the fridge, lit a cigarette and drank while she thought. After a while the silence became oppressive, and she put on a CD. She went into Mary's room, but her diary was missing, along with anything else of importance. She slammed the last drawer shut and wished, for the umpteenth time, that she had not been so blinded by jealousy and anger that she had taken absolutely nil interest in Philippe's story. Now she would have to ask Jack for help; he had access to almost any bit of information one could possibly require. There was one drawback, however: Jack would leap on the opportunity to get involved, and the price for his help would be Mary. Laura returned to the living-room, trying to think of a way to keep Mary all to herself.

A male hand closed her mouth, another gripped her wrist and pulled it right up her back. She bit at the hand and kicked back, aiming for her attacker's knee. He was ready. Her heel missed and Laura found herself doubled forward. She jabbed her elbow at his ribs, but her position robbed her of sufficient power.

His voice hissed in her ear. 'Quite the little spitfire, aren't we? Move another muscle and I'll break your arm!'

He felt strong enough to carry out his threat and sounded determined enough. Laura decided discretion was the better part of valour. She went limp. His hand left her mouth, grabbed her free wrist and she felt handcuffs close. He shoved her face down into the settee. Before she could struggle to her feet, her mouth was plugged with a ball gag fixed by Velcro straps behind her head. She gurgled her anger as he pulled her upright. She caught a glimpse of herself in a mirror. It was one of her own gags.

He turned her round to face him. At any other time, Laura would have gone gooey. He was tall, fit and strong, about thirty, with short fair hair, steady, cool grey eyes and a handsome face. For a moment she studied him, filing away everything, including the little scar on his chin, for use in a future ID parade. In his turn, he stared at her, and she could tell he liked what he was seeing.

'Now, Miss Jenkins –' Christ! He even knew her name '– why don't we go somewhere a little more private? We don't want your landlady interrupting us, do we?' He took her elbow. His grip was firm. He was in charge, even if he didn't know Mrs Theodopolous wasn't her landlady.

Laura let him guide her out. Once in her own flat, Laura began to struggle again. Effortlessly, he pushed her into her bedroom, on to the bed, and without a wasted second used the cuffs she had fixed to her bed to chain her ankles. Sitting her up, he released her wrists for just as long as it took to fasten them once more, outstretched. Then he left her alone.

Laura fumed silently. Bastard! Using her own bloody gear! Shit-head! He was so bloody arrogant, showing off how bloody clever he'd been, searching her flat and then sneaking up on her.

In the midst of her silent rant, he returned grinning. His aggression seemed to have been replaced by curiosity.

'If I remove the gag, will you behave? No shouting or girlie screeching?'

Laura nodded, and he leant over and took it off. As he did so his face came very close. She smelled his musky, spicy aftershave. His skin was good, and she noticed that his grey eyes were shot with greens and russets. Before he stood up again, his hand brushed her shoulder lightly. Laura shivered. He bent his head and kissed her. Despite herself, despite what he had done to her, Laura found herself responding. Her lips opened, their tongues met and she felt her nipples stir. The kiss went on and on. She felt his hand stroke down her body to her hips and the beginnings of dampness between her thighs. The contradictions of Laura's sexuality were asserting themselves strongly once more, and when he broke the kiss she was breathless and wanting more.

He looked thoughtful and surprised. 'Would you like a drink?'

Laura raised an eyebrow, pretending he had not moved her, and answered curtly. 'You know where it is, I suppose?' He nodded. 'Mine's a Scotch.'

While he was gone, Laura decided to use his hots for her as a tool, so she would try to be friendly.

He brought her cigarettes and lighter back with him, released her wrists and helped her to sit up, putting her Scotch, cigarettes, lighter and an ashtray within reach.

She sipped her drink and lit a cigarette. Smiling, she asked, 'May I have the name of the gallant who has just attacked me?'

His eyes twinkled. 'Adam, Adam Hardcastle.'

Laura peered up at him. 'Under normal circumstances, I'd say I was pleased to meet you.'

'Under normal circumstances, so would I, and you wouldn't be chained to your bed. But these are strange times – made stranger by the fact that you have a wardrobe full of bondage gear and chains fitted to your bed.' He sat down. 'What were you looking for in Mr Banton's flat?'

Laura automatically lied. 'A book I lent his flatmate.'

'In her knicker drawer and his briefcase? Taking an hour? A very strange kind of book, and very, very special. What did you lend Miss Coppen?'

'*Far from the Madding Crowd.*'

He looked at her coolly. 'It was on the bookshelf, next to *Sons and Lovers*.'

Clever bugger, and very thorough. She dropped her defiance. 'I was trying to find some clue to Mary's whereabouts.'

'So she's disappeared too.' He looked shrewdly at her. 'Is she with Mr Banton?'

'Why do you want to know?' Laura panicked suddenly; had there been an accident? 'Are you the police? What's he supposed to have done?'

'Nothing, as far as I know, but they might be in trouble.' He sipped his Scotch. 'Can I have one of those?' He pointed to her cigarettes. Laura nodded; he could take them anyway, so what was the point of refusing? 'Thanks. I don't usually, but this is kind of difficult.'

She gave a wry smile. 'You're telling me.'

He seemed to summon up courage. 'You deserve an explanation, Laura. May I call you Laura?' She nodded. 'It's a long story.'

'Well, I'm hardly likely to run away, am I?' Laura hinted.

He did not move to release her. 'I'll keep it brief. When I was ten, my older sister, Anne, went on a working holiday to France. She never came back, and we couldn't find out what had happened. The police could not, or would not, help. Eventually my parents gave up. Just before Mother died, she made me promise to find Anne. I was in the army then, but as soon as I got out, a couple of months ago, I got down to business. I found her death certificate in Paris, which said she died from complications after childbirth. She had the name du Bantonne, and her child's name – Philippe. There was no mention of where she died or what had happened to him.'

Laura made the connections but kept quiet; she wanted to know what he knew before she told him anything.

'I came here by pure chance. I was dealing with some of my investments. There was a letter signed by one P. Banton. It was a long shot, but the name is unusual. I wondered if he was my man, so I rang his employers and they confirmed he was about the right age and he'd just been given indefinite leave to go to France, but they couldn't tell me where. A lot more digging brought me here.'

'Why do you think Philippe and Mary might be in trouble?'

He drew on his cigarette and sipped his Scotch, looking as if he wanted to avoid the question. 'How much does Mary mean to you?'

Laura considered her answer: should she reveal her relationship? He looked and sounded genuine. 'We're very good friends, and I feel responsible for her. She's never been away from home before. She's very innocent.'

'So how come you don't know where she is?'

'We had a tiff.' Laura looked down at her feet, ashamed.

83

'A lovers' tiff?'

Laura coloured. 'Sort of.' She looked up at him.

That twinkle in his eyes reappeared. 'How far would you go to find her?'

This was getting ridiculous; every question met by another. 'Why don't you get to the point?' He said nothing, waiting for her answer. Laura shook her head. 'I'd do anything, go anywhere I had to.'

Adam smiled, possibly relieved, as if she had passed a test he wanted her to pass. 'From the little I know, it appears that Philippe's father, the Comte du Bantonne, is a recluse, but he is held in high regard by the sort of people who revere the Marquis de Sade.'

Laura's heart thumped. This was too close to home. She knew the sort of people who revered de Sade. She felt a surge of hope. 'Adam, I might be able to help.'

'I hoped you might.'

He crossed to the bed and kissed her again. Laura opened herself to him. He took her wrists and pushed them above her head. Laura let him; she felt surprisingly safe. She murmured when he reattached her to cuffs above her head and sighed as he moved away. He left the room then, returning with the bronze and the little table it was mounted on.

For a while, in silence, he just looked at Laura and the scaled-down simulacrum, before readjusting her legs until, albeit horizontally, she was in the same position as her image. Laura began to get impatient. Her body ached for his touch again. He stood back and took a pair of scissors from his pocket. A flutter of anticipation travelled out from her belly.

'You know, I've always wanted to have a beautiful woman in this position, especially one who doesn't seem to mind.'

'That rather depends on what you're contemplating.'

'A little research –' he smiled and waved the scissors towards the bronze '– into female body jewellery and the submissive personality. My preliminary findings suggest that you would be a good subject.'

Laura suppressed a giggle, trying to match his academic approach. 'The subject is willing.'

He removed her trainers, stroking her ankles and, like a true gentleman, refrained from commenting on her travel-soiled feet. Laura held her breath as he moved towards the hem of her skirt. He took it between the fingers of his left hand and opened the scissors. The snip as they cut the hem almost echoed in the silence. Violently, he grasped each side of the cut and tore the cotton asunder, ripping it all the way to the waistband. Laura closed her eyes and felt her clitty jump. She was naked from the waist, her wet, bald sex hidden only by shirt-tails. She felt cold steel softly push between skin and skirt. He could have used the button holding the skirt, but of course he did not, nor did Laura want him to. The waistband fell away. Now all she wore was the thick shirt. Snip, snip, snip, he cut away every button. She felt each plastic disc tumble and bounce away. He cut the buttons at her wrist, severed the hem and tore each arm in two. Laura gasped as the scissors sounded close to her ears as he cut from shoulder hem to collar. Adam laid the shirt back, exposing her last item of clothing. Laura enjoyed the irony; it was the first time she had worn an ordinary bra for all of two years, and now it was her only remaining clothing. She laughed quietly, but he did not understand. She explained, and he cut the strap between her breasts.

Laura looked into his eyes as he stared at her flattened mounds. He threw away the scissors, and they clattered loudly on the floor. Adam straddled her waist and took each of her nipple rings between finger and thumb. He was fascinated by them, gently pinching and twisting, flicking the rings lightly, until each nub was hard and throbbing. Laura could not suppress a moan of pleasure. He kissed her open mouth and nibbled her ear lobes. Without releasing her thick, tingling nipples, he licked her throat and plunged his tongue into her mouth. Laura's hips arched under him, and he sat down, pinning her. Laura revelled in her inability to move and in his complete mastery. She longed to see him naked and feel him inside, but simultaneously she wanted him to draw his lovemaking out until she screamed for release.

Adam rolled her aching nubs between his forefingers and thumbs as he edged down her body to kiss her navel. His face hovered over her soaking, hot, open pussy, but instead of kissing he blew cool air. Laura moaned as he dried her stickiness. She felt her lips open and her clitty grow. He blew directly on to it, and her hips bucked. He blew into her vagina, and she twisted, fighting her bonds to open wider. He blew down towards her bottom crack, and her buttocks clenched and bounced. Then he left her again.

Laura lay panting. He returned with a reel of white cotton. He made a loop and dropped it over her left nipple. He tightened the little noose until it felt as though it was cutting the base of her nub. He soaked it in his saliva, and it shrank a little more. Adam led the cotton down to her labial rings, measured the length back to her right nipple, and bit off the cotton. He fed the thread through the left ring then looped it through, repeating the operation with the right-hand ring, leaving a little slack between them. Laura gasped as he tied another loop around her clitoris, as near to its emergence as possible. The cotton was tied off to her right nipple ring. The web was taut. He tested it by tugging, each tug sending exquisite darts of sensation through her body.

Adam produced the blindfold then, and in her darkness he applied dripping ice cubes to each delicate, looped node. Laura laughed and giggled, writhed and stuttered. She gasped and bit her lip hard to suppress screams as he chilled her clitty. Ice melted in her vagina, her anus and mouth. He washed her in body-melted ice straight from the freezer. She strained and wriggled, pleaded and, when she thought her nerves could stand no more, climaxed as his hot mouth laved heat to her pierced and tied bud.

Still clothed, he took her then, her sheath tightened by the ice, his stem thick and long. His balls bounced between her thighs. She felt his fingers hard on her hips as he gripped. She heard his breath and kissed his mouth. He plundered her mercilessly, plunging deep and long, almost

86

withdrawing, touching everywhere. Helpless and blind, Laura cried as he drove her towards orgasm. She tried to slow herself, to time her climax with his, but he undid her resolve with a final icecube pressed quickly into her rear.

Laura guessed he had loosened the chains to her ankles while she recovered, for he lifted her hips and followed the rapidly melting ice cube into her bottom with a slow, slow penetration. Her sensitised anal ring registered every minute change in the contours of his cock; from the smoothness of its helmet to the veins along its length. When his ticklish pubic hairs tickled her cheeks and his fly buttons ground into her thigh, he withdrew almost entirely, and she sighed with the sense of loss. He pushed in again and stayed deep inside, letting her muscles work. To encourage her, he began describing circles around her recovering, bloated clitoris with a fingertip lubricated with her honey.

Laura ground at him until he was ready. She felt his balance change as her ankles came free. He lifted them, and pressed them back to her chest. Then he plunged rapidly three times and burst inside her, splattering his semen so deeply she thought she could taste it on her tongue. Laura held him tight while he let her feet down and slipped out, soft and drained. Before they slept, he removed the blindfold and kissed her eyelids tenderly. Laura felt an overwhelming sense of security and happiness as he slipped into sleep in her arms.

Seven

Mary lay awake as the new day's light began to spread through the shutters, illuminating the bedroom. She longed to close her legs and roll up into a ball, but the chains held her fast. The frames of pictures began to show, and she realised that the ceiling was covered in moulded and painted images. For the first time she had both the light and the time to look closely.

Most of the pictures on the walls were either at the wrong angle or as yet indistinct, but the ceiling decoration could be discerned. A chain of masked men and women ingeniously connected in a continuous act of sexual congress, and driven on by devils with wicked goads, formed a frieze round the edge of the ceiling. Painted in loving detail, the whole of the centre was dedicated to a beautiful young woman, with long flowing auburn hair, shown in a variety of situations. She was tied to frames, bent over trestles, hung upside-down and upright. In some she wore wisps of clothing, but everywhere she was belaboured by masked monks. In one image, her breasts were lashed; in another her buttocks were branded with a heart in chains. Her shaven sex was whipped, her mouth filled by a giant phallus, her nipples ringed, her labia pulled apart by chains.

The artwork was nowhere crude or brash, and by the generous proportions of the girl Mary guessed the work was quite old in origin. The longer she looked, the more Mary became involved in the drama. The girl appeared, despite the physical stress, to take a perverse pleasure from the abuse against her body, reminding Mary of colour plates from religious books of old saints and martyrs; pictures of suffering always showing the victim in a trance, eyes closed and smiling. Mary drank in the images, her body reigniting but in an agony of frustration thanks to the chains.

When Beatrice came, Mary knew she could see how excited she was. Silently, the older woman released her. She made her stand and removed her nightdress to reveal Mary's hard nipples.

When Mary stood naked with her pubic hair in sticky tendrils, Beatrice finally spoke. 'Today, mademoiselle begins her education proper. The first lesson is self-control and humility. We will go to the bathroom together. You will allow me to attend to your entire toilet. Afterward, you will be prepared for the day before breakfast is served.'

Meekly, Mary allowed Beatrice to lead her to the bathroom as she tried to come to terms with her instructions. Was this woman really going to be with her throughout her ablutions? Only her mother had attended to these most intimate bodily functions when she was a baby. Beatrice pushed her towards the strange low toilet.

'Squat, please.' Mary took her place and bent her knees. 'Lower.'

Mary bent her knees more, feeling totally exposed with her legs parted so wide. She blushed, and, though her bladder was full, nothing would come. Beatrice looked disappointed. She crossed to the sink and turned the cold tap. Water trickled. Almost immediately Mary's bladder began to respond. With a sigh, she heard her own water tinkle into the porcelain bowl. Nature took over. She closed her eyes, and hardly noticed Beatrice's presence until she was taken to the shower and sat down under a strong flow of hot water.

Automatically, Mary reached for the shampoo, but Beatrice pushed her hand away and began to shampoo her hair herself. Mary closed her eyes and remembered her shower with Laura. As these older hands began to massage her shoulders and breasts with a soapy flannel, Mary felt her wanton nipples thicken in response. The flannel was rough, and Beatrice scrubbed hard. Mary began to glow. Beatrice asked her to stand and scrubbed her back, thighs, stomach and, after nudging her willing legs apart, her pubis and buttocks. Mary parted her legs yet wider, seeking the flannel between them, wanting the roughness against her swollen slit. Beatrice obliged, rhythmically washing Mary's sopping sex. Mary's hips pushed back, but Beatrice withdrew, denying her the ultimate pleasure. Instead, she scrubbed her bottom hard, but if she thought Mary would get no pleasure there she was wrong. Mary gasped and opened herself. She wished Beatrice would penetrate her, but the chatelaine declined.

When Mary stepped out, and a towel had been wrapped around only her hair, Beatrice asked her to sit on a towel-covered chair. As soon as she sat down, Beatrice pushed a long, low stool in front of her.

'Put your feet at each side of the stool, please.'

'Why?'

'To remove your body hair, of course.'

Bemused, Mary did as she was asked, though she found that, with her feet in the desired place, her entire pubis and at least half her buttocks projected beyond the seat and she had to lean right back to keep her balance. Beatrice placed a tray by her side with a bowl of hot water, a shaving mug and brush, a pair of scissors and a cutthroat razor.

'Raise your arms.' Beatrice lathered the brush and then Mary's armpits. With two strokes under each arm she removed every trace of both small bushes of ginger hair. Mary felt very naked and soft.

'Now, do not move your legs or hips.'

Mary watched Beatrice kneel between her thighs and begin snipping away at her pubic thatch with the scissors, reducing it to a stubble. Every now and then she would brush away the clippings, and slowly Mary began to see the shape of her delta as her lips came into view. Beatrice applied the soapy brush, tickling and caressing. Mary murmured as the soft bristles brushed over her lips and clitoris. When the whole area seemed to be under an inch

91

of foam, the chatelaine started to wipe it, and the hidden stubble, away with the razor. Using the fingers of her left hand, Beatrice stretched Mary's slit wide and tight, and located her folds. The blade even cleared the hairs on the most delicate skin inside the top of her thighs. Finally, Mary felt the chill steel against her inner lips as the fine hairs on her outer lips were removed.

Before the foam was rinsed, however, Mary watched with a tingle of fear as Beatrice brushed some foam into the crack of her bottom and, with a finger pressed against her anus, she shaved the few hairs there too. Despite her fear, Mary felt her knot dilate against the finger, and a little honey flowed under the soapy mask over her sex.

Beatrice brought fresh water and washed away the last traces of the soap and hair. Mary felt so bare and delicate, every splash sent a shiver through her body, exciting her still further. Beatrice checked every inch, plucking stray hairs with tweezers and inducing gasps. Then she produced a pot of muddy yellow cream.

'This may hurt a little, but it will also soothe your skin. It helps slow the growth of hair.'

Mary closed her eyes as they began to water. The cream seemed to contain menthol as well as alcohol. She felt Beatrice's fingers rubbing slowly over her naked, bare belly. Some of her own running juices thinned down the cream, and it ran into her bottom, which made her hips jump and twist. Beatrice slapped her thigh, and Mary struggled to control herself.

'You may stand now and look in the mirror.'

Mary, her hips still wriggling, obeyed. The cream had disappeared, and instead of that familiar ginger bush she could see a pink triangle split vertically by her wrinkled pink inner lips. Mary felt absolutely naked and very young, as if she had regressed back to pre-pubescence without losing her hips and breasts.

Beatrice appeared behind her. 'That is better, is it not?'

'But why?'

'Because this is the way Le Comte wishes all the women in the house to be.'

'All? Including you?'

'Of course. Now, hurry up, we have to dress you.'

As if by magic, clothes had been laid out on Mary's bed. Today's corset was a pale cream colour and so much shorter it did not reach up to her breasts, but it was just as severe as its predecessor. Once laced inside, Mary expected to be dressed directly in the long cream woollen dress. Instead, Beatrice told her to stand with her legs apart. She held a tangle of leather in her hand.

Beatrice held it up. 'This is a chastity belt, and you will wear it most of the time – the master and I do not want you indulging in your selfish little games again. It will also protect you from any unwanted advances from the male members of the household. Only I have the key, to allow you to perform your natural functions.'

Mary looked with horror on a small, shield-shaped piece of thick leather attached by steel rings to narrow straps at top and bottom. In turn, these were connected to a narrow belt.

In a trance, and feeling like a naughty schoolgirl, Mary let her fit the belt. First, the belt was attached to her corset with small padlocks at front and back. As she did so, Beatrice explained, 'These locks also prevent your corset being loosened.'

Then the shield was positioned so that Mary's entire sex was hidden. The inside seemed to be shaped so that the leather touched her everywhere, even around the inside of her entrance. Then the strap underneath was led between her buttocks and up to the lock at the back of the belt. Beatrice tightened it until Mary's sex felt almost crushed and the leather pressed on her anus.

'There, safe and sound.'

Mary felt as if she had a bicycle seat between her legs, and even though she knew it was much smaller she wanted to walk bandy-legged. Every step made the leather rub against her clitoris, labia and rose, and she realised that her whole day would be filled with this rubbing. When Beatrice turned away for a moment, she tried to rub herself through the leather to see if she could increase the stimulation, but the shield was too thick and unyielding. Mary suspected this was deliberate, and that the shaving had been necessary only to heighten the belt's effect.

The dress clung to her every curve and covered her from her throat almost to the ground. It was so tightly fitting that as they walked downstairs the soft fabric caressed her naked buttocks and nipples, her thighs and calves and, as a novelty, her smooth underarms, where, on this hot, humid day, sweat was already dampening the wool. Mary knew her patience would be severely tried.

Just as soon as Mary finished her light breakfast of freshly baked bread, home-made jams and huge cups of delicious, strong coffee, the rain began. Beatrice, her only companion, assured her it would last all day. They discussed what Mary might do, given that any walking in the grounds was out of the question. Mary found herself describing life in the Community and the daily round of chores inside and outside the home. Beatrice heard her out and seemed disappointed.

'You need no training in your domestic duties. In that case, you will be free until six to amuse yourself. You will find, in your suite, some books, and you may make use of the salon across the hall into which you were shown last evening. However, you may not, today, explore further. I will fetch you for lunch at one and will be in your suite at six to prepare you for dinner, which you will be taking alone with Le Comte.'

Thus dismissed, Mary made her way back to her room, wondering what was so unsuitable for her to see. All traces of her morning toilet had been eradicated. A tray with mineral water, a flask of hot water, a small teapot and a jug of milk had been placed on the table in the window. She looked at the row of leather-bound books. Some were printed; others appeared to be journals, written in fading inks. One diary was in English. Mary settled, as comfortably as her corset allowed, in the chair by the window, and began to read.

9 May 1902

At last, after three whole weeks, I am able to record all that happens in my diary. Oh diary, how I have missed you!

It was hard, leaving home, but Father was determined and Mother promised I should be happy. A daughter's duty is difficult when her dowry has been lost. At least I know that Father's business is now secured; the count has ensured that.

He is a charming old man, and all my worries have been dismissed by his kind devotions to me – his 'dear little Victoria'. He is, however, much older than I had been led to believe, at least forty years older then me. His hair is quite grey, and his face is wrinkled. My maid, Natalie, who is from the West Indies, says he looks like a prune, but she is just a silly Negro.

I have two maids. The other is Jasmin, who was born in Egypt. Both are eighteen, just a year older than me. They help me dress in all the best Paris fashions and are improving my French.

Tonight, when they bathed me, they insisted that I stand completely naked and said all kinds of nice things about my little bosoms and nether regions. I think we are going to be very good friends.

10 May – afternoon

I discovered the most curious thing about Natalie. We went walking in the grounds. The sun was very hot, and she suddenly removed her hair! It was a wig, and underneath her head was shaved shiny smooth. She told me that the count liked her head like that, and every few days he watches Jasmin shave her. I touched her head and tingled all over. She told me that the count likes all his female servants to be clean of body hair, except for head and eyebrows, for he says that body hair harbours all manner of vapours and disease. I will be shaved tonight, but I am not sure I like the idea very much.

10 May – after midnight

Natalie came to my room, undressed me, and lay me down upon a towel to shave my intimates. I was afraid, but she bared her lower half to show me her bare naughtiness. She is very beautiful, with ebony skin, long legs and a waist so narrow she has no need of stays. Her intimates are very prominent, with bright red lips peeking between her dark mound. She let me touch her. Her skin was soft and silky and, when I happened to stroke her lips, they were hot and oily. I made her hips wriggle, and her little man poked out his head before she asked me to stop in case we were caught.

After she made me smooth, I looked at myself in the mirror. My nether lips were quite hard to see, being pale pink and very narrow. Then Jasmin arrived, and she showed me her mound. Her skin is pale brown, with darker pink lips that pout. She also has a pair of rings, one through each outer lip. She said that is a custom of her country, where they often pierce the nipples of harem girls as well. I was shocked to hear such a dreadful thing, and she bared her bosom to show me her long, almost purple teats with gold rings in them. I touched them, and it felt very odd. Jasmin told me that the beys and pashas mark their concubines with tattoos or brands, and she presented her round, firm bottom to show me a scimitar tattoo on her buttock.

Natalie then showed me her small, high boobies, which were also ringed. Then they played a game, pinching my teats and nether lips and making believe I had rings. I grew very hot and wet, and we were very naughty and our fingers entered each other, and we sucked boobies, but although I grew very excited, they would not let my crisis come, saying that only the count may have that pleasure.

12 May

I dined alone with my dear count. In the music room afterward, he bade me play the piano as a prelude to an entertainment. Natalie and the groom entered after a few minutes. To my horror, she was naked except for a collar, the chain lead to which was held by the groom, who wore only leather trousers and a white shirt. The count calmed my distress and bade me sit by his side on a chaise longue and then instructed them to begin. Natalie, he told me, was due punishment for cheeking the cook. She knelt on the floor, with her bottom raised high, and then the groom began to lash her behind with a thin whip. The whip scored fine, glowing lines of purple across the dark chocolate globes, and, although it must have hurt her terribly, Natalie barely uttered a sigh but opened her legs even wider until her red, wet gash was clearly evident.

When the groom completed his task, he made her kneel up and, by means of the whip being fed through her nipple rings, held her to him while she unfastened his trousers. The count clasped my hand as the groom's member was exposed to my view. 'This is a lesson for you. You must watch and learn,' he said to me.

The groom's member was enormously long and as thick as my wrist with a dark purple knob. Natalie opened her lips and almost swallowed it whole! For a long time she bobbed her head up and down, sucking it and stroking his hairy balls. At last, when he looked ready to burst, she held his stem just outside her open lips, and I could see his thick spend spurting into her mouth.

The count dismissed them, but he held me by his side, kissing my ears until I consented to kiss his mouth. Commanding me to be still, he stroked my boobies, making me feel all hot, before demanding I do for him what Natalie had done for the groom.

I did not like to do something so disgusting, but he is my master, although we are not, as yet, man and wife. Thus I fought my reservations and released his member. Unlike the groom's, his was quite small and soft, and pale in colour. As I held it, however, it began to grow somewhat. At his urging, I knelt before him and lowered my head. He was very kind, encouraging me in my clumsy efforts. I kissed the end, and he twitched, growing bigger, and the smooth tip began to emerge. I sucked and licked on the end, and it grew bigger still until it filled my mouth. When I looked at it again, it more resembled the groom's example, somewhat thinner, but as hard as iron.

He told me to rub him up and down as I licked and sucked, and like Natalie I stroked his balls as well. I loved the way they are both delicate and strong. Soon, my master began breathing very hard and thrusting his member into my mouth. He reminded me to breathe through my nose to stop me gagging, but it was difficult. Quite suddenly, he jerked harder and pumped his spend into my mouth, telling me to swallow it. It tasted strong, though it seemed less thick and copious than the groom's emission.

Afterward, he seemed to faint away for a few moments, but when he was recovered he bade me sit upon his lap while he reached up inside my skirts and, at last, brought on my own pleasure with his fingers.

Mary closed the book, suddenly angry. This was part of some plot to pervert her. She poured herself a glass of mineral water, but as she moved she felt that pressure again on her sex, and the heat and wetness inside. Her nipples itched against the woollen dress. She drank, trying to beat down her need for self-gratification. She so wanted to touch herself. Maybe cold water on her face would help? Mary made her way to the bathroom, each step a subtle caress, but the door was locked. Immediately, she wanted to pee. The clock on the wall told her it was only ten o'clock. Three long hours until Beatrice would be available to release the belt.

Mary sulked back to her chair then changed her mind. If she lay down, perhaps her bladder would forget its need to pee. She picked up two more books at random and lay down. The first book was in French: *Travels with Chevalier du B.* by Marie D., dated 1773. From what she could make out, it had been produced as a private edition.

For several wearisome pages, the arch Marie D. chatted on about the court at Versailles and the dreary inns in which she and the Chevalier stayed as they travelled by coach to his château. Unlike silly Victoria, Marie was obviously a sharply observant lady, and occasionally her pointed and witty words reminded her of Jane Austen. However, once the pair reached their destination, Marie D. became quite excited:

The Chevalier and I dined late, but well, and drank several bottles of burgundy before withdrawing to enjoy the night and a fine cognac. He led me at once to his famous pleasure chamber, which will be found beyond the wine cellar. There, a most exciting and ingenious tableau presented itself. A pair of young women, sisters so he informed me, were chained outstretched in a wooden frame. Both were blindfold and dressed only in cheap cotton shifts. The Chevalier informed me that their father had failed to pay his rent on time and so, as was the local custom, his daughters had presented themselves to settle the debt by offering their bodies to the landlord.

When we came close, the Chevalier introduced himself and, much to my regret, promised that, though chained as if for punishment, neither would come to any harm unless they should offer any resistance to his whims. Upon spying my disappointment, he promised me such sport as I should never forget upon the morrow when he would sit as magistrate and serve sentence upon the various malefactors whose crimes had been committed in his absence in Paris.

From beyond the shadows cast by several torches emerged four members of the household, whereupon the Chevalier announced that the girls were to be washed and prepared for his pleasure. The girls whimpered as their shifts were cut from them, displaying their firm young flesh to our view. They were, I was informed, virgin twins of seventeen summers. Each had long dark brown hair, full, cherry-tipped breasts, narrow waists

99

and shapely thighs surmounted by thick bushes of Venus hair. The servants washed them with wet cloths before trimming their bushes to neat triangles, like arrows directing our eyes to their unspoilt slits. By articulating the frames, the servants bent the girls forward and shaved the hairs from around their roseholes before each was set upright once more, tears trickling from their blindfolds as they contemplated their maidenly ruin.

The Chevalier and I approached and feasted our fingers and lips on their trembling bodies. I pressed and pinched the resilient breasts of my girl until she cried out, and bit her nipples until they became hard and red. The Chevalier, I observed, used her sister with less violence, caressing the slut as if she were one to be truly loved. I, of course, treated my quarry as she deserved, for such peasants are mere slaves to our enjoyment. Understanding that the slut's maidenhood was due to my companion, I merely tested her sheath before pinching her lips and bud until she squirmed and squealed most delightfully. Her buttocks were strong and firm, excellent material for the whip, and her arse as tight as any good man could want. I slapped her posterior playfully, and when she did not object, tested my palm against her udders likewise. Observing that her juices flowed more quickly, I ventured to suggest she be warmed up a little before her combat. The Chevalier agreed, and the frame was adjusted so that I should have a good target.

With her sister trembling with consternation and anticipation, I set about burnishing the girl's bottom to a bright red with a paddle. The Chevalier now unleashed his stem and, adjusting his virgin to a horizontal position, introduced his lance, tearing deep with a single thrust. Overcome with passion, I hoisted my skirts and held my girl's mouth to my gash, demanding that she satisfy me while a servant was called to belabour her haunches and thighs. I was surprised by her adeptness, and as my passion rose I commenced pinching her dangling teats as the Chevalier, in his now-familiar

100

fashion, fainted away as his semen jetted into the virgin sheath. In due course, and with the slut's tongue deep inside my hole, I reached my crisis and staggered away for a restorative glass of cognac.

The Chevalier, once restored, seemed even more eager to take on his second bout. I remarked upon his increased vitality, and he told me that there was nothing like the taking of one cherry to increase his appetite for another.

Mary lay the book down and closed her eyes. Her bladder was bursting, and under the belt her mound itched. She pushed her hand underneath her dress and tried to rub through the leather. Her clitty jumped, throbbing to life, and she was agreeably surprised to find that the need to pee receded. For a while she casually rubbed on, and though the leather diluted the friction, a comfortable titillation spread from her congested delta. Casually, she picked up the first volume again, not caring, for the moment, to struggle with archaic French, but, before she could return to Victoria's adventures, the dinner gong sounded.

The rain continued to fall throughout the afternoon, and before Beatrice came to dress her for dinner, Mary was forced to light the candles. She had read more and learned much. The château, she concluded, had been a house of sexual excess for many years, with generations of du Bantonnes indulging in the art of debauching maids. All the girls seemed to have thoroughly enjoyed themselves in the process, even when caned or strapped for lapses of manners and other mild infractions of the rules. Certain themes recurred: the shaving of pubic hair and the enforced wearing of corsets and long dresses. The piercing of nipples was mentioned repeatedly, but not one of the journals suggested that the writers had been pierced themselves. Not one book reached the point of marriage.

As Mary took her place for dinner, she was more aware of her isolation. Tonight there was no Philippe, and Beatrice, too, was absent. Yvette, silent and keeping to the shadows, flitted around, filling glasses and serving the meal. She was dressed in a long, plain grey dress that disguised her figure. Mary, in contrast, felt almost naked. Her shoulders and arms were completely bare, and the pale orange silk of her dress seemed to break like waves over the very points of her uplifted and separated breasts, so that every time she breathed in she expected her nipples to leap into her host's sight. In any case, the silk was so fine that the equally pale corset and the straps of her chastity belt were revealed by the flickering candlelight. Le Comte complimented Mary on her appearance and promised fine weather for the morning, but beyond pleasantries nothing much was said until after the main-course plates were removed, which suited Mary because she was ashamed of the incessant excitement generated by her sole activity.

'You enjoyed your reading today?'

The inevitable question surprised her, and she realised he controlled her every action through Beatrice. She stammered and blushed. 'I, er, I um –'

He smiled disarmingly. 'I shall take it that you did. Books are a great source of learning, I think you agree, and I take a small measure of pride in the fact that every single book in my home contains at least something worth learning.'

Coming from another's lips, his words would have sounded unbearably pompous, but his twinkling eyes introduced an almost satirical irony. 'Young Victoria, for instance – you did read her diary?' Mary nodded, feeling uncomfortable.

'Young Victoria hiding her emotions behind an unhealthy edifice of euphemism and false modesty. In some ways, you are quite like her, in your strict and sheltered upbringing.'

Mary bridled at being compared with that stuck-up and coquettish little madam. Le Comte shook his head and smiled again. 'Do not mistake me, my dear, I mean no insult. You do not have her airs and graces, nor have you spent so much of your youth spying on the sexual exploits of others. Victoria, though the diary you have seen does not reveal it, peeped into rooms, behind haystacks and into barns to see what men and women do.'

'Were all those tales in those books true?' Mary was trying to work out how he knew so much about the past.

He answered enigmatically, his eyes blank jet reflections. 'Some of the writers may have embellished the truth.' He abruptly changed the subject. 'Has Beatrice treated you well?'

'Yes, sir, I believe she has followed your wishes.'

'And nothing has discomfited you?'

Mary felt the belt biting into her congested, soaking sex and the rise and fall of her almost exposed breasts. Was she discomfited, or merely excited by her accession to his demands? She answered truthfully. 'No, sir, though everything is still strange.'

'And you remain willing to agree to anything I ask of you?'

'Yes, sir,' Mary replied, anticipating a test to her resolve.

'Yvette, please bring the dessert.' This second abrupt change of subject left Mary wondering what he would require her to do next.

The maid produced a bowl of gleaming fresh fruit. Cherries, raspberries, peaches, pears, nectarines, slices of cantaloupe and watermelon, oranges, apples and small bananas. Beside this she placed a large crystal bowl of stiffly whipped cream and a smaller bowl of pale lemon ice-cream. After placing a single plate before her master, Yvette poured him a glass of champagne and withdrew to the shadows.

'Mary, will you stand by my side?'

Mary raised her eyebrows but moved none the less and stood as he requested, looking down on his white hair and noticing that, though the hair was like fine spun sugar, his scalp was nowhere thinly covered. His eyes were level with the base of her throat. He took a plump red cherry and dipped it first into the champagne and then into the cream.

'Open your mouth.'

Mary formed her lips into an 'O' big enough to take the fruit, and he popped it inside, holding the stem until she bit into the morsel and sucked the soft pulp from the stone. Mary had never tasted a cherry so perfectly ripe.

'It is nice, no?'

'Very nice.'

He carefully cut open a peach, slicing it into quarters, and repeated the operation. The peach, too, tasted wonderful.

'Please expose your breasts. Yvette will assist.' Mary stared unbelieving. Expose her breasts? His eyes narrowed. 'Not five minutes ago you agreed to do anything I wished. I wish your breasts to be bared, now.'

Mary felt Yvette's fingers fiddling between her breasts and then the floating ruffle of silk was whipped away. She blushed and looked down at her elevated mounds and soft pink nipples. Almost immediately, as if chilled, they began to harden, and under the belt her clitty throbbed.

'Put your hands behind your back and do not move them.'

Mary did so, and Yvette tied them loosely with the silk. Her heart jumped.

Instead of looking at her, he dipped another cherry into the cream and ate it. Mary felt foolish and embarrassed and resented the maid, who stood by the wall facing her. Le Comte took a spoonful of cream in one hand and a slice of peach in the other and turned to her.

'It is one of the great pleasures to mix the flavours and textures of one's food with those of the body of a young, fresh, unspoilt woman. You have such magnificent breasts that I can deny myself that pleasure no longer.' Mary watched as he wiped the cool, wet peach over her right breast, leaving traces of pulp and a sheen of sweet juice. Her nipple swelled and her breathing accelerated. After an age, he took the peach away and let drips of cream fall across the peach juice until the upper slope and nipple was coated.

'Come closer,' he whispered with excitement.

Mary shivered, shuffled and sighed as his pink tongue flicked out and licked the mixture away, before kissing her nipple and popping the battered slice of peach into his mouth. The touch was so gentle, sensual and subtle that, Mary's fears dispersed in a moment. She opened her mouth and closed her eyes as tiny shudders of incredible excitement ran down her spine to where her body boiled.

He took a teaspoon of ice-cream next and placed it above her left nipple. Mary shivered and almost jumped away as the cold stabbed her, but she held her ground and waited with him, watching the blob slip slowly down, melting and stiffening its target. At the last second, before it slipped off, his mouth closed. Mary wriggled her fingers and toes as his tongue held the ice-cream against her until it melted away. Then he sucked the tip hot again. When it emerged from between his lips, her nipple was red and thick. He repeated the treatment, alternating between breasts, until both tips glowed. For the next dish, he let cream run over her slopes before dipping cherries, now matching her shade, into the gathering of cream in her cleavage. He fed her sips of champagne and crunchy apple, and then, taking the chilled bottle, ran it against the tips of her breasts and her lips.

At every touch, Mary felt her crushed sex throb, pulsing deeply. Her breasts seemed to swell, and the little ledge holding them up began to press into the mounds weighing down. She looked down. He was removing two steel gadgets from his pocket.

He looked up, his eyes burning. 'Something to remind you of dessert.' Taking one of the devices, he placed it around her left nipple and flicked a tiny catch. Steel jaws shut, trapping her flesh at the base, and he tightened it with a twist of a small nut. Mary gasped. The constriction made her whole breast throb. It felt as if her nipple would burst.

'Don't worry, my dear. You will become used to it soon, and no damage can be done.'

Mary breathed deeply, desperately trying to contain her moans. As she did so, her right tip was similarly gripped. Now waves of intense, throbbing excitement coursed out of her bosom, connected with the heat in her womb, and set up a low, liquid vibration that made her feel faint. She closed her eyes as her legs began to shake, and she felt every tiny shift as her lungs worked hard. Contractions pulsed through that part of her under the belt. She felt her anus touch the leather and her vagina clutch at thin air. Mary moaned, heat boiling in her loins.

His hands came to her breasts then, cool and dry, and the intensity diminished, as if his hands were drawing out the intoxication, absorbing her orgasm. She heard him catch his breath, as if surprised by the waves of pleasure wracking her body, and she looked at him as he stood before her. His eyes shone with excitement and pride, his lips were open, and somehow he looked less venerable, less like a grandfather than a father.

Suddenly, he released his hold and both staggered apart, Le Comte into his chair, Mary into the arms of Yvette.

Eight

Laura awoke in an empty bed, but not an empty flat. Adam was in the shower, and an aroma of coffee drifted in from the kitchen. She smiled to herself and straightened out from a foetal curl. Under sheets crumpled from last night's excesses, she ran her fingers over the trails of broken cotton. Her nipples were still sore, and her labia puffed by penetration. They had made love three times before exhaustion took them, and her thighs were sticky and coated with his semen. Laura stroked herself gently and wondered if her strong feelings for Adam were reciprocated.

He was different from most men. Only Jack had ever given her reason to trust the male sex before. Callow students and sad, emotionally stunted lecturers had made passes, but she had rejected them all. Adam seemed quite like Jack – self-contained, respectful, sexually unselfish and masterful. Perhaps she might come to call him master . . .

Adam emerged from the bathroom clad only in a towel around his waist. Daylight revealed well-defined six-pack and a series of old scars to his left chest and upper arm pale against a light tan. His legs, too, were tanned and strong, and immediately she ached to remove the towel and reveal his tight bum and silky, beautiful cock.

He smiled down at her. 'Morning. How do you like your coffee?'

'Black and strong.'

'Like your men?' He raised an eyebrow as he filled the room with infectious humour.

107

She smiled back and looked meaningfully at the towel. 'Not necessarily.'

'Time for that later, young lady.'

The promise started her fingers moving again as he went to get the coffee. Soon they were slipping around in her warmth and soothing the tenderness away.

'I said later, Miss Jenkins. Do I have to restrain you once more?' Mock anger belied shared desire.

Laura snatched her hand away and rolled on to her side to reply in kind. 'My apologies, Mr Hardcastle. Your lover will restrain herself, at least for a while.'

'Good. We're going to have a busy day, so you'd better get showered and we'll grab some breakfast on the way to my place.' Laura reluctantly levered herself from her bed. 'You will dress so that, at any time, I can reach your rings. Oh, and I do like stockings.'

Laura smiled as she bowed to acknowledge his request, her inclination to call him master growing by the minute.

Adam drove Laura to a quaint cottage in a village tucked away in the midst of rural Essex: thatched roof and a barely tamed mass of ancient roses, hollyhocks and fruit trees for a garden. Inside, the beams were exposed and wood smoke clung to everything, and everything was in its place, clean and tidy, a bachelor's home with family memorabilia. Laura found herself feeling, despite her Welshness, at home in a classic piece of England.

'It's lovely.'

She wanted to say more, but he was already opening drawers, pulling out documents and switching on his computer. She looked at the family photographs. They included one of a pretty, slim young girl with dark curly hair.

'Is this your sister?'

'Yes, that's Anne.'

'I can see the resemblance to Philippe.'

Adam turned away thoughtfully and finished organising. Laura decided to make herself useful. 'I'll make the coffee then.'

'Please. You'll find everything you need, including an ashtray if you feel you must smoke.'

Laura realised suddenly that she had not even thought about a cigarette all day – indeed, she had started smoking regularly only in the last couple of weeks, since Mary's rejection and things with Jack had started to go wrong. She smiled and raised her eyebrows. Was she falling in love with Adam? Laura did not take the ashtray back into the living-room.

Late in the afternoon, just as the low sun, slanting into her eyes, made Laura squint, she finally found something of interest in Adam's pile of research. It was an address: 17 Place Dubias, Paris.

Laura turned to where Adam sprawled on the sofa and pointed it out on the paper. 'I know this place.' Adam sat up. 'Princess Leila has an apartment there.'

'Who's she?'

'She did the bronze.' What a strange coincidence, she thought, that Leila, with her proclivities, should live in a house tentatively linked to the mysterious count. 'What made you note it?'

'I wondered if the first count had a house in Paris. It used to be called the Hôtel du Bantonne until it was sold in the 1920s.'

Laura reached for the telephone. 'Why don't I give Leila a call, see if she knows anything about it?'

Adam nodded. 'Maybe we could visit.'

'She won't be there at the moment – nobody stays in Paris during the summer, except tourists.' Laura looked up the number in her diary and tapped out the digits. Her call was answered. After a pause, while a maid went for her mistress, Leila came on the line, her exotic accent strong.

'Darling, how lovely! Did you like your statue?'

'Lovely, really good, and at least three people have admired it with me.' The niceties over, Laura got down to business. 'I wondered if you might be in Paris soon? I'm going over for a few days, and I'd love to see you, and so would my new friend, Adam.'

109

'A new friend? Your new lover – he's tall, strong and handsome, yes? And very sexy and masterful, yes?'

Laura laughed. 'How did you guess?'

'I know you. But why go to Paris in the summer? Spring, autumn and winter suit Paris so much better.'

Laura tried to disguise the reason. 'Adam's doing some historical research, and I'm going to show him around. Just thought, if you were going to be there, we might pop in.'

Without a word from Leila, Laura was put on hold. She turned to Adam, but he had left the room. She waited a long time for Leila to come back on. She sounded flustered.

'Sorry, darling, lost my diary.' Laura caught the dissembling tone. Leila's diary was never more than an arm's length away. 'I find I have to be in Paris tomorrow – how silly of me to forget. I'll meet you the day after, at about noon?'

'It's a date.'

'Ciao.'

'Ciao.' As Laura replaced the handset, a feeling of unease settled on her stomach.

Laura and Adam drew up outside Leila's apartment. Unlike the rest of the buildings in the square, all of which were terraced, number 17 stood a little apart, and its roof suggested much greater age. Laura wondered who else lived there; Leila occupied only the top floor, but Laura had never seen anyone else, even though the other three floors and the basement were clearly in use. Laura followed Adam to the entrance. The intercom gave no clues: just five blank buttons. Laura pressed the top button and announced herself to Leila's maid. The door opened with a click, and they entered the small lobby and went to the lift. Another locked door prevented them from investigating the ground floor.

Adam looked round. 'Why don't we take a look at the other floors on the way up?'

Laura pressed all four buttons, starting with the basement, but the lift ascended directly to the top. 'Must have some automatic control tied to the door lock so only invited guests can enter.'

Adam barely nodded. Laura sensed his nervousness. He was closer to the mystery than he had ever been before, and about to meet the creator of the erotic bronze.

The lift delivered them to another secure lobby. A maid waited, new to Laura. She curtsied stiffly, and Laura guessed that under her demure knee-length dress she wore Leila's speciality underwear designed to accentuate her figure and impose strict control on her body. Laura wondered if Adam had divined as much. The girl stood a little taller than Laura, with straight, shoulder-length, almost mousy hair, a peaches-and-cream complexion and a large bust.

In clipped upper-class English, she invited them in. 'Follow me please, sir, madam.'

She showed them into the apartment where Leila lay like Goya's Maya on a couch draped in silks and cushions. Like the Maya, Leila was virtually naked, her opulent figure dressed in almost transparent gauze that merely shaded her skin, emphasising ripe nipples and a thick, dark triangle between lasciviously parted thighs.

Laura quickly looked at Adam before she kissed her friend's cheek. His face was stiff as he tried to hide his surprise. Secretly, she was pleased with herself for not warning him what to expect.

'Darling!' Leila squealed, as if their appearance was a surprise, and returned the kiss.

Laura stood back and waved Adam closer. 'This is my friend Adam.'

Awkwardly, Adam reached to shake her hand. 'Pleased to meet you, Princess.'

Leila pulled him down and kissed him on either cheek. 'Pleased to meet you, Adam.' She released him. 'So, are you my little Laura's new master?' He coloured. 'Make sure you keep her in order. She can be very wilful. I recommend the crop for her bottom at least once a day as a matter of course, and on her little tits as well if she gives you cheek – she likes that, don't you, dear?'

111

It was Laura's turn to blush. Although Adam was her master, as yet, apart from a little bondage and orders defining what she wore, they had not ventured further. Leila's indiscretion was threatening Laura's relationship before they had time to get to know each other well enough to swap secrets.

Leila ignored her reaction and ordered the maid, Camilla, to fetch drinks while Laura and Adam took their seats on the other couch.

Leila stretched like a cat. 'What do you think of Camilla? Twenty-two, English landed gentry, well educated, very spoilt. Her fiancé sent her to me for training. She was reluctant at first, but after only three weeks she's as docile as a lamb.'

Adam looked startled. 'Training?'

Leila smiled knowingly. 'Yes, dear. The sort of thing Laura underwent with a certain Greek we do not now mention. When Camilla returns, she'll show you.'

Laura swallowed nervously. Adam would get seriously sidetracked if Leila went on like this. She urgently wanted to talk to Leila alone, so that she could explain her relationship to Adam, but the maid returned with their drinks. As soon as they had their glasses, Leila addressed her charge.

'Camilla, show these nice people your markings.'

Without complaint, but without making eye contact, Camilla began to undress. Laura licked her lips surreptitiously and heard Adam's sharp intake of breath. Camilla exposed her white shoulders and generous bosom laid on a stiff leather corset. Her breasts were like ripe melons, with faint green veins and small pink nipples in the centre of wide pale haloes. Laura glanced at Adam's groin and smiled to herself; he was becoming stiff inside his tight jeans. The maid dropped her dress, turned and bent to display her round, full, crop-marked behind. Tattooed on her right cheek, curving into the crease and lined up with her anus, was a heraldic shield, and as the cleft came back out to her left cheek, crossed riding crops below a heart in chains.

Leila explained. 'His family coat of arms and his personal seal. Turn round, dear, and show them your rings.'

Camilla turned to face Laura and Adam, parted her legs, bent her knees and pushed her hips forward. Her mound was completely shaved, and her prominent outer lips were linked by three heavy steel rings. From the middle ring hung a large disc engraved with the initials H D F C.

'Her fiancé's favourite book is *L'Histoire d'O*, although he had her tattooed, not branded. Camilla requested the adornment and is now considering how to improve her nipples, aren't you, dear?'

'Yes, mistress.'

The maid seemed inclined to return to silence, but Leila indicated she should explain.

'They are rather small and pale. My master would like them larger so I can wear matching rings. Princess Leila has suggested a course of stimulation by clamps, weights and binding. My master has offered to have them surgically enlarged. I have to decide by the end of this week.'

Leila interrupted. 'Laura, I thought you might be able to help her make up her mind. Camilla – kneel!'

The girl dropped to the floor and sat on her heels, her thighs parted and hands behind her neck so that her breasts were out-thrust and the rings hung clear of her soft, rounded thighs.

Laura felt uncomfortable, put on the spot like this. Leila was presuming too much of her nascent relationship with Adam. She glanced at him, seeking his approval. He nodded, looking curious.

Laura looked at Camilla. The mixture of excitement and fear in her eyes sparked Laura's honey. 'My nipples were just as small as yours, but they were enhanced by the sort of stimulation Leila suggests, and I'm really pleased with the results.'

Camilla nodded, but her eyes betrayed her worries. Laura reinforced the benefits. 'It sounds painful, and it is, a bit. But you get so much pleasure as well.' She lowered

113

her voice, imparting her intimate secret. 'I had loads of orgasms. They enlarged my pussy lips and clitty the same way.'

Camilla licked her lips. Adam coughed. Laura saw disapproval in his face.

Leila smiled. 'Has that helped you, Camilla?' The maid nodded. 'Adam, we've embarrassed you. Camilla, get dressed and leave us. You're upsetting my guests.'

Adam jumped in. 'No, please, don't dismiss her yet. I'd like to know what other training she has undergone.'

Camilla blushed deeply and lowered her eyes. Leila laughed at her discomfort and chided her.

'Camilla, the gentleman is interested in you, You should be proud. She turned to Adam. 'Camilla was reluctant to conform to her fiancé's preferences – oral and anal sex. I have no doubt she's quite happy to be fucked normally, but that pleasure is to be saved for their wedding day and thereafter only for procreation.'

Adam seemed genuinely interested. 'Do you use live rounds, as it were, for practice?'

With English being her second language, Leila was slow to get the joke. 'Sorry? Oh, no, well, not so far. She has been practising on artificial pricks, each one bigger than the last, but so far she has not tasted semen, either in her mouth or bottom.'

Laura raised an eyebrow. Was this an invitation? Leila turned to her trainee. 'I am sure you would like to show Adam just how far you have come, wouldn't you, Camilla?'

The maid replied in subdued, reluctant tones. 'Yes, mistress.'

'Then use your mouth, please. He might have your bottom later – if you're lucky.'

Laura looked hard at Adam, but he showed no sign of refusing the offer. Automatically, she hunted in her handbag for her cigarettes. Jealousy had defeated her resolve never to smoke again. She had left her cigarettes at Adam's. Searching for nicotine, she looked round the room as Camilla crawled across the carpet to kneel

114

between Adam's knees. She spotted a gold cigarette case on a table behind Leila. As she heard Adam's zip open, she went across to where Leila lay, thighs wide and lips parted as she contemplated her trainee's performance.

'May I smoke?' Laura asked quietly.

Leila reached out and took her hand. She whispered in reply. 'Mm, I'll have one too.'

Leila sat up a bit, raised her left leg and indicated the space she had made. 'Why don't you sit here and watch.'

Laura tugged her hand free.

'Jealous?' asked Leila.

'We only met the other day,' Laura hissed with annoyance.

'I think, darling, that you're going to have to get used to it. He's gorgeous, and very masterful.' Leila was, for once, being absolutely serious.

Laura collected the cigarettes and lighter and sat against the Princess. She lit up and watched as Camilla stared suspiciously at the cock held between finger and thumb.

Leila leant closer and whispered in her ear. 'That's only the second penis she's ever seen. Henry's was the first, and she only saw him once. I hope Adam's got enough self-control.'

Laura could not prevent herself from defending her lover, even though she felt angry with him for accepting the offer of another's mouth. 'He's as good as they get.'

'I'm sorry, darling. I have dropped you in the deep end.' Leila put her arm round Laura's shoulder and kissed her lips. Laura settled against her soft, cushioning bosom and watched the maid displaying her new-found skills.

Tentatively, Camilla opened her lips and touched the purple helm of Adam's penis, as if testing the taste of an ice-cream. Leila coughed meaningfully, and she began to move her hand, now trying to encompass his thickness, up and down.

'Your mouth, Camilla, it's supposed to go in your mouth.'

The girl closed her eyes and forced herself to swallow the dome. Laura felt sorry for her; Adam was quite large for a beginner to have to take. He closed his eyes and stroked her head gently. Slowly, as more of his length disappeared from view, she began to suck, her cheeks hollowing. Laura looked at the curve of the girl's spine and full buttocks.

'Her skin's very soft. Doesn't she cry a lot when you smack her?'

'Delightfully, and she gets so wet I want to drink her up, but I'm not allowed. Her fiancé says she must learn to pleasure women, but only get pleasure from men, via her breasts, anus and mouth.'

Laura was appalled. 'And she agreed to this?'

'Yes, I was there. Apparently, her mother has had a long and happy marriage on the same terms. They're strongly Catholic and practise contraception by natural means.'

Laura wondered at the strangeness of her sex. How could anyone agree to deny herself natural pleasures? The girl was trying hard, all the same. Adam was now buried deep in her mouth and murmuring his pleasure as her head bobbed up and down. Despite her misgivings, Laura began to enjoy the spectacle, and Leila's fingers, which were now stroking her breasts and thighs. She stubbed out her cigarette and returned the gesture, dipping her fingers between Leila's thighs, into the thick, humid bush. Leila's heavy, oiled lips opened, and they slid up to the tender, thick, ready bud. Leila kissed her again and sought Laura's smooth slit with her hand. Laura opened her thighs. They heard a groan and broke their kiss to watch the maid.

Adam urged his hips gently. She almost had all of him inside; just two fingers gripping at the base. Her other hand now rolled his balls softly and stroked his thigh. Adam pushed his jeans further down, exposing his lightly haired buttocks, and lifted up, hoping she would touch him there.

Leila whispered encouragement. 'Remember his anus, and the gland inside. He wants you there. Wet your finger and enter him.'

Camilla murmured a sort of protest, but she released his cock to wet the finger and hesitantly obey. Adam writhed and sank back into her mouth, his grip tightening on her scalp. Now that his thighs were spread almost parallel to

116

the sofa, Laura could watch the maid's heavy breasts swing, and she reached for Leila's and took a thick, turgid nipple between her lips and bit hard, knowing that Leila loved rough treatment.

Leila speared her, three fingers thrusting deep, thumb flicking across her clitty. Laura stabbed her own fingers rhythmically in time with Leila's fingers, in time with Adam's increasing grunts. She looked across. His eyes were screwed shut, his body tensing. Laura watched as he came, thoughtfully holding Camilla's face away so that he did not hit the back of her throat. She gagged none the less, her face registering shock as the thick goo pumped into her mouth in salty strong jets. Leila, managing to retain some control, ordered her maid to swallow. Camilla did so, struggling against her scruples.

'Lick off anything you've missed and then come over here.'

Leila and Laura slowed their hands, receding from orgasm. The girl rose to her feet, licking her lips, and approached.

'Display.' Leila's voice was thick and low with lust.

The girl stood close, parted her legs and put her hands back behind her neck. Leila reached out the hand that had not invaded Laura and stroked the open, plump, ringed sex.

'Laura, she's as wet as you. Feel and reward her. She's done well.'

Laura used her wet hand to spread those thick outer lips. She was indeed wet and hot, with a gloss of arousal spread across the tops of her thighs. Camilla's inner lips were almost invisible, her little man just a small pink bump. Laura tested her entrance and found wet tightness. She urged the girl closer and stroked her bottom as she began nipping gently at that little bean, making it grow and glow. She spread her lips far apart, and pressed. Camilla thrust back and bent her knees as Laura spread her buttocks and reached with a wet finger for the soft pink hole. Laura looked up at her looming breasts shaking with excitement. Her finger entered the delicate ring, she pinched the bean

117

again, and Camilla shuddered. She pinched once more and thrust her finger deep, and Camilla groaned. Leila put her hands to the maid's breasts and pinched the little, hard nipples just as Laura pinched and thrust for the third time. Camilla jerked, shuddered and cried and nearly collapsed.

Leila took Laura's hand. 'Come, sweetheart, let us leave them to recover while we catch up.'

It was time for Laura to take her own pleasure, to take this woman as she liked to be taken, and Laura liked to take her: violently, greedily and quickly. She waved her fingers at Adam as she followed Leila through a door. Unexpectedly, she found herself in a stairwell.

'Where are we going?'

'I thought you wanted to look round the building, darling.' Leila squeezed her hand and grinned conspiratorially. 'This leads down to the first floor, which has not been changed for simply ages, at least since the count sold up.'

Laura missed the opportunity to feign ignorance. 'Oh, I'd love to see.'

'We thought you would.'

Laura went quiet and swore to herself. Who was the 'we'? And how did Leila know she was interested in the count? They arrived at the first floor and Leila ushered her into the past. The room was straight out of the end of the last century, all in heavy reds and blacks, with heavy brocade curtains, leather armchairs, tasselled lamps and ornate crystal chandeliers. There was no mustiness or dust, and a decanter of cognac and two glasses lay twinkling on a silver tray. Above the fireplace hung a great painting. Leila led Laura over and left her looking at the picture as she poured a cognac each.

Laura stared up. Hooded monks with exposed and gigantic phalli goaded a group of naked young women with whips and sticks into a dance at the feet of a Pan-like figure. From the pack of frightened women, monks took individuals for their pleasure. Whips and birches beat down, turning buttocks pink before the giant cocks plundered the nearest orifice. Several of the female faces were turned towards the viewer, and Laura recognised at least one: Adam's sister. Horrified, she turned to her friend.

'Leila, what is this?'

Leila stood between three tall, menacing men.

'What's going on?'

The oldest of the three men answered in rich, Middle Eastern tones. 'You are sticking your pretty little nose into things you are not yet ready to understand, Laura.'

Laura interrupted. 'How do you know my name?' The other two men came and stood by her side.

He ignored her question. 'One day, my master may admit you into this knowledge, but until then you have to be dissuaded. Your accomplice is receiving the same message from my colleagues as we speak.'

Laura started to protest. 'But I don't know –' The men took her arms in their grip. She could not escape.

'You already know too much! The Princess Leila has reported you, and your friend. Precautions must be taken.'

'But what –' His palm stung her face.

'Quiet, girl. I understood you knew your place!' Laura subsided into a moody silence. 'You will come with us as a surety against your partner's continued interest.' He turned to Leila. 'The Prince sends his greetings and thanks. We shall take care of her.'

Laura looked daggers at Leila. He snapped his fingers and Laura was frogmarched out of the room.

Nine

After breakfast, and having nothing better to do on a hot, sunny day, Mary took a walk in the grounds around the château. She considered which way to go. North and west, only the open grass separated the house from the forest. To the east, at the back of the house, the dark, protective woods edged up to the walls of the kitchen garden, but to the south lay a straggly orchard and the forest appeared to be a long way off. She moved towards the heavily laden apple, pear and plum trees gradually absorbing the grass, discouraging mowers so seared grasses grew tall, waving in the dappled shadows between the solid trunks. Light twinkled from beyond, beckoning her with the promise of fresh discoveries.

She strode out as if she were walking the hills of home. It was the first time since Beatrice fitted the belt that she had stretched her legs, and immediately she felt the arousing friction. She cut her stride, and the rubbing eased a little. Crickets chirruped in the tall grasses, and butterflies fluttered amid splashes of colour made by wild flowers. She quickly grew hot, and her chest, constricted by her corsets, felt tight, but before she became uncomfortable she was beyond the orchard and under the shade of oak and beech. Bees buzzed and small birds fluttered the leaves. She followed a twinkling and, after a minute or two, smelt water. A hidden lake; how romantic. Mary reached the shore and breathed the cool air.

The lake was surprisingly large, maybe a quarter of a mile long by a hundred yards wide, with an island towards the middle. Away to her right she could see a landing-stage and an overgrown boathouse. Her way right was blocked. She went left and sat in the shade on a strong branch overhanging the water. The water was utterly clear, and she could see right down to the rock-covered bottom. Small fish swam, and once a trout flashed by, shining and plump. An electric-blue dragonfly hovered and skittered. The trout took it in a clean leap. Mary sat back against the tree trunk. Reeds wavered in a gentle breeze, ducks and a pair of black swans pootled. In the peaceful, warm air, her thoughts wandered over the events of the last few days, the things she had seen and experienced, and how she seemed to be coming to terms with it all.

She had to admit that she was, on many levels, enjoying herself; the physical sensations, the sudden acquisition of sexual awareness and the insight into the actions of other people or characters in books. She had discovered that romantic love, the only love she had considered proper, possessed a physical side. Now, she wanted to be with Philippe, to be naked in his bed, to smell and touch and taste. Even her guilt over Laura was gone, replaced by longing and happy memories of the love they had shared. Even Le Comte touched her emotionally, not as an old, nice man, but as a suitor. She chided herself for pride, but she was sought by all three, they said she was beautiful, and now she wanted to repay those compliments.

Mary looked up, searching for the source of a big splash. Someone was swimming from the boathouse. She shaded her eyes. A dark head shot from under the water and shook. Philippe! She smiled and wanted to call to him, but something held her back, perhaps the urge to spy. He dived again, smooth skin pale in the water, his body almost liquid, a ripple of shoulders, naked buttocks, thighs and calves. His feet kicked and all that was left was a widening circle. Captivated, Mary waited for him to resurface, naughtily wanting to see him reverse the dive; to emerge on his back so she could see his torso, thighs and, she blushed to herself, his cock.

Twenty yards nearer, he emerged, swimming strongly,

face down. She froze as he came nearer, not wanting to be seen watching, to keep this moment for herself. He was so strong, manly and handsome, with his hair plastered to his skull, his shoulders and arms sweeping, fingers cutting the water. Suddenly, when it looked as though he would swim right up to her, he dived into a turn, rolled on to his back and headed away with an effortless backstroke. She peered, hoping to see his secret, but there was only a dark shadow among the streaming, foaming water as his legs scissored. He returned to the boathouse and, hidden by the jetty, climbed out and began drying himself, too far away to be seen.

Mary sat back with a sigh, excited and exhilarated. She let her thighs fall open and stroked them, closing her eyes as she thought about Philippe's naked body; the splash of dark hair between his flat breasts, the shading at his groin, his small, dark nipples and hard belly.

'Get down from there this instant!'

Mary jumped and almost fell off the branch. Beatrice stood on the bank, her face bright with anger. Mary scrambled on to dry land.

'I'm sorry, mistress.' She apologised, though she had no idea why she should.

'And so you should be, spying and playing with yourself!'

'But I wasn't!'

'I saw everything, mademoiselle.' Beatrice glared and then walked round her, sneering as she noticed smears of moss and bits of twig stuck on her dress. 'You look hot, sticky and dirty, like a little girl. You need a bath.'

Mary gaped at her. 'But, I only –'

'Who gave you permission to speak? Get undressed and into the lake. You obviously like the water.'

Mary stared disbelieving. Beatrice's right hand, hitherto held behind her back, snapped round. The stick she was carrying slashed across Mary's flank.

'Ow!'

'I said, get undressed.'

Mary obeyed, sulking at the injustice, but strangely

123

stimulated by the threat. She kicked off her shoes and reached behind to unbutton the high-necked dress, at once feeling the tight material part. She drew the top forward, and tugged her arms clear of the clinging sleeves before shimmying her hips to work the dress down over her bottom and thighs. Now clad only in her corset and chastity belt, she bent down and gathered up the dress, shaking it straight. Beatrice indicated a suitable hanger created by a broken branch. Mary lay the dress carefully over the protruding, shattered finger. Mary presented her back to her mistress and suppressed a sigh of pleasure as the tight corset was opened. Then, unexpectedly, the chastity belt was removed too. She looked down at the pink marks left by the corset and belt across her stomach.

'Well? Get in, then! You can swim, can't you?'

Mary nodded and began, hesitantly, to make her way through the leaf litter, twigs and stones down to the lake edge. Suddenly, the water didn't look so enticing. She dipped a toe and thought of the fish she'd seen in there just a few minutes before, and how they would view this pale invader. She heard Beatrice behind her and went to step out. Then she was flying through the air, impelled by Beatrice's left hand thumping her between the shoulder blades. Splash. The water was deep. She kicked out, and a foot touched the bottom. It was breathtakingly cold. She kicked out and regained the surface, coughing and spluttering. She waved her arms and came to a standstill, gulping in air and spitting out mouthfuls of water. It tasted sweet. Beatrice said something. Mary looked round and saw a short bit of branch flying towards her. She ducked and dipped under the water again. She opened her eyes, and the water was clear except for her flailing arms. She kicked out and swam out of the chatelaine's reach, stretching her limbs into a breaststroke. She shook off the chill and stretched out across the lake, until something slimy touched her leg. She squealed, spluttered and turned back to the bank.

Beatrice beckoned her out, and she rose, thinking herself brave and bold as she walked from the lake, water pouring from her long hair, her breasts and thighs. 'Hands out.'

Mary complied, expecting to be dried. Instead, her wrists were captured by a length of rope and bound securely together. Beatrice led her to a tree and hooked her wrists over a branch, forcing her to stand on tiptoe facing the trunk, and deep in shade. Then she flipped Mary's long, straggling wet hair over one shoulder, leaving her whole spine bare.

'Wait there while I get something to dry you with.'

Mary heard Beatrice go into the trees, and the regular snapping and tearing of twigs. She was gone for several minutes, and Mary began to get cold.

'I think this will do.' Mary looked round. Beatrice held a bunch of wands, most with their leaves intact. She had tied them together at one end, forming a handle. 'In your country, I believe this is called a birch. In Sweden they use them during their saunas. Invigorating, so I'm told.'

Mary yelped as Beatrice plied the wands to her back, but as the rapid, gentle whipping proceeded she realised that it was not really painful. The leaves cushioned most of the sting as Beatrice covered her back and flanks, slashing away the water. Her skin began to tingle, feel warm as toast. The birching extended down, over her thighs and calves.

'Spread your legs, so I can dry you there.'

Mary, in an almost dream state, obeyed, and the twigs whipped between them, stinging and tickling, scratching lightly. She wriggled on tiptoe, gasping as new areas were kissed. The birch extended up her sides, clipping the edges of her breasts, her armpits, her ribs.

The whipping halted. Beatrice lifted her wrists.

'Turn round.'

Mary turned to face her mistress. She felt nervous as her wrists were hung up again. Now her tender breasts and naked belly were exposed; was the softest, smoothest skin she knew so much better than the unseen flesh of her back now going to be lashed dry? She looked warily at the bundle of wands. The leaves had almost all been shredded away, and now the instrument looked likely to produce a far more painful result.

125

The chatelaine ran a forefinger across Mary's stomach. Droplets of water still stood out. Then she flipped her hair back out of the way again.

'You are still wet, child.'

She drew her arm back. Mary closed her eyes and heard the whoosh of the birch.

'Ahh!' The wands caressed her shins, rattling, skimming.

'Oww.' Her knees and lower inner thighs.

'Sss, ahh.' Arms and shoulders.

'Ahh, ahhh.' Belly and ribs, almost ticklish light stings.

And then back and forth, constantly sweeping and stinging over those same areas, extending a little way up her thighs, between her legs, sometimes catching the outer slopes of her breasts or the lower curves of her belly. Mary sagged, her legs wider, hips reaching out and vulva parted with a weird, dark longing to know the stinging birch. Her nerves tingled as the birch still avoided her swinging, excited breasts and sex. Her mouth opened in a moan as, at last, she felt the sting on her nipples. Beatrice worked up and down, back and forth, catching every angle and crease. Mary squealed and yet found her bosom thrusting out for more.

Suddenly, the whipping stopped. She opened her eyes. Her breasts glowed, nipples hard and red. She was breathing heavily and was not sure if the wet between her legs was water, sweat or arousal. Beatrice also breathed heavily, and as Mary looked at her she smiled crookedly.

The birch whipped across the hitherto untouched front of Mary's thighs. Mary swung on her wrists and cried as millions of tiny stings swept across her tender flesh, scouring, slicing, scratching. Her vulva throbbed, her thighs flared with heat. Swish-whip; the wands stung her wet, open lips and upstanding bud. She moaned. The twigs were slowly drawn up her body from thighs to breasts, catching protruding flesh. She gasped. Swish-whip; her breasts reignited. Swish-whip; her sex screamed.

Beatrice grabbed her then, her mouth clamping Mary's lips, her hands grabbing sore breasts and molten, swollen mound. Mary ground back at the grasping fingers, but they left her, gasping.

'My apologies, Mary, forgive me.' Beatrice looked ashamed at her outburst of passion.

Mary implored her with her eyes, begging for a release of her pent-up arousal, but Beatrice ignored her, instead fetching more rope. Leaving Mary bound by her wrists, Beatrice wound the rope round her waist and threaded the long end between her legs, under the loop round her waist and up to her shoulders. She formed another loop under Mary's armpits and above the upper slopes of her breasts, and made two more loops and knotted them at her shoulder blades and fixed them tight round her breasts. Then she tightened the loops until Mary's breasts bulged pink and lined by the birch. These loops were anchored with another loop below her breasts knotted to the waistband. Mary hung, disbelieving, as Beatrice fed more rope down between her legs, on either side of her slit and up to her back again. All the loops were tightened again, and the coarse rope rubbed into her sore, tender flesh and squeezed her lips tight.

She let Mary down, and made a few minor adjustments to get the tension right. Mary looked down at her obscenely bulging, throbbing boobs. She was dressed again in the tight wool dress and shoes. Mary squirmed as the dress was buttoned up and the tight wool tickled and rubbed her sore skin, and as she squirmed the rope tightened and rubbed harder, and every movement became a trial, and a pleasure, and another step along a path Mary was beginning to recognise, a path leading to reliance on physical pleasure spiced with pain. As Mary came to understand this, Beatrice, very tenderly, combed and brushed her hair.

Finished, Beatrice took Mary's hand. 'Come, child, Le Comte desires your company.'

She led Mary through the trees but stopped her just before they left cover.

'Mary, I am very sorry for what I nearly did back there. I, er, lost control. It is not good for a woman to lose control. We should always keep something back, just a little bit, five per cent, something we only give to the one we love most, and who most loves us most in return.' She added sadly before her eyes lit up, 'Never forget that, child, never forget.'

With a tug, Beatrice led Mary into the sunshine and added no more to that enigmatic, vehement injunction. Mary speculated about what she really meant, and what lay in the older woman's past to have made this piece of advice sound so important. Whatever the history, Mary decided to follow her advice and lock away five per cent of herself. Mary had no idea what that five per cent nugget consisted of, yet, but she vowed that only Philippe would ever be given it.

'Thank you, Beatrice. Mary, please stand by my side.' Le Comte indicated to his right. He was sitting at his desk with a large book closed in front of him. 'Did you enjoy your walk, Mary?'

'Yes, thank you, sir.'

'And your swim?'

He knew everything. 'Yes, sir.'

He looked up at her. 'I see you are not wearing your corsets. May I ask why?'

Mary blushed. 'Beatrice bound me with rope after drying me.'

His eyes never left hers. 'And how did she dry you?'

Mary's blush deepened and spread, her bound parts throbbed anew. 'With a bundle of long twigs.'

'I am sure she gave this bundle a name.'

Mary's voice dropped. 'Yes, sir. She called it a birch.'

'And you enjoyed it.'

Her reply came in a whisper of embarrassment. 'Yes, sir.'

'And not merely for the exhilarating effect upon your skin.'

Mary shook with humiliation. 'No, sir.'

'And so Beatrice bound those places with rope to remind you.' Mary was silent. 'Are the bonds very tight? Do they cut deep into your very soul and make your breasts yearn for my touch?'

A tear of confusion and shame gathered; her body did yearn for the touch of his cold, dry, bony old fingers and lips. Ignoring her lack of response, he opened the book with his white cotton gloved left hand and carefully turned some blank pages and a sheet of tissue until a print was uncovered. It showed, in colourful and precise detail, a girl and an older man in a stylised Turkish costume. His plump cheeks were pink with exertion, and in his right hand he held a switch. The girl, standing but bent forward with her wrists hanging from a chain on the wall, was naked from the waist down. Her plump white buttocks displayed the red lines made by the switch, her pretty face, looking over her shoulder at her master, was barely obscured by a transparent veil, and her breasts were held in a sort of metal brassiere. Underneath, in French, the inscription explained *A Slave Girl Meets Her Master*.

Shocked, Mary stared, and felt Le Comte's right hand slid up her thigh. Rooted to the spot, she watched him turn the page once more. Mary's eye went first to the title, *The Master Makes His Mark*.

She shuddered, recalling those pictures on her bedroom ceiling, and closed her eyes. His hand gripped her thigh, where it was soft and sore from the birching. Mary stiffened and opened her eyes under his prompting. The same girl, now naked except for the veil, was strapped on her back to the table, her thighs stretched as wide as they could be. Her mound was devoid of hair, with every crinkle and crevice of the pale pink lips, each point where the light caught her wetness, lovingly described. Against the inside of her flawless white thigh, a gnarled little man was tattooing an intricate design with his needle. The girl strained against the ropes tying her down, but not, Mary guessed, as a result of the tattoo. Another man, in a blacksmith's leather apron, was piercing her right nipple with a red-hot needle; a big gold or brass ring already hung from her left.

'The artist drew from life,' commented Comte Henri in a conversational tone. 'She was French. Taken by the Barbary pirates in 1796 and sold into slavery. Her master

129

commissioned her to record the life of his concubines and odalisques. Although the artist rose to be his wife, she had a happy, long life as an odalisque. He was so taken with her work that he had it reproduced for a private edition. This is one of the eight copies.'

He turned the page. Now the girl wore bracelets round her wrists and ankles, and between her plump breasts hung a light chain. Smiling, she lay on a couch attended by young girls with nothing but little shirts just covering their pubes. The girl displayed her tattooed thigh as her hair was brushed and she ate grapes. *Scenes from Harem Life: After the Hammam*.

The next scene showed her with her master once more. She knelt between his thighs, her veil removed but wearing floaty clothes that hid almost nothing. Mary sucked in her breath. She held his penis elegantly in her hand with the tip between her lips. The penis was enormous, its base fringed with black hair, the tip bright red, almost purple. Her master's eyes were on a scene in the background; a slave girl was being whipped by eunuchs while another danced. *The Slave Pleasures Her Master*.

The next plate was a close up of the girl's face as she pleasured her master's penis. The depiction of the lips distended by the immense, almost glowing cock, Mary thought, reflected the artist's enjoyment of the act, but Mary could not understand why the slave girl appeared to be getting so much pleasure herself; her eyes were half closed with contentment. The question formed in Mary's head: how can a woman get pleasure from an act that can only give a man orgasm when she gets no physical contact? As if in answer, Le Comte spoke as he revealed another plate, this time with the penis almost completely swallowed.

'Can you see how much the slave enjoys bringing pleasure to her master?' He turned another page, and this showed the moment of ejaculation, the tip of the spurting penis between her open lips. 'She receives his sacrifice, the concentrate of his masculinity, as the reward for her efforts to gratify him and as the confirmation of her status as lover and subject.'

His hand moved round to her hip and gently insisted that she half turn to face him.

'His sacrifice is the spray of seed into the infertile depths of her throat. She will be aroused, her con –' Mary was uncomprehending. 'You English use the word cunt.'

Shocked at the crude word, Mary pulled away.

He persisted. 'Her fig, or yoni if you like, her vagina if you want to be clinical, will be running with juices.'

He pulled her back to his side. 'These are ideas and words you must learn, my dear, if you want to be a good wife. You should choose a word for your sex that suits you. Cunt clearly offends your sensibilities, though it is a good, honest English word. You might consider pussy, or cunny, slit, gash, hole, breach, cranny, crease, gap, nick, nook, clam, notch, vent, wound, fanny. Crude words, I agree. More lyrical are muff, minge, coynte, quaint, quim. Snatch is an old Yorkshire word, or placket, delta, or even that American term – beaver.'

Mary's head whirled with the rush of words and disgusting, erotic images. He turned another page. The girl lay on her back, with her hairless sex spread almost life-sized between thighs raised vertically to expose her bottom. Le Comte used his gloved forefinger to point at specific places.

'What do you call that?'

Mary peered at the glowing tip of exposed clitoris. She blushed like a schoolgirl caught with her homework not yet done. 'Um, clitoris?'

'Other, more poetic names include bean, bell, button, dot, little man, praline, nubble. The Chinese use "the jewel terrace", which I find rather enchanting. And here?'

His finger stroked the inner lips. 'Labia minora?'

'Accurate, but consider "love lips", or nymphae. What about here?'

He tapped the pouting, slightly open anus. Mary swallowed. 'Anus.'

'You English lack poetry. What about rose, ring, starfish or freckle?'

He turned to her. 'And your breasts, have you personal words for them? Expose them for me, and we can find out.'

131

Mary blushed, but none the less she reached behind her neck to unbutton the dress once again and pushed the wool from her shoulders until her tight-bound breasts stood proudly at his eye level, still hatched with pink-red lines from the whipping. His hands came as she made to free her arms from the long, clinging sleeves and pushed her hands away before relocating the shoulders, so tightening the wool into another binding. Mary's arms were held stiff by the tension, helpless.

He breathed deeply through his nose and stroked the drum-tight mounds softly. 'What do you call these?'

Mary had no particular name. 'Breasts, bosom?'

'Not boobs, or Bristols – a very British name – or tits? No? Perhaps balloons – no, these are not balloons, and nor are they melons or knockers. Charms? They are indeed charming, and so very sensitive.' He rubbed her nipples gently and they thickened.

Wordlessly, Mary moved her lips.

He looked into her eyes and asked again. 'Nips, nubs, teats, haloes, grapes, olives, buttons?'

His fingers pressed the tips rhythmically, sending reflective throbs through her entire breasts. The word 'boob' came to Mary's mind; something mindless, thick and easily led, like her breasts. His mouth closed on each peak in turn, sucking and nibbling. He took something from his pocket and held them up to her misty eyes. Two silver roses, each with a hole in the centre where the hip would form. He took one and spread the petals until the aperture grew, and then pressed it against her halo so that her hard, bright, wet nipple filled the hole. Gently, by pressing the petals, the hole closed, clamping her once again. She drew in her breath sharply as the pressure grew. With a pinch, Le Comte locked the rose so that the protruding tip bulged tight. Mary's shoulders shook as he repeated the operation, making her breasts tremble.

Le Comte turned back to his book. Succeeding prints showed the girl being pierced with rings in more and more places; her ears and nose so that chains could decorate her face and hold her veil; her navel and both sets of sex lips.

After each piercing, and after new tattoos on her breasts, mound and buttocks, the slave girl took her master between her lips in gratitude. Mary saw her tickle the little slit at his tip with her tongue, saw her suck his hairy balls and even lick his anus as she used her hands on his cock.

'Is that wanking?' she asked, shocking herself with crudeness.

Le Comte nodded and turned to her. 'Your education is coming on apace. Would you like to show me what you have learnt today?'

Mary nearly started to tell him about the words and the whipping and the cords, but she stopped herself. He had said 'show'. He wanted a demonstration, and there was only one thing she could demonstrate: oral sex. She wondered what that particular act was called, and in his disconcerting way he answered her unasked question.

'Fellatio. I believe your American cousins call it a blow job. They are so brutal.'

'Do you want me to perform, er, fellatio?'

'If that is what you wish, to grant me the gift of your mouth.'

Mary breathed in deeply and stood very straight. He waited, graciously allowing her time to decide. Mary tested the pros – his wit and humour, the orgasm of last night, the sensuality he was drawing from her – and the cons – her lack of love for him, his age and threatening directness, his frightening ability to read her mind. He smiled, a welcoming 'I'm just an old man who couldn't hurt you and it's only a little thing' smile; an 'I'm your favourite uncle and I deserve a little pleasure in my old age' smile. He wasn't the dirty old man the aunts warned me about, was he? No, he is a lovely, dear friend, and I can't deny him something so seemingly insignificant.

Mary nodded her assent. He moved his chair away from the desk and turned it, his thighs parted. Mary sank to her knees and discovered that the extra pull on the bonds around her loins sank deeper, squashing her vulva and rubbing with exquisite roughness over the throbbing peak of her clitty. Her bottom came to rest on her feet, and for

133

the first time she felt a ticklish soreness on the outer surfaces of her rose. Her breasts, flattened slightly by the changing tension of her bindings, rubbed her clamped nipples against his legs. Before her, filling her vision, was the buttoned flap of his archaic trousers. Her hands reached out and unbuttoned it, fumbling in her inexperience.

The flap fell forward, revealing white silk pants, also buttoned. Behind the buttons, he bulged softly. His scent rose to her nostrils, rich, earthy and slightly dry. Mary undid the pearl buttons with greater skill but a little more trouble because his bulge grew as her fingers perforce caressed him. Inside, exposed and relaxed, his sex. Brown, as if tanned, with surprisingly long, fine, white curly hair. Mary stared at his penis, summoning up her will. It was long, like a sausage, and when she did touch, taking it between finger and thumb, it felt heavy and flexible. Her fingers stroked lightly, and it moved heavily, as if a snake breathed, thickening and lengthening. From inside the crinkled corolla at the tip a smoother, pinker surface began to emerge, with a slit at the end; his snake uncoiling. Her other hand cupped his balls, weighing their delicate potency.

Mary took a deep breath and leaned closer, opening her mouth and kissing the emergent head. The snake twitched again, and grew. How big would it grow? With her fingers, she peeled back the tightened foreskin. His scent grew stronger, musky, but clean. She opened her lips wide and encompassed that head, the plum, and licked around it, moistening a surface that looked as if it had been too long in water, delicately wrinkled. The wrinkles disappeared as her tongue worked, the plum growing and hardening. His balls felt firmer in her hand. He was getting too big. She turned her head aside and kissed the stem to its base, first one side, then the other, until it was slick. She held him tight, wanting to control how much she took inside, and licked and sucked the head.

His scent filled her nostrils; heady now, and she bobbed up and down a little way. Each movement was relayed via the bonds to her own sexual core. Her breasts, her boobs, bobbed, silver-girt nubs twanging. Shivers ran down her spine, and her mouth took more of him and her hand moved of its own accord, unconsciously mimicking the prints. His breath, like her own, came louder through the nostrils. He was big now, and very hard, like steel, only slightly yielding. Her tongue-tip flickered, and a saltiness came from the little eye. She backed away, looking at the bright red stem and deep purple head. His balls felt tighter, stronger, and his breathing grew deeper.

For the first time, he moved. His ungloved hand began to gently stroke her head, and his hips grew restless. She sucked him in again, and sucked as her tongue slurped. Her hand jerked up and down, and she sucked harder. He grunted rhythmically, and her own pleasure grew, but not in her sex. She was surprised, and pleased, to discover that this pleasure came from her heart, from, as he had said, the giving. Her hand moved faster, her head bobbed faster. His hips jerked, threatening to bump his cock against the back of her throat. She pulled back but did not disengage. She wanted him now, wanted to taste his semen. His balls clenched, his hips jerked, his cock swelled. She felt the pulsing start and sucked again, and gripped him tight.

The first spurt splashed against the roof of her mouth, thick and creamy and salty and strong. Another spurt, longer, filled her, and she tried to swallow before she choked. He gripped her head as the third, lesser spurt erupted, and some escaped, trickling from her lips. She cupped her tongue, catching as much as she could, licking his already softening plum and stem. His grip on her head relaxed completely, and she felt his entire body go slack as she slurped and swallowed the last dribblings, cleaning him and her lips. He shrank away, and she released him. Her forefinger wiped the trickle on her chin, and she licked it off.

Mary sank back, breathing heavily, thrumming with pent-up sensations and a sense of pleasure in her handiwork. Her first cock, her first – what did he call it? Fellatio. She had enjoyed it, and that was a very pleasant surprise.

Ten

Laura leant back against the cold stone pillar and stared out over arid mountains, watching a circling bird of prey. The bird, eagle or buzzard, rode a thermal for a few moments longer, its great wide wings barely moving, and then swooped from the frame created by the narrow window. She felt a twinge of sympathy for its target, a target as incapable of escape as she seemed to be. Her legs ached from standing, her feet burned on the woven straw mat covering the stone-flagged floor. She shuffled, and her chains rattled. She considered sitting down again, shook her head, and continued the shuffle. Laura had been sitting on the hard floor all night. Her bum still hurt from the cold that had seeped through the thin mat, and the stiff caning the female jailer had administered on her arrival.

Daydreaming took her mind off her suffering. She imagined Adam pursuing after her in an old biplane, silk scarf streaming. He landed in a field, mounted a waiting stallion and raced towards distant mountains, his steed leaping stone walls without breaking its stride, devouring the miles that separated them. Was he all right? Had the thugs beaten him up?

Her calves threatened to cramp, and she sat. Her bum might ache, but not as badly as her feet. She winced as each individual straw bit into the red weals across her buttocks. Time hardly moved. How long had she been here? The slit window faced north, and there were no clear shadows in sight. Laura closed her eyes, willing sleep to come, but knowing it would stay away.

The journey here had been swift and disorientating. Once out of Leila's sight, the men had buckled a heavy belt round her waist and snapped her forearms into built-in cuffs. Helpless, Laura submitted to a gag and the shapeless shroud they shuffled over her head. Adjusting a small gauze slit so that she could just make out where she was going, they set off at a pace, hauling her as she tripped on the long habit, to an underground car park. A black car appeared, they shoved her in and the car squealed away.

Jammed between two men in the back seat, her sight restricted both by the shroud and black windows, Laura had tried to use her ears to record the route, but the car seemed airtight. Traffic was muffled, and it was only when they neared an airport that she heard any discernible sounds. The car doors opened, and seconds later she was inside an executive jet, belted in, and the jet was moving. Not one word had been said since she last saw Leila, and not one word was to be said until she came to this cell, but she thought she was probably in Spain.

Laura was sure they had flown south on the three-hour flight; a clock above the cabin door gave the time, and the car windows for the last leg had not been blacked out. Through them she had seen small Roman Catholic shrines at the sides of mountain roads, goatherds and black-dressed men and women scraping a living in the barren land. The castle was undoubtedly Moorish; outwardly strong and inwardly beautiful. It had fountains and intricately carved stonework, mosaic floors and marble staircases, but gave no clue as to the identity of her captor. The three men had made her climb a long spiral stair to this lonely tower before leaving her with a tall, blonde woman. This woman had immediately locked a steel collar round her neck. Laura was going no further. The collar was chained to the pillar she had stood or sat against ever since.

Laura scratched her ear. Her hands were free to move, a little, with a short chain between the shackles. She could, when sitting, reach her legs and rub them. Now, as she finished scratching, she stroked her thighs in memory of what had happened next.

The woman had spoken, taking Laura by surprise after the hours of silence.

'My name Irina. Me mistress.' Laura nodded to show she understood. 'When I take gag, you not make screaming. No one listen.' Laura had guessed as much. 'When I take belt, no fight. Be good girl, not get this.'

She swished a crop. Laura nodded again, and Irina removed the gag as promised. Laura rubbed her wrists and moved her jaw. Irina handed her a mug of water, which was gratefully accepted.

'I take clothes.'

'What?' Laura protested.

'I take clothes.' Irina pointed to a corner. A large bowl steamed, and there were towels. Laura relaxed. 'I wash and give clean dress.'

Though rather humiliating, the experience had been relatively pleasant. Irina thoroughly washed her from head to foot with scented soap and soft flannel. Indeed, it had been quite arousing when the older woman – Laura guessed she was in her mid-thirties – lingered over her breasts, ringed nipples and between her thighs, cooing and clucking. As her fingers pushed softly into Laura's sheath, she whispered.

'You very beautiful. Prince like you. Rings good.' She tickled the clitty ring, making Laura jump and sigh. 'This ring very good. I like.'

Laura decided to test the limits of this intimacy. 'Who is the Prince?'

There was no adverse reaction – indeed Irina's thumb began to circle her clitty. Irina put a finger to her lips. 'Shsh, girl. He come soon.'

Laura sighed, and that index finger eased into her bottom, stopping that hole just as surely as she stopped Laura's questions. The circling thumb circled on. Laura looked into Irina's cool blue eyes. She gasped as a third finger entered her tight, wet sheath. For the second time that day, another woman was bringing her close. Irina smiled slyly and bent to lick Laura's breasts. Her tongue teased Laura's rings, the finger in her bottom urged her up on to tiptoe and her thighs crudely parted.

Suddenly, Irina abandoned her, open, throbbing, on the precipice. Laura moaned her disappointment as her hips writhed emptily. She moved her hands towards her gaping, soaking vulva. Irina smacked them away and picked up a towel to dry her. Irina locked her ankles into manacles chained to the pillar, then snapped a spreader bar between Laura's feet, and retreated to the other side of the cell.

'You fuck with fingers.'

As an order it was blunt, crude and challenging. Laura was being tested, but the circumstances were hardly conducive. Laura looked at her adversary under lowered lids, trying to measure her resolve. Her body pulsed with the frustration of incomplete business. It wanted that completion, but her mind was frozen. Yes, she had masturbated in public before, but then she had known the rules. Here she knew nothing and nobody, but her clitty still ached. As she hesitated, Irina showed impatience.

'You do now, or I lock hands behind back and no dress.'

To be naked in a hard, cold place, displayed for anyone who cared to see, settled matters. Laura closed her eyes, and her hands went to her hard right nipple and wet, soft cleft. Her fingers were cool from being washed, her arousal hot. The nipple grew, her sex lips parted, and she began, slowly, to rub and twist, to pinch and tug, filling already swollen tissues to the brim with excited blood. Her oils flowed, and her middle finger hooked inside, while index and ring fingers spread her lips wide. The ball of her thumb pressed and squeezed her swelling bead, the gold ring transmitting and amplifying every subtle shift directly to the dense network of nerves behind.

A noise caused Laura to look up. Across the cell, Irina reached for a wooden stool without taking her eyes off her prisoner's delving fingers. Her eyes were bright, her lips parted with excitement. Their eyes met and held. They probed each other's weaknesses. Laura felt as if an invisible bridge ran between them, a pathway transferring every nuance of pleasure and emotion. Laura released her breast and joined her hands together as she liked to, slipping two fingers already lubricated with her juices into her anus. The thumb gripped in her sheath, the second hand took her clitty, and hooked a finger inside, located the G-spot and squeezed rhythmically, but just as she was about to deliver the *coup de grâce* the warder's voice rang in her ears.

'Stop!'

Startled, Laura looked up. Irina held a cane in one hand and a set of manacles in the other. Irina's eyes carried the threat, she needed no words. Reluctantly, Laura dropped her hands. The manacles closed around her wrists, then the chain to her collar was loosened. Irina brought over the wooden stool and sat down.

'Kneel.'

Using the whippy cane, Irina indicated that she wanted Laura to kneel in front of her, facing Irina's knees. It was awkward, with the pole between her ankles, but Laura managed to comply. Irina spread her knees and pushed her skirts out of the way. She was naked underneath. Laura could see pouting, glistening outer lips hung with heavy steel rings and a smooth, hairless mound. A third big ring pierced the flesh above her clitoris. The cane tapped lightly on Laura's bottom. She crawled forward until her face touched Irina's upper thighs. The older woman's musk invaded her nostrils. Laura felt another tap of the cane between her shoulder blades. She dipped her spine, offering her buttocks up to the cane.

Laura licked her lips. She knew what was wanted, and what was going on. Irina wanted Laura's submission. She had induced Laura to bring herself to the brink of orgasm, and now she was testing how far Laura would go without more coercion. Irina shifted, spreading her thighs and pushing her sex closer to Laura's face. Her fingers stroked Laura's hair.

'So short. Master like it long, like me.' The fingers gripped and tugged, forcing Laura forward until her nose was pressed against the ringed pouch. Laura squealed. 'Lick.'

The cane scored Laura's right bum cheek. She stuck out her tongue and parted Irina's heavy inner lips. The cane

141

whistled again, harder, bucking Laura's nose against the top ring. Irina thrust back, and Laura's tongue poked inside her hot, soaking, pulsing sheath. The cane came down, softer for the next few minutes, determining the rhythm of her thrusts against Laura's tongue, then she shifted again, raising her buttocks. Laura's tongue slipped over the ridge to Irina's anus. The cane whistled harder. Laura licked, even as the pain snatched her breath away. She licked the musky, tart knot. The cane came again. Laura yelped and stabbed her tongue into the opening.

Irina then changed hands with the cane, crisscrossing Laura's cheeks with lines of fire. Tears formed in Laura's eyes as the cane snapped at already sore weals. Her tongue, rolled tight, penetrated deep, her nose was pushed into Irina's pulsing vagina. She heard Irina's grunts and gasps. The cane lost weight for a few strikes, and then Irina shifted again, dragging Laura's tongue up to her clitoris for the first time. Now the blows came harder and faster, building to a crescendo. Laura cried around her out-thrust tongue as her hair was gripped and tugged again. Irina began fucking her face, slashing with the cane, until, in a line of fire, the cane sliced down the length of Laura's crease, snapping at the tissues of her anus and open, wet, swollen sex. Irina twittered as she soaked Laura's chin and crushed her face into her gaping, heaving slit.

She threw Laura down, leaving her rubbing her bottom and writhing in a sea of frustrated arousal and pain. After a few moments she removed the bar, shackled Laura's wrists and left her to relieve herself as best she could.

The sound of a key in the door brought Laura out of her reverie. Guiltily, she snatched her fingers from her vulva. A woman in black shuffled in, pointedly ignoring the prisoner, unloaded a tray, and left. Laura had tried to speak to her before, but to no effect. She glanced at a bowl of steaming stew, a hunk of fresh bread and a flagon of wine. All the utensils were made of wood, to stop Laura from trying to use them to effect an escape. In a while the woman would return with a lidded bowl which she would leave close at hand, and take the tray away. If Laura had not used the bowl before she returned once more, it, too, would be removed until the next mealtime.

Irina, whom Laura had not seen since the caning, had left Laura dressed in a very simple knee-length dress made from coarse grey cotton. It was fastened at the front by two large buttons, one between her breasts, the other at navel height. From time to time her three kidnappers would come, make her pose and undo one or both buttons. Then, with great solemnity, they would step back and watch. Nothing else, just watch. They did not speak. They might smoke cigarettes and change her pose, so that her hands were behind her neck and her legs wide apart, or kneeling with her back to them, knees parted to expose her body. Once they made her cup her breasts, as if offering them to a lover, before she had to hold her thighs wide, ready for penetration.

The cell door opened and the maid returned for the tray. The men followed her. Once the maid had left, they rolled her dress up above her waist and made her squat over the bowl. Then they waited. Laura's stomach churned with butterflies. They had sat for hours yesterday, and they would sit for hours again today until she used the bowl. She could refuse to pee and let the maid take it away empty, but dismissed the idea. She was dying for a pee, and if she didn't use the bowl now she would end up in a pool of her own mess. She pleaded, but their faces were set in stone. She swore at them, and one smiled. The other lit a cigarette. Laura sighed her resignation. Her legs threatened to go into cramp. She closed her eyes and tried to blot her audience out. Finally, legs shaking with exertion, she heard a trickle. She forced herself to relax, and the trickle became a flow. As she finished, the three men gave her a round of applause and left.

On the third morning, just after breakfast, Irina returned, accompanied by two of the black-dressed women. In marked contrast to their first meeting, Irina looked stunning, blonde hair glossy with brushing, eyes and lips

143

painted, and dressed in a flowing scarlet dress that swept the floor. In her hand she held a riding crop, and around her waist was a gold cord, tied so the loose end hung between her legs.

'The Prince come. Stand.'

Laura hauled herself to her feet and let Irina remove her dress; it might have been morning, but she had slept badly on the hard, cool floor. The black-dressed women washed her face, hands and sex. They took her dress away.

Irina paced backward and forward. 'Call him master or Prince. Not look at eyes. Not speak unless he ask you. OK?'

'Yes, mistress.'

Laura heard her words from a distance as she tried to prepare herself for the forthcoming interview. She had racked her memory for clues to this prince's identity, and only one person she had heard of fitted the bill: Leila's estranged husband, Farouk. Laura knew little about him, save that Leila had some kind of hold over him which prevented divorce and that they still communicated. Laura guessed it was Leila's money. She had come to the marriage with a huge fortune. He had been politically well placed but relatively poor. Now he had to keep Leila in the manner to which she was accustomed. Something like that, anyway.

A tall, dark man in a white, collarless silk shirt and white cotton trousers strolled in. He appeared to be in his forties and had kept himself fit. Laura glimpsed piercing brown eyes and quite long black hair highlighted with grey before she obeyed the order to look down. His moccasined feet stood before her.

'Irina, why is she chained like an animal? I sent no such instructions to you.' He sounded angry but controlled.

Irina fumbled for English words. 'Mr Ali, he order me.'

The Prince harumphed. 'I will deal with both of you later. Free her.'

Laura looked up, smiling her thanks. He smiled back and nodded an unspoken welcome. Laura wondered if she was the object of a charade, a suspicion almost confirmed by a glance at Irina, who showed not one jot of remorse or worry as she quickly unlocked Laura's chains.

Laura rubbed her wrists and neck, and then fell still as she became aware of the Prince's unwavering gaze.

'Has she been a good girl?'

'Yes, master.' Irina stood behind him, a crooked, supercilious smile on her haughty face.

'That is reassuring.' He stepped closer, took Laura's chin between lean, beautifully manicured fingers and tipped her head up. His brown eyes smiled back. He released her chin and cupped her right breast.

'I am Prince Farouk. I think you know my wife, the Princess Leila?'

Laura nodded. 'Yes, master.'

He gently squeezed a ringed nipple. 'And you know why you are here?'

'I think so, master.'

His hand travelled lower, flat over her tummy. She felt the cold metal of his fat gold signet ring as his fingertips met the stubble now covering her mound. His middle finger rubbed lightly against her clitoris and parted her lips. Held by his eyes, she looked inside his head. Power, confidence and wealth poured forth, but underneath she read an ambiguity. He seemed a little hesitant, as if he had a genuine interest in her body and personality. Her hips began to move to his fingers.

'You are here as my guest, until any fuss dies down – perhaps a month or two. I hope you will be home in time to resume your studies, if you still want to.'

His voice oozed like cinnamon honey, hinting at pleasures beyond her imagination and tripping a switch inside her head. Until now, she had made up her mind to suffer his attentions and this prison, but his fingers, clever and devious, undermined her determination. His voice, his handsome, dangerous face and apparently honest eyes appealed to her heart. He was making her want to share his bed. For a moment Adam was almost forgotten.

'Let us hope that your time with us will be short and pleasurable.' He grinned broadly and then began to speak

145

to Irina in a businesslike tone. 'Have her hair trimmed, make it spiky. Colour blue, like her eyes. The rings to be standardised – replace her sex rings with sapphire studs to match the lips. Make her ready –' he pinched Laura's cheek '– and I may choose number eight tonight.'

His eyes sparkled with the promise and danger of an adventure. Laura felt as if the floor had been taken from under her feet and she were falling into a pit of pleasure.

Dressed in a loose, long dress, Laura followed Irina down staircases and along corridors from her tower to Prince Farouk's harem. On the way, while walking through a colonnade around the central courtyard, she had her first glimpse of the layout of the castle. Five pointed towers marked the corners of the irregular ground plan. The castle nestled against a mountaintop, and its walls surmounted the ready-made foundations of several spurs. Inside the walls, but rather to the back to make room for the courtyard, a four-storey central square tower, containing the main accommodation, rose above the outer walls. Laura had been imprisoned in a tower beside the main gate. Before they turned into another tower, Laura noticed a side spur of the mountain running down towards a section where the outer wall was just a few feet from the main tower. One of the many decorative balconies adorning the inner tower projected over this narrow spot. She filed this all away in her memory.

Irina led her through an iron gate and down into a cool, narrow open passage between the outer wall and the inner tower. It ended at a heavy locked door which Irina unlocked. Laura found herself in a private courtyard overlooked only by windows on the ground floor. Above, every arrow slit had been skilfully blocked up. In the centre of the courtyard a pool gathered the outpourings of a pretty fountain below which lilies twinkled and splashed colour. Shaded by almond and peach trees, stone benches awaited sunbathers, and formal herb beds added a drift of sweet aromas to the warm, comfortable garden. The door slammed solidly and permanently behind her.

'This harem. No way out, unless Prince let you.'

Though the news was hardly unexpected, Laura felt a chill in her heart.

'You are number eight girl. Remember number. I number one. Prince tell me you trained.' Irina took her arm, gently, hooking round her elbow and holding her hand. 'We friends, yes?'

Laura, still trying to absorb the message, just mumbled. 'Yes, Mistress Irina.'

'Good little girl.'

They entered an empty hall. Laura looked up to a dome. The complex geometrical delicacy of the Moorish architecture was beautiful. From hidden rooms came the chatter of women and soft spicy perfumes, but she did not see anyone as they turned aside through an arch and into a low-ceilinged baths.

'This is hammam.' They skirted the steaming pool and into a bare changing-room. 'You undress. Into shower then pool. Quick!'

Under Mistress Irina's cool gaze, Laura undressed. An older black-dressed woman appeared and took Laura's dress away.

Laura ran across the room, following Irina's finger, awkwardly aware of her bouncing breasts, and into the showers to wash away the soiled sweatiness of the last few days. Though they had washed her every day, Laura had never felt clean until now. After that, the water in the pool was fragrant and thick with oils and salts. Slowly, the warmth and vapours infused her body, reviving and enlivening her limbs and soothing away the soreness of her bondage. Relaxed, invigorated and with restored self-confidence, Laura obeyed the call to leave the waters and, wrapped in a towel, go into a salon to be beautified by yet another black-dressed woman.

Under Irina's watchful eyes, the silent woman indicated that Laura should sit on a luxurious version of a dentist's chair. Laura let the routine impose itself on her; she was being prepared, again, to suit a new master's tastes. A second woman joined them and began to cut her hair. The

147

first woman urged Laura's legs apart and lathered foam over her pubic area. Laura lay back and enjoyed the rare pleasure of not having to shave her own pubes. Chill steel slid over her skin, along her lips and around her anal crack, removing the light stubble.

Irina leant over. 'Cream, make growth slow.'

The cream was cold against her skin, but heat suddenly infused the zone immediately underneath. Laura winced and wriggled until it was rinsed away. A warm oil was rubbed in, and Laura's vulva awoke as fingers stroked. She breathed deeply, and the woman slid her lubricated finger inside both vagina and anus. Laura wriggled and sighed. Irina pinched her right nipple hard. Laura squealed.

'No pleasure. Only master or I give pleasure.'

So that was the way the wind blew. Laura filed the comment away and accepted, with as good a grace as possible, the cessation of activities.

The hairdresser was still clipping away as the first woman began to massage her legs. Laura was assailed by overwhelming tiredness in the quiet room. Her eyes closed, her mind drifted, and, although she registered the masseuse moving up her body, she let herself doze, even through another tactile assault on her vulva which fuelled images of sensual splendour. Her doze was cruelly disturbed by cold metal. Her eyes snapped open as she felt a steel band close round her wrists. Irina stood beside her, looking down. Laura looked down. More clasps snapped over her ankles and neck, anchoring her to the chair. A belt around her waist completed her immobilisation. Then the chair began to move, opening her legs wider and flattening into a table.

Irina beckoned, and one woman drew a trolley alongside. 'New rings. You not move.'

With an aerosol spray, Irina numbed her ear lobes and removed Laura's gold sleepers. She heard a loud click and felt the punch as the holes were enlarged, and then the weight of the heavier steel rings that replaced them.

The Russian now began to pinch and tug Laura's nipples with latex-gloved hands. Laura shrank back. Ice cubes were produced, chilling and stiffening the dark pink peaks. Irina sprang open the fine gold rings and pulled them out. The spray numbed her, and she closed her eyes as the punch was lined up, close to the base of her left nipple. Distantly, she felt the punch, a little pulling, and when she looked again her breast was crowned with a thick steel ring closed so cunningly she could not see the join. A tear, misunderstood by Irina, trickled.

'There, there, very quick.'

The discomfort did not matter. Laura had been proud of her fine gold rings. They were the manifestation of the discovery of her sexuality, and a link to her first and most enduring love, Penny.

She felt a needle just above her navel, and, while the local took effect, the spray again on her vulva. Laura tried to look down, but the collar held her. Two punches in her outer labia, and tugs as rings were installed. Her navel was pulled, and she felt a weight, and then her clitoris jumped and began throbbing deep inside. Irina fiddled around for a few minutes while the black-dressed women painted her nails and face. Irina moved, and she felt the sting of alcohol as her nipples and vulva were swabbed. Laura opened her eyes to see her nipples being painted a pale, bright blue, like her fingernails. Soon she was helped off the chair-cum-table and shown her reflection. Laura gasped.

A spiky, blue- and blonde-haired punk stared back, with bright blue lips and painted eyes. From her ears hung strong steel rings, matched at the blue peaks of her breasts. Another ring pierced her navel, and above the peak of her sex a yet bigger ring framed a clitoris now pierced by a short sapphire-tipped bar. Matching studs showed in her blue inner lips behind the new thick rings through the outer lips, which were joined by two more rings to form a short chain from which hung a disc, decorated by a crossed whip symbol and the number eight. The disc bumped heavily against her sex. As she stared at the transformation, manacles, without chains, were locked around her ankles and wrists. These were also stainless steel, round and smooth, anchoring four rings each. Around her neck went a similar, but wider, collar.

Irina smiled gently and stroked her arm. 'No chains, not now. Later, if Prince want.'

That familiar sense of capitulation swept through her. Such concrete signifiers of submission had irrecoverably altered Laura's life once before. Avenues of pleasure and knowledge had opened up then, but now, two years on, she wondered if she wanted to be owned again in this most direct way. The Prince had given her no choice, apparently, but in a way she did have one. She could let the comfortable habit of submission take over her mind and body, or she could resist. Resistance seemed, right now, to be useless; they had all the means to coerce her. Acquiesce, she persuaded herself, and probe for their weaknesses. Although the countryside looked hostile and the castle strong, Laura felt sure she would get away, given time and opportunity.

They dressed her in wedged sandals and a long, almost transparent blue skirt anchored by a heavy gold belt low on her hips. Under her breasts, supporting and lifting but not covering the small orbs, came a gold halter-neck bra lined with silk. There was nothing else.

'Come. Meet friends.'

Irina led her back to the hall and into a hubbub of female voices, walking swiftly. Laura's skirt flowed and parted, split from the belt down, revealing the length of her legs right up to the dangling chain. They entered a large room with lots of low tables, cushions and low couches. The chatter stopped abruptly. Laura looked round. There were six women dressed much like herself and perhaps a dozen of the older black-dressed women. Irina clapped her hands, giving an instruction obviously understood. The black-dressed women moved towards the walls while the six others came forward and stood in a line. Each was different in height and body shape, and they were colour-coded; their fingernails, lips and nipples, like Laura's, a specific colour. Some had hair shades to match.

Irina made the introductions. 'This is Laura.' She pronounced it 'Lara'. 'She is come to stay. The Prince expect you make her welcome.' The girls smiled back nervously, surprised by her unexpected appearance.

'Dava.' Irina indicated the woman at the left-hand end of the line, a tall Scandinavian girl with very long ash-blonde hair, shocking black lips, huge black nipples and endless dancers' legs. She bowed, looking like a magazine model, with her high breasts and flat stomach.

'Fatima.' The next in line, a short, plump Levantine with heavy, soft breasts and hips that craved to belly-dance. Her colour was purple.

'Polly.' Tall, lithe, *café au lait*, arching eyebrows, smiling eyes and a mass of soft curly black hair. The nipples of her high, melon-round breasts were picked out in coral pink. She nodded and smiled.

'Marissa.' Italian-looking, medium height and generous build, hair very dark brown overlaid with green, dark eyes staring hard. She looked jealous, as if Laura had come to steal something precious. Laura let her eyes linger with defiance. Marissa, she thought, need not worry. She's beautiful, with lovely curves and juicy, firm, pear-shaped breasts.

'Saba, sister of Fatima.' Slimmer and shorter than her sister, with mauve lips and, like her sister, long, lustrous black hair.

'And Chai.' Chai, probably from South-east Asia, smiled as if she were blushing. She looked very young, with narrow hips, rounded, high breasts peaked with magenta and long, long straight black hair.

Irina beckoned to Polly. 'Polly American. Speak English better. She tell you.'

The tall, dark girl stretched out a long, slim, elegant hand. 'Hi, girl-friend.'

Polly's accent sang with all the romance and mystery of New Orleans, and her teeth gleamed with fun. Laura liked her immediately.

'New girl on the block, and so sweet! Girl-friend, we are going to have some fun!'

Eleven

Mary turned the handle of the door. Well oiled and well used, the door made not a sound as it opened. For some reason she could not explain, she was surprised to find the corridor and spiral staircase unchanged from her last visit, on that memorable first night. She entered, eager to reach the gallery from where she hoped to find Philippe. No candle was required as the sun, filtered through windows high above, washed the walls in gold.

She was missing Philippe more every day, missing a friend and her native tongue. That her French was improving by constant use meant little when her innermost thoughts were conducted in English, and she needed a listener to those thoughts. She turned the corner into the gallery and saw her surroundings in detail. Here the roof came down low, and there were no windows behind as she looked down on the seemingly empty room below. Mary felt a little disappointed, but she was prepared to wait.

At first Mary supposed drawn curtains cast the ruby glow suffusing the entire room, Philippe having just risen late from his slumbers, but the bed was made and everything was neat and tidy after Yvette's morning visit. Maybe the sun's light came through stained-glass windows. She could not see the outside wall from here, but she could see the room's décor. Even more than her own suite, this room was decked with erotic imagery: statues of naked women entwined and in congress, friezes of explicit sex acts and fetishes, pictures and prints, carvings and wall-hangings depicting every conceivable byway of human sexuality, and some more Mary could not interpret at all. No wonder Philippe seemed so changed, living in this blood-red chamber, his senses assailed by the deeply sexual decorations, all washed in the colour of heat and lust.

Mary's speculations ceased abruptly as she heard a movement. Yvette, stiffly dressed in a freshly starched uniform, rustled into the framed view. Mary drew back into deeper shadows, watching the maid calmly undress to corset and stockings. As if following precise instructions given in advance, Yvette knelt on the bed, head down, haunches raised and knees apart. From her vantage point, Mary looked down on the maid's broad bottom. It was vertically bisected by a deep cleft, pierced by a dark circle, leading down to her prominent darker red slit. Mary's eyes, becoming more used to the light, noticed that Yvette's slit glistened in anticipation. Mary imagined her tongue lapping up and around the softly lined, deep cleft and dusky rose, her tongue probing the moist, humid orifices of the enigmatic maid.

She shook her head, ashamed and angry. Shocking, depraved ideas like that were entering her mind more and more often these days. Le Comte and the chatelaine were to blame. They wound her body up every waking moment, with their books and clothes and little sensuous punishments and games. Always, her nipples throbbed, her sex poured and pounded, and her boobs seemed to be permanently sensitive to every breath of air or touch of material. Most of all, her little jewel, the seat of deepest arousal, felt as big as a broad bean and was pushing out from its protective folds.

Mary heard a door open and close. Philippe, hair tousled, wearing a padded silk gown, came into view. For a few moments he stood between Mary and Yvette, contemplating the view presented so delightfully and patiently. He said something, his voice indistinct at this distance, and Yvette turned right round to face him, still kneeling, still bowed. She looked up, her eyes betraying nervousness. Mary believed that she had been given no precise reason for assuming her flagrant pose. For a

154

moment the maid waited, and then Philippe removed his
robe. Underneath he was naked. Mary noticed how much
fitter he looked since she first saw him with Laura. His
muscles were more clearly defined, his buttocks tighter
despite the flattening effect of the red light. Yvette bowed
her head and moved closer. Little sucking wet sounds rose
from the bed. Mary knew what was happening. The maid
was sucking Philippe's cock. Mary felt jealous again. That
was her cock, promised now; the cock that filled her
naughty dreams.

Mary's body began to stir under the restraints of her
outfit. She felt her breasts swell against the coarse wool
dress and satin linen cups of her corset; her sex thickened
under the belt and began to dampen the leather straps.
Philippe's buttocks clenched as the maid used her mouth,
head bobbing. He pushed her away and told her to return
to her original position. Yvette obeyed, spreading her
knees and flattening her breasts on the brocade bedcover.
Philippe stood behind her and pulled her hips towards him.
For a moment or two he tried to get Yvette into the exact
position desired, then he made her move further up the bed
and knelt between her thighs.

Mary moved to the end of the gallery to get a better
view. From there, her face pressed up to the screen, she
could just see what he was attempting to do. His hand
grasped his cock, the wet purple end pointing between the
maid's buttocks. Mary bit her knuckle, suppressing her
gasp of surprise. His cock was not pressed against Yvette's
gaping vagina but her bottom-hole. The maid gasped. He
pressed harder, and the bulbous end began to force its way
inside. Revulsion knotted Mary's stomach as the rose
opened, stretching to encompass his thickness. It was
unnatural, another mechanism seemingly designed to
prostrate women under men's power, another device for
the satisfaction of male lust. The cock forced its way
deeper, until the helmet disappeared. Yvette's muscle
closed round the thinner stem. He pushed on, wringing a
small cry from the maid. His hand went round, under
Yvette's hips. She bucked. He had gathered some of

155

Yvette's own juices and smeared then over his stem. He pushed again, and she crooned as he went deeper.

Mary discovered that her fingers were going white with tension as she gripped the balustrade. She was fascinated, almost enjoying the awful, enthralling spectacle. Yvette's hands closed into fists, but she pushed her hips back into Philippe, forcing him deeper until his pubic hair flattened against her buttocks. He groaned, his lips drawn back. Mary slipped her fingers into her dress and rubbed a nipple. Philippe began to move slowly back and forward, each inward drive wringing a groan, each outward pull a sigh from his increasingly willing maid. The clouds of confusion and jealousy began to clear from Mary's mind as she observed Yvette's evident and increasing pleasure in this abominable act. Mary suffered a sudden spasm in her own anus, as if being invaded herself. Her hips moved in time to Yvette's, and she began to imagine the sensations the maid must be feeling.

Each push of Philippe's hips was now being answered by a backward push from Yvette. Philippe leant back. Mary could just make out the effect his thrusting phallus was having; Yvette's rose was pushed in with his column, and when he pulled out again, the inner tissue came with him. Yvette's head came up, her eyes closed, teeth biting her lower lip. She hissed and screwed up her eyes, and gasped out the intensity of her feelings. Philippe reached forward, grabbed her tossing black mane, and dragged her head back further. He leant forward on an in-stroke, her head turned, and their mouths met. Philippe's other hand dived back under her writhing belly, his fingers obviously caressing her sex. Mary sighed, longing to touch herself there, too, instead of twiddling her nipples between finger and thumb.

Below, Philippe's thrusts became ever more urgent and rapid. From Yvette's mouth, open since the savage kiss, came grunts and howls. Her body undulated, now raised by her arms to allow more movement, breasts swinging, nipples just rubbing the bedspread. Mary gripped her own nipples hard, trying to reach her crisis through indirect means. Philippe ground against the maid's buttocks, jerking as he emptied deep inside. Yvette cried out. They went rigid for a moment and then slowly collapsed, Philippe flattening his lover.

Frustrated and confused, Mary reluctantly released her breasts. They slid back into place behind the bodice of her dress, disordered and red. She sat back, her bottom settling on the cool stone. Her rosehole twitched and itched, sensitised by the awareness of another avenue of possibilities. After a while, with Philippe showing no signs of waking, and Yvette none of departing, Mary stood up and retraced her steps slowly. As she opened the door into the corridor outside her room, she bumped into Beatrice.

'Where have you been – as if I can't guess?'

Mary mumbled her apologies. 'Sorry, madame. I was just looking round – ow!' Beatrice took her by the elbow so violently it hurt.

'Sorry? You'll be sorry, miss, poking your nose into private places.' She opened Mary's door and pushed her inside. 'Undress and present yourself for punishment.'

Mary obeyed, but tears began forming and trickling. With babyish pouting bottom lip, she shoved and tugged at her dress, uncaring if buttons pulled or threads broke. Loneliness and frustration saw the dress in a heap and her sandals being kicked across the floor. One came to rest against Beatrice's ankle. Mary froze, frightened about the consequences. Instead, Beatrice came to her and put her arm round her shoulder.

'Mary, what is the matter?'

She flopped against the older woman, and the tears poured. Between sobs and sniffs, she attempted to explain. 'I saw Philippe with Yvette. I want to talk to him. You, and Le Comte . . . I, I'm not . . . I'm all confused. My body wants . . . I need . . . Please . . .' Mary came to a halt, tongue-tied, mind scrambled with emotion, and her French failing altogether.

'Oh, my poor, poor dear. Come, lie down.'

Beatrice led her to the bed and drew her down, cradling Mary's head against her bosom. Slowly, Mary's sobs

157

subsided until her breathing matched the slow, soft strokes of her mistress's hand over her hair. Beatrice produced a handkerchief and wiped the teardrops away. Her face was filled with concern, and her body felt soft and yielding.

'Oh, my little one. We have not tried to hurt you. We love you, Le Comte and I, and we want the best for you. It is we who should be sorry.'

Mary looked up, needing to be convinced, and for the first time those subtly oriental features displayed love. She kissed Mary on the cheeks and forehead. Mary smiled, and Beatrice kissed her on the lips. Her lips were soft and warm. Mary found herself responding. Her mouth opened and they moved closer together, breast to breast, the friction reawakening Mary's nipples. Her mouth was invaded by Beatrice's tongue – long, hot and wet. Her hands moved round, clasping the older woman's corseted waist. They rolled over, until Mary lay underneath. Beatrice pulled away. Mary looked into smouldering almond eyes, and she noticed how free the chatelaine's face was of even the few wrinkles one would expect in someone of her age.

The older woman's face descended, kissing her mouth, her neck and chest, all the way down into Mary's cleavage, across the upper swells of her breasts. With her tongue, she released Mary's nipples from the cups, and with her teeth she gently chewed. Her hands stroked Mary's thighs and buttocks, across the impenetrable belt, up to the band of flesh below her corset. Mary wriggled, suddenly ticklish. Beatrice nibbled her ears, her shoulders and the nape of her neck. She rolled Mary back on top and whispered in her ear. 'Don't tell Le Comte of what I do now. Our secret, for ever.'

Mary nodded her assent and felt her belt loosen as the lock was removed. It came stickily away, and she was rolled on to her back again. Beatrice bent down, examining Mary's naked sex.

'Oh, how red and wet you are. You enjoyed watching Philippe and Yvette?' She rolled Mary on to her side and reached round. Her fingers slid over Mary's bottom. Her rosehole clenched as it was touched. 'You wonder what it's like?'

Blushing furiously, Mary said nothing.

'I can do something to help.'

She left Mary and went across to the small chest of drawers from which all manner of instruments and devices for Mary's titillation were to be produced. Unlocking the top drawer, Beatrice took out a short, stubby phallus with a flared base, and a pot of lubricant. Mary watched, wondering what would happen next. Beatrice paused at the side of the bed.

'Undress me, and I'll make you feel better.'

Mary hovered uncertainly, knocked out of her stride by this sudden outbreak of affection. Beatrice questioned her hesitation with her eyebrows, encouraged her with a smile and offered Mary her hand. Mary moved to her. They kissed again, and Mary began to unbutton her mistress's high-neck blouse. Beatrice held up her cuffs. The buttons were small, pearly and fiddly, as were those on the blouse's front, and there were lots, so that long before she reached the skirt Mary's fingers tired. After releasing the wide leather belt, she found the buttons at the waistband, undid those and tugged the blouse gently free. It fell softly to the floor. Instinctively tidy, Mary picked it up and laid it carefully over the back of a chair. Only then did she look at the older woman.

To Mary's surprise, Beatrice was dressed, like herself, in a corset with no more than platform cups for her breasts. The breasts thus presented were soft, larger than her own, and hardly touched by the effects of age. Facing Mary, in the centre of wide, dusky pink haloes, protruded two fat, long, barely aroused nubs bearing thick gold rings at their bases. Beatrice cupped and raised them, offering them to Mary's lips. Mary bent and took them alternately, at first kissing just the tips. She grew bolder as the nubs stiffened, filling out and lengthening. She took the rings into her mouth. They were big, much bigger in every way than Laura's fine rings, heavy and cool on her tongue. Beatrice sucked in her breath, her breasts wobbling slightly, as

159

Mary moved the rings. Mary moved back and knelt. Her fingers unbuttoned the long skirt. Underneath, Beatrice wore no knickers, just black stockings clipped to the bottom of her corset. Mary folded the skirt and reached to the chair. As she turned back, Beatrice imperiously raised her right foot. Mary bowed to unbuckle the stout shoe. Beatrice did not lower her foot.

'Kiss me.'

Her foot was warm, smelling strongly of leather, an intimate, personal, enticing smell. Mary kissed her toes through the silk stocking, taking them one by one into her mouth, and placed kisses on instep and ankle. She carried on, stroking the calf, kissing behind the knee, all the way to the naked flesh above the garter. The leg was lowered then, and the performance was repeated up the left leg. This time, as she reached the bare upper thigh, and when Beatrice lowered her knee, she held Mary's head to her, urging it upward. Mary kiss-licked the soft, delicate skin. Beatrice opened her legs and drew her upward. Mary's nose touched cool metal.

She was allowed to sit back and investigate. Of course, Beatrice was shaved, her mound smooth until cleft by a dark succulent cowl arching over a thick, peeking clitoris. Mary remembered Le Comte's phrase, the jewel terrace. This one was like a wedding ring, a ruby mounted on gold. The clitoris was pierced by a gold bar at least an inch long almost half an inch from the tip. The bar held the fleshy tip out, pressing back a hood that seemed detached from the shaft. Below, the inner lips blossomed, heavy and thick, between pouting, firm outer lips. Just above the entrance to her body, they were pierced by a pair of thick gold rings, and joined by a disc.

Beatrice pulled Mary to her feet and kissed her lips before sitting on a chair without arms. 'Lie across my knee, and I'll start putting things right.'

Nervously, Mary obeyed, balancing herself on her hands and toes. Her breasts softly fell out of their inadequate platform; her hair covered her shame. Her bottom, pale and naked, quivered high above her head. Beatrice urged her thighs a little wider, and then Mary felt something cold and wet between her cheeks. A gel-coated finger left a glob of cold in the centre of her freckle. Mary liked that word, freckle; it seemed respectable, affectionate. The hard, smooth tip of the stubby phallus pressed against her tight freckle. Instinctively, she tightened. Taking her time, Beatrice caressed the flesh around the knot, massaging, relaxing her protégée. Mary, knowing that the invasion was inevitable and wanting to feel something of what Yvette had experienced, tried to relax. The thick stem was reluctantly accepted, opening, filling the tight passage. As it invaded, Mary felt the stretching. The bulbous cap slipped inside, and Mary felt the odd sensation of hardness inside the ring of muscle. She squirmed; the bung went deeper until the base met her exterior flesh. Her mouth opened, a silent 'O'.

'You like that, don't you?'

Mary had to admit that she did, though its very presence made the emptiness of her vagina suddenly important. Beatrice gently moved the phallus in and out, and Mary's hips moved against it. She ruminated on the new words for her body, dissatisfied with the clinical terms she still used in her head. She felt the muscles in her front passage clench. Snatch, he said that was from Yorkshire. Home, a homely word, she tried it out. Her snatch ran with honey. She liked it. Snatch, freckle, boobs, jewel, nubs, leaves. She wanted them all touched, kissed and caressed.

Beatrice's hand smacked down, shattering her reverie. She tried to turn her head, to question the abrupt punishment. Beatrice held her down with a light touch. 'Just to remind you. I caught you spying.'

The hand smacked down seven more times. She felt heat spreading under the sting. With each smack, the phallus moved, touching her inside and out. Her hips bounced up and down, sending rhythmic shocks through her mound. The honey ran more freely, her jewel swelled. Mary gasped and cried, and then, just as suddenly as it started, the onslaught ceased. She felt hands stroking her pink soreness. Lips kissed, and then they were crossing the room to the bed, and falling, and rolling, kissing and clutching, heavy breasts bumping between them.

Mary found herself underneath, her mouth full of ringed breast, sucking and nibbling as hands gripped her own breasts, revelling in their weight and mass. Beatrice moved further down, presenting her sex to Mary's face. As the older woman's mouth descended on her own snatch, Mary was able to examine the rings at the base of those heavy inner lips. They were engraved with some kind of lettering or design, and the disc bore that heraldic device Mary had seen so often around the château: crossed whips under a burning heart. Comte Henri's mark of ownership. The disc descended. Mary opened her mouth and sucked in the heavy, hot, dripping lips.

'Your fingers,' Beatrice gasped, 'use your fingers.'

Mary freed her hands and assaulted the hungry, drenching sex vigorously, transferring her own desperate need to her partner. First one, then two and three fingers plunged into the soaking, gripping sheath. She watched her fingers pumping, becoming slick, the squashing lips and the pull of the rings in their holes as Beatrice's body moved. Mary added her other hand to the churning melting pot, soaking thumb and forefinger, and then applied them to the dark, sex-soft ring just inches further away. Beatrice wormed and gasped as Mary slid her thumb into the tight ring. In glorious Technicolor close-up, Mary watched the older woman's body react to her manipulations.

Beatrice nipped Mary's jewel softly between her teeth and began turning the phallus slowly in her bottom. Her jewel was sucked deeply, and felt as if it was being sucked out of her body. Fingers pressed the surrounding pad of flesh back, extruding her jewel still further. Mary giggled and flexed, trying to follow her jewel, to reduce the pressure. She felt again that emptiness in her snatch. She needed just a slim finger inside, pressing against the back of her jewel, to make her feel complete. She opened her thighs more widely than she thought possible, contorting her limbs. Beatrice allowed her fingers to rim the opening. Mary reached out her tongue and flickered across the outer edges of Beatrice's inner lips. Beatrice bore down, and Mary's tongue became a stabbing tool, batting the folds before rolling over the impaled boss of her clitoris. She sucked at the strange fruit and felt it grow. The gold bar moved out, freeing the folds behind it.

They bucked together, mouths clamped as fingers plunged or played. Mary ground her hips upward, felt Beatrice's nose enter her body, and as the older woman exhaled, rhythmically filling her sheath with air, she felt her body climb towards an unstoppable explosion. Beatrice flicked her tongue over the very tip of her jewel. The phallus seemed to grow, the fingers at her entrance withdrew and spread her labia wide. The tongue flicked up and down the length of her slit. Mary lost hold of Beatrice as she came, her head arching back against the bed, hips raised up, taking the older woman's entire weight.

When Mary resurfaced, Beatrice had turned round, and her mouth and fingers were playing with her heaving, tender, flushed breasts. The older woman trapped Mary's right thigh between her own and began rubbing herself, the wet, sticky streak growing. Mary understood what she was desired, and rolled her over. She now knelt between Beatrice's thighs like a man. Feeling her power, she began to ride the older woman with her thigh, grinding down. From her superior position, she kissed Beatrice's mouth, tongue stabbing, and then bowed to grip and suck a nipple deep. Beatrice moaned and bucked. Mary drove faster, felt sweat dripping from her face and chest, loving the bouncing of her breasts. Beatrice groaned softly, suddenly limp. Mary slowed and let herself relax into her mistress's arms.

'The master was right. You have made love to a woman before,' Beatrice said a few minutes later.

They had moved on to their backs, recovering. Beatrice leant on her elbow and covered Mary's breasts with light kisses. Mary closed her eyes.

'And yet you are a virgin. Your lover was careful too, no?' Mary nodded, resigned to losing her secret.

'An experienced woman, no? And you were not shocked by my rings.' The kisses stopped as she moved up, her face now above Mary's. 'I know our master has been showing you these things, but touching them is different. Your lover has rings?'

Mary nodded. 'Much smaller than yours.'

'The master made them for me. He is a skilled goldsmith.' Beatrice lay back. 'He engraved them with my name in my mother's tongue – Vietnamese. He found me there, a bastard child of a French soldier, and rescued me from the whorehouse. I've been with him ever since.'

Mary tried to imagine why her companion sounded so infinitely sad. Had she failed to meet Le Comte's standards? Why weren't they married if she had been with him so long?

Beatrice lay silent for a while and then leant on her elbow again. 'You remind me of a girl who came here once. She was English, too, and pale-skinned like you, but with brown hair. A truly exceptional woman, she gave Le Comte his first legitimate son. She was Philippe's mother.'

'How did she die?'

Beatrice replied in a sad voice. 'Of love. An excess of love.' She kissed Mary's cheek. 'Never love a man too much, Mary.'

She lay back again. 'She asked the master to give her rings. She asked for steel, but he refused, her flesh was too delicate and fine. She cried, so he tattooed his name across her belly, and his coat of arms on her breast. Indelible marks she carried to her grave.'

Mary wondered if any man would do the same for her, mark her as his possession, as a promise of eternal love.

Beatrice suddenly stood up. 'Mary, you will not feel well later. The master must not know of this afternoon. He will see it in your eyes, and read your mind. Tomorrow, well, he has plans for you tomorrow and will miss the clues. Sleep well and eat all I send you. You will need it.'

Twelve

Polly lay back along a couch, ushering Laura to lie at the other end, their feet intertwined. They had spent the remainder of the morning and all afternoon together while Polly showed her round the harem and introduced her to the girls. The harem consisted of a dormitory with eight wide single beds fixed to the floor by iron plates, each with an iron ring above the bedhead; training rooms where the girls worked out, perfected dances and other routines for the amusement of the Prince; and the dungeon, as Polly called it, where punishments were carried out for infractions of the rules. The dungeon walls were festooned with chains and racks of whips, paddles, canes and birches. Set in the floor were a pair of upright frames and three padded trestles, for restraining the girls during discipline.

The rules, Polly had explained, were essentially simple: obey Irina instantly and without question, love their master and love doing whatever he wants, and don't play with yourself, ever. Simple, but apparently both Irina and the Prince made difficult, capricious demands. On the upside, when Farouk was in residence, any girls not chosen for his bed would, unless under punishment, be allocated a partner for the night.

'Irina nearly always takes a girl for herself, which ain't so good.' Laura, having had a taste of Irina's style, grimaced. 'And nor's having to go with his guests. We do shows for them.'

Laura had guessed as much. Polly had avoided one thing. 'What happens when the Prince is away?'

165

'No sex. Every night chained so we can't touch. That way we all get horny for him. All but Irina. She still gets us to do her, but she never lets us come. The maids watch all the time – they got TV cameras all over, and they'll always tell, even on Irina. But –' Polly brightened up again. '– the food's fine and the place is really cool, and tonight we get to fuck.'

Laura asked a question that was troubling her. 'What happens in the long run? You're all young, except Irina. Did he use to keep the maids the same way?'

'No. Don't know much about them. Very close, don't say much. No, if he gets bored with Dava, Marissa, Irina or me, we get to retire with a great fat bank balance. Won't happen to the sisters, maybe not to Chai either. I reckon he's going to keep them as wives.'

Laura peeked at her new friend from under her eyelashes. The rings in Polly's coral nipples must have been all of a quarter-inch thick, but her nubs were so thick and long the metal seemed as thin as Laura's old gold rings. Laura's new rings had a somewhat smaller gauge but were still fat and heavy. Polly noticed Laura's interest and unselfconsciously opened her thighs. Her skirt, slit like Laura's from navel to hem, parted to expose a smooth, ringed mound interrupted by a very long clitoris and droopy, pouting inner lips. Polly reached out, flicked open Laura's skirt and touched the studs in her sex.

'Very nice, girl-friend,' she murmured. 'In your beanie and little flaps.' She leant forward and took Laura's hand in a gentle, sympathetic gesture. 'You already been around the block a few times, ain't ya?'

Laura agreed with a little nod.

'How come you're only here for a little while? We're all here as long as he says.'

The truth might be dangerous, so she tried for an enigmatic one-liner. 'Princess Leila sent me.'

Polly looked surprised and uncertain. 'Never met the lady, but her name's poison round here. Madam Irina and a couple of the maids knew her.'

Some pieces fell into place for Laura, but Polly clearly

wanted to know more. Laura temporised. 'I must have upset her, so she sent me here to teach me a lesson.'

Polly appeared to accept the explanation, for she changed the subject, extending a foot until her toes brushed the inside of Laura's thighs.

'How do you like our Prince?'

'Only met him this morning.'

Polly's eyes widened in astonishment. 'Shit! You kidding me?' Laura shook her head. 'He bedded most of us before we came – except Fatima, Saba and Chai. They were virgins, but he met them first.' Polly reached for a sweet as she chewed over Laura's story. 'So you didn't come here of your own free will?'

'No. One minute I'm in Leila's bed, the next I'm on his private jet.'

'Jesus, girl-friend, that's tough.'

'I'll survive.'

'Guess you will.' The big toe began to stroke Laura's inner lips.

Laura thought about everything she had seen and heard so far. A girl laughed loudly. Laura looked up to see Fatima in a fit of giggles and noticed soft, swelling breasts shaking behind wide silver shields worn over her nipples.

'How come Fatima's wearing those shields?'

'Oh, she's just had his child. His first boy. He's really proud – you know how these royals value boys?' Laura nodded, getting the drift. 'So's Fatima. Mind, 'til your friend Leila gives him a divorce, the boy's technically a bastard.'

So Leila had got him in a corner when she got married in London; outside Islamic law, he could not get a divorce unless she agreed. That way he had to keep her sweet.

Polly returned to Fatima's shields. 'Anyway, the Prince likes Fatima's milk. The shields stop anyone else getting at it.'

Laura shivered. Not so long ago, she had tasted a mother's milk, and the idea brought back all kinds of dark, lewd memories. 'Does she see the child?'

'Oh, yeah, most every day. The boy got his own

wet-nurse and rooms not far from here. A lovely little thing.
Pretty soon the Prince'll get Saba pregnant too. Another
nice little Arab baby. That's why Marissa's so jealous. She
wants babies. I don't, nor do the rest of us, yet.'

'Ow!' Laura winced as Polly's toe flicked the new ring
above her clitty. The numbness had worn off, leaving a
slight soreness behind, which was a considerable damper
on the arousal brought by the presence of seven
semi-naked gorgeous women.

'Sorry, girl-friend.' Her eyes narrowed to smouldering
slits. 'Later, I hope.' Laura almost blushed.

Laura looked round at the other girls. They had been
surprisingly welcoming, even Marissa, once the temporary
nature of her stay had been explained. They were all
attractive, but Laura was especially taken by Chai, who,
apart from Laura, was the slightest of the girls. She giggled
and blushed like a convent schoolgirl; which she had been
when the Prince had met her only a few months ago. Like
Laura, he was drawn to her petite body and almost
childlike innocence.

Chai caught her eye and came over. Polly licked her lips
lasciviously, reached out and stroked her bottom. Chai
blushed. Laura held out her arms, and the girl hid her face
in Laura's lap.

Polly laughed. 'If you think she's blushing now, you
shoulda seen her when she first arrived! Only ever been
kissed by one man, our Prince, never been touched or seen
naked. Sees us like this, then has to dress the same way –
Chai blushes all the way to her toes. And he made her wait,
really wait, for her first fuck. Didn't even let us get our
hands on her until she'd been here a month, just made her
watch.' Polly playfully smacked Chai's firm, rounded
bottom. 'Her butt's still virgin, ain't it, kid?'

Chai giggled and wriggled deliciously. Laura could not
keep herself from stroking her head.

'Yeah, we all got our own trick – I blow good, Irina does
the dominatrix thing, Marissa's a sorry little submissive –'
Polly declined to continue. 'You'll see, soon enough, 'cos
he always takes us least two at a time.'

A gong rang. All the other girls jumped to their feet; Chai disappeared in a blur.

'Gotta get ready for parade.'

Polly grabbed her hand, and they almost ran to the beauty parlour, Laura gasping as her new rings jiggled. They were last in; the other girls were already in a frenzy of hairbrushing and repairing make-up.

'Hurry up.' Polly pointed to a spare dressing-table. 'You gotta be perfect for parade, or Irina'll make your sorry ass sting!'

Laura sat down last in the line. Her mirror had a large number '8' on the wall above it. Everything she needed – all the shades of blue used this morning, even gel for her hair – lay before her, labelled. She looked round. Beside her, and with a complete lack of self-consciousness, Chai was hunched over wide-open thighs, painting her labia. Laura noticed she was also rubbing herself, as if making herself ready for sex. Chai looked up at her with big dark, serious eyes.

'Master and mistress like us wet. It help to get picked. Look sexy.'

Laura copied her, but almost as soon as she touched herself the ring above her clitty set off such strong vibrations that she had to stop or cry. She had only just finished touching up her lip-gloss when a second gong sounded and everyone hurriedly finished as they set off for the main hall. Laura followed, more slowly to save herself the discomfort of heavy rings bobbing about in sore breasts, and joined the line next to Chai. For a few moments, until Irina took her place before them, they remained standing with their hands at their sides. For once, Irina was dressed like the others, and Laura could see her heavy, full breasts tipped in scarlet and hung with the thickest, heaviest rings of all.

Irina clapped her hands. Laura looked right to see what the others did, and copied them, putting her hands behind her neck, thus raising and pushing out her breasts. Irina clapped her hands again, and the line of girls spread their feet apart, bent their knees and pushed their hips forward.

Chai whispered, catching her attention. Laura looked round. Chai and the others had trapped their skirts as they moved, opening the split at the front of their skirts. Laura adjusted and felt herself melt into a blush of excited shame. Like this, her newly ringed and painted mound was exposed, pouting and wet. He had been away for three weeks, and the atmosphere of pent-up female sexual passion was heavy in the air.

The Prince strode into view. For a few moments he stood looking at his women, his possessions. Irina clapped her hands, and the line of girls sank to their wide-parted knees and bent forward until their noses almost touched the floor. Laura felt her skirt part behind, the halves sliding over each other until air kissed her bottom. She heard movement and peered out as best she could. Irina was kneeling too, kissing the Prince's gem-laden slippers. For the first time Laura began to understand the depth of her companions' love and submission to their master. Even haughty Irina abased herself before him. He tapped her bottom with an ornate riding crop, and slowly, as if reluctantly, she stood up. They exchanged a few whispered words and then came over to the line. Laura kept her head down as she heard Dava kiss his shoes. Then she heard shufflings, little wet noises, and eventually a moan of pleasure and regret. The sequence of sounds came closer as Irina and Farouk moved along the line. Laura heard Chai's little mew, and then his feet were by her face.

Laura licked her lips. Did he really expect her, his hostage, to kiss his feet? The crop tapped her bottom in warning, and he spoke softly: 'Perhaps Polly has not done her job?'

'I cane both?' Irina stood behind him, anticipating some fun.

The idea that Polly would be beaten if Laura didn't obey harem convention was enough to make Laura taste his sandal. Laura heard Irina walk round behind her. Fingers began stroking her sex and bottom. One slid into her partial wetness and moved around. Like the others before her, Laura began to become aroused. Another finger

170

entered her bottom. She jumped, and her hips rolled with the thrusts. Abruptly the fingers left her, and she, too, moaned.

Irina reported her findings. 'Wet. Rings sore. Kneel up, girl.'

Laura straightened to find that the other girls were already upright and had witnessed her humiliation. Their hands were still behind their necks. Laura copied them. Her Prince bent down to touch her nipples. She winced as thrills of pain and excitement ran through her. He smiled kindly into her eyes.

'Mmm, too sore for tonight. Have her rest. Tomorrow, perhaps, I might take her. I'll take two and three.' He turned away and headed for the door, then seemed to change his mind. 'No. It's good to see you all again, and the turnout has been so good I've changed my mind – you will all come to my chamber.'

With a broad smile, Farouk left his harem. As soon as the door closed, excited chatter broke out until Irina, whose eyes twinkled like the rest, cut it short with a handclap.

Laura was chained by her collar to a pillar again. She looked round the palatial bedchamber at her companions. They, too, were chained to pillars – except Irina, who stalked the room with her cane watching for any slacking. All were all in a traditional harem costume: transparent silk veils, baggy pantaloons with separate legs, and little turned-up sandals decorated with precious stones. Their unsupported breasts were hardly covered by tiny, jewel-embroidered jackets, their nipple rings, all but Fatima, linked by glinting chains forming a 'Y' with the rings in their navels and mounds. From both their labial rings and earrings hung strings of gems that weighed heavy on Laura's new piercings. Fatima's nipples were hung with two small silver cups.

The air was heavily scented with sandalwood and female arousal. Even Laura, sure she was only a mere spectator, felt a longing in her loins and breast, even though the new

171

rings irritated. She tried to take her mind off it and looked round. Over Fatima's shoulder she could just make out a portrait. It was the only one in the room; all the other decorations were in the abstract Islamic tradition. It was specially lit and showed a middle-aged, distinguished man in Napoleonic uniform. Above his grey head was a coat of arms, obviously considered as important as the man: a pair of crossed riding crops below a heart in chains.

Laura did not know why, at that moment, a spasm of pleasure gripped her, setting the dangling gems and chain tinkling. Irina stared at her with utter contempt. Laura closed her eyes in shame, but she could not avoid the snap of the cane against her flank.

Four maids entered and noiselessly brought champagne and glasses, sweetmeats and cognac, then left. Another door opened behind drapes, and, at last, the Prince made his entrance fresh from the bath, a towel across his shoulders and a robe over his body. Laura glimpsed a couple of maids behind him, their comely, middle-aged faces creased by smiles, and again she wondered just who they were.

Irina, mistress of the harem, knelt before her master, his concubines followed suit, their lead chains being just long enough, and all, having bowed their heads low, sat back on their feet with hands clasped behind their necks and their elbows back. He smiled down, proudly surveying his slaves. Laura felt the waves of love emanating from the Prince and his subjects. Then he laughed, at first to himself, and then for them all, a rich, deep, rumbling laugh of pleasure and happiness that infected the air and broke the solemn, constrained atmosphere. Laura watched the concubines' faces crack into smiles and relax. Farouk walked round the room, skirting the enormous bed, touching his girls on head, cheek or chin, saying little private words. Laura's understanding of the harem grew. He loved them all, but she suspected his capacity for love was shallow and no one could touch him deeply. This insight explained Leila's attitude to him. She was greedy by nature, possessive, wanting all of a lover with no capacity for sharing.

172

Finally, he came to Laura. She looked up at his face. He cupped her cheek. Hitherto, his eyes had shown predatory interest in his latest acquisition, but now she saw something apparently deeper and more meaningful. She wondered if he was one of those men able to switch on whatever his audience wanted to see. Then he spoke, and her doubts diminished.

'Laura, my new, special girl. This is my playroom, my soul's recovery room. Soon, you will have me all to yourself, but tonight, enjoy.' He urged her to stand and kissed her, a deep, long, warm, loving kiss that melted her resistance away.

'Now, my children, let us begin.' He lay back on his bed, eyes twinkling.

Irina deployed her troops. Laura remained by the head of the bed as the others were released. Polly and Dava began a slow, sensuous dance to hidden music. Chai and Saba crawled across the wide expanse of heavily embroidered fabrics to undress the Prince and, without touching his sex, arouse him slowly with kisses. Fatima and Marissa, meanwhile, moved back into the shadows and added scarves and bells to their costumes.

Dava and Polly, a contrasting pair of tall, leggy dancers, coiled sinuously together, kissing, touching breasts and buttocks, moving round the bed. Slowly, and without missing a beat or losing contact, they climbed on to the bed and formed an arch above Farouk's head. As he looked up at their pulsing, writhing thighs, Saba insinuated herself under his shoulders to make a human pillow. Chai nibbled his nipples and wormed her tongue into his navel, her fingers stroking the inside of his thighs as his cock rose, still untouched, the brown, slim, circumcised tube filling and extending. Laura moistened her lips and wanted to touch herself.

Irina, who had been circling the action, came to her then and kissed her mouth as she attached short chains to Laura's wrists, restraining them behind her back. Laura gasped as a finger ran the length of her wet slit, followed by a tongue as Irina knelt and chained her ankles wide apart to the pillar. Unable to touch herself, and abandoned by Irina, Laura felt cheated.

Marissa and Fatima now began their belly dance, plump breasts and bellies shaking, hips describing figures of eight, thighs parted, becoming slick with perspiration. They tinkled and clinked their bells and belts of gold discs and began to discard the scarves that hid their charms. Farouk turned on his side, opening his thighs with one leg bent and the other straight. Chai slid behind and put her mouth to his firm buttocks. Polly and Dava took it in turns to lower their loins to dangle the strings of gems hanging from their labia into his mouth. Farouk's cock hardened as Chai's tongue wormed between his cheeks, the bulb purple and long.

Laura imagined her mouth stretched round it, and the fullness in her sheath. She wanted him inside, wanted his jism. Irina came to stand beside her as she watched. She rubbed herself over Laura's thighs and shoulders, sometimes offering a breast to her mouth. Laura tasted the heavy rings, soft breast and hard nipple, and felt the persuasive contrast of metal, gems and hot, slick flesh press her thigh.

In a powerful display of sensuality, Fatima and Marissa brought their dance to a climax, each shuddering with intensity as they simulated, maybe even experienced, orgasm. Irina gripped Laura tight and came too. Farouk's untouched cock quivered. Dava and Polly pressed their mounds together, mimicking intercourse. Polly gasped, a fine spray spattering the Prince's face as she climaxed, surprising Laura. Saba rubbed her thighs aganist his shoulders, seeking relief, and Chai's hips and thighs moved, longing for a touch.

The Prince clapped his hands with glee and beckoned the belly dancers to his side. The other girls became still, Dava and Polly parting, Chai escaping from under his relaxing back. He reached up to Marissa and pulled her head down to his mouth, thanking her. Then he brought Fatima's mouth to his own, and then her breast. For a few moments he suckled, then he beckoned Polly to take his cock in her mouth. Each girl kissed him, taking turns, until Irina went forward. He whispered instructions and left the bed. The six girls arranged themselves into numerical order.

He came to Laura, his cock sniffing out her hunger, glistening with Polly's saliva. He kissed her, and Laura smelt the fragrance of Polly's extraordinary burst of pungent honey and the rock-hard poke of his manhood against her. He kissed her for a long time, stealing Laura's breath, gripping her buttocks and breasts, and once dipping to lever her up with his cock between her thighs. Laura nearly came then, her clitty reaching for him, his wiry, curly, thick pubic hair tickling her mound.

He moved away. Six pairs of buttocks swayed in a line at the foot of the bed, their owners' wrists chained to the brass rail in front, their knees on a long padded seat. Their ankles had been chained to the ankles of the girls beside them so that each was open and available. Their hanging breasts shook; they were blindfold and gagged. Irina stood at the far side, a training whip in her hand. He nodded and stood by Laura, cupping her buttock.

The whip whistled, snapping a red line across Saba's cheeks, then Polly's, then Chai's, and so on, without any particular sequence, until each had received six light, sharp starts, three red lines on each rounded, taut cheek. The Prince moved away then to stand behind his targets. Irina moved Laura to another pillar, so that she could clearly see his cock and their open bodies.

He entered Dava's cunt, and she moaned as he moved in and out three times, soaking his cock. He moved to Saba, and plunged up to the hilt in her bottom. She hissed, more in relief than pain at the sudden invasion. Chai, her sex still tight, produced a muffled yelp as his girth and length stretched her lips to a tight circle. Polly rolled her buttocks as he took her anus. Marissa dipped her back and moaned with disappointment as he left her sex unfulfilled. Fatima muttered her love, Saba sighed when he went back to her clutching bottom. He entered them all in both places, except for Chai, somehow withholding his ejaculation, those who had not already come getting more of him, but none managing to climax before he left them, gaping and desperate.

Irina pushed Laura to her knees. The Prince looked round and saw her in place. Laura licked her lips, guessing what was going to happen next. He thrust twice more into Fatima and then came over, presenting his slippery, shining, intensely fragrant and almost bursting stem to her mouth.

'Taste your new friends, Laura.'

She opened wide, he guided himself in, filling her mouth. Laura breathed through her nose and tried not to choke as he thrust, as careless of her pleasure as he had been of his other girls. She tongued and sucked as best she could. He grabbed her head and exploded, his semen splashing the back of her throat in thick gouts. She swallowed as his movements slowed and the spurts subsided. Sad, Laura felt him slip away, and she was left, alone, empty, with just the taste of his come as her reward.

Laura knelt meekly by the desk, her ankles linked by a chain, waiting. Irina had left her here some minutes ago, called away suddenly and without giving any clue as to why Laura had been called from her lunch. Over the last couple of days the harem girls had become aware of an odd mood emanating from the Prince's quarters. Guests had appeared, their pleasures served by the older girls, leaving Saba, Chai and Laura to twiddle their thumbs, but Polly reported that she had been unused for the entire night, and Dava returned fuming after being buckled into a harness and then ignored too. Now Laura had been called, and again she did not seem to be needed.

An internal door opened. 'Ah, Laura, good.'

Framed for a moment by the drapes of his bedchamber, Farouk, in casual shirt and jeans, smiled, but his mind seemed elsewhere. He sat down behind his desk, opened some files and switched on a computer.

'I have some business to attend to. I'd like you to make it more interesting.'

Laura looked through the gap between the drawers on

either side of the desk, smiled up at him and crawled forward as he parted his legs. Before she opened his fly, she decided to spin out her seduction. She trailed her fingers over his moccasins and the bare tops of his feet. She bent lower, removed his shoes and took each toe into her mouth before kissing his feet all the way up until his legs disappeared under the denim. She heard the keyboard tapping, and little murmurs of annoyance and interest as he worked.

She knelt up as far as she could and undid his jeans, drawing the zip down slowly, extending the moment. Underneath, he was naked, his turgid cock nestling in its wiry bush. She eased his manhood free and popped the soft tip between her lips. He grew, and she felt moisture between her legs. She was full of suppressed desire, untouched since the other night.

Soon, as her tongue and cheeks worked, he filled her. She scooped out his balls, cradling them in her fingers and squeezing gently. He tasted clean but strong. A droplet gathered at the tip and she licked it away. Laura was getting to like his penis, and she wanted it inside her, so she took her time, stretching out the pleasure to encourage him to break off from his work. A telephone rang, shrill and discordant in the quiet. He answered in a foreign language.

'Damn,' he said to Laura. 'I have to go. Stay here until I return.'

Impatiently, he stood, zipped up and sped from the room. Laura followed him to her feet and looked round. The files were dry financial statements, and the computer had been switched to a screensaver. Laura didn't understand the figures, so she ignored them and, in her chain clinking way, crossed to a small bookshelf by the window, looking for something to read. The harem was, as Polly had said, very pleasant, but it was an intellectual desert. No books or even television, just fashion magazines and cartoons. She ran a fingertip along the shelf of books. Dull, all business directories. What's this? She pulled out a small, slim, untitled leatherbound book. It was handwritten in French, being a fragment of the diary of *Comte Henri B*. Laura's pulse quickened. She began to read, scanning quickly.

The entries ran through the summer of 1877, explicitly detailing the seduction and debauch of a young girl, Antoinette, by this Comte Henri. At first she was described in tender, loving terms, but as the summer proceeded she became first an object and then the means to an end. The man, if the narrative were not the imaginings of a lunatic, described how the girl was deliberately aroused to a point close to madness before her virginity was taken, in order that Le Comte could feed on her sexual power and somehow, as he put it, 'become myself once more, invigorated, youthful and hungry for the next such meal'. At the end of the extract, he merely noted that, after thorough debauchery, 'the girl expired in a surfeit of emotion and pleasure'.

Footsteps neared the door. Laura pushed the book back into place and looked out of the barred window, thinking hard. Comte Henri; Philippe's father's name; the coat of arms she had seen in Paris and Farouk's bedchamber; the means of poor Antoinette's seduction, a sensuous education involving pain and pleasure; and some comments about de Sade's misuse of 'the technique' – all seemed to tie this diary into Adam's enquiries. But the year was 1877, more than a hundred years after the first Comte du Bantonne's ennoblement. Was it his son or grandson? Was Philippe being led down the same path?

The door handle rattled, but the hand decided otherwise and the footsteps carried on past. Outside the castle, the sun burned down on barren rocks. The bars were on the outside of the window, the shutters were open. Laura poked her head out as far as she could, looked down, and saw, to her surprise, that this was the point where the outer wall came so close. The ground level was only some five yards or so below the window. She looked right, to the bedchamber. That was the projecting balcony, with an unbarred window. Her mind raced. She checked her calculations, counting the stones. She could escape.

A door opened. Laura spun round, guiltily. Farouk's face was black with anger and looking for a scapegoat.

'Who told you to move?'

Laura dropped to her knees, offering herself, her true offence conveniently mistaken by her captor. 'I'm sorry, master.'

'Sorry isn't good enough!' He swept the files into a drawer. 'Bend over the desk. I will deal with this myself.' He brandished a leather strap in his hand.

Laura stood up, nervous, tingling, and with a glimmer of hope in her head. If she could make him want her in his bed, then she might get that chance to escape. Without a hint of defiance, Laura walked to his desk, bent over and put her hands behind her neck. For a few moments she lay against the leather and wood, the cool rings in her breasts and belly pressing into her softest flesh. His hand opened her pantaloons, exposing her silky cheeks. She shuffled her feet apart, and felt the rings in her sex slip apart. She was open and wet for him. He stroked her thighs, and she stretched her legs wider still. She felt the leather handle of the strap on her sensitive inner thighs, stroking up and down, then heard the whistle and sting of his controlled anger. She tried not to whimper.

The strap rapidly slashed backward and forward, double strokes stinging the inward curves of her cheeks and thighs. He drew back and leathered the outer curves. Her breath came in ragged gasps, out of rhythm with his fast-moving assault. Her hips bounced, driving her mound into the desk edge, rubbing her clitoris. He began slapping up and down, closing on her exposed slit. Laura pushed her bottom out, towards the stinging strap, urging him to hit her there and release the bubble of lust between her thighs.

He hit cleanly along the crease, once. Laura cried out. His hand stroked her puffy, red wetness and murmured. She heard his fumbling fingers on his jeans. His fingers grabbed her hips, rough on sore skin. He entered her violently, filling her in one breathtaking plunge. Laura grunted. He began pumping hard. Her fingers gripped the desk. She shook her head as he drove her. Her new ring ground in her mound, the stud in her clitty scratched across the wood. His pounding took her to the edge.

Suddenly, she was gurgling as he pulled her head up, twisting and kissing. Their lips meshed together, and he came in uncontrolled spurts, his cock still thrusting, his semen splattering, some hitting, some missing, her gaping, pulsing pussy.

Laura, unfinished, tried to keep him moving, but he drooped over her, pinning her to the desk. His kissed her neck and whispered his promise.

'Tomorrow night, you and Chai. Then you will know my love.'

Thirteen

'Not going to the lake?' Mary could not believe that she didn't have to dive naked into the cold lake, swim until she was thoroughly chilled and be birched dry. It had become such a big part of her routine, a brisk, arousing start to the day.

'No. You are to go directly to the master's study once you have dressed.' Beatrice handed her a pair of soft white slippers and then a long white cotton dress. 'Nothing else is required.'

Mary was even more surprised; no swim or birching, and now no corset or chastity belt, which had already been removed for her morning toilet. Mary felt free, in that her body moved naturally, but quite naked despite the dress. She found walking without the constant rubbing belt really nice after so long, but the lack of tight corsetry was rather unsettling. The thin, tight, white cotton dress displayed, for the first time since her arrival, the natural roundness of her tummy, the cleft of her buttocks and the haloes of her nipples moving softly with every step. Once her hair had been brushed to a shining, wavy curtain, Beatrice accompanied her to the foot of the stairs.

'Wait here.'

Mary watched Beatrice disappear through a door, troubled by the older woman's demeanour. There had been something regretful in her last glance. Since their lovemaking there had been a change in Beatrice's attitude. Formerly, Beatrice had been concerned only with Mary's physical appearance and behaviour, her eating and drinking and dress. Twice she had asked if she was worried about anything. When she had bathed Mary last night, Beatrice was much more tender, almost maternal. Mary began to confide in her, expressing her yearning for Philippe's company. Beatrice seemed to understand, hinting at a cause of dissatisfaction in her own life.

At the same time Mary was noticing changes in herself. She felt as if she was floating through a sensuous, erotic dream. Not a dream of her own, but Le Comte's dream. Her mind was changing. Gone were the old certainties, the list of sins, the axioms that had ruled her existence. In their place, desire and physical gratification had come to dominate her every moment. She was aware that she willingly, compliantly accepted things she could not possibly have countenanced, or even imagined, just a month ago.

Twice now, the old man had requested her attendance in his study. Each time she had been asked to stand beside him naked but for corset, chastity belt, nipple clamps and the stubby ebony rod Beatrice pushed into her bottom after her morning swim. The first time, nothing physical happened, except that he might stroke her bottom or breasts from time to time as he read or wrote.

The second time, he requested, after an hour or so, that she kneel on one end of the desk, presenting him with an intimate view of her sex and bottom. He removed the belt and rod, and then read out a long, explicit and erotic description of harem life by the woman whose drawings she had seen earlier. Initially, she felt deeply embarrassed, used, a mere object for his impersonal gratification. However, after just a few minutes of kneeling with forehead resting on forearms, nipple clamps just touching the mahogany surface, strange sensations and thoughts zigzagged through her body and mind. She imagined Philippe sitting in his father's place, and her delicate pink nubs weighed down with rings of gold. She longed for her young master to make her his own, to use her, on this desk, right now, his cock between her thighs or buttocks. Le Comte remarked, as she dreamt, how beautiful her sex was becoming, and how copiously her honey flowed. Mary said nothing, unwilling to admit her incessant, unfulfilled lust for physical pleasure.

She shook her head as she remembered it all and realised just how desperate her need to be wantonly displayed had become. That one orgasm with Beatrice had not cooled her ardour; if anything it had increased her need.

Le Comte appeared through another door. 'Good morning, my dear. Today, a treat. Come.'

Mary followed him along the hall to a door almost hidden in the panelling. She followed into a dim passage and down a flight of stone steps. He stopped at the bottom of the steps and waved his arm, encompassing the lamplit vaulted void before them.

'The cellars.' He indicated right. 'Through there are the wine and food stores.' He moved to the left. 'And this is my workshop.'

Beyond an arch, sunlight slanted in through a series of windows up at ground level, illuminating a series of long benches. The nearest was cluttered with strips of leather, wood and metal, hammers, files and boxes of nails, all covered in a patina of dust from long disuse. The next workbench was more interesting, and in current use. Little trays of silver and gold, stands holding magnifying glasses with adjustable clamps to hold pieces of jewellery or precious metal, and trays, lined with felt, indented to hold an array of delicate, miniature tools. Like her guide and master, Mary moved closer. Beside one of the stands lay an inlaid box, lined with purple velvet, containing several gold rings. Each was about an inch in diameter, an eighth of an inch thick, and inscribed with letters. Curious, Mary picked one up. Around the outside ran the legend *Philippe had me made* with the familiar armorial crest, and inside, the words read: *Mary's body holds me.*

A shiver ran up Mary's spine. 'Are these for me?'

He took the ring from her. 'Yes, my dear. Philippe asked me to make them.'

The news thrilled her. She was getting close to her goal. But you only need one wedding ring. 'Why so many?'

His eyes twinkled. 'Ah, that is for you to decide.'

'What do you mean?'

'Have you not seen my pictures and heard those stories? It is a family custom for our women to wear several signifiers of their love and submission. Remember the girls in the harem, with rings through their intimate flesh?' His eyes dropped momentarily to the dark discs under her cotton dress.

Mary stiffened as she caught the implication. Her nipples hardened as if anticipating pleasure from holding the gold bands.

After this pause for thought, he added: 'One, which cannot be adjusted, is for your finger. You may decide where the others go.'

Mary fingered another ring, feeling its weight, contemplating, listening both to Le Comte and her inner feelings. The idea of wearing these rings in the way Laura and Beatrice wore them, in her flesh, at once repelled and excited her. Her sex became wet and her nubs thickened as he continued.

'In centuries past, our women were always marked by the branding iron. Somewhere hidden, on the buttocks, inner thighs or breasts, to show their fidelity and ownership to any man who might venture into intimacy.' Mary quailed at the thought. 'But fashions change, even here, and the choice has always been the woman's. She is, after all, choosing to give her heart and soul into our hands.'

Mary slowly replaced the ring with unsteady fingers. To choose the pain of branding or piercing, to make a choice to endure pain for her lover, how could anyone be so brave, so certain of his love?

The old man moved away from her, towards an arch behind. She followed, wondering what sacrifice Philippe was asking of her, and whether she could choose right without talking to him. Could she stand to have those gold rings pierce her most tender flesh? Even her ears hadn't been pierced, but most girls had, so it couldn't hurt that much. A tattoo? All the rage, a fashion accessory for her generation, so that can't be too painful either. Not a brand, that was a form of torture, the sort of barbarity endured by the saints or done to horses. She could not decide.

With a huge, old-fashioned key, Le Comte unlocked a heavy, bolt-studded door under the arch. Inside, the light flickered. He stood aside, letting her enter before closing the door behind them.

'Even Philippe has not been here. This is my Chamber of Pleasure.'

Mary's mouth opened in horror. Belying his description, the low, wide space was filled with what looked like instruments of torture; racks of whips, canes, leather paddles, frames with cuffs and chains, chains hanging from iron bolts set into the ceiling, walls and floor, what looked like a rack, an iron maiden without internal spikes, hoods, a great wood fire, torches, chairs and trestles, bars … Mary backed away.

His arm caught her. 'Don't be afraid, Mary. No one has been tortured here for over two hundred years. This is a sacred place now, dedicated to pleasure. Look, there are couches, furs, cushions. Only those who desire the ultimate sensuous experience may enter.'

He turned her to face him, and looked into her eyes. Mary tried to look away, but she could not. His eyes burned, not reflecting the flaming fire but an internal fire. 'You and I, Mary. We are the seekers of ultimate pleasure. I can see it within you!'

Mary felt herself trembling in his grasp. Comte Henri's eyes burned into her head, into her mind.

'You want to know the pain of ecstasy and the pleasure of surrender. You seek the answer. Are you strong enough to wear those rings? Are you strong enough to love completely, to abandon yourself, heart and soul, to your lover? Do you not want to know?'

Mary felt herself nod, her rational mind bypassed by deep, dark impulses. The chamber triggered dark imaginings, answered some of her questions, fed the need to be owned, taken by Philippe, marked and used. All this Le Comte now knew, because he was plundering her mind.

He continued. Mary wasn't sure if he was talking or communicating directly with her brain, without recourse to the crude instrument of speech.

'Test yourself now, my dear. I know you would rather Philippe did this, but he, too, is learning, and he is not yet ready to match you.'

Mary didn't understand, but because his mind still probed he was able to offer his explanation.

'A young man's passion is too hot and quick. They rush. Philippe is learning how to control his passion, to extract pleasure from giving pleasure, to measure his ecstasy by his lover's ecstasy. Woman's capacity is bottomless, immense. Your gift is the female orgasm, the supreme physical manifestation of humanity. With Philippe, we teach control. With you, we need only to open a few doors to expose the potential and show you how to intensify and prolong the event. One day, soon, you shall be allowed to climb the heights of sexual experience, and the world will change.'

He released her and she staggered back, shaken by the force of his mind and the promise. For a few moments she leant against the door, breathing hard, regaining control. Her vision, dazzled by his eyes, slowly cleared. She saw him through new eyes, taller, straight-backed, his face less wrinkled by age. She thought he looked handsome, vital and strong.

Le Comte turned away, releasing her from his presence, and walked over to the sturdy frame that dominated the centre of the chamber. Mary watched as he stroked the wood with his long, pale fingers, lovingly caressing the blackened, polished wood.

'English oak, from one of your ships we took during the Seven Years War.'

Mary looked at him curiously, detecting an odd, almost nostalgic note behind his words. His eyes seemed misted over in memories, memories he could not have for his own.

He continued for a few moments, lost in his own little world. 'They fought well that day . . .' His eyes suddenly focused on her. 'Imagine the memories locked away in this timber, eh? Could you stand here, bound fast to the frame, pleading to be kissed by the whip?'

Mary, who had begun to walk into the room, hung back. Not, she thought, unless Philippe asked.

'Or perhaps the chair.'

He moved across to a heavy wooden chair, oddly constructed, with high arms and a deeply reclined back but without much of a seat. Rather, the seat was a semicircle of wood polished by years of wear set far back from the front legs. The back, legs and arms were connected to each other by iron rods and levers. Thick, strong leather cuffs were attached to the arms and legs.

'Yes, the chair.' He walked round to the back, facing her, still stroking the wood lovingly. 'The seat where a thousand unthought dreams can be made flesh.' He looked up, entrapping her eyes once more, speaking directly to her brainstem. 'Can you imagine the pleasure to be had from abandoning yourself to the chair?'

Swimming in his mind-pool, Mary pictured herself sprawled open-legged, bound, eyes wild, mouth wide, her breasts and belly pushed out under the attack of the cowled monks from the paintings, penetrated, beaten and howling for more. His eyes beckoned. Mary walked forward, her thighs wet, bosom heaving, automatically licking her lips. She halted before the chair, arms held up to ease the removal of her single garment. Le Comte nodded. Although she thought they were alone, Beatrice materialised from behind and began to unbutton the dress, her hands appearing in front of Mary, methodically revealing Mary's body to an old man who was not so old any more.

Proud, naked, unable to believe that she was offering herself so easily, Mary stood looking directly into his eyes, meeting his challenge. She glimpsed, from within the shrouded glow of his eyes, her own power for the first time; her power to surprise and to give what he, with all his powers, could only plead and connive to obtain. As if to deny her this insight, a helmet was pulled down over her head. She understood and did not struggle when her sight

187

was blocked by stiff leather, her ears muffled and her mouth covered by the tightly buckled helmet. She felt hands turn her round, and let them sit her down until her back lodged against the wooden frame. Mary smiled to herself; this was what she wanted, and she breathed deeply through her uncovered nose.

Gentle hands drew her limbs, one by one, to the straps on the legs and arms of the chair. She felt the tight, comforting constriction as she was fixed. She heard the clicking of a ratchet, and the chair began to move. Her arms moved back and down, the back reclined until she was almost flat and her breasts stood out and sideways. Now her hips were almost suspended, her body open, her hot wetness evident. They could do anything now, and they stroked her, caressing away any remaining fear. Fingers stroked her breasts, and gently pinched her nipples to hardness. Something hard, metallic, ringed her rubbery nubs, pushed down by hot wet lips and teeth to the base of her nipples.

The fingers stroked between her legs, circling the jewel. Lapping wavelets of pleasure moved Mary's lips to an inner moan. A mouth kissed the firm peak, sucking slightly. The jewel elongated, and hard, metal cold ringed the tip. It was pushed delicately into place at the base, the folded tender base. The tongue continued sucking, harder now. Mary gasped and wriggled. She felt as if the fleshy jewel was being strangled at its base, squeezed in a vice.

Le Comte's voice whispered in her ear. 'Rings to enhance and beautify.'

The mouth took her nipples, one by one, sucking, nibbling until the pressure came to them, even tighter. Teeth tugged as she grew, forcing the rings further down. The lips went away.

The rustle of leaves came to her ears. Was she going to be birched now? Soft filaments brushed across her thighs and breasts. For a moment she felt cool, and then the touched skin burst into life, itching, squealing hot. Nettles. The brushing came again, between her thighs, across her belly, between her buttocks. Zinging prickly heat. The

188

exposed, wet tissues of her sex, her rose and her nubs burst into singing, soaring awareness and throbbing. She sucked in her breath, and tried to retreat, straining at her bonds, wriggling so her bottom almost lost its precarious purchase on the inadequate seat. She felt something draw tight round her waist and just below her knees; more straps to hold her still. Where the rings gripped, flesh bulged tighter, hotter, tingling.

Crack! Slicing heat burned across her inner right thigh, then her left. She bucked. Her nerves translated the overlaying band of pain; a strap, probably, now alternating the bands of heat from side to side, advancing on her molten core. Mary bit her lip as the smarting warmth infused her thighs. Her hips moved, instinctively trying to escape the biting strap as it closed on her belly.

Beatrice, Mary imagined, worked assiduously, subtly, inflaming her skin but not touching her sex. The strap travelled slowly over the upper surface of Mary's right thigh and down into the crease between thigh and mound. The soft, hairless delta danced. Mary gasped in time to the beat of the leather, which moved on, circling its ultimate target, closing inexorably. As the circle was completed, Mary sucked in her breath in anticipation, unable to imagine anything but pain from the next stroke. Instead, the leather came like a kiss to her outer lip. Her breath escaped in a hiss of relief.

On and on, the strap kissed the reddening, swelling flesh, now beginning to work across the thickened leaves, the crevice between, the wet cup of her entrance. Sensations of pleasure and pain darted about, she felt splashes as the leather whipped her honey to a froth. Tremors ran round the intricate nerves and muscles inside her pelvis. Mary's breath came in tiny gasps, rising in tone inside her enclosed, isolated head. Her head tossed uncontrollably. She wanted it to end, and she didn't, all at the same time. She squealed as Beatrice set up a rapid tattoo along the length of her puffy slit, sending shocks through to the mass of nerves behind the as yet untouched tip of her clitoris. That jewel felt enormous, as long and thick as a thumb beyond the ring. Her body shook, disturbing her breasts and stinging, swollen nipples.

The sensations reached a plateau, filling her with fire, a rumbling earthquake somehow capped. Her limbs were rigid, jerking against their bonds. Mary felt sweat pouring from her, trickling between her breasts and down her spine. She cried, with frustration, with exhaustion.

Everything stopped.

Mary only slowly noticed the absence of tapping smacks. Her breasts jiggled and heaved as her lungs worked overtime. But this was not to be the end. Mary felt someone stand close to her right, and another to her left. A line of fire snatched across her right breast, high up, then her left, a rapid incising of slashing heat. Her breasts twitched and bounced, swelling, heating to cauldron temperature from the outside. The lashes closed on the peaks, went round, snapping under the swell. Simultaneously, she felt her nipples pulled, tugged between fingers, raising the bulk of her breasts to expose the under-creases, the soft, untouched creases.

Mary jerked as the fire came to that softest skin. She bounced off the reclining back of the chair, and yet they held her breasts high for more. She felt coated in fire, her trapped nipples squealed. They let go, but she knew why. The fire bit the swollen, tender tips. She screamed and felt as if she would burst. Stinging darts shot outward. She pleaded for them to stop, to go on, to leave her, to take her. Partly, they responded to her muffled call. She felt a weight straddle her belly. She felt fingers on her helmeted head.

Le Comte's voice was loud and hoarse. 'Can you bear the kiss of the strap on your clitoris?' Mary swallowed nervously. 'Do you want that release?'

Her body screamed for just that. She nodded, mumbling incoherently.

He spoke to his accomplice. 'You may start.'

She felt something hot and hard fall heavily between her throbbing, tortured breasts. Like light bursting in, she saw herself through his eyes; helpless, masked head thrown back, breasts red, thick and desirable, infinitely desirable.

190

Suddenly, she could read his thoughts as if they were her own, feel his desire and look down on his hard, swollen cock as if it were her own. She saw herself violated, splashed with his semen. Mary tried to understand what was happening. She was looking inside his mind as he had so often looked inside hers. She felt his uncontrollable lust, the need to ravage and abuse her offered, vulnerable breasts. Every thought, every action in his body was concentrated on that one thing.

His hands gripped her breasts roughly, pulling them round the hot column of his penis. She screamed as the leather smacked beside her jewel for the first time. The strap came down again, on the other side. She tossed her head as her nipples were crushed in his palms. Mary felt fingers press down on the flesh on either side of her clitoris, pressing it further out, pushing the ring further down. His cock began thrusting, somehow lubricated, slippery in its hot, tender flesh cushion. The end bumped on her throat. The strap came down, softly, thrilling, biting, stinging, clinging. He pumped back and forward, setting her breasts on fire. The leather, wet with her own juices, struck again, harder this time. Mary screamed. Her stomach clutched and burst, and his semen, thick and heavy, splashed across her throat and over her bright red breasts.

Mary slowly entered the dining-room. Walking was a trial with her skin still pink and tender, even after a long hot bath and an application of soothing oil. The three little gold rings were still in place, keeping the three nubs of nerve-filled flesh swollen and delicate to the touch of the silk dress she now wore. The corset was the most severe yet, bulging her sore breasts high, nipping her waist and making her buttocks swell. To make walking more difficult still, Beatrice had inserted another, thicker rod into her bottom and fitted her into a new chastity belt; a suede pouch which cupped her puffy labia below the trapped jewel.

Philippe turned from the fireplace and came to her. 'Mary, you look wonderful.'

She grinned and blushed. They kissed, cheek to cheek in the French fashion, under the eye of his father. Philippe looked so full of longing, she thought she would cry. She never noticed what she ate, nor what was said, though she was aware of Le Comte maintaining conversation despite the virtual silence of two companions eating and drinking mechanically, looking into each other's eyes, smiling and blushing. Only when they finished, as the cognac accompanied coffee to the table, did their host make a determined effort to disengage them.

'Philippe, I believe you have something to give to Mary?'

For a moment Mary looked questioningly at Philippe, who hesitated before standing up, then she remembered the rings in the workshop. Was she going to have to make a choice so soon? But then, this was a formal proposal of marriage. Her heart thumped, butterflies took wing in her stomach. Philippe returned to the table with the inlaid box in his hand. He hovered uncertainly and then came round to her.

'Mary, this is for you.'

With trembling hands, Mary took the box and placed it on the table. There was a little gilt key in the lock. On top, above the rings, lay a sheet of vellum, folded once. She opened the note.

Dearest Mary,
It is the custom of this house for the women to wear a mark of their fidelity, service and love. I offer you these rings to wear as you will. Our wedding ring is safe, elsewhere.
Philippe

Mary folded the note and put it to one side. Seven identical rings lay on the velvet, and she began to choose their destinations. Two for her ears, without doubt, but the others? Her body gave her hints, fresh throbs coming to the tips of her stirring breasts and un-pouched jewel. She considered having a chain between her sex lips, or perhaps a ring in her nose, like the fashionable girls in London. She thought of Laura and Beatrice, of the delicious feel of gold through clutching, hot tissue. She saw herself kneeling, bowed in submission before her master, rings named and loved. She took a deep breath, looked at Le Comte, who waited patiently, and at Philippe, back in his seat, eyes on fire with excitement, and made up her mind.

She started to tell them, but the words dried up.

'May I have a pen?'

A pen was pushed towards her. On the note, below Philippe's words, she drew a simple diagram of her body, and added circles for each ring. Folding it, she passed it across to Philippe. He looked, and passed it in silence to his father, who responded on both their behalves.

'I applaud your choice, my dear. You will look yet more lovely. Shall we do it now?' Mary blinked with surprise. 'I have everything ready, and there is no time like the present, for the sooner it is done, the sooner the nuptials can begin.'

Philippe looked so eager, Mary agreed without thinking. Le Comte rang a bell.

'Beatrice, take Mary to the chamber. Philippe and I will join you shortly. Yvette, bring the cognac.'

Mary stood and followed Beatrice down to the cellars again, this time with head high and heart thumping. She let Beatrice remove her dress and pin her hair away from her ears. Nearly naked, she suddenly realised that Philippe was about to see her body for the first time.

'So, you have decided to wear his rings.' Beatrice stroked her hand before strapping it down.

Mary nodded.

'You would like to be numbed?' Beatrice adjusted the chair so that Mary lay back slightly.

'Will it hurt?'

'Without numbing, yes. With, just a little, you'll hardly feel a thing.'

Mary nodded again.

'First, I will clean you with alcohol. A little sting, perhaps, and then the anaesthetic spray.'

Beatrice stroked her cheek and leant forward and kissed Mary's lips. 'You must be strong now.' Mary chewed over those last words. Was she making a mistake?

Beatrice pushed over a trolley, took a bowl, opened a dressing pack and began to cleanse the targets. Carefully, she tugged the little collars away from the bases of her nipples and clitoris, but did not remove them altogether.

'They will serve to make the piercing easier.'

The alcohol stung the tender flesh so exposed. It stung a little more as her inner lips were swabbed. Mary closed her eyes and prayed she had made the right decision.

Philippe and his father came in. Mary smiled to allay Philippe's concern. Beatrice sprayed her ear lobes and nipples, and a few moments later nipped them between her fingernails. Mary watched but felt just a dull pressure. When she looked up, Le Comte stood before her, his face set, eyes hooded.

'Mary Coppen, as a mark of your love for your master, you have chosen to be pierced through your nipples, ears, clitoris and inner labia. The rings, once in place, may only be removed by your master. This is your last chance to change your mind. Do you wish so to do?'

Mary's answer escaped in a whisper. 'No.'

'Then it shall be so. My son, will you look once upon Mary before she is for ever marked with your rings?'

Philippe nodded uncertainly and shuffled into his father's place. Mary blushed. Philippe blushed. He could see all but the strip of stomach beneath her corset; breasts still tender and swollen from earlier, nipples bright, the glistening, open, heavy drooping lips of her smoothly shaved mound, and even the end of the rod obscenely peeking from between the cheeks of her bottom. Mary detected hesitation in his eyes, a weakening of his resolve. She smiled, and noticed the thick bulge in his trousers. A tremor of desire ran through her body.

Beatrice stood ready, waiting for permission to start. It was Mary who commanded her, cutting off Le Comte. 'Please do it.'

The chatelaine brought the piercing gun to her left ear. There was a loud click, a slight pressure, a sense of flesh on metal, and then the weight of the gold. Mary closed her eyes and heard the second ear being pierced. She felt fingers on her breasts and looked down to see Beatrice lining up the gun while Le Comte held her right nipple firmly by the tight ring. Mary meant to close her eyes, but somehow failed, so she saw the gun shoot an open-ended metal pin through the nub, right at the base. Putting the gun down, Beatrice placed the opened end of an engraved ring into the hollow end of the pin and then, with a push, send the ring through. Removing the pin, she closed the ring with a distinct click and laid it carefully down. The cold gold chilled where she wasn't numb, and weighed heavily.

Mary did close her eyes for the second nipple ring, and then felt the chair move. Her back came up. She opened her eyes. Her breasts hung somewhat, the rings free of their cushions. Beyond, between those mounds, Mary could see her mound as the spray was applied to the opened petals of intimate flesh. Somehow, Mary managed to tear her eyes away before her swollen jewel was nipped and the gun lined up. She felt a deeper punch. Her stomach lurched as the pin punched through, but no pain, nothing compared with the nettles or the strap. Fingers fiddled lower down, and she felt only the extra weight.

They left her bound by her legs as the numbing spray wore off. Le Comte handed her a fresh glass of cognac, which she drank thankfully, and they toasted her. Soon the rings made themselves known with a dull throb. She was released and shown herself in a mirror; the gold rings opening her lips, holding her clitoris out between the folds, keeping her nipples erect. Naked, she was taken to her bed, and bound, spread-eagled, to sleep.

Alone in the dark, Mary sighed for her lost innocence and smiled, aware of her own, secret power.

Fourteen

The parade was almost over. All the girls awaited was word of their duties for the night. Laura licked her lips nervously. The Prince had promised to take her to his bed tonight, and it was Irina's custom to name the Prince's choice first. The mistress opened her mouth to speak. Laura's heart thumped loudly; so much hung on her next few words.

'Seven and eight. You serve master.'

Laura didn't bother to listen to any more, but she noticed Saba's little sigh. The poor girl was becoming desperate to lose her virginity and try to bear Farouk's child. Instead, it was Chai's virgin bottom he intended to breach. As the others were paired off, Laura and Chai made their way to the preparation room accompanied by four black-dressed women. This was a ritual time, one Laura had not yet experienced, and she was curious because none of her new friends seemed prepared to explain.

Laura and Chai were led to a room new to Laura, with two dentist's chairs, tiled walls and ceilings. Their clothes were taken away and they were asked to sit down. As straps secured their ankles and wrists, Laura resigned herself to some unpleasantness. She turned to Chai, who looked nervous. Laura smiled reassuringly. The chairs tilted back until their hips were above the level of their shoulders. At the same time as their legs were parted and bent at the knee, two trolleys were brought in. Laura smiled again at Chai. The little girl looked terrified, even

197

though she had been through this many times before. The trolleys held plastic containers of blue and green liquid from which clear plastic tubes ran. Towards the end of each tube was a small tap. Laura awarded herself no prizes for guessing what was going to happen next, but she was surprised at her physical reaction. Her nether mouths spasmed, her nipples tingled, her sheath lubricated, and her tummy muscles fluttered in anticipation. She heard Chai whimpering as the maids inserted the first tube into her vagina, and then a maid knelt between Laura's knees and gently inserted an unnecessarily oiled tube inside her own sheath.

Taps were opened at each end of the tube and the green liquid moved like virgin olive oil. The oil was cool, at least at first, but when the tube was removed and the maid closed her sex with gloved fingers, it grew warm like chocolate. Laura sighed and eased her hips. The maid smiled up at her, for once abandoning stony indifference, and began to move her fingers against Laura's pouch, palpating her lips and clitty. Laura gasped as she flicked her rings, and let her body relax into the subtle arousal. The chair moved her upright, and the hand slid regretfully away. Out glooped the liquid, warmed to a less viscous state, leaving behind a sensation of sparkling, plump warmth. The chair tilted back again.

The blue liquid was introduced to Laura's bottom. She heard Chai's tears of shame and discomfort and steeled herself as this liquid bubbled and filled. It felt like gallons poured in before two fingers stoppered her clenching, spasming muscle. Laura's guts went into cramp. She shook, knowing she could not expel the seething fluid until the chair lowered her again. After an age, the chair let her down and the fingers left her, followed almost instantly by the fluid and a moan from Laura's lips.

She was refilled, though not with so much, by the green oil. As it eased the discomfort, she noticed that her vagina seemed to have thickened softly. She could feel every sensation inside; the heat of flowing lubrication, pumping blood, the slop of the liquid in her rectum. When the last drops left her bottom, she found the same super-sensitivity, oiliness, and sensation of cleanliness there too. The maid who had so gently caressed her mound before, now repainted Laura's swollen labia and lengthening clitty with a soft, cunning brush before covering the bright blue with a sheen of oil. Laura clenched and relaxed her knuckles as the fine sable tickled and the fingers repeatedly spread and stretched her most intimate membranes. She heard Chai's sighs and giggles. The maid also anointed her anal ring with purple oil, making her jump and squeal, before wiping away her nipple paint and using fingers and some warming oil to erect the nubs before colouring them blue once more.

Laura heard Chai sigh with pleasure. She looked over. A maid was inserting a small dildo into the younger girl's vagina. Her own maid produced something similar, a wrinkled, flaccid phallus with firm balls. As it was pushed in, the maid pumped one of the balls, and Laura felt the phallus inflate until she felt comfortably full. When the maid took her hand away, Laura noticed another soft protrusion dangling from the outside of the pretend testicles. The straps holding her down were released, and the maid held out her hand.

'Please stand. Hold it in.' Laura struggled to comply, gripping the now-smooth dildo as tight as she could with her slick sheath. She gave up as she moved, holding it in with her hand.

She was placed, facing Chai, to be dressed in a web of purple leather straps and steel. She grunted as her breasts were pushed and pulled through the circular holes in a curious article that seemed to be a cross between a cuirass and a corset. As the tapes at the back were tightened, so the holes tightened until her breasts swelled to pointed cones and the stiff corsetry made her gasp. For a moment, while the maids tidied up the tapes and buckles, Laura looked at her changed figure, comparing her new curves with Chai's and wondering if her own bottom swelled as enticingly. The maids buckled thin steel plates mounted on leather to their forearms, biceps, shins and thighs, slipped their feet into sandals, and attached a skirt made of strips of leather to the bottom of the cuirass. Finally, their new male parts were anchored with fine, tight chains to the cuirass, chains that ran down each side of their mounds and back up across their bulging buttocks.

At the end, looking at her dusky twin in her magenta outfit, Laura smiled with amusement; a pair of savage hermaphrodites, with pointed female breasts and obscene black, flaccid male genitals. The maids produced chains for their wrists and collars and then clipped clamps to their swollen nipples, making Laura shiver. The clamps were linked by a length of chain that weighed heavy, adding extra bite to the spiteful jaws.

Laura followed Chai and a maid along the corridors and up the stairs to the Prince's chamber, every movement adding to her arousal as the phallus worked inside her steaming sheath. Her whole body throbbed with lust, her honey gathered and trickled down her thighs.

Farouk already lay on his bed in the chamber. Like his concubines, he was dressed as some kind of warrior, in breastplate, tight leather trousers, knee-length boots and a silk shirt. He lounged, smoking a hookah and sipping wine from a gold goblet, but sprang to his feet as the maid chained their leads to a pillar. This was a game, and Laura would play along until she found an opening to her own advantage.

'So, vanquished slaves brought to their new master.' He stroked their chins.

'Strange warriors, aren't you? Brothers, or should I say sisters, in arms against me.' His hands wandered to their breasts, as if touching rare works of art.

'Tits.' He squeezed hard and then snapped the clamp from their left nipples simultaneously. Both girls cried out. Laura closed her eyes and absorbed the pain-pleasure as the remaining clamp dug deeper under the extra, swinging weight.

'And pricks.' He gripped their sacs and squeezed, pumping the cocks thicker and longer. As she gasped at the expansion, Laura guessed there must be a non-return valve to keep the thick balloons inflated.

He stepped back, and Laura saw that her external penis was now hugely erect, maybe ten inches long and a couple across. It bobbed slightly, transmitting shivers through her sex. He released Chai from her lead and brought her round to face Laura. They were the same height, more or less. Chai looked uncertain, almost frightened. Laura wondered if she understood the game in any way. Their black cocks nodded at each other, as if in greeting. Farouk took Chai's hanging nipple clamp and closed it on Laura's left nub. She closed her eyes as a new wave of pleasure-pain swept through her. When she opened them again, Chai was biting her lip as the other spare clamp bit into her sore, bright teat.

Now he released Laura from the pillar and led them to the bed, Chai shuffling backward, Laura trying to keep the chains slack. As Chai's thighs touched the bed, he helped her lie back, and then drew Laura forward so that they crawled on to the fur covers. However hard Laura tried, she could not stop the chains from tugging and bringing more little yelps from the gentle young brown girl under her.

She felt Farouk join them on the bed. 'Now, my little slaves, show me how close your brotherhood is. Let me see you make love.'

Laura looked down into Chai's big brown girlish eyes, smiled and moistened her lips. What a night this could be; Chai for starters, Farouk for the main course. Chai tried to smile back, her smile reflecting her nervous unease and, to Laura's surprise, innocence. The sweet little thing had been here for three or four months; she must have witnessed many scenes like this, and been called on to make love with the other girls. Laura had seen her with Marissa only last night, when she'd been a full participant . . . Laura corrected herself. Chai had been supine, almost completely inactive, letting Marissa caress her, only then meeting Marissa's demands. Chai was not happy making love with her own sex, and their master no doubt knew it. This was going to be difficult.

'Come on, soldiers, make love. Let me see how you take your pleasure!'

He tapped Laura's bottom with a riding whip, as if he knew what Laura was thinking. She dipped her head, but kept her hips as high as possible so that Chai might not be disturbed by Laura's huge phallus. Laura knew it had to be a slow, gentle, feminine seduction. The other girls, even Saba, had a self-confidence in their sex play that must intimidate shy, sheltered Chai. Their lips came close and, as Laura expected, Chai closed her eyes and lay still. Laura kissed her eyelids, her forehead and her nose. Laura breathed a whisper as she kissed.

'You are beautiful, little Chai. Innocent and pure. Let me love you, sweet Chai, let me show you that the love of a woman can be just as good as the love of a man.' Chai's eyelids flickered.

Laura kissed her lips, fleetingly. 'Let me in, sweetest child.'

She brushed Chai's lips with her own again. The lips fluttered. Laura kissed them again, for longer. Chai's eyes opened in a smile. Laura pressed her lips harder, and Chai pressed back. In the background, Farouk grunted. Laura hoped it was a grunt of satisfaction.

Their kisses became deeper. Laura's tongue slipped between Chai's lips, and Chai's chains rattled as her hands moved, first to hold Laura's hips, and then to pull them closer. Their breasts, hard and pointy, joined by steel, touched lightly; their rubber cocks collided, obscenely rubbing, passing that friction into their bodies. Chai began to relax, her body moving under Laura. Laura lowered her head and licked around the base of her breasts. Chai shivered. Laura kissed and nibbled her way round Chai's collar, neck and ears. Chai sighed and began offering kisses in return.

The kissing game went on. Laura began to feel frustrated; she wanted to take those magenta nipples in her mouth and kiss her way down Chai's delightful little body, to open her sex and plunge her tongue and fingers inside, but all these things were denied by their costume. Perhaps Farouk was getting frustrated too, for he tapped her bottom with the whip again. Laura pushed herself up on her arms, gratified to hear Chai's sigh of sadness that the game had come to an end.

'Roll over. Brown one on top.'

Carefully, for the clamps were still attached, they complied. He pushed Laura's thighs wider apart and back, and then released the right end of her wrist chain, but only to snap it to her left ankle, keeping it short to hold her thigh bent almost double. He released Chai's wrists, and used that chain to fix Laura's right wrist and ankle. Then he pushed Chai down, so their cocks rubbed against each other for a few moments.

'Take her, brown one. Show me how you warriors make love.'

Laura's eyes opened wide. Chai's dildo was so big, and he wanted it up her arse! Chai looked shocked too, and completely at a loss. His hand gripped the black phallus and pushed it down until the tip lay against Laura's tight, oiled knot. Laura raised her legs, opening herself as far as possible, and tried to relax. The rubber pressed, hard and unyielding. Chai hesitated. Laura watched as he took aim with his whip and lashed it down.

'Fuck her!'

Chai bucked and cried out. The phallus jabbed and lodged. Laura moaned and bore down. The whip slashed again, and the phallus punched deeper. Laura sucked in air and tried to kiss Chai in reassurance. The whip descended again, and the head pumped inside. Laura had never felt so stretched before. Chai's buttocks jumped again, and it went in deeper. Tears dripped from her eyes. Laura felt his fingers, and her internal cock grew again. Chai screwed up her face, and she guessed he'd done the same to her.

The whip set their rhythm. Laura gripped Chai as best she could, trying to get her into her own rhythm and save her from more pain. The phallus was plunging now, and Laura's double dildo ground both deep inside and against her thrumming clitty. Pleasure began to overcome the discomfort. Laura was full to bursting, every thrust felt through the thin membranes to her sexual core. Their breasts were rubbing together, the clamps becoming painful. Farouk must have noticed their winces as the clamps dragged back and forth, for he released them, gently this time.

Chai, too, was starting to get pleasure. Her eyes closed. She grunted and moaned as her own dildoes worked. Laura felt hands, and Farouk, his trousers open, presented his cock to her mouth. She opened wide and licked him.

He whispered, 'Get it wet.'

Laura slurped saliva along his length, and then, as she expected, he left her, moving behind Chai. He steadied her hips with one hand and pushed himself into Chai's virgin anus.

Chai froze and cried out. He slapped her cheeks.

Laura tried to pull her head down. 'Relax. Push out.'

But Chai resisted, and he slapped her again and pressed her head flat, ignoring her pleas. Laura bucked her hips, trying to take her friend's mind off the invasion. Farouk jabbed again, and Chai's eyes bulged. Laura kissed her mouth, sucking in her cry. Then he was in and moving, his thrusts repeated through Chai and so stronger, deeper and heavier inside Laura. She felt crushed, engulfed by their crouching bodies. Her mouth opened, sucking in breath, gasping. Chai's tears fell on her cheeks. She kissed Chai's unbelieving lips and chin.

Gradually, the younger girl became accustomed to the novel experience, and her face relaxed. Her breath rasped excitedly with Laura's, and perspiration replaced the tears. Laura felt every jab of the rubber cocks in her body, and the bouncing cock between her belly and Chai's. Chai's rings rubbed against Laura's swollen mounds. Laura laughed, cried and howled as orgasm took her. For a few moments her limbs flopped, and she became an inert receptacle. Perhaps it was her relaxed body taking the pressure off Chai, but the lovely young girl began to come too, her muscles rigid, triggering Farouk's orgasm. He arched his back and buried the spitting head of his penis deep in Chai's super-stimulated rectum. They collapsed, pinning Laura.

After only a few moments Farouk withdrew, dragging a

204

long, sad sigh from Chai. He unlocked their chains and deflated their ersatz gonads. Laura closed her eyes with relief. Chai rolled off, and the three lay exhausted in a heap while Laura began to plan her escape. After a while she whispered into her master's ear.

'Master, I need to use the toilet.'

He muttered and rolled over for a set of keys, handing her a small brass key. She took it, and he waved her towards the bathroom door. As Laura extricated herself, Farouk slurred his request for Chai to clean his shrunken cock with her sweet, pure mouth. Laura slipped away to unburden herself of the codpiece. When she returned, walking normally again, she found him once more erect. Chai knelt across his thighs, sucking as he drank deep draughts of champagne and smoked his hookah. Laura's nostrils twitched at the aroma rising from the pipe; hashish. She curled up beside him and began to lick and nibble his nipples and belly. He was getting quietly, deeply stoned.

Chai sucked and wanked him, her little hand delving under his thighs to play with his anus and balls. Laura mimicked wetting her finger. Chai smiled in recognition and proceeded to insert a digit inside. Laura made a stroking gesture, and Chai nodded. His breath became harsh as that finger stimulated his hidden gland. Laura took the empty glass from his almost lifeless fingers. Sucking deeply on his pipe, he pumped his sperm into Chai's throat and passed out.

Laura slid away and looked round the room, seeking watching cameras. None were apparent. Silently, she began to pull down and knot together wall drapes until she had enough to get her to the ground. Chai looked on, uncomprehending. Laura secured one end of her improvised rope to a ring on a pillar and fed the rest out of the unbarred window. Chai caught on.

Laura went over and whispered. 'I've got to go, sweetheart.'

Chai kissed her. 'I won't tell. Good luck.'

'Thanks. Be good.'

Summoning all her energy and will, Laura went out on to the balcony and tossed the rope out. It fell outside and clear of the outer wall. Laura gripped the drape-rope and took a very deep breath. She smiled once at Chai, confirmed that the Prince was still unconscious, and began to let herself to the ground.

Outside, the night was cool and quiet. She concentrated only on shinning down the improvised rope and wondering just how silly she must look, with her naked arse white and sticking out. When she came level with the top of the outer wall, about halfway, she looked down for the first time. The rope disappeared into shadow. She looked up at the sky. The moon itself was hidden, but there was bright starlight. A good night for escaping. A twig brushed her leg, making her tense, then her foot hit the ground. She stood still on terra firma for a few moments, getting her breath. She looked up. Chai's face looked down. She waved and began to pull the rope back up. Laura waved her thanks, worrying about the little Thai. Removing the rope would buy Laura a bit of time, but Chai would catch it for assisting her escape.

Laura turned away and began to move downhill when a thought struck her. They were bound to search the easy way first. She found a gully and clambered uphill, into the shadows.

'Laura!'

The whispered call brought her to a frozen stop, her heart beating loudly. It couldn't be, not here.

'It's me, Adam. Up here.'

It was! She looked up and right. His teeth and eyes gleamed from just six feet away.

'Three yards left, you'll find a path up.'

She found the goat track and crept as quietly as possible up five stones making a rough sort of stairway. At the top, his hand came out of a pool of shadow and drew her in to a sort of cave formed by a camouflage sheet.

'Welcome to my den.' He kissed her.

'How did you get here?'

'I'll tell you later.' He scrabbled in a bag. 'Put these on

and we'll get moving. I've got transport a couple of miles away.'

Laura took a black sweatshirt and combat trousers and shuffled her way into the warm, rather more discreet clothing.

Adam started removing her sandals. 'Your trainers, madam.'

Laura took her shoes gratefully; miles of walking over rocks in flimsy flat sandals had not appealed. He shoved a woolly hat over her head and smeared something black and greasy on her face and hands.

'That'll make you harder to spot.' He dismantled his hideaway and bundled it into his rucksack. 'Let's go. I'll lead.'

Like a shadow, he moved away into another gully. Laura followed, conscious of the noise she made picking her way among the loose stones and dry, prickly bushes. For a while they climbed until, just below a ridge, he turned sharply and led her round a boulder and over the rim.

A few feet down the other side, he stopped. 'We're out of direct sight now. Want a drink?'

'Please.' Laura was puffing with the sudden exertion. 'Christ, I thought I was fit.'

'You've had a hard night, even before you let yourself out of the window.'

Laura was horrified. 'You were watching?'

'Mm, and very nice it was too. I'd like to have joined in.'

'How long have you been here?'

'Since this afternoon. I spent ages working out why I shouldn't go through the only unbarred window. It was too easy. I was just coming up when I saw you go in.'

'How d'you find me?'

'Jack. He's working on the Count's whereabouts. You fit?'

Laura nodded, and they moved off into the night, away from Farouk's harem. On the way downhill, Laura fretted over Chai and what would happen to her when they found Laura gone. After a while she gave up, too tired to think. As dawn came, Laura was put to bed in a villa by the sea.

* * *

Adam slipped the automatic pistol into a shoulder-holster. 'Just in case, although I think we're clear now. We've got seats on a plane at four. Geneva, then Bordeaux.'

Laura wiped her lips with a napkin. 'Why Bordeaux?'

'Your Jack has come up with an address. He'll meet us there, with some fresh clothes.'

'Jack? You've met Jack?' Laura was sure she'd never mentioned him to Adam, but she was relieved to have some more help.

Laura suddenly felt guilty. She had hardly given a moment's thought to Adam since her arrival in Spain. He must have been frantic, and what had Farouk's heavies done to him? Laura reached for his hand.

'Sweetheart, I'm sorry. I've been so wrapped up in my own adventures, I haven't even asked you what happened in Leila's flat.'

Adam stared out of the window for a moment, then turned back, smiling, trying to play things down. 'Not a lot, really. After you and Leila left, I sorted myself and Camilla out with a drink and then these three armed gorillas burst in. One took Camilla out of the room while I was told to sit down and shut up. A few minutes later, Leila came in. She told me they'd taken you hostage, as an insurance against me causing problems for her friends – not that she told me who her friends were.'

He took a cigarette from Laura. She lit one too.

'Then I felt a needle in the back of my neck and I passed out, drugged. I woke up in my car, in a train going through the Channel Tunnel. I had my wallet but my notebook had gone. When I got home, I found they'd wiped my computer and stolen every paper about the Count they could find. Your flat had been raided too. I'm afraid your computer got the same treatment.'

Laura sighed; a year's work down the drain.

'Anyway, to cut a long story short, your friend Penny rang up asking after you, and from there I got to Jack, and from Jack to Farouk. Jack seems to be able to find anybody, anywhere. What does he do?'

'I don't really know, except he's somehow tied up with

208

the CIA and Interpol – that's where he gets all his information – investigating major drug dealers and slave traffickers.'

Adam nodded absently, as if his mind was racing ahead. 'What I'd like to understand is the tie-up between Farouk and the Count.'

Laura remembered her few minutes alone in Farouk's office. 'I read something very interesting. A diary for 1877, and I saw a portrait of the Count and his coat of arms – that chained heart over crossed whips thing we saw in Paris. The diary was either a satire, or frightening. Like he was like Dracula, but instead of drinking blood he used virgin girls' sexual essence to stay immortal.'

Adam started to laugh. Laura dared him with a look. His eyes widened. 'You're serious, aren't you.'

'Absolutely. Unless it was some kind of sick fantasy, he described the seduction of a young girl, how he made her have stronger and stronger orgasms, and how those orgasms rejuvenated him. Eventually, she died of exhaustion and pleasure.'

Adam absorbed the new information. 'There is no record of the first Count's death. There are some records of a series of marriages, and reports that his wives died young. He earned the reputation of a Bluebeard, and eventually none of the nobles would let their daughters marry him, though nothing was ever proved.'

Laura felt suddenly nervous, thinking the unthinkable. Adam put his hand on her shoulder. 'He can't be a vampire, Laura. They don't exist – legends – like werewolves and the yeti.'

Laura smiled sardonically. 'That's what they always say in the movies.'

Fifteen

Laura gazed at the château while Adam rang the bell. This was it, the moment they had been working towards for what seemed to have been a very long time. Laura ran over her mental checklist: don't panic, be ready for anything, don't forget the man might be innocent, play the slave and let Adam do the talking, get Mary and Philippe alone at the first opportunity, don't panic. She tugged at her plain blue skirt and white blouse, hoping that the correct, demure message would be conveyed. Mind, all this might be wrecked if Farouk had already put the Count on his guard against them. Farouk was the unknown factor; they still had no idea what the relationship really was.

Jack had not made any concrete progress on that front, despite the revelation of the Count's address. All he could find was rumour, hints of a secret society worshipping Comte du Bantonne as a mythical figure. They believed that by following the Count's methods, as read in three surviving accounts, they could achieve a transcendental state of sexual freedom. Farouk was one such believer. Laura was sure that Leila was not. Leila could not keep secrets from her lovers, and Laura had spent a long time with her. As far as could be determined, Farouk and his friends had no idea that a Comte du Bantonne still lived, but there was a chance . . .

The great door opened and a woman's face peered out, forties, hair in a tight bun, high cheeks and oriental eyes.

'Can I help you?' she asked in French.

Adam produced the note from Philippe they'd found in

Mary's flat and replied in clumsy French. 'Is this the home of Philippe du Bantonne? He said we could call if we were in the area.'

The woman eyed the note suspiciously and then grudgingly invited them in, showing them into a reception room. Laura took up position a few feet behind Adam, unobtrusively sizing up the other woman. She looked just like the dominant, protective housekeeper she played; statuesque, starched blouse, razor-sharp pleats in her long black skirt, sensible shoes, large breasts and a softness to her full, red lips that hinted at strong passion.

'If you would like to wait here, I will inform the young master you are here. Who shall I say wishes to see him?'

This was a question Laura had anticipated. Philippe didn't know Adam from, well, Adam. Adam gave the agreed answer.

'This is Laura Jenkins, Philippe's neighbour.' Laura nodded and smiled pleasantly. The woman barely acknowledged the attempt to establish contact. 'And I am Adam Hardcastle, Laura's master. Philippe may remember me – we once met at a family gathering.'

The woman sniffed, evidently disbelieving, and shut the door firmly behind her as she left.

Adam waited until her footsteps faded and then turned, suppressing a laugh. 'Is she for real?'

Laura looked round the ornate, plush room, not finding the woman a joking matter. 'In my experience, she is not to be underestimated. She serves only her master, the Count. Treat her with respect, Adam. She probably knows more about all this than anyone.'

'Sorry. Nervous.' They both were. He walked over to the picture above the fireplace. Laura looked out of the windows. She took in the line of dark trees and spoke her thoughts out loud. 'I wonder if Mary's all right?'

Adam came over and wrapped his arms round her shoulders. 'Now we're here, she is.' He kissed her cheek. 'You really love her, don't you?' Laura nodded. 'Maybe I will too. I'm looking forward to seeing her.'

The woman returned. 'Comte Henri and his heir

212

welcome you to their home. They invite you to join them for dinner tonight and apologise for their enforced absence until then.'

Laura wondered if they were being played with, whether Comte Henri already knew who they were but had decided to trap them with a false sense of security.

Adam answered. 'We would be honoured, madame. I'll get our bags from the car.'

Adam left, leaving Laura alone with the housekeeper. They stood warily watching each other for a few moments.

The woman broke the silence in awkward English. 'You are a friend of Mary?'

Laura answered in fluent French, attempting to break the ice. 'Oui, madame. I am her neighbour and we go to the same college.'

'She is a very nice girl. We have become friends.'

'Then I hope we can become friends too.' Laura held out her hand. The older woman shook it with surprising warmth and without a trace of deeper suspicion, giving Laura hope that Farouk had not sent a message because he really did not know that a Comte Henri still lived.

'My name is Beatrice, chatelaine of the house. Rooms are being prepared for you.' She caught the look in Laura's eyes as she spotted the plural. 'The master is somewhat old-fashioned in such matters. If you were man and wife, you would be allowed to share, if your master desired it.'

Laura raised her eyebrows; no late-night hanky-panky then. 'That's all right by me.'

To underline the message, Beatrice added, 'Your room will be in the north wing, near Mary's. Your friend will be in the east wing.'

Adam returned. Beatrice addressed them both. 'I will show Mademoiselle Jenkins to her room. A maid will escort Monsieur Hardcastle. The master prefers that you wear the costumes provided for dinner and begs you to forgive his little eccentricities.'

As the small procession reached the top of the stairs, an old man appeared in front of them. Laura nearly jumped out of her skin; it was the man from the portrait.

'Welcome to my home,' he said in English.

He held out his hand, first to Adam. Laura took her first look at the man she now knew as her enemy. His appearance was contradictory; he had the white hair and stooped shoulders of a man well over eighty, and a face with that mix of wrinkles and substance of someone in his early sixties. When he shook her hand, Laura felt strength but saw liver spots and almost transparent skin. As he raised his head from a formal bow, she found herself looking into eyes of arctic blue, absolutely clear and malevolently cold for the briefest instant. Spicules of ice, needle-sharp, probed her, seeking her purpose. Laura blinked deliberately, fighting back just in time to break the link. Then he smiled, and the eyes thawed.

'And you must be Laura. You are beautiful, Laura, an English rose. Alas, you are no longer a maiden.'

Laura's smile of gratitude for the compliment was stillborn. He had thrown down a challenge. For a moment she considered retaliating, but thought better of it; if his suspicions had been aroused by Farouk, fighting back might confirm them. She bowed.

'Thank you, sir, for welcoming surprise guests.'

'The more the merrier, I always say. See you at dinner.' And he was gone with amazing speed and agility.

Laura watched him go, unable to make up her mind about him. The meeting had been too brief, and his mild animosity perhaps understandable, given that she and Adam had turned up out of the blue without his personal invitation. He could have turned them away, or worse, but he had not. Well, the game was afoot and there was no going back.

In the event, Laura still had not seen Mary by the time she had bathed. According to Beatrice, Mary was temporarily indisposed, and she wasn't to be disturbed in case her recovery was delayed. Laura was amused by the dissembling; everyone seemed to be too busy to welcome them.

She roughly towelled her hair dry. The blue hair dye was

fading slowly, and she wondered if it was time to try to cover it with a more natural colour; she had a new hair colour in her bag. Laura decided against; the streaks might not disappear and the blue did somehow go with the steel rings, though she wished there'd been time to swap them back to gold. She unwrapped the bath sheet and looked at herself. The new rings still looked odd, but their greater size made them much more arousing; her nipples would not go soft, and her clitty throbbed, keeping her juicy and hot. Adam had removed the telltale disc bearing the coat of arms, but he liked the chain and it didn't get in the way. The sight of her long, bright red clitty, held out by the bar, reminded Laura to slip on a pair of loose knickers in case she was interrupted by Beatrice or the maid. Revealing all her piercings might reveal Laura's encounter with Farouk, if they knew of him and his particular style.

She was looking for her underwear when she heard a knock at the door. Before she could even open her mouth, the chatelaine walked in, followed by a young woman carrying dresses and shoes.

'Good, you're ready to be dressed.' Beatrice cut across Laura's instinctive protest while the maid laid the dresses down and left. 'It's a pity about your hair, but that can't be helped, unless I can find a suitable wig. Now, get rid of that towel.'

Laura tried to penetrate the cheerfully businesslike stream. 'If it's all right with you, I can dress myself.'

'Oh, no, my dear, we can't have that; the master wouldn't hear of it. It's my task to dress you as he wishes. Anyway, I doubt you're familiar with this sort of dress.' She held up a long pale blue satin dress of nineteenth-century vintage. Over the maid's arm hung a corset. 'No zips and Velcro, young lady; this is all hooks, eyes and laces. Anyway, I might have to make some alterations – as we haven't had time to measure you properly.'

Laura was still wrapped in her towel. Beatrice just looked, eyebrows raised. Reluctantly, Laura let the towel drop. Beatrice kept one eyebrow raised as she looked her up and down, taking in Laura's figure and rings. She shook her head slowly, genuinely surprised by what she saw. Laura's doubts about Farouk were diminished by the look in her eyes; if Beatrice had never heard of Comte Henri's secret admirers, then Laura doubted Comte Henri knew either.

'London fashions have changed much since I last visited. I suppose the girls in Paris are much the same, no?'

Laura grinned, touched by the older woman's obvious surprise. 'Yes, and tattoos are very in as well.'

'Mary is not a follower of fashion?'

'No. She wouldn't be seen dead with dyed hair and rings.'

Beatrice smiled smugly but said nothing, leaving Laura with the impression that Mary had somehow changed.

Beatrice spoke to herself as she picked up the corset. 'I wonder what Comte Henri would think if he saw you like this, or Philippe?'

Or Mary. Laura kept her own smug smile to herself. Philippe, like Mary, might be surprised at recent developments, but they had been prepared. Laura looked at the approaching corset with interest. She rather liked the tight supported elegance of well-made stays; her waist was not naturally narrow, nor her bust and bum all that pronounced, so a basque always improved her figure. Beatrice began lacing the corset up.

'Ooh, that's very tight.'

'And your figure needs it, young lady.' Beatrice tugged the laces even tighter and tied them off. 'Have a look. It suits you.'

Laura turned to face the mirror and admired her new hourglass figure. Her small breasts looked twice their normal size, blossoming over the top of the little cups, and her waist was nipped in more sharply than ever before, making her bottom bulge high and round. Once in the floor-length, low-cut bustle, and with her hair dried and brushed as close to neat as the spiky cut allowed, Laura felt a foot taller and very elegant, if rather too upright and narrow to eat very much. She was getting pretty hungry. She'd have to be careful not to drink too much tonight.

Together they fashioned her make-up to suit both hair and dress with the toned-down punk look, adding a modest amount of jewellery round her neck and hanging simple stones to her earrings. Laura thought she looked quite *fin de siècle* and was quite happy with her appearance when she went down to the reception room to meet the others before dinner.

Adam stood at the window breathing in the warm, scented evening air. He turned. Laura giggled. He was attired in a buff tailed jacket, white open-necked shirt, tight buff breeches and soft riding boots.

'My God, Mr Darcy!'

He bowed theatrically. Laura curtsied in return, as best she could remember, then went up to him. They kissed.

'You look incredible,' he whispered.

Laura blushed, unused to heartfelt compliments of late.

He turned towards a huge tray of glasses and decanters. 'In the absence of the staff – all busy dressing the inmates – I am empowered to offer you an apéritif. What would you like?'

'Something very small. This corset's murder.'

He poured her a small dry sherry. 'Have you seen Mary yet?'

She shook her head. 'But I don't think they know about Farouk. Any sight of Philippe, or anything?'

'Not a sausage.'

The door opened. Philippe, looking taller and even more handsome than ever, entered. 'Laura, how wonderful to see you!'

Laura embraced him. 'Phil, you're looking great.' He, too, wore breeches, with a green tail-coat and very loose and frilly shirt.

He broke away and held out his hand to Adam. 'So you must be Adam Hardcastle. Have we really met before?'

'You came to my father's funeral, about ten years ago.'

'Oh, yes, I remember, vaguely.'

Adam reassured him. 'Not surprising really – you were, what, ten? I can't say I've much memory of it either –'

He was interrupted by two more arrivals, Comte Henri

217

and Mary together. Laura greeted her with a hug while coming to terms with the changes in her appearance and bearing. Gone was the awkward, well-built, self-conscious, embarrassed girl. In her place stood a refined, elegant, curvaceous young woman with perfect, understated make-up, controlled coiffure and expanses of bare skin. Her breasts threatened to spill from the daringly low-cut full-length emerald-green dress at any moment, a situation she would never have allowed just a few weeks before. As they hugged, Laura noticed the lack of perfume overlaying Mary's natural, soft scent. Big gold earrings, dripping with emeralds, surprised her. Mary used to be so firm in her refusal to tamper with her body in any way.

'Oh, Laura, it's so good to see you. I've missed you so much.'

Laura stood back, holding both Mary's hands. 'I've been missing you too. You're looking great.'

Mary blushed a little and smiled coyly. 'Who's the friend?'

'Adam.' Laura introduced them.

Adam took Mary's hand and kissed it. 'So this is Mary. I've heard a lot about you.'

The maid Laura had seen earlier offered Mary a glass of anise. Mary took it. 'Thank you, Yvette.'

Yvette's eyes were on Philippe, barely flicking to Mary as she was acknowledged. Laura detected jealousy. Yvette must have something going with Philippe.

Comte Henri, having finished a hushed conversation with Beatrice, came over. He was dressed in the same style as Philippe and Adam, but more formal, with waistcoat, sash and buckled shoes.

He embraced all four with his warm welcome, his mouth smiling but his eyes, Laura thought, ever watchful.

'What pleasure an old man can find in seeing young friends reunited. Come, let us eat.' He smiled at Laura. 'May I escort you to the table?'

Laura remembered a snippet of etiquette and offered him her arm. 'I would be honoured, sir.'

She felt a thrill of energy, like a soft electric shock. She glanced at him. His mouth smiled, but his eyes tried to probe her again. Laura looked away quickly, and the tingling faded. Laura dreaded the moment he caught her off-guard, for then he would break through. She tried not to shiver, but suspected he picked up the vibrations none the less.

Comte Henri, of course, sat at the head of the table, with Mary on his right and Laura on his left. Laura's feeling of exposure was reduced by Adam's presence at her side, but for the first two courses – chilled soup and oysters in champagne – it did not matter; the conversation was general and amicable. Only when the meat course arrived did the chat become more pointed.

'Tell me, Adam, what in your opinion makes for a good wife?' Comte Henri enquired lightly.

Assuming the offhand manner of the public school educated, Adam responded after a mere moment's thought. 'Oh, she should be beautiful, dutiful and demure – the last only in public,' he added with a wicked grin.

The old man turned to Laura. 'Do you agree with that, my dear?'

Laura summoned up all her enthusiasm for the part she had to play. 'Yes, sir. A woman must make every attempt to be attractive, always, and serve her master's will with all her being.'

'So this modern talk about equal rights for women is not for you?'

Laura had often thought about this difficult question. 'I know of women who can be both equal at work and serve their master at home. It is no longer possible for most women to stay at home.'

Comte Henri seemed quite shocked. He shook his head sadly. 'I did not realise how much has changed.' He sipped his wine. 'Is this true, Adam?'

'I'm afraid it is, sir. When Laura goes off to college, she is her own woman. At home she will do anything to satisfy me.'

The old man's eyes twinkled. 'Anything?' Adam nodded, smiling. 'So if it pleased you that she bare her breasts, she would do so without hesitation?'

219

'Of course.' Anticipation set Laura's body thrumming into renewed life.

'And would it please you now?'

'It would indeed.'

Adam looked at Laura. She felt all eyes on her. She swallowed and wiped her lips with her napkin. The test had come. Looking directly at Mary, Laura undid the two tiny buttons at the front of her dress, folded back the satin and scooped her breasts up and out. Mary blushed, but her eyes held a question as she saw the new rings. Laura's nipples swelled. The rings moved gently. Goosebumps shivered across her shoulders and up the back of her neck

Comte Henri admired the view for a moment. 'What a delightful sight, but she must not be alone in this display. Mary?'

Mary's blush deepened, spreading down her neck. Her fingers shook as she brought up her fingers. Unlike Laura, her dress was not equipped with any ready opening, and she had to lift her breasts out from their barely adequate covering. Laura suppressed her surprise. Mary's nipples stood long and proud, with heavy gold hoops linked by a golden chain.

Comte Henri sighed with pleasure and turned back to Laura. 'You see, Laura? Mary shares our views.' He raised his glass. 'To beautiful women.'

The men drank. Laura felt used, a pretext to expose the submissiveness she had long suspected in Mary, and reveal those shocking rings.

Their host put his glass down. 'But I don't think that only our guests should go bare-breasted. Yvette, Beatrice, reveal yourselves.'

Laura looked to where the maid and her mistress stood waiting to serve the next course. Without a flicker, Yvette opened her bodice and let her breasts spill out, violet-tipped, full and soft. Beatrice's back stiffened, as if insulted, but she unbuttoned her dress to reveal melon-round mounds tipped with dark, gold-ringed nubs.

Hard though it was to concentrate on the food, Laura resumed her meal. Dampness gathered between her legs as

220

the combined effects of three other pairs of gorgeous breasts and the eyes of three men worked on her mind. The dessert came, a chocolate soufflé, luxuriously rich and smooth. Laura tucked in. When the cognac came out, their host snapped his fingers.

'Yvette?' Comte Henri called. 'Please bring some ice and take a seat. Beatrice, bring the jewellery box and join us.'

The two women took their places, looking uncomfortable.

Comte Henri explained. 'A little entertainment, gentlemen, and a little exhibition of the ladies' sense of duty.' He sipped his cognac appreciatively. 'That is, of course, if Adam doesn't mind me directing Laura?'

Adam bowed. 'Of course not, sir.'

Comte Henri bowed in return. 'Thank you. Ladies, we would like to see the full beauty of your breasts. Please make your nipples hard.'

All four women looked at each other briefly, and then, led by Laura and Beatrice, raised their hands. Laura smiled reassuringly at Mary, and took each nipple between finger and thumb, giving her a lead. She felt rather strange, almost detached. Her fingers rolled the firm nubs, pinching and tugging them out. Opposite, Mary worked with less confidence but no less response. Her nipples thickened and darkened as the blood pumped in. Her areolae swelled, bumps standing out, turning a deeper pink. Laura glanced down. Her new steel rings were subtly adding to the extension with their weight. Mary's chain swung, their breathing grew rapid.

Softly, Comte Henri interrupted. 'If you would take some ice, ladies.'

Adam passed the bowl to Laura. She took two cubes. In their turn, Mary, Beatrice and Yvette followed suit. The cubes were very cold on Laura's fingers. This was something she had never done for herself, but she had experienced ice on her nipples before. She took a deep breath and put them to her breasts. Her eyes closed as the cold spread, numbing but contracting the soft tissue, leaving her nubs wet, slippy and incredibly sensitive.

Round and round the ice slid, and the numbness became a fire, nipping at the throbbing, excited nerve-endings.

After what seemed like an age, Comte Henri let them stop. 'Philippe, be so kind as to open the box and pass it round. Ladies, apply what you find in the box to your breasts.'

The box went first to Mary. Her eyes opened in horror. She produced two silver devices. The box was passed to Laura, and she was able to see why Mary was so shocked. Laura took two of the narrow, sprung, silver clothes pegs with teeth around the notches. Mary was waiting for her lead. Laura left one peg on the table and took her right breast in her palm. With her right hand she opened the jaws. The spring was strong, and she knew this was going to hurt. That foreknowledge produced a remarkable effect. Her pussy poured, her clitty jumped and her breasts trembled, swollen hard. Taking a deep breath, she presented the peg to her tingling nub and let the jaws slowly shut.

Her eyes closed as the spring gripped and squeezed. Thick, dark darts stabbed through her breast. She felt her pussy clench and knew she was making a wet patch on her chair. Her eyes opened. Mary was trying to copy her. Laura took the other peg and made the inevitable pain start again. She shivered and gasped. Mary moaned loudly, as did Yvette. The teeth seemed to tug, as though the pegs were twisting themselves. Laura closed her eyes again, aware that her boobies were shaking. She reached for her cognac and sipped, the fiery spirit briefly diverting her attention. A kind of heat throbbed inside, a line of direct communication opened between nipples and clitty. She spread her thighs to stop herself squeezing herself to orgasm.

Comte Henri waited until all eight nipples were undergoing the devilish torture. 'Well, gentlemen, what do you think?'

Adam took Laura's hand and gave it a little squeeze. 'Very nice. If I didn't know better, I'd say Laura was just about to come.' He looked into her eyes. 'In fact, I'm sure she is.'

She hissed under her breath. 'You bastard.'

Philippe mumbled and flustered his reaction. Laura sympathised with his confusion and embarrassment, though she suspected his cock was just as hard as Adam's was.

Comte Henri clapped his hands with glee. 'What do you think? Should we gentlemen have some fun too?'

Adam agreed. Philippe looked even more uncomfortable.

Father reproved son. 'My dear boy, this is what all my teaching has been about. Enjoyment, the sating of our pleasure. Oh, it is a pity that Mary's maidenhood is not for taking, yet, for I am sure we men feel the need of a tight orifice to furrow.' He started to rise to his feet. 'But we cannot do with the others what cannot be done with Mary. Let us take their bottoms, which at least will relieve Mary of that virginity. Beatrice, please blindfold the young ladies and arrange some lubrication.'

Laura had been keeping her eyes on Mary throughout this speech. Her face registered a mixture of excitement and fear. Laura digested that new information: Mary was still a virgin, except, perhaps, for her mouth. And, judging by their reactions, Philippe and Mary had not yet slept together. So with whom had Mary been having sex – the old man? Beatrice? Both?

The men were on their feet, clearing the table in front of them. Yvette was brought to the top of the table and blindfolded. Laura felt Beatrice's hands on her arms and she stood up. The blindfold was tied, concentrating her senses. The chairs were pushed back. Laura felt a pressure on her shoulders; she leant forward and reached out her hands, seeking Mary's. She took hold of them, trying to reassure her friend. She heard the sound of rustling silk and Mary squeal quietly. She guessed the lubrication was being applied. Laura recalled licking that pale beige-pink knot, and a throb of excitement pulsed between her thighs.

Yvette giggled and sighed, and then Laura's own dress rustled up and over her head. A tongue, that could be Beatrice's, lapped wet and hot. She heard sucking round a cock, and then she felt a hand on her hip.

'Let us begin.' Comte Henri's voice came from in front. He was having Mary, so who was about to thrust his cock up her bum?

Laura felt a hard cock press against her anus. She relaxed, and it stretched inside. She hoped it was Adam. The cock's owner was well controlled, loosening her with slow, circular movements. He bent forward and whispered.

'Does it feel as good as that girl in Spain?'

She smiled. It was Adam. She turned her head and they kissed as he pushed his cock deep, filling her, thrilling her, and crushing her ringed mound into the tabletop. Her piercings rubbed and moved, giving her the friction she craved. Her breasts rubbed hard, the pegs dragging, deepening the sensuous pain. Laura moaned, but listened out for Mary. Mary's hands gripped tight. She cried out, and her nails dug into Laura's palms. The table began to bump as the three men began pounding, every vibration transmitted through the rings into Laura's body. She felt her clitty grow, and the running honey pour down her thighs. Mary gasped. Laura felt Yvette's hips moving in time to her man; Laura's were already doing the same. Finally, she felt Mary moving as well, and she felt able to concentrate on her own pleasure in the knowledge that Mary was getting some too.

The congested mass of Laura's sex began to clamp her muscles. Adam's cock filled her almost as completely as Chai's dildo, but felt much more fulfilling. Adam gripped her hips, and she thrust back at him, head shaking from side to side. She heard Philippe shout as he came, and the vibrations from the end of the table faded. Adam was taking his time in comparison. She heard Comte Henri's grunts coming faster. Adam leant forward again and tore off her blindfold. Laura caught sight of Beatrice, skirt raised and hand plunging deep underneath. Yvette was lying, red-faced and dripping with perspiration. Philippe lay across her back watching his father sodomise his fiancée through eyes green with envy.

She looked up at the old man. His face was cool, but his eyes were on fire, staring down at his cock plunging in and out of Mary's parted buttocks. A tear escaped Mary's blindfold, her mouth was open and gasping. Her hands gripped and relaxed in time with the old man's thrusts. Comte Henri howled. Laura looked up. He thrust violently three times and then collapsed across Mary's back, utterly spent. Beatrice dashed up and took his shoulders to guide him into a chair. He was virtually unconscious, his arms dangling, head floppy.

With that crisis past, Adam reached round and pulled Laura to him, cupping her breasts. He thrust harder now. One hand slipped down, delving under her hips, locating her swollen, throbbing, pouring pussy. His cock drove deeper and harder. He gently released the peg from her left nipple, and Laura felt a soufflé of unctuous, chocolate pleasure start to rise in her womb. He stroked her clitty gently, the soufflé expanded, bursting with warm, pulsing energy. He removed the second peg, and his fingers oozed inside her pussy. Laura clutched at his cock, arching her back, gripping tight as he pumped out his seed. The soufflé burst, filling her whole body with warm, heavy, indulgent gratification.

Mary grasped Laura's fingers nervously. Her nipples, distended, squeezed by the pegs and still tender from the new rings, chafed against the tabletop. Down below, she experienced the novel feeling of her ringed jewel against a hard surface. Her vulva squashed down inside the little suede pouch temporarily serving as a chastity belt. It was soaking wet with the juices that had been flowing from her like syrup since the order to bare her breasts. Now it clutched like a sucking mouth. She felt the wetness of a tongue, and then the touch of fingers between her buttocks. Who was it going to be? Philippe, oh please let it be Philippe. To feel him, for him to know her body, that's all she asked. Hands held her hips; hard and bony. Her heart sank. It was his father, again.

She felt the tip of his cock press against her rose. He pushed, but despite the stretching rods he could not enter. One hand left her hip, and fingers began to press round the rim of her rose. The cock-head pressed again, and fingers reached under her belly. She groaned as the one exposed ring was touched. She felt as if her jewel were being pulled out. Her hips bucked involuntarily, her rose relaxed and he gained a foothold. She felt as if an elephant had filled her with its trunk. Under the blindfold, her eyes popped wide. The cock pressed on slowly, acquainting her with the stretching, unfamiliar feeling. The end was in. Her rose contracted somewhat around the thinner stem. He pushed on and on, so big and long she thought it would reach all the way to her heart.

But, apart from the stretching, it didn't hurt. Even more surprising, Mary discovered that she was enjoying the whole experience, the act of penetration and the knowledge that she would soon be filled with his semen. Her jewel throbbed, her vulva thickened and her poor boobs loved every rubbing, fricative impulse. Mary let her hips do what came naturally. They drove back at him, taking him all the way. His thrusts became rapid; she felt her belly bump against the table. Her head came up for air, tossing with joy. She felt almost complete, doing what she had been wanting to do for so very long; riding a cock, any cock. Her orgasm began to build; she now recognised the signs. His balls bumped against her pouched sex, his fingers tight on her hips. Suddenly he was pumping, faster, jerky. Stars expanded in her head, ready to burst, his semen pulsed and splashed. She cried out with frustration.

The old man's body slumped over her back, pinning her still-writhing body. Mary shed a tear. In those last seconds, when all the signs had been so good, the ultimate pleasure had been stolen from her. All the symptoms of success were present – the released tension, the gentle softening – but something had been taken away in the moment of his orgasm, and the starburst had flopped, a damp squib. She felt his body being pulled away, and when Laura's hands clutched then went limp, Mary slowly clambered upright and removed the blindfold. She smoothed her dress down as she looked round.

Le Comte was collapsed in a chair, his eyes closed, face flushed but lips unnaturally pale. Beatrice knelt at his feet, washing his shrunken penis. Yvette was leaving the room, walking stiffly. Philippe, his cock flaccid but shining with sex, sat smiling idiotically. Laura was at Adam's feet, sucking his cock, slurping, licking him clean. Mary looked at Philippe again. He looked up, ashamed, questioning, begging for her forgiveness. Mary glanced again at his cock, and glanced at Beatrice, who nodded. Mary dropped to her knees, and as she felt his father's semen leak from her body, she began to clean Philippe's shrinking, slimy, wonderful cock with her lips and tongue.

She shoved the knowledge that it had been inside Yvette to the back of her mind. She wanted him, wanted to show her love. He tasted strong. His sticky pubic hair brushed her nose. His hands stroked her head. She mumbled her love into his body. He began to thicken again. She wanted him hard, wanted him inside her, in the proper place, and now. She needed her pleasure, unspoilt by his father's theft. She heard him moan. Beatrice pulled her away, not roughly, but urgently.

'Stop,' she hissed. 'The master is waking.'

Sixteen

The disordered table was quickly tidied by Yvette, and fresh glasses of cognac handed round. Laura regained her seat, the sticky mess on the back of her thighs penetrating her dress. Adam turned from his conversation with their host.

'Laura, Comte Henri has graciously offered Beatrice's services for the duration of our stay. You could do with a bit of discipline, and I am sure you can assist Beatrice with Mary.'

Laura put down her brandy glass and bowed her head. Good, now I'll get a chance to talk to Mary.

Adam continued. 'Philippe's going to show me just how much fun young Yvette can provide.' He grinned wolfishly.

Laura looked across at Mary. She looked sad. Bastard, thought Laura, he's making us both feel jealous now.

'Before we part for the night, I have an announcement to make.' Laura turned to the speaker. Comte Henri looked pleased with himself. 'The nuptial ceremony will take place the day after tomorrow, at noon.'

Laura looked in turn at Mary and Philippe. Both were completely surprised.

Comte Henri continued: 'Our tradition maintains that neither partner shall engage in any consummated sexual activity between now and then, although they should be maintained in a constant state of arousal. Therefore, I charge you, Adam, and you Beatrice, with the responsibility for ensuring that this tradition is followed.'

Comte Henri reached for Mary's hand.

'And there is a further stipulation. It has always been the custom for the father to open the way for his son. I have already opened two ways, and I am looking forward to removing the burden of your hymen during the first act of the marriage rite.'

Mary flushed, and tears began to gather. Laura sympathised, knowing Mary had promised her virginity to her future husband. All her suspicions seemed confirmed. Comte Henri looked younger now than before his thorough ploughing of Mary's behind; fuller around the shoulders, less lined, more coloured in the face. He was feeding from Mary, and he planned to feed some more. A cold certainty gripped Laura. Unless she and Adam acted now, Mary would never leave this château and Philippe would become a monster like his father. Laura dutifully followed Beatrice and Mary from the dining-room, her heart heavy with foreboding.

Beatrice came early to Laura's room, opening the shutters on a morning bright with the promise of a hot day ahead. Laura looked up hopefully as the older woman leant over. She had spent a wakeful, fretful and frustrating night. Her wrists and ankles had been chained together after the chatelaine had fitted her into a chastity belt, an arrangement guaranteed to arouse her and ensure she could not find fulfilment.

Beatrice unlocked the shackles and belt and took her to the bathroom, before reattaching the chastity belt and dressing her in a long, simple, tight cotton dress. Never once did her eyes leave Laura. Laura responded with pleasant smiles, even as she squatted over the toilet; after all, it was a situation she had been in before, and she needed this woman's trust.

After a glass of orange juice, Beatrice beckoned to her to follow. They went along the corridor to where Mary waited, also chained to her bed. Laura slowly drank in the sight of her naked friend and erstwhile lover. She was spread-eagled. Laura licked her lips and raised an eyebrow as she peered between the defenceless thighs. She

230

remembered an almost translucent pink fullness under a thick dark ginger thatch. Now the lips were thicker, bare and pierced by three gold rings. She had to fight an urgent desire to dive in and drive Mary wild with her mouth and hands.

Beatrice, perhaps sensing her lust, gently shoved Laura to a spot just outside the bathroom door. 'Kneel there, please, hands at the back of your neck.'

Laura watched Mary's toilet proceed with mounting excitement as the whole of Mary's full, firm, generous body was systematically displayed by the older woman. Laura suspected this was deliberate teasing, perhaps even a challenge, as if Beatrice knew they had been lovers. When Mary was dressed identically to Laura, Beatrice bade Laura stand.

'Now we shall go for your morning swim. Mary, lead the way.' Beatrice followed Laura, a crop in one hand and a basket in the other.

As they left the house and crossed the grass towards the lake, Laura tried to divine the significance of the covered wicker basket. It was no way big enough to hold towels, but it looked heavy. And why the crop? Was it just a symbol, or did Beatrice plan to use it? Mary looked happy enough, walking with the exaggerated hip movement the belts provoked. How did Mary cope with it? Every single step sent tremors through her own clitty and swelled her lips with the friction. Laura, her arousal initiated by watching Mary's toilet, felt deeply randy by the time they reached the lake's edge.

Immediately, Mary began to undress. Laura followed suit, hoping the belt would be removed. She wanted desperately to be free to caress herself, and Mary, too, once they were in the water, beyond the older woman's control. Alas, Beatrice showed no sign of getting the keys. Mary took her hand and led her to the water's edge.

'This is a good spot to get in and out. The bed shelves slowly here. It's very deep from about ten feet out.'

The water was cool, still warming up in the sun. As they walked in, holding hands, Beatrice called out a warning.

231

'You must stay in sight all the time, no stopping, and return when I call.'

Laura launched herself into the refreshing water, stretching out into a brisk crawl. Mary matched her until they were fifty yards out, then slowed. Laura slowed too, and they began a breaststoke.

'Laura, I want to apologise.'

'What for?'

'For breaking us up the way I did.'

Laura had almost forgotten in all the adventures since. 'Don't. My fault. I was too pushy. It's forgotten.'

'Why have you come here?'

'To make sure you're all right.'

'Why?'

'Because I love you, and you seem to need a lot of looking after. So does Philippe.'

They turned back the way they had come, keeping away from the shore. As they settled on their new course, Mary asked, 'What do you mean?'

'You're both in the deepest danger.'

Mary stopped in mid-stroke, swallowed a mouthful of water, spluttered and tried to speak. Laura stopped too.

'Danger? What sort of danger?'

'Adam had an older sister. She came here, married, produced Philippe, and died. As far as we can tell, every girl who marries Comte du Bantonne dies very quickly. Oh, and only virgins ever get to marry him.'

Mary looked shocked and fell silent. Beatrice called them back.

Laura set off. 'I'll explain more later.'

Swimming back, Laura began to notice what was happening to the leather belt. It was shrinking in the water, tightening, and now every movement dragged and rubbed, deepening the frustrating arousal. One-handed, Laura tried to loosen it, but it was too tight.

Beatrice came to meet them as they emerged, not with towels but with manacles. Mary offered her hands automatically, and Laura realised this was part of the routine. In turn, she offered her wrists to leather cuffs,

fastened by straps, and linked by a foot or so of chain.
Mary moved towards a particular tree, Laura followed,
looking round. Two bundles of leafy twigs and two of long
grasses lay near the tree.

Mary stopped below a broken branch and held her arms
up. Beatrice took hold of the chain and tossed it over the
branch. Mary stood comfortably on her feet. She turned to
Laura.

'Now you. Face Mary.'

Laura obeyed, adopting the same pose. As she was
shorter, her chain could not reach the branch. Beatrice,
revealing remarkable strength, just picked her up by the
waist and hoisted her until the chain was hooked
satisfactorily. Laura dangled, her toes brushing the grassy
ground, all her weight on her shoulders. Beatrice produced
a broad belt, took Laura's weight with one shoulder, and
fastened the belt round both girls' waists, crushing them
together, Laura's breasts just above Mary's, their faces
level. Now Laura's weight was transferred on to Mary.

Laura felt Mary's nipples crushing into her, and the
slight swell of her stomach against her pubis. Automatically, they rubbed together, wet skin warming and
squeaky. Laura felt Mary's breath against her cheek and
wanted to kiss her full lips. She heard Beatrice moving
beside her, a swishing, and then a blaze of twigs exploded
across her shoulders.

She looked round, shocked. The chatelaine held a
bundle of twigs in each hand. Her left arm drew back, and
the twigs fluttered and snapped across Mary's back. Mary
closed her eyes and sucked in her breath. Laura jerked as
the birch slashed the water from her middle back, feeling
both heat and friction. Her nipples, cooled hard by the
lake, warmed and thickened. She felt her sex flood. Mary
jerked into her, and the delicious warmth and friction
spread. It was like being rubbed in a coarse electric
blanket.

The gentle beating proceeded, covering her arms, legs,
bottom, flanks, the outside curve of her flattened breasts.
They swung together, gasping now, their hips trying to

gain a foothold, desperate to get direct friction between their pussies. Now Laura understood why Mary had been so happy to go swimming. It was a glorious sensation, being dried by the birch. Her back felt hot to the touch, ticklish, deeply sensitive. Her thighs rubbed together, her ringed nipples throbbed, aching. She buried her face in Mary's neck and wished they could make love while Beatrice carried on.

Suddenly, the birching ceased. Laura felt the belt loosen. Beatrice turned her round, and then Mary, until their shoulders rubbed together. Laura was hoisted again, so her bum rested somewhat on Mary's. Laura and Mary squirmed together, their reddened, hot, dry flesh squashed together. All three were breathing deeply. Beatrice had a wild, hot look in her eyes. She unlocked Laura's chastity belt, but not Mary's. Beatrice picked up the bundles of grass. The grasses were long, almost dried to straw by the sun, with fully developed seed heads, soft and hairy.

She smiled at Laura, a glint in her eye. 'Mary has been used to the twigs all over, but now she has her rings, like you. The birch might catch in the rings, but this will take longer.'

She drew back her arm and lashed the soft spray across Laura's thighs. A light tingle. Her arm came back. More scratchy now, and her skin pinkened. The bundle worked down Laura's legs and across her feet, ticklish like gnat bites that faded quickly, leaving behind a heat growing deep inside.

With the grass bundles, Beatrice had to deal with each girl in turn, so stretching out the whipping dry. When she turned her attention to Mary, Laura heard her gasps and moans, and it was Mary's body that flexed and twisted. In these intervals, Laura found herself missing the subtle, tingling pain. She was wet between the legs, so wet she imagined she was dripping. Beatrice returned and whip-dried her belly and breasts. Laura crooned as the fraying grasses flogged her tight-stretched mounds and hard nipples. The grasses caught the rings and tugged slightly. It was like a thousand tiny bites. She trembled, rings shaking, every pore wide awake and feeling the fresh air anew. Her loins began to boil, and as her legs thrashed from side to side she was sure she felt her juices flowing down over her thighs.

'Oh, please,' Laura heard herself plead as Beatrice moved away. She wanted the exquisite, elegant torture to go on and on for ever. It was too much and not enough, so light and so dense. She panted as she heard Mary get the same treatment, and felt her friend buck and swing. Just as her internal fires damped down, Beatrice appeared before her once more, holding the bundle down, lined up with Laura's streaming, steaming pussy.

She smiled. 'Shall I?'

Her desperate need for completion and the deep heat of pleasure-pain made her wanton. Laura nodded.

'Ask properly, then.'

Laura licked her swollen, dry lips and tried to frame the appropriate, shaming response. 'Please, mistress, dry my pussy.'

'Open your legs so I can do it properly.'

Laura forced her legs wide until her toes could barely feel the ground, closed her eyes and let her head fall back on Mary's shoulder.

'Ahh, eee.'

The grasses scratched and slithered and slapped into her molten, open slit, flicking the honey, stinging the delicate tissues. Laura's back arched, pushing her pussy out, opening her swelling, tingling lips. The light scourge came again, snapping, slicing into the inner surfaces. Laura squealed as her hips chased the escaping wands. Her whole sex felt unbelievably alive, sensitive to an unprecedented degree. She wanted more, just two or three of the unique caresses to get there. But Beatrice stayed her arm.

Laura opened her eyes, feeling tears trickle. 'Please let me finish, please.'

'You will do whatever I ask?'

Laura's reply was immediate and unthinking. 'Yes, yes.' She screwed up her eyes and reached out with her hips. 'Ah, ah, ah. Ahheee, yes.'

Three strikes were enough. Her sex flowered and opened like a ripe fruit. As her hips bounced back, Beatrice was on her, mouth plastered to her mouth, hands fumbling for her shackles. Laura felt herself lift and drop. Beatrice followed her down, grabbing her hand, pulling it up under her skirt. The kiss never stopped, hungry, greedy, thrumming. Laura's fingers found the hot wet cleft and dug in as the older woman ground down. They rolled over, and Laura plunged three, then four fingers inside the sucking, pulsing mouth. Her thumb rubbed across the thick, long, ringed clitty. Beatrice was coming already, humping at her hand, holding her face to her as their tongues darted and penetrated. Beatrice climaxed.

They lay in an heap, Laura held down as Beatrice gasped her gratitude.

'Thank you, ma chérie, thank you, thank you.'

Laura relaxed in their mutual glow and realised that her new mistress was a deeply frustrated woman. Only Beatrice had not taken pleasure during last night's orgy, and Laura wondered when she had last been allowed, or able, to have sex. She seemed loyal to her master, but was she really happy?

Exhausted, Mary lay on her back on her bed, naked and bound once again, but this time she was not alone. Laura, tied by wrists and ankles to the bedposts, stood at the end of the bed; she, too, was naked. For once Mary was not spread-eagled; her ankles were joined by a three-link chain between sturdy leather cuffs, and her arms were above her head, chained to the headboard. Every now and again, Laura would twitch and gasp, screwing up her eyes as sets of balls, inserted in vagina and anus, held by her chastity belt, played a cunning game. Mary held some balls in her behind as well. They moved in an odd, eccentric way, sweeping involuntary spasms through her pelvic region, little rubbery bumps on the surface picking pangs of pleasure.

Mary wriggled unintentionally, setting the balls in motion. As she did so, her breasts jiggled, causing the heavy clamps on her nipples to shift, supplementing the subtle excitement. Laura smiled with her eyes, her hips thrusting of their own accord.

Mary knew that, if Laura could speak, she would echo her plea. 'God, I just want to come –'

But Laura could not speak. She was gagged, just like Mary. So all they could do was look at each other, watching the other's frustrated excitement rise and rise, because the balls did not bring release. Since returning from the lake, Mary had been subjected to the almost continuous stimulation promised by Comte Henri, and as promised by Beatrice she had not been allowed to climax. Her vulva and nipples throbbed, her bottom and breasts itched, and her thighs were soaked in the honey leaking from under her chastity belt.

Her buttocks clenched again, still affected by the strange treatment her bottom had been given, and the balls shifted again. Once back from her swim, Beatrice had made her kneel in the bath, with her bum in the air. With Laura's assistance, Mary's bottom had been filled with some kind of liquid which made her belly swell and her rectum itch. They let her squat over the loo, and did it again. Mary blushed just thinking about the awful humiliation and, even more shaming, how much it had excited her.

Then she had been taken to the Pleasure Chamber, and put in the chair once again. Mary squeezed her thighs together as she remembered, trying to get some friction against her sex. Laura and Beatrice had spent hours toying with her. They used lips and fingers, cotton and clamps to make her nipples as long, hard and dark as almost-ripe cherries. Mary had watched helpless and gasping as her poor nubs, already tight and stinging from the grass switch, turned purple under the constant stimulation.

After that, they turned to her bottom, still itchy from the douching. Laura had rubbed oil into her freckle, slowly opening the tight muscle, before pushing a thing like a feather duster inside. For ages, Laura had twirled it around, the filaments inside tickling and touching everywhere, sending Mary mad. As Laura twirled, Beatrice had begun pinching and pulling at her leaves. They grew swollen and puffy. Oil was rubbed into them, weights were hung from her rings, and then the rings had been tied to her thighs, opening her slit wide.

Mary had been screaming for climax for ages by this time, her cries muffled by a gag. Every muscle had ached with tension, and she was drenched in sweat. Beatrice had licked her slit, up and down, up and down, and tickled it with a feather, but she did not touch Mary's jewel once. Then she had shown Mary a very fine, long feather, letting her see every tiny filament and feel its wicked tickle on her cheek before inserting it into Mary's pee-hole. Mary could still feel the echoes of that appalling, unimaginable invasion; the incredible delicacy of the tickle, feeling like it went right up to her teeth.

The gag removed, they let her rest for a while, giving her ice-cold champagne and orange juice to drink. Mary had been grateful, until her bladder began to ache. The feather had been left in. The feeling grew, and Mary asked to be allowed to go to the loo, but Beatrice merely produced a bowl. Mary pleaded, and the feather was slowly removed. Laura ran her tongue round and round the entrance to her sex, Beatrice twiddled the thing in her bottom, and then told Laura to stop. She pressed her hand on Mary's tummy, low down, almost on the pubis, and Mary knew she had to pee. Laura held the bowl and caught it all, but the tickle didn't go away.

Eventually, Laura had wound cotton round and round her jewel, and they adjusted the seat so Mary could see the bright red tip peeking from the cotton sleeve. They hung a weight from her ring, and again she nearly came. Then Laura and Beatrice had gone to lunch, and Mary had spent at least an hour in a throbbing seethe of frustration still bound to the chair. Later, she had been brought back to her room, the balls inserted, and then Beatrice had left them alone.

The door opened. Beatrice came in with a wicked smile on her face. 'Enjoying ourselves? Well, it's time for a change.'

238

She gently removed the clamps on Mary's nipples. Mary gasped as blood rushed in, but Beatrice did not release her arms and legs, only removing her gag. But she released Laura, even taking off her belt and gag.

With a little knowing smile, Beatrice took Laura's hand. 'Now, I'm sure you would like to renew your acquaintance with Mary. Please lie, face down, on top of Mary.'

Mary licked her dry lips and wondered what new torture the woman planned. Laura climbed on to the bed and arranged herself, knees apart, leaning arms beside Mary's shoulders. Their nipples touched, sending a shiver through Mary.

Beatrice produced leather belts and proceeded to strap Laura's legs and arms to Mary's. The hard points of Laura's nipples pressed into Mary's breasts, her wet sex rubbed across her belly. There was a slap, and Laura's hips bounced against Mary.

'Ow!'

Beatrice slapped her bottom again. 'Enjoy, and remember, Mary can't climax.'

As soon as the door closed, Mary's mouth opened for the kiss she had wanted all day. Laura probed with her tongue, and then bit her ears and neck. Mary felt her friend undulating over her body, rubbing her wetness. Laura could move enough to grip Mary's thigh. Mary groaned. Laura somehow bent enough to kiss the upper swells of her breasts, and her mouth over and over again. Mary groaned with frustration. The balls in her bottom and her sore, tingling nipples were all she could feel. The leather pad over her sex was too thick and tight for any friction.

Laura's body moved faster and faster, humping her thighs, spreading the slick all over. Her breathing grew heavier. Mary kissed her back, helpless to do anything except provide a firm surface for Laura's greedy snatch. Suddenly, Laura went rigid, rubbed twice and collapsed.

'Oh God, I needed that,' she breathed.

'I still do.' Mary didn't mean to carp. She was starting to enjoy having Laura all to herself.

'Oh, Mary, I'm sorry.'

'Doesn't matter. It's just nice to be with you again.' Tears appeared from nowhere. 'Laura, I've missed you so much.'

'Shush, sweetheart. I've missed you too.'

Mary needed to know. 'Do you still love me?'

'Why else would I be here?'

There was still one worry to put to bed. 'I thought you might have come after Philippe.'

'Why on earth –' Laura stopped. 'Is that why you went off like that? Because of me and Philippe?'

'I saw you. What do you think I thought?'

'Oh, Mary, I'm so sorry. I didn't mean anything. It was just a one-off.'

Mary had to be sure. 'Really?'

'Yes, really. It's you, and Adam, now.'

'Thank God for that.' They kissed again, and Mary suddenly felt free.

'Mary, do you believe me now?'

Laura still lay on top of her, and she was clearly worried. Mary tried to clear a path through all the sex feelings to the important question she was supposed to be thinking about: Comte Henri's true intentions. Laura had some crazy notion that the old man was sucking her sexual energy like a vampire would suck blood, and that she would not live long enough to marry Philippe. It seemed nonsense, at first sight, but on reflection she wasn't so sure. But was Laura being honest? Did she have another agenda, like revenge for being dumped, or her desire to take Mary for herself? Mary hated herself for thinking like that. She looked into Laura's eyes. No lies lay therein.

'Well, I suppose he does seem to be getting younger,' Mary admitted, 'and last night, when he, er –' she couldn't bring herself to say the words 'buggered me'; she had never talked so candidly about sex before '– you know, on the table.' Laura nodded. 'Well, I remember I was having a really good –' she hesitated again.

Laura helped out. 'Orgasm?'

'Yes. Well, it was like he somehow stole it.'

240

Laura's eyebrows arched. 'How do you mean? Did he finish before you were ready?'

'No, I did get there, but afterward it was as if the heart of it had been taken away.'

Laura turned her head and stared towards the window, deep in thought. 'Does he always faint like that when he comes?'

'Mm, and for longer every succeeding time.'

'And he looks younger afterward?'

Mary nodded. Laura was right, and she remembered that none of the diaries had gone on after the wedding. 'But what can we do about it?'

'Jumping ship tonight must be favourite, but I don't know if Philippe will come with us, and if he doesn't, well, I'm afraid he'll go the same way.'

Mary felt a surge of clear thinking. 'I think he would, but I don't think Comte Henri would just let us go without a fight. He has a very strong hold over everyone here, especially Philippe. You can feel it. When he wants you to do something, you just can't refuse, even when you want to.' A vague idea began to form. 'Leave it to me. I think I know how it's going to be done.'

Seventeen

At some point in the night, Mary's feverish, disordered mind returned to the central problem. The long day of arousal had not ended until midnight, and even when put to bed, with wrists shackled together and tethered to the headboard, and ankles chained wide apart, her body had not been left in peace. Before refitting the chastity belt, Beatrice inserted a fat, squeezable bung into her bottom, clamps along the length of her swollen inner lips, and tight spacer rings behind her nipple and clitoral rings. Mary felt attenuated, stretched on a rack of unfulfilled arousal. All attempts to sleep had been unsuccessful. Sheep counted became gambolling male genitals, fleeces transmogrified into bundles of feathery whips. She turned and tossed, as best she could, and chewed on the leather bit strapped around her head.

The moment of clarity came when she gave up the idea of sleep and concentrated instead on trying to make herself cool. A brief draught caressed her throbbing, glistening body like a cold sweat, chilling her breasts as it passed. Her breasts, the boobs so embarrassingly prominent since the moment of their emergence at puberty, were the answer.

She shook her head in exasperation. Why hadn't she realised their power before? Comte Henri was a fool for her boobs; playing with them, eating off them, having them in his sight all the time, even coming between them. She could have kicked herself. He had lost control because of them, and instead of his mind dominating hers she had been able to look inside his. Her breasts, large, firm and bulging with feminine fertility, were the chink in his armour, and tomorrow they would expose him for what he was – a monster.

Mary relaxed and tested her theory. Through Laura, Adam had confirmed that Philippe was still in thrall to his father, and although he had started to worry about his father's intentions towards her, he would not leave. Philippe's stance, and the fact that Adam's car and mobile phone had been sabotaged, had scuppered the plan to leave overnight. Mary had been able to reassure herself on one point. This Farouk, who had kidnapped Laura, was not known to Le Comte, nor any secret society. Mary had spent so long in Le Comte's study that she had had time to observe all his writings and hear him chatter about his work. It was all for himself and Philippe. No letters received or sent; no contact with the outside world. If this Farouk had been in touch, Mary would have known. Le Comte was suspicious, of course he was. No one came uninvited to his home, and now three had come in just a few weeks, and his plans for Laura and Adam after the 'nuptials'? They were anybody's guess.

Everything now hinged on finding an opportunity during the so-called wedding ceremony. Mary now thought she had a way of exploiting that opening. And one thing was for sure: Mary had made up her mind not to surrender her virginity willingly to the old man. To Philippe, yes; to his father, no.

For the first time since entering the château, Mary's thoughts were all her own, and at this moment they did not include an incessant desire for sexual pleasure. Her body cooled, ignoring the pressure of rings and clamps, and she slipped into a dreamless, refreshing sleep.

'Good morning, Mary.' Mary prised her eyes open as Beatrice threw back the shutters and sunlight poured in. 'It's your big day. First breakfast, and then we'll get you ready. I'm going to make you the most beautiful virgin in the world.'

Mary yawned and stretched as the shackles were removed. 'I'd like to use the bathroom first.'

244

Beatrice unlocked the belt and removed the bung and the clamps. Mary's bottom and lips relaxed. Unsteadily, she got to her feet and tried to walk. Her delta felt so thick and heavy she parted her knees. Grateful to be alone in the bathroom, she took her time, not touching herself, just waking slowly.

Breakfast consisted of just orange juice. Beatrice fussed round the room, laying out clothes and cosmetics and hairbrushes. Afterward, she took Mary back to the bathroom.

'Kneel on the floor, bottom up, knees apart.'

The tiles were cold. Mary foresaw what would happen next, and resolved to keep her queer enjoyment of the operation from her mistress. She felt the lubricated tube push inside her bottom, expand inside and out, and a deluge of what seemed like gallons of water plunge into her guts. The now-familiar cramps began, and she tried to get up even though the tube was still inside.

'Stay down. The liquid must stay inside for five minutes. It cannot escape.'

Mary swallowed nervously. Her insides churned and her anus spasmed, but neither tube nor liquid escaped past the valve and balloon arrangement. The five minutes seemed like hours, and a cold sweat broke out as the liquid seemed to boil and bubble. At last, Beatrice helped her to her feet, made her squat over the toilet and deflated the valve. The tube popped out, and the pain, like the liquid, went away.

'Kneel down again.'

Mary obeyed, her stomach rumbling; no solid food had passed her lips since breakfast yesterday. A second tube was introduced, and something slow and oily filled her, soothing the irritated tissue. Only a minute passed before she squatted again and let the balm escape. Now her bottom felt warm and soft.

Beatrice showered her then, slowly, caressing her all over with soft suds and a gentle exfoliating pad. Mary leant into the soft hands, offering her breasts, her bottom and her mound to the slippy fingers and almost imperceptible scrubbing. Her snatch grew oily, her nipples firm, but without the ache of yesterday. After shaving her armpits and mound, Beatrice played the hose over her, rinsing with cooler water, and then dried her with the softest towels.

For a long time Mary sat in front of the mirror as Beatrice brushed her hair to a glowing sheen, long and natural as it had not been since arriving. At Beatrice's request, she stood while the chatelaine knelt and took her jewel into her mouth, sucking until Mary moaned. She took hold of the ring and pulled insistently but gently. Mary looked down through eyes slitted with agitated arousal. Unbelievably, the little nub was even longer. She added a second spacer ring, and, when Beatrice let go, the head and piercing ring were completely clear of the pouting lips. Then Beatrice oiled and rouged her sex and anus, giving her lips and jewel a thick, glossy fullness. Mary breathed deeply, fighting the incredible pleasure that seemed just a touch away.

The French woman produced an ebony rod, perhaps four or five inches long, rounded at the end and fat, except for a short narrow section before it flared to the base from which a short, heavy chain hung.

'Bend over, dear.'

Mary obeyed. The rod was pushed inside her bottom. It was thicker than anything yet but, once in, could not escape. Beatrice fixed the chain to the rings in Mary's lips, pulling them together, and to her clitoral ring. Mary stood up and the chain pressed against her, at least symbolically preventing access to her virgin entrance. The arrangement pulled as she moved, setting off little darts and explosions of sensation through her loins. Beatrice turned her attention to Mary's nipples, sucking and tugging and oiling until they, too, grew longer, and spacer rings were added as well before a chain was fixed, heavy and gold, between the throbbing, aching nubs.

Mary shivered, her eyes closing as waves of pleasure, intense, almost orgasmic, swept through her. Beatrice made her stand still, to dress her in a floaty, long, almost transparent white dress through which her coloured nipples showed pointy and proud. Mary took a very deep breath and looked at herself in the mirror while flowers were woven into her hair and round her forehead in a wreath. A garland was placed round her neck, and her hands bound in front of her with thick, soft rope from which a length hung loose. Beatrice slipped out of the room for a moment.

Mary revealed her inner self to the mirror, upright, shoulders back, breasts proud, tied wrists held at waist height. Pagan goddess Mary, Mary the nymph and earth-mother; sensual, erotic, fecund and, she now knew, powerful. Her body throbbed with desire, but now that desire was focused, controlled. The château had done its work too well. Mary was supposed to be pliant and submissive, the source of sustenance for a monster masquerading as a man, even possibly the mother of another of his children. She knew otherwise. Comte Henri had no future, for she knew his secret. Philippe would have his chance to love her, but if he failed too, well, there was always Laura . . .

The door opened. Mary resumed the mask of submissive modesty, relaxing her shoulders and looking down just a little, hands in front of her maidenhood. Her handmaidens, Laura and Yvette, entered. They wore peasant-girl costumes, breasts swelling above tight-laced buff leather bodices worn over white dresses with flowers embroidered round the hems. On their heads they wore garlands of flowers matching Mary's, on their feet soft slippers. Mary felt the cool floor with her bare feet. Laura came over, her eyes sad because she had no idea what Mary planned.

Mary smiled back bravely. 'I'm ready.'

Laura took hold of the dangling rope. 'Good luck.'

Laura looked round the Pleasure Chamber. Adam, standing next to a worried Philippe, nodded. She passed the rope's end to Beatrice and took her place behind Mary's left shoulder. The outline of the ceremony had been given at dinner last night. Mary must signal her submission to her master by asking to be whipped by Le Comte. After the whip, she would be deflowered by him, and then whipped by Philippe, as a prelude to taking first his ring, then his cock. Laura wondered when, and how, Mary was going to act, and why her friend seemed so confident.

A terrifying hush fell on the wedding party. Comte Henri entered, his confidence and lust palpable even before she saw him. As usual, he wore archaic breeches and tail-coat, but now he had a sword buckled to his left hip. In his right hand he held a thin whip. He stood before Mary, looking taller, stronger and younger than ever, his eyes glittering with unquenchable hunger. Laura trembled and lowered her eyes as he looked round at the small gathering. Everyone held their breath.

'Mary, how do you wish to mark your submission to the will of your master?'

Laura bit her lip nervously.

Mary replied in a small but certain voice. 'I wish to be whipped across my breasts, master.'

Laura couldn't believe her ears. Her delicate, trembling breasts, no.

Mary must have noticed the disbelief. She responded with reiteration, her voice stronger. 'I wish to hold my breasts to the whip, master.'

Clever girl, Laura thought, getting her hands free.

Comte Henri raised his eyebrows and drew his sword. 'So be it. You are a very brave girl, Mary.' He cut Mary's bonds and passed them to Laura. 'If you will kneel on the block.' He indicated a raised stone plinth by his side.

Mary coolly knelt on the smooth stone block. Le Comte waved his whip, inviting the audience to gather round for a better view. Laura's feet felt like lead as she saw Mary draw her shoulders back and cup her gorgeous mounds. The rings and chain glittered. At a sign from Le Comte, Beatrice stepped up and removed the chain. Mary's breasts trembled as she waited, eyes staring into the distance beyond the walls of the cellars.

Comte Henri flexed the whip. 'You will receive six blows on each breast – two on top, two underneath and two to the tips. You will count them out loud.'

Mary's knees shifted a little apart. Laura licked her lips

and wished she could stop this now and save those long, thick nubs from their fate. The whip swished, and a red line scored across the upper slope of Mary's right breast. The crack echoed around the chamber. Mary sucked in her breath.

'One, thank you, master.'

A red stripe appeared across her left breast. 'Two, thank you, master.' Her voice wavered slightly.

'Three, thank you, master.' It came out as a whisper.

Mary licked her lips, and Laura found herself doing the same. Mary's eyes closed slowly. Laura's breasts throbbed in sympathy, remembering such a whipping, and the deep fire it had sparked in her womb. Mary's knees edged wider as she licked her lips yet again, her breath coming in gasps. Again the whip cracked.

'Four, thank you, master.' The words were barely audible.

'Take hold of your rings and hold your breasts up.' Le Comte's voice was hoarse with lust.

Mary's fingers gripped the dangling rings. She stretched her breasts upward, exposing the soft, delicate flesh of the undersurfaces.

The whip made the right breast shake and jiggle. Mary carried on counting, refusing to acknowledge the pain with a cry. A red line marked her left breast, followed rapidly by a crossing line. Laura felt the wetness between her thighs and looked at Adam, now standing beside her. His hand took hers, and he squeezed. His tight trousers bulged. Laura found it hard to believe that Mary's sacrifice could be so erotic, but it was.

Now a cross had been scored across Mary's right breast. 'Eight, thank you, master.'

'Put your hands behind your neck and keep your elbows out of the way.' His eyes burnt bright in a face red with lust.

Mary bit her bottom lip. He lined up the whip, aiming to bring it down on the trembling gold and red tips. The whip slashed down, the tip unerring in its accuracy. Mary's torso jerked back, and a little moan escaped.

'Nine, thank you, master.'

A tear trickled down Mary's cheek, but she forced her breasts back into line. His arm raised and fell again. Mary jerked again as her left breast bounced. Now both nipples looked like blackberries squeezed in gold. Her eyes were closed, so she did not see him change his aim, striking horizontally. Mary bit back a scream as the whip scorched across the median line of her left breast, right across the thick tip. Sweat sprayed from her face.

The whip cracked for the last time. Mary gasped and bent over, her hands covering the burning orbs. 'Twelve, thank you, master.'

He bent forward and gently tugged her hands away. 'You have done remarkably well. Très formidable, mademoiselle. Display your trophies, my dear.'

Mary straightened up. He tipped up her chin and kissed her before stepping away. Mary opened tear-filled eyes and looked at her audience. Laura suppressed a gasp. Triumph shone from Mary's eyes. She knew she was in charge. Laura squeezed Adam's hand hard. He looked round. Laura nodded towards Mary, silently communicating her new-found confidence.

Mary gritted her teeth as she looked at the admiring or appalled faces of the four watchers. Laura nodded back, Philippe looked totally shocked, but his breeches bulged almost obscenely. Beatrice curtsied, almost mockingly. Yvette surreptitiously rubbed her own breasts. Mary fought the pain as she turned back to Le Comte. His eyes told her all she needed to know. His lust was almost overpowering at such close proximity. Her thighs were slick with her juices, her nubs and boobs longed for a soft, wet, warm mouth to soothe the pain away. She took her breasts in her hands once again, not to rub the pain but to present them.

'Master, in what way may I please you now?'

He was, for once, lost for words. His eyes drank in the sight of her red-striped, swollen, heaving boobs. Her cleavage was slick with beads of sweat. She looked directly at his cock. It stretched his trousers. His aura seemed weaker already.

'Shall I take you in my mouth, to make you wet and ease the way inside my tight, virgin *con*?' Mary felt her knife twisting in his depraved soul.

He nodded absently, consenting. She kept her eyes from his in case she gave the game away. She reached out and unbuttoned the flap in his breeches slowly. His cock sprang out. Mary took a deep breath and shuffled closer, taking his thick, hard stem in her hands. She could never take him; he was already bigger than ever before. She opened her mouth and licked the tip. His stem jerked. He moaned. Opening her mouth as wide as possible, she sucked in the purple head. He tasted strong. She sucked, and he whispered incoherently. She licked up and down and around his length and his balls, lapping and kissing. She heard little shuffles and whispers from her audience.

Le Comte's hands gripped her head. This was her greatest fear, that he would come to his senses and stop her too soon. She needed more time. Was he going to pull her away? His hands rustled through the flowers, crushing them, releasing their scent. She let him out of her mouth and straightened up, close to him, his cock between her aching breasts. He grunted and began rubbing himself up and down.

Mary felt a flash in her head. She saw his rotten, devastated soul, the soul devoured by hundreds of years of emptiness and cruel hunger. Mary brought her hands up to her sore, throbbing breasts and trapped him. Her nipples rubbed his trousers, harsh, stabbing pains. She gasped but gripped harder, entrapping his being in her web. From his mouth came animal groans and angry need. He pumped harder in reflex. Her breasts hurt deep inside. She felt his cock pulse and grow, his balls hard, tight against her stomach, opened her eyes and looked up, knowing he was lost.

The purple end bumped against her throat. She held her breath. He crushed her to him, and spurted his thick, strong, copious semen over her face, neck and shoulders.

251

It went everywhere, in ribbons and splashes. His entire body went rigid. His mouth opened. He howled. Mary felt his body deflate. She pushed him gently away. He fell back, unconscious.

Adam took Laura's hand as they watched the erotic, demonic frottage, leading it to his cock, but Laura pulled it away and began making a loop in the rope she was still holding. Adam looked down. She shook her head; this was no time for idle wanking. She felt Le Comte's power ebbing as his monstrous needs overtook his power for rational thought. Mary him had trapped.

Comte Henri came, crying out in a strange hollow bellow. Laura pushed Adam towards Mary and spun round on Beatrice. Taken by surprise, Beatrice was no match for Laura as she spun her round and kicked her to her knees, grabbing Beatrice's wrists, pushing them up her back and passing the loop round them. Yvette jumped on her back, but she ignored her, tightened the knot to leave Beatrice on her knees, and helpless.

Yvette yelped and stopped pulling at her hair. Her weight disappeared. Laura stood up. Philippe was holding her, confused and indecisive.

'What's going on?'

Laura glanced over to Mary and Adam. They had gagged the still-unconscious old man and were shackling him to the chair. She turned back to Philippe.

'We're saving your bacon. Take Yvette to the frame. I'll finish with Beatrice.' She ran over to fetch a set of shackles. None too soon, she was back to immobilise the older woman. Beatrice was getting her breath back. Laura stopped her mouth with a gag and then went to help Philippe.

Yvette fought, but Philippe was too strong, and Laura too practised with using chains, and soon she was shackled to the frame, arms and legs outstretched, with a gag in her mouth. Adam brought Beatrice over and soon she, too, was spread-eagled in the frame.

Laura finally had time to catch up with Mary. The

heroine of the moment was standing over her victim. An Amazon, magnificent and terrible, naked from the waist upward, striped breasts jutting, sperm dripping and sliding down her body, her eyes triumphant. For a ghastly moment Laura thought that Mary had somehow absorbed the old man's evil, but then Mary turned towards her and began to use the tatters of her dress to wipe herself down. Her eyes grew soft as she became preoccupied with the task, her limbs softer as the martial stance melted into the old familiar, if different, Mary.

Everyone waited on her. Even the captive women stopped struggling and spluttering through their gags. Mary looked up shyly and beckoned to Philippe. He went to her, trying to keep as far as possible from his unconscious father.

Mary smiled coyly and reached out her hand to him. 'Shall we finish the ceremony now?'

Laura snuggled into Adam's side as Philippe reached Mary. For a moment Philippe just looked at his intended, fingers fidgeting. Mary took his hands, looked up to his face and spoke privately, her voice only just audible to the others.

'Phil, you do want me, don't you?'

'Er, yes, its just –'

'Master?' Mary sank to her knees and bowed her head. For a moment more, Philippe stood still, seemingly cowed by his father's presence. Mary reached out for the whip his father had dropped and held it up to him in both hands, the image of the perfect slave.

Philippe took the offering, looked at it as he tested its flexibility, his mind working again. Laura smiled. Resolution was suddenly written all over his face and bearing. 'Adam, would you bring a trestle over, please?'

'Of course, old chap.' Adam placed the trestle in front of Comte Henri's shattered body.

Philippe drew himself to his full height. 'Mary, are you willing to submit to my pleasure in every way?'

'Yes, master.'

'Then bend over the trestle and bare your behind.'

253

'Yes, master.' Laura, and no doubt Philippe, caught the flicker of a smile playing across Mary's lips.

Mary let her dress fall, spread her legs wide and bent forward until her belly rested on the padded apex of the whipping trestle. Laura moved closer, noticing the strange bung and chains. Philippe reached forward and stroked the offered orbs. Mary sighed. The whip whistled again, snapped across the pale domes, and left behind a diagonal red line from hip to hip. Mary gasped and gripped the trestle harder. The whip fell again, crossing the other line, making a cross. Philippe was breathing hard now. He struck just twice more, doubling the pair of lines, before throwing the whip down.

Laura heard the clatter as she turned into Adam's kiss. He whispered in her ear.

'Let's make things a bit more comfortable for them. See those furs?'

He pointed into the shadows, and they set off as Mary stood upright, turned, and knelt between Philippe's knees. When they returned, laden with thick furs, Mary was nuzzling Philippe's cock, sucking and licking noisily, joyfully. Laura lay her load of furs down, leaving Adam to arrange them; Philippe was still fully clothed.

Laura stood behind him, reached round, and drew his jacket from his arms and shoulders. Mary, her hair disordered, had her lips stretched about the object of her desire. Laura undulated against Philippe as she unbuttoned his shirt and untied his neckerchief, thrilling her breasts with his shirt, feeling his hard buttocks with her belly, kissing his bare back as she pulled the shirt away. She knelt, caressing Mary's hands as her hands ran down his thighs. She reached round and eased his feet from his shoes, reached up and began to unbutton his breeches, pulling them down and away from Mary's face. As she straightened up from tugging the breeches free, Mary turned to her, holding Philippe's cock, rubbing it gently up and down, and met Laura's lips with a smile of pure happiness. Laura kissed her, tasting him.

Hands ran over Laura's shoulders. Adam pushed her

dress down and scooped out her breasts. He pulled her away, kissing her neck and grabbing at her skirts. They ripped. He tore them away from beneath the bodice and led her on to the furs. He lay on his back.

'Your mouth, slave.'

Laura laughed and bent to extricate his bulging manhood.

Mary looked up at Philippe. He was ready. She drew back and lay on the furs beside Adam, nearer to Comte Henri. His eyes were opening blearily. It was distasteful to gloat, but she couldn't stop a smile as she spread her legs wide to welcome his son.

Philippe lowered himself to her. She raised her hips; he needed to take the bung from her bottom to uncover her. She burned for him, her breasts tight swollen, the red lines hard. The fur tickled and stung her buttocks. His fingers located the ebony rod and eased it from her with a twist that tugged deep inside. As it left, she felt empty. Philippe lay the bung on her belly, and she reached to open herself. At last, at long, long last, she was going to feel him inside her hot, sopping, tight tube. It pulsed as his fingers held his cock to her. Mary grabbed his shoulders.

'Now, my love.'

Philippe complied. Her entrance spread and clutched. He felt huge. Her feet left the furs and climbed up to his back as she made herself as open as possible. His weight pressed on the insides of her thighs, the ebony rod slipped as she undulated. His length slid in, wide, immense, forcing and stretching. She gasped and sucked in her breath. He lodged deep, momentarily held against the obstruction of her hymen. He seemed to hesitate, but she wanted it over now. Mary grabbed his hips and pulled hard.

He burst through and plunged on. Mary heard a squeal, and realised it was hers. Her head began to rock from side to side. She caught sight of the old man. He was awake; grey and old, his eyes bulging with fear. Philippe began to withdraw slowly, and she gripped him, unwilling to let him go. She wanted him there, inside, filling her for ever, but he slid out almost all the way before thrusting again. Mary grinned and gasped and found her hips moving without control with him. He went as far as he could go up her tight tube, but still his pubis had not met hers and nor had her cervix felt his tip. She wanted him entirely, to drown him in her honey as he drowned her in his semen. Her rings shivered as he retreated and thrust, every time his pubis getting closer. They kissed, and she cuddled his head on to her sore nubs.

Mary felt movement. Laura leant over. She was kneeling with Adam behind. Her mouth descended and Mary welcomed her blessing. Laura bumped, taking Adam's thrusts. They smiled at each other, each in heaven. Mary was full to the brim with emotions: happiness, relief, love, self-confidence. Mary said the first thing that came to her.

'Thank you, Laura.'

Laura moaned as Adam filled her. 'What for?' she managed to gasp.

'For being my first love.' They kissed again and then Philippe reached bottom, his curly hairs crushing down on her ringed, extended jewel. Mary moaned as the pleasure shot through her. When she regained some semblance of awareness, Laura was suckling her nipples, soothing their hurt.

Philippe's thrusts came faster. Mary cried out, tears rolling down her cheeks. She was engulfed by her two lovers and a bursting, whole, unfettered orgasm. Philippe kept moving, faster, grinding because he hadn't come. Successive smaller waves rippled through her body, her fingers clawed his back. Philippe went rigid, his cock crushed against her cervix. A peal of joy issued from her mouth as he pumped and pumped, and a second tidal wave engulfed her. Vaguely in the background she heard a guttering croak.

Laura crawled out from the tangle of soggy, sated bodies and looked round the room. The two women hung listless in the frame. Beatrice was crying softly and looking at her master. Laura turned to him. His face and hands had

256

become parchment-skinned,
stretched under the apparent
white hair.

She went over to remove th
wrong for an old, sick man
dangerous. It came away from a
lips were blue, his eyes closed, a
mouldy and dry, rose from his coll

Laura sighed and opened one alm
The pupil was filmed with a mil
moved. There was no pulse. The croa........ ....
his last. Mary's orgasms, the essence he needed to extend
yet further his vile career, had finally ended his life. Laura
released the captives. Neither said a word as they made
their way slowly and sadly from the cellar. Laura turned
back to her friends. They were slowly regaining their wits.
Philippe looked from his father to Laura. She shook her
head.

Silently, they gathered their clothes and made their way
out. Adam took Philippe under his wing, whispering
consoling words. Laura hung back, waiting for Mary.

Mary looked round the Pleasure Chamber for the last
time, a tear trickling down her cheek. Laura put her arm
round Mary's shoulders.

Mary finally turned away. 'You know, I rather liked
him, in a funny sort of way.'

Nexus

A Dozen Strokes Various
August 1999   Price £5.99   ISBN: 0 352 33423 1
This, the first in a series of themed collections from Nexus, is a paean
to the delights of discipline. Mixing extracts from hard-to-find genre
classics with new material, this is the definitive CP compilation, and
an indispensable guide to the joys of a freshly birched bottom.

The Master of Castleleigh by Jacqueline Bellevois
August 1999   Price £5.99   ISBN: 0 352 33424 X
When Richard Buxton is forced to leave the delights of 19th century
London, marry and run a country estate, he assumes that the
pleasures of the whip are no longer his to be had. Both the estate,
and his new wife Clarissa, however, provide unexpectedly perverse
opportunities, and he is diligent in making imaginative use of them.

His Mistress's Voice by G. C. Scott
August 1999   Price £5.99   ISBN: 0 352 33425 8
Sensing a powerful, animal drive within Tom that echoes her own, Beth
decides to make Tom's initiation into bondage a swift one. His hesitant
first steps soon quicken as he is drawn further into her dark and intimate
web. Just when their relationship seems to have reached its peak, Beth
introduces him to Harriet – and the games suddenly become even kinkier
and more convoluted. This is the seventh in a series of Nexus Classics.

Confessions of an English Slave by Yolanda Celbridge
September 1999   Price £5.99   ISBN: 0 352 33433 9
Introduced to the joys of bare-bottom discipline by lustful ladies,
naval cadet Philip Demense, posted to the far east, painfully learns
true submission from the voluptuous dominatrix Galena. Escaping
from her lash, he is kidnapped to serve in an English school of female
domination, transplanted to the emptiness of Siberia to escape do-
gooding restrictions on corporal punishment. His male arrogance
utterly crushed, Philip gladly submits to total enslavement by women,
with unlimited flagellant discipline of naked males – and females . . .

become parchment-skinned, his head lay over, neck stretched under the apparent weight of his long, thin, soft white hair.

She went over to remove the gag. Somehow it looked wrong for an old, sick man to be gagged, however dangerous. It came away from a mouth slack and dry. His lips were blue, his eyes closed, and the smell of decay, mouldy and dry, rose from his collapsed body.

Laura sighed and opened one almost transparent eyelid. The pupil was filmed with a milky opacity. Nothing moved. There was no pulse. The croaking gasp had been his last. Mary's orgasms, the essence he needed to extend yet further his vile career, had finally ended his life. Laura released the captives. Neither said a word as they made their way slowly and sadly from the cellar. Laura turned back to her friends. They were slowly regaining their wits. Philippe looked from his father to Laura. She shook her head.

Silently, they gathered their clothes and made their way out. Adam took Philippe under his wing, whispering consoling words. Laura hung back, waiting for Mary.

Mary looked round the Pleasure Chamber for the last time, a tear trickling down her cheek. Laura put her arm round Mary's shoulders.

Mary finally turned away. 'You know, I rather liked him, in a funny sort of way.'

NEW BOOKS

Coming up from Nexus, Sapphire and Black Lace

A Dozen Strokes Various
August 1999   Price £5.99   ISBN: 0 352 33423 1

This, the first in a series of themed collections from Nexus, is a paean to the delights of discipline. Mixing extracts from hard-to-find genre classics with new material, this is the definitive CP compilation, and an indispensable guide to the joys of a freshly birched bottom.

The Master of Castleleigh by Jacqueline Bellevois
August 1999   Price £5.99   ISBN: 0 352 33424 X

When Richard Buxton is forced to leave the delights of 19th century London, marry and run a country estate, he assumes that the pleasures of the whip are no longer his to be had. Both the estate, and his new wife Clarissa, however, provide unexpectedly perverse opportunities, and he is diligent in making imaginative use of them.

His Mistress's Voice by G. C. Scott
August 1999   Price £5.99   ISBN: 0 352 33425 8

Sensing a powerful, animal drive within Tom that echoes her own, Beth decides to make Tom's initiation into bondage a swift one. His hesitant first steps soon quicken as he is drawn further into her dark and intimate web. Just when their relationship seems to have reached its peak, Beth introduces him to Harriet – and the games suddenly become even kinkier and more convoluted. This is the seventh in a series of Nexus Classics.

Confessions of an English Slave by Yolanda Celbridge
September 1999   Price £5.99   ISBN: 0 352 33433 9

Introduced to the joys of bare-bottom discipline by lustful ladies, naval cadet Philip Demense, posted to the far east, painfully learns true submission from the voluptuous dominatrix Galena. Escaping from her lash, he is kidnapped to serve in an English school of female domination, transplanted to the emptiness of Siberia to escape do-gooding restrictions on corporal punishment. His male arrogance utterly crushed, Philip gladly submits to total enslavement by women, with unlimited flagellant discipline of naked males – and females . . .

The Rake by Aishling Morgan
September 1999   Price £5.99   ISBN: 0 352 33434 7
Henry Truscott is a dissipated rake even by the standards of the late
eighteenth century. When his eye catches the beautiful Eloise he
expects either to be thrashed by her footman and dumped in a ditch
or to take his full pleasure in her magnificent curves. He gets more
than he had anticipated, in every way, trading seduction and revenge
and finally using her and her maids in an increasingly perverse
manner as they are pursued across France by bloodthirsty
revolutionaries.

Citadel of Servitude by Aran Ashe
September 1999   Price £5.99   ISBN: 0 352 33435 5
Tormunil: the mysterious citadel of erotic mastery from which there
can be no excape. Sianon is the beautiful love-slave whose breasts
weep milk; Josef the outlander who tries to save her, only to be drawn
ever deeper into a vortex of perverse desires. In the Citadel of
Servitude, every avenue of sexual love must be tested, every strange
pleasure explored, and every taboo broken. The eighth in a series of
Nexus Classics.

A new imprint of lesbian fiction

All That Glitters by Franca Nera
August 1999   Price £6.99   ISBN: 0 352 33426 6
Marta Broderick is an art dealer with a difference. She has inherited
the art empire of her Austrian uncle, and has been entrusted with
continuing his mission of retrieving art treasures lost in the Second
World War. When an investigation is set up into Marta's activities,
the chief investigator discovers to her horror that Marta is a former
lover, and one with especially kinky tastes. When another of Marta's
innocent lovers appears on the scene, can the investigator keep her
mind on the job in hand?

BLACK
lace

Confessional by J. Royce
August 1999   Price £5.99   ISBN: 0 352 33421 5
Faren Lonsdale, an ambitious young reporter for *Splash!* magazine, searches for the scoop that will rocket her to new journalistic peaks. Fascinated with the question of celibacy in the priesthood, she is convinced this is the feature that will achieve her goal. To prove her theory, Faren infiltrates the local seminary where she plans to unearth the priest's nocturnal entertainment. She meets maverick priest Karl Sterling who takes her on a journey of ungodly sensual pleasure and the debonair Simon Murray who has some dark surprises of his own.

Like Mother, Like Daughter by Georgina Brown
August 1999   Price £5.99   ISBN: 0 352 33422 3
Although they are not aware of it, mother and daughter are very much alike. Stella is mature, sure of what she wants and not afraid to take it. Rachel, her daughter, won't admit to inexperience and isn't sure how experimental her sex should be, and relies on her increasingly perverted fantasies to help her – but she won't fully drop her guard. In the meantime, Stella is busy seducing men half her age. Both are about to learn things about themselves and, gradually, about each other.

Out of Bounds by Mandy Dickinson
September 1999   Price £5.99   ISBN: 0 352 33431 2
When Katie decides to start a new life in a French farmhouse left to her by her grandfather, she is horrified to find two men living there already. But her horror quickly becomes curiosity as she realises how attracted she is to the two men, and how much illicit pleasure is to be had by becoming involved with them. The world in which they live knows no rules, and for the first time she can explore her darkest desires to the full.

A Dangerous Game by Lucinda Carrington
September 1999   Price £5.99   ISBN: 0 352 33432 0
Jacey, tired of the opportunities available to her at home and deciding to push her boundaries, takes a job as a doctor in a hospital in Guatamàl, South America. It's the ideal environment for experimental sex, and she soon finds herself loving the kinky medical games she can play. But Guatamàl is not a safe place to play around with men – how soon will it be before Jacey realises she is playing a very dangerous game? By the author of *The Master of Shilden*.

Nexus

NEXUS BACKLIST

All books are priced £5.99 unless another price is given. If a date is supplied, the book in question will not be available until that month in 1999.

CONTEMPORARY EROTICA

THE ACADEMY	Arabella Knight	
AMANDA IN THE PRIVATE HOUSE	Esme Ombreux	
BAD PENNY	Penny Birch	
THE BLACK MASQUE	Lisette Ashton	
THE BLACK WIDOW	Lisette Ashton	
BOUND TO OBEY	Amanda Ware	
BRAT	Penny Birch	
DANCE OF SUBMISSION	Lisette Ashton	Nov
DARK DELIGHTS	Maria del Rey	
DARK DESIRES	Maria del Rey	
DARLINE DOMINANT	Tania d'Alanis	
DISCIPLES OF SHAME	Stephanie Calvin	
THE DISCIPLINE OF NURSE RIDING	Yolanda Celbridge	
DISPLAYS OF INNOCENTS	Lucy Golden	
EMMA'S SECRET DOMINATION	Hilary James	
EXPOSING LOUISA	Jean Aveline	
FAIRGROUND ATTRACTIONS	Lisette Ashton	
GISELLE	Jean Aveline	Oct
HEART OF DESIRE	Maria del Rey	
HOUSE RULES	G.C. Scott	Oct
IN FOR A PENNY	Penny Birch	Nov
JULIE AT THE REFORMATORY	Angela Elgar	
LINGERING LESSONS	Sarah Veitch	

THE GOVERNESS AT ST AGATHA'S	Yolanda Celbridge		
THE MASTER OF CASTLELEIGH	Jacqueline Bellevois		Aug
PRIVATE MEMOIRS OF A KENTISH HEADMISTRESS	Yolanda Celbridge	£4.99	
THE RAKE	Aishling Morgan		Sep
THE TRAINING OF AN ENGLISH GENTLEMAN	Yolanda Celbridge		

SAMPLERS & COLLECTIONS

EROTICON 4	Various		
THE FIESTA LETTERS	ed. Chris Lloyd	£4.99	
NEW EROTICA 3			
NEW EROTICA 4	Various		
A DOZEN STROKES	Various		Aug

NEXUS CLASSICS
A new imprint dedicated to putting the finest works of erotic fiction back in print

THE IMAGE	Jean de Berg	
CHOOSING LOVERS FOR JUSTINE	Aran Ashe	
THE INSTITUTE	Maria del Rey	
AGONY AUNT	G. C. Scott	
THE HANDMAIDENS	Aran Ashe	
OBSESSION	Maria del Rey	
HIS MASTER'S VOICE	G.C. Scott	Aug
CITADEL OF SERVITUDE	Aran Ashe	Sep
BOUND TO SERVE	Amanda Ware	Oct
BOUND TO SUBMIT	Amanda Ware	Nov
SISTERHOOD OF THE INSTITUTE	Maria del Rey	Dec

- -

Please send me the books I have ticked above.

Name ....

Address ....

....

....

.... Post code........................

Send to: **Cash Sales, Nexus Books, Thames Wharf Studios, Rainville Road, London W6 9HT**

US customers: for prices and details of how to order books for delivery by mail, call 1-800-805-1083.

Please enclose a cheque or postal order, made payable to **Nexus Books**, to the value of the books you have ordered plus postage and packing costs as follows:

UK and BFPO – £1.00 for the first book, 50p for the second book and 30p for each subsequent book to a maximum of £3.00;

Overseas (including Republic of Ireland) – £2.00 for the first book, £1.00 for the second book and 50p for each subsequent book.

We accept all major credit cards, including VISA, ACCESS/ MASTERCARD, AMEX, DINERS CLUB, SWITCH, SOLO, and DELTA. Please write your card number and expiry date here:

....

Please allow up to 28 days for delivery.

Signature ....

- -